Eleanor McDowall

About the Author

CHRISTIE DICKASON started writing at the age of three, before she could spell. She went on to study English at Harvard, then won an MFA in Directing at Yale Drama School. After spending fourteen years as a theater director and choreographer, with the Royal Shakespeare Company and at Ronnie Scott's, among others, she returned to her secret passion for writing while convalescing from illness. In addition to her novels, she also writes poetry, music lyrics, and for the theater. As a child, she lived in Thailand, Mexico, and Switzerland, and has now lived longer in London than anywhere else. For more information and to contact her, please visit her website, www.christiedickason.com.

Also by Christie Dickason

The Firemaster's Mistress

·:- *The* -:·
KING'S DAUGHTER

A NOVEL

Christie Dickason

HARPER

NEW YORK · LONDON · TORONTO · SYDNEY

For my Beloved Tom

HARPER

First published in Great Britain in 2009 by HarperCollins Publishers.

HarperCollins books may be purchased for educational, business, or sales promotional use. For information please write: Special Markets Department, HarperCollins Publishers 10 East 53rd Street, New York, NY 10022.

FIRST U.S. EDITION

Library of Congress Cataloging-in-Publication Data is available upon request.

ISBN 978-0-06-197627-8

10 11 12 13 14 OV/RRD 10 9 8 7 6 5 4 3 2 1

ACKNOWLEDGEMENTS

JOHN, my husband and personal Google. Theatre producer and consultant, who knows more than seems possible for any one person (and remembers everything he reads). Who, yet again, tracked down much that I needed to know.

Again and as always to my friend, the award-winning radio and television writer, STEPHEN WYATT, for his generous offerings of sudden thoughts, 'what-ifs', and articles 'you should read' – and for his patient, constructive listening during all those working park walks.

DAVID DIBOSA, for his gift of insight and inspiration in helping me to see and feel the reality of Tallie.

CHUK IWUJI, a charismatic actor who has inhabited the 17th century as the Royal Shakespeare Company's Henry VI, and helped me to make the imaginative time leap.

GARRICK HUSCARED (aka 'King James') friend and colleague, the gifted artist, writer, actor-manager and film-maker, for those conversations about black pirates and other unexpected Englishmen that lit the slow fuse of Tallie. And for making history so much FUN.

JANEY HUSCARED, friend and fellow-writer, for introductions, bodices to wear and inspirational good talk, among much, much more.

LINDSAY SMITH, passionate historian and side-saddle expert, for advice, information and farthingales.

RICK EVANS, (aka 'Captain Stanton' and Hampton Court's HENRY VIII). I owe his 'trans-temporal' sensibilities far more than I suspect he knows.

SUSAN SOLT, long-time friend, for our stimulating discussions about women of African descent in Early Modern England.

My son, TOM FRENCH, for designing and building my website.

EMMA FAULKNER, my sharp-eyed literary PA and conscience.

JEREMY PRESTON, of East Sheen Library for research and support.

LYNNE DREW, Publishing Director at HarperCollins, for launching my little ship of state and for keeping a steady hand on the tiller.

SUSAN OPIE, my editor, and JOY CHAMBERLAIN for accompanying Elizabeth and me on the journey. (Every writer should have such editors – inspirers, whip-crackers, friends.)

NB In my last novel, *The Principessa,* I smuggled the names of Susan Opie and Joy Chamberlain into the text, as a literary game. This time, it's Lynne Drew's turn . . .

ROBERT KIRBY, of United Agents.

ORLY (Café Strudel) and LEO GIANNINI (Café Al Fresco) for giving me working places away from home.

Francis II [1] m. MARY, QUEEN m. [2] Henry Stuart
King of France OF SCOTS Lord Darnley
r. 1542–67 d. 1567

JAMES VI and I m. Anne of Denmark
r. 1567–1625 (Scotland) d. 1619
r. 1603–25 (England)

Henry   Elizabeth m. Frederick V   Margaret
1594–1612   1596–1662   Elector Palatine   b. 1598
                                                        d. in infancy

Sophia   m. Ernest Augustus
1630–1714   1630–98
                Elector of Hanover

Elizabeth's Family Tree

CHARLES I   m.   Henrietta   Robert   Mary   Sophia
King of England   Maria   b. 1601   1605–7   b. & d. 1607
and Scotland   d. in infancy
r. 1625–49

George I   m.   Sophia Dorothea
Elector of Hanover   of Celle
King of England   1666–1726
and Scotland
1714–27

(via Victoria)   Elizabeth II
1952–

For more information see page 461

Rex fuit Elizabeth: nunc est Jacobus Regina.
Elizabeth was King. Now is James Queen.

Popular saying

I am ever for the medium in everything. Between foolish rashness and extreme length, there is a middle way.

King James

Be wary, then, best safety lies in fear.

Hamlet I, iii

PROLOGUE

1

WHITEHALL PALACE, LONDON, JUNE 1610
ELIZABETH

Today, I learned what I am for. I think that the information has always been there, but I've chosen to ignore it. Then, this morning, when the Duc de Bouillon looked me up and down and allowed that I was indeed 'handsome enough', my grip on wilful ignorance began to slip.

I felt a tide of unbecoming red begin to rise from the top of my bodice. I tried to imagine that I had turned into a tortoise so that I could pull my head inside my shell and close the flap.

I was standing in the Great Presence Chamber on show as a prospective bride, weighed down by a pearl-crusted blue satin gown, with a chain of bright little enamelled gold flowers draped across my (still-improving) breasts. My hair had been savagely disciplined. My finest pearl and sapphire ear-drops knocked at my jawbones. Ten pairs of adult male eyes, including my father's chilly gaze, stared at me as if I were a greyhound or horse for sale.

'Good breeding,' I imagined them saying. 'Shame about the cow hocks.' 'Nice deep chest, not certain about the set of the ears . . .'

'Handsome enough,' the duke had said. I tried to think what had made me so uneasy.

Such guarded praise might have squashed my vanity, if I had any.

I know how I look – tall and skinny with wild amber-red hair and fair Scottish skin. I may not be beautiful, like Frances Howard or fair, dainty Lucy, Countess of Bedford, but I'm not a trowie *crept from under a stone, neither. But there was more to my sudden unease than hurt feelings.*

Since I can remember, I've known that my father will marry me off, when and where he pleases. Marriage meant exile. I would be forced to leave my brother, to go, again, to a strange country to live among foreigners, with a man I didn't know, to be his queen. Just as my poor mother had to leave her home in Denmark for Scotland to live with my father. And then had to follow him here to England.

I know that my brother Henry has no more choice in his fate than I, but at least he knows where he will be when he becomes king. He can let himself learn to love England. It's his country now. My heart must not settle here.

That is the price of escaping from my father.

'She's tall for her tender years,' said the Duc de Bouillon. The marriage broker for the German state of the Palatine slid his probing eyes over me again with a private adult male gleam that made me squirm and look away. My chest and face burned. My grip on wilful ignorance slipped a little further.

My father, a smallish man, moved his mouth as if chewing and scratched his neck. He didn't trouble himself to reply. He knows that his wits are quicker than those of most men. And he's the king, so he can play the fool if he wants to.

'Of course, there's no harm if the wife is taller than her husband,' de Bouillon added quickly.

My mother is taller than my father.

My father still said nothing. He was behaving well, for him.

I rested my hands on the shelf of my farthingale and looked at the floor. The white ostrich plumes of my fan trembled in my fist. I felt a secret meaning in the duke's words, which I did not yet grasp. I saw secret understanding gleam in other male eyes.

I know that I would be married even if I had tiny eyes like a badger and the stumpy legs of those German hounds they send down the badger's hole – which I don't. I am the First Daughter of England. Whoever marries me marries England. 'Handsome' has nothing to do with it.

The Dauphin of France, the most likely of my possible husbands according to my old nurse Mrs Hay, is a sulky, big-nosed boy not handsome enough for any purpose that I can think of. And yet his mother means to arrange a good marriage for him, in spite of his nose and absence of chin, like a trout – although I wrong the trout, which is a beautiful creature, all polished pewter-brown and speckled silver with the flush of dawn lining its gills. Also, its wits are sharper than his from what I hear. And its temper is less haughty, irritable and melancholy.

Handsome enough for what, then? I glanced up.

The duke's eyes were now unlacing me, searching under the pearl-crusted silk for the swelling curves of my breasts. They lifted up my petticoats. They rested on my mouth. They dug through the layers of silk and linen looking for my most secret parts.

'His highness will be pleased,' he said.

He didn't care that I could read his eyes. With a private smile, he nodded to himself. She will do, said his eyes. With her amber hair and blue eyes, which are much larger than those of a badger, and long legs under those petticoats. She will do very well.

For . . .

The cold edge of understanding slid into my heart. My thoughts scattered. I struggled for breath like a fish cast-up on the rocks. But I could no longer blind myself to what I hadn't wanted to see.

I'm no looby. Of course I've known. I listen to gossip. I have observed dogs locked together and the noisy, terrifying breeding of horses. I can draw conclusions. But I never thought it might happen to me. To my flesh and skin and heart beat, to this thing that lives behind my eyes and breathes and fears and is me. Here is what I saw slithering through the duke's eyes and let myself understand at last:

I am no more than a greyhound bitch or a mare to be bred.

Marriage is not mere exile and strangeness. Marriage means that I must serve my country with my body. On my wedding night, Spain, or France or some German state – as our father chooses – like a dog or stallion, will push its designated cock into my private parts to plant an infant treaty.

Into that prim, closed mussel shell with its new amber fur, mysterious even to me. Closed like a book, even to me. Closed like a peach. Closed like a dark eye, still blind.

That is what I am for. How will I bear it?

PART ONE

The Dangerous Daughter

*To make women learned and foxes tame has the same effect –
to make them more cunning.*

James I & VI

2

5 NOVEMBER 1605 – Combe Abbey, Warwickshire

It was my fault, but the sun had to share the blame. Because of the sun, I had escaped alone. It had been a wet November in England. To judge by the purple-edged clouds hanging just above the horizon, the rain would return before nightfall. But just then, bright sunlight spilled down through holes torn in a bruised cloudy sky.

Like contented hens, my three ladies had spread out their feathers on the river bank and settled in the patches of sun. Tipsy with unexpected sunlight and greedy for more, they agreed that I could come to no harm here on my guardian's quiet estate.

'I won't go far,' I promised. 'Just a little way along the forest track across the ford.'

I was learning. When I was younger, perhaps six years old, I could never grasp why I should always seem to do as I was told. Then I learned. When people trust you, they watch you less.

My greyhound Trey splashed across the river Smite beside me as I balanced from stone to stone. Then he raced off after a squirrel and now barked furiously in the distance. My favourite toy spaniel, Belle, with her little short legs, had stayed behind on the riverbank.

Under cover of the forest canopy, I stopped to look back. No one had followed me.

Around me, the sun poked wavering holes through the wind-stirred trees and scattered spots of light across the ground like golden coins. I set off along a twisting leafy tunnel, through occasional pools of sunlight, to discover what adventure lay around the mysterious bend ahead of me. Under my leather riding boots the crumbly leaf mould of the forest track was sharp-smelling and black from rain in the night.

I stopped in a clearing, took off my hat and held up my face and hands to the rare, wonderful heat. A day like this tempted me against my better judgement to fall in love with England after all.

Something struck my hair lightly and slid down my chest – a yellow oak leaf, so bright and smooth that it seemed precious and mysteriously purposeful. I picked it off my bodice and held it up to the sun. It was so perfect that it made me want to cry. I tucked it, smooth and cool, into my bodice to press later in a book.

The voices and laughter of my attendants arrived only faintly on the wind from the far side of the river. I picked up a piece of fallen branch and threw it as far as I could. I listened to the satisfying crash. I wanted to shout with joy.

Unwatched, unattended. A miracle of freedom.

I spread my legs wide. Happily, I emptied my bladder like a mare under the cone of my skirts, felt the steamy warmth and smelled the friendly barnyard odour from my own body.

Ever since my family came south, I had lived in a cage of eyes. Scotland had been far more free. In Edinburgh, while we waited to travel down to London, I rode almost every day with my older brother Henry, one of his hawks on his wrist.

Accompanied only by a single groom and my greyhounds, Trey, Deuce, Quattro and Quince, we escaped together up onto the crags above the city under a sky of bright luminous grey. There, we stood side-by-side looking down on Edinburgh from the Cat Nick, a rocky point higher than the castle where our father had been born, higher even than the gulls. In the waters of the Firth beyond us, an island crouched low and dark in the water like a dragon waiting to spring on Fife. We would watch the mists blow in from the sea to cover it before we rode back. On the last day before we left Scotland, I took a small piece of sharp granite from the crags and hid it in my writing chest. I hold it in my hand now when I can't fall asleep.

I paused again in a little glade pitted with rabbit holes. The only sound was a leafy whispering. Trey had stopped barking. I stood so still that five rabbits popped out from under the roots of an old oak and began to forage on the forest floor.

I imagined that I became a rabbit. My nose twitched. I hopped forward to nibble a fresh tuft of grass, then pulled my hindquarters up after me, as if I had almost forgotten and left them behind.

One of the rabbits lifted its head. In an explosion of movement, they all disappeared into the ground.

I turned.

A handsome young man stood on the track watching me. Coins of sunlight danced on his shoulders and fair hair, which was almost the colour of the oak leaf.

I felt a thump of startled interest and grew a little breathless. He had materialised silently in the forest glade as if by magic. I knew that I had just stepped out of my everyday life into something far more interesting.

As we stood regarding each other in silence, I grew more and more certain that he was one of the magical creatures from my nurse's bedtime stories, who lived in forests and lochs and under stones. Always in our world but invisible unless they choose to show themselves.

I tried to think how to speak to him. He might have been anything, a tree-soul or a magic stag like those that roamed the Highlands, which had taken the shape of a man.

I wanted to reach out and pick the coins from his broad shoulders and put them into my purse, knowing that they would turn into real gold.

I was not afraid. His handsome face, though pale, was gentle and seemed made for cheerfulness. In any case, I was protected by the fairy shot, an ancient flint arrowhead, which my nurse, Mrs Hay, had sewn into my petticoat.

I smiled in greeting. When he did not smile back, I nodded encouragement.

He did not respond. We stood in silence.

'Are you a spirit of the forest?' I asked at last.

He opened his mouth as if he wished to speak but still remained silent.

I thought I understood then. I looked at his hands, clasped tightly in front of him. 'You're under a spell so that you can't speak? Must I set you free?'

'You must come with me.' His voice cracked a little, as if I had indeed just lifted a spell and his words were still rusty.

'Why?' I told myself that this adventure was exactly what I had secretly hoped for when I set off down the mysterious, twisting path. All the same, I suddenly wished that Trey were there. 'Where do you want me to go?'

He held out his hand to me.

I considered the urgency in his voice and gesture. But he was not threatening me. On the contrary, his words and reaching hand were a plea, not an order.

'Are you an enchanted prince?' I knew from Mrs Hay how the story went. He needed a kiss from me to set him free from a curse, but if he explained beforehand, he would stay cursed forever.

12

I looked at his mouth. I had never kissed a man, only my dogs and monkey and horses. Until this moment, I had not thought I would ever want to. To my surprise, I could imagine kissing him. My chest felt thick and full, making it hard to breathe.

I closed my eyes. It would be impossible to kiss a man while looking at him.

'Please come, your grace!'

I opened my eyes. With his uncertain eyes and fierce words, he now reminded me of Baby Charles playing at being a soldier, though he was taller and far more handsome than my puny five-year-old brother.

I saw now that his hand shook. Now I detected the reek of ordinary human fear, stronger than the sharp tang of leaf mould and comfortable smells of dog and horse on my own clothes. Unease stirred.

He wasn't doing it right. This no longer felt like the story I'd been imagining. With a thud, I dropped back into my everyday self. He was not an enchanted prince, and I was far too old to believe such things. A flush of shame began to creep up past the top of my bodice.

I smiled coolly, as I had learned from watching my present guardian's wife, Lady Harington. He was most likely nothing more than an importuning courtier. Even at my age, when the tender pebbles on my chest were just beginning to swell into breasts, petitioners pursued me, imagining that I might at least put in a good word for them with my father or mother, or older brother, even when I was locked away here at Combe.

The young man did not smile back.

But then, people were often too overwhelmed to smile back at royalty, even young female royalty.

I eyed the silver buttons on his doublet and the fine Brussels lace edging his collar. In truth, he didn't look like one of the usual awe-struck. More like one of those well-born Englishmen who sniggered behind their hands at my father

and the 'barbarian Scots'. A gentleman, in any case, importuning or not.

'I beg you!' he said.

'Are you a footpad?' I asked, to punish him because I had
imagined foolish things, and thought of kissing him. 'My
purse is empty, but my amethyst buttons might be worth
taking.'

He looked so startled and indignant that I almost smiled
at him again.

The lace on his collar was vibrating against his coat.

But then, many people trembled before my father. Some
even trembled before me, young as I was and only a girl.
But such people were not often gentleman like this one.

Suddenly, I heard my father's voice in my head, 'Trust *nae*
man.' Then with that little flick of cruel disdain, '*Nae* woman
neither.'

Beyond the beech saplings and arching bramble framing
the young man, the forest track was deserted. Suddenly, I
felt very young and alone. I had gone too far. My screams
would not carry back against the wind to my attendants on
the riverbank.

'Where must I go with you?' I asked.

'Please trust me, your grace. I take you to some true friends.'

'What do you and these friends want with me?'

He shook his head.

'I won't come unless you give me a good reason.'

We stared at each other again.

'You must be queen,' he said desperately.

I did not like that 'must'. 'Very likely, in time,' I agreed
cautiously. That had always been my eventual fate. 'But of
which country?'

He looked away. A branch creaked in the silence.

'Where am I to be queen?' I repeated. My voice sounded
reedy and caught in my throat.

'England.' He spoke so quietly that I almost couldn't hear.

'Queen of England?' My heart lurched into a gallop like a startled deer. A giant foot seemed to step on my ribcage. 'England already has a king! And a queen!' I took a step back. 'My father is king! My brother Henry will be king after him!'

He set his hand on his sword.

I was alone in the forest . . . the king's oldest daughter . . . alone in the forest with an armed, unknown man, who wanted to . . . I wasn't yet sure what he intended, but it was not good . . . fool! Fool! Should have seen the danger at once . . . not magic deer or enchanted princes.

I took another step back. I could not believe how this scene had turned. Mrs Hay had also told me tales of politics and treason, and they were true. Those who laughed at my father's fears were fools. Demons pursued our family everywhere. This young man, with his urgent voice and smell of fear was one of the demons.

I looked around, as if someone might come to my rescue. No ladies, no grooms, no guardian. No instructions what to do next. Not even Trey!

'When am I to become queen? What do you mean to do?'

Henry! I could never become queen while my father and older brother Henry were alive! This young man spoke treason and meant to harm my brother, Henry.

Treason. A word with a huge sharp beak that bit off people's heads. It had bitten off my grandmother's head. It could bite off my head.

I might die, I suddenly thought. For the very first time, I understood that my life could end. I would die. Now . . . one day . . . or very soon.

My wits scattered. My eyes blurred. I had never before in my life felt such fear. A dark, cold hollowness at my centre grew larger and larger until the thin shell of my being seemed about to crack. I wanted to sit down on the track. To imagine this scene away and make it back into a story.

But he stood there waiting, reaching out to take me. And there was no one to help me but myself.

'I won't come,' I said.

'You must.'

I slid my hand down to my dirk, hanging at my belt. But, though sharp enough, it was only a short-bladed, jewelled woman's toy.

'Don't make me call the others,' he begged. 'I swear I won't harm you.'

He drew his sword and stepped closer.

I wanted to scream at him. 'You may have killed me already.' I kept my voice steady. '. . . killed me without touching me!' Did he think I didn't know my own family's history?

I knew I could not outrun him but my body would no longer stand still. I turned and ran.

My skirts jounced up and down, swayed out of control, knocked into my legs. Though dressed for riding in a soft-hooped farthingale, I was still too wide, too heavy, too ornamented, too stiffened and pinned together.

I snagged on bushes, tore free. I heard his breathing close behind. A weight hauled at my skirt. I yanked free of his grasp. Felt a fumble at my sleeve. Then his hand clamped tightly around my upper arm.

His face was distorted, no longer handsome nor amiable. No going back for him now, not after laying hands on me. Not after those words. No going back for me, neither. With my free hand, I tried to hit him, to claw at his face, lost my balance. We fell together into a tangle of scrub.

Treason! I thought, now as desperate as he. As I fell, I clutched at leaves that tore away in my hands. I landed on the side of my ankle, lay wedged, half-toppled, my skirts caught in the thicket, my bodice twisted tightly around my ribs so that I could not breathe.

Our fall broke his grip on my arm. I snatched a tiny breath

16

with the top of my chest, pushed myself out of the scrub and hit him hard in the face. He stepped back.

'My grandmother had friends . . .' I yanked at my bodice, tried to breathe and run again. '. . . like you! She died on the block because of . . . friends . . . like you!' I could already feel the axe falling towards my bared neck.

Even the loyal Mrs Hay was willing to whisper how the Scottish king had been happy to take the English crown from the same hand that had signed the warrant for his own mother's death.

The young man picked up his sword, dropped in our struggle. 'I can't let you go.'

He must know as I did that he was almost certainly a dead man now, sooner or later, no matter what happened to me.

And I could no longer scream for help, even if I could be heard. Not now that I knew what he intended.

I shifted my weight onto my hurt ankle as slowly as a cat stalking a bird. The ankle felt cold and watery with pain but held, just. I tried to read him as I would a new dog or horse. 'I also see that you don't want to do this. I think you'd rather let me go.'

Startled eyes met mine. I hopped my good foot back beside the other. 'I think you're a good man and something has gone wrong.'

'If you knew . . .!' he agreed fervently. 'But I have no choice now.'

Our panting seemed to fill the low vault of arching trees. In his face, I could still see a last gleam of my enchanted prince. 'I thought at first you were under a curse,' I said. 'I wasn't entirely wrong, after all.'

And in a different story, we might have been friends. I hopped another step.

'I'm damned,' he whispered.

I begged my courage rise up to fill that cold hollow space inside me. 'I trusted you when I first saw you,' I said.

'That's why Robin . . .' He caught himself. '. . . why I was sent alone. For fear that you would take fright at a group of armed men.'

I straightened my back to give my courage room to rise. Please, I begged. At first it felt as fluid as water, flowing into my limbs, rising through my belly and chest. Slowly, another stronger creature, that was both me and something else far greater than I was forced its way up through the tight column of my throat until it reached my eyes.

I burned my attacker with a wolf's fierce gaze. 'Is my father already dead?' Even stiffened by courage, I didn't dare ask about Henry.

'I don't know. But it makes no difference now. It's too late to turn back!' He looked at me, his mouth slightly open. 'I beg you, forgive me, your grace, I never meant . . .'

'I think you should run,' said the young she-wolf steadily. 'As fast as you can.'

He closed his eyes. 'Holy Mother, protect me . . .!' His sword shook in his hand.

I had to tempt him to rewrite this story. I felt certain that he wanted to. 'It doesn't have to be too late,' I said. 'I don't know who you are, or what you truly intend. If you go now, I won't raise an alarm.'

He shook his head.

'You don't believe me? Don't you see why I can't raise an alarm? Why I must not even admit that you exist?'

I might be just a slip of a girl, but even I could see why no one must ever connect me to him and his friends. I knew suddenly that, though he was a grown man armed with a sword, my wits were quicker than his.

He kept shaking his head.

'You're a fool! But not wicked enough.' I eased back another step. 'They sent the wrong man. I swear I won't betray you. Save yourself, if you can.'

I watched his eyes as I watch those of a new hound to see

whether it means to lick my hand or bite. 'Whatever you and your friends are plotting, you must stop it, so I can try to save myself.' I saw struggle in his blue eyes. 'Neither of us wants to be here.'

'No,' he whispered.

'Then we must simply agree that we're not here and never were. If I don't betray you, what crime will you have committed?' I held my breath.

'You're scarce more than a child and don't understand men's affairs.' Then he went still, in that moment-of-just-before. Just before a dog is unleashed. Just before a bow-man releases his bolt or the dangling pig's throat is cut. I had seen men gather themselves up like that before, when they had to do something unpleasant.

'You must come with me,' he said. 'Please don't make me hurt you.'

I had lost him.

But I wouldn't die on the scaffold like my grandmother! Because that was how I would end, if I let him take me to these 'friends'. Better to die now, with only a short time for fear. Struggling, perhaps not even noticing the fatal blow. Better that than to wait blindfolded for the first blow of the axe, and the second and third. Better that my Belle not creep whimpering out from under my skirts, like my grandmother's little dog, covered with my blood, to sniff at my severed head.

'I won't come!'

He shook his head, avoiding my eyes.

I tightened my grip on my dirk.

'I can't be queen if I'm dead.'

'I swear that I won't kill you.'

'But I will.'

He stepped towards me.

I placed the tip of the dirk in the hollow at the base of my throat. I felt the point prick my skin. I took another step back.

Don't think! Don't think! Be ready to push . . . twist . . .
Just do it!

'It's harder than you imagine,' he said. But I had made
him uncertain again.

I hopped back another step. He started to follow.

'Don't misjudge my age or sex! I'm not a child, whatever
you may think.' The young she-wolf looked him in the eyes.
'And I'm not one of your delicate English ladies, neither. I'm
a Scottish barbarian. I cut the shoulder of a stag when I was
seven.' I hobbled another step. The she-wolf still knew that
I would use the dirk. My eyes told him so.

And another step.

He wavered, sword half-raised.

'God speed you!' I turned my back with the knife still at
my throat.

Breathe in. Hop. Breathe in. Hop.

The courage-wolf inside me gobbled up the pain.

Breathe in. Hop.

I listened for his footsteps over the sound of my own
breathing.

Around a bend in the track, then past a hazel clump. I
began to hope. Unreasonably, that fragile physical barrier
between us made me feel safer.

Breathe in. Hop. And again. And again.

Suddenly, the pain returned. I stopped, dizzy with pain. I
looked back. Through the screen of brown hazel leaves, I could
see him only in parts. He sat on his heels in the middle of the
track, rocking, with his head in his hands.

Get out of England! I urged him silently. As far away from
me as possible!

'Robin,' he had said, 'a band of armed men.'

There were others, but how many? And what were they
doing at this very moment? What did they intend? Oh, God!
I begged. Please let Henry be unharmed!

The snake word 'treason' coiled around my throat and

tightened. I must warn Henry. But how, without entangling myself in treason?

A fine deep tremor began in the bones of my legs. I leaned my hand on a beech trunk. My heart felt smothered, as if it didn't have room to beat. I tugged at my stomacher and bodice again. Distractedly, I picked broken twigs and leaves from my skirt and sleeves. The smell of fear rose from under my arms. I felt small and empty. My wolf had left me. I was on my own again.

I hobbled on. Now I had to return to my attendants and try to lie.

Trey raced up covered with mud and bits of dead leaf from rolling on the ground. Then he galloped ahead and back again, reproaching me for my slowness.

I had been such a fool!

If only our thoughts could leap across distances.

Take care, beloved brother. Take care! I don't know where you are. I don't even know what I must warn you about

'*You don't understand men's affairs,*' *my would-be kidnapper had said. Please, God, let someone tell me what is happening.*

Henry and I had been kept apart from birth, he at Stirling Castle under the rod of Lord Mar, I at Dunfermline and Linlithgow with Lady Kildare. But when we met at Holyrood before coming south to England, we had recognised each other as true kin in our first shy glance. Henry, who would one day be king, would know what I should do next.

Are you still alive?

It did not seem possible that Combe would still be standing when we got back.

On the riverbank, the grooms were asleep on the grass.

Lady Anne Dudley Sutton, a niece chosen by my guardian to be my chief companion, was making a necklace of plaited grass.

'What has happened to you?' cried one of the two older ladies with the beginning of alarm.

'Twisted my ankle,' I said. 'Slipped from a fallen log.' Only half a lie.

The ladies clicked their tongues over my ankle and promised a poultice. They exchanged amused glances while they re-pinned my sleeves and skirt without further questions. This time, at least, past misbehaviour worked in my favour.

To my relief both my guardian and his wife were away when we returned to Combe and would not return that night. But I had to let Mrs Hay resume her former role as my nurse, and order my fire built higher and fuss over my ankle with cool cloths and ointments. I agreed to eat my supper propped up on pillows in my big canopied bed. I stroked the four upright carved oak lions that held up the canopy and protected me from bad dreams. But tonight they stared past me with blank, denying eyes.

There was no help for it, I decided as I tried to force down some pigeon pie. I must risk implicating myself with guilty knowledge and warn Henry. If any harm came to him that might have been avoided, I would have to kill myself after all. I would not let myself think that the harm might already be done. I pushed aside the chicken broth. I asked Anne to fetch my pen and ink.

'You don't understand men's affairs,' the man in the forest had said. He was right. My life was being shaped by events I might know nothing about until it was too late. But I knew enough to know that my father's demons had followed us here to his Promised Land and threatened both Henry and me.

3

When I was younger, Mrs Hay had often put me to bed with tales that kept me wide awake in the dark for hours, tales even more terrifying than the servants' whispers of a ghostly abbot who sometimes stalked through my bed-chamber, which had once been his.

Vivid against the shadowy canopy overhead, I saw the sword tip held to my grandmother's pregnant belly while my father still lay curled inside. My grandfather's sword tip, threatening his own wife and unborn son. My father almost killed by his own father, Lord Darnley, while he was still in the womb. Then I saw Darnley murdered, his twisted body blown out of his bed by a mysterious explosion, lying dead under an apple tree. I saw my grandmother, Mary, Queen of Scotland, beheaded because Protestant Queen Elizabeth believed her guilty of plotting with Catholics to usurp the English crown.

'Papists,' whispered Mrs Hay. 'The devilish spawn of Rome.' She kept her voice down because my Danish mother was a Catholic and one never knew who might be listening. But she did not hesitate to call my Grandmother Mary by her Scottish nickname – 'The Strumpet of Rome'.

I learned that there had been two Catholic plots against

my father here in England, before his backside had even touched the English throne. The Bye and The Main, I repeated silently to myself.

When very young, I did not understand. Then, shortly after we came south, I had lost my own sweet governess, Lady Kildare. Her husband had plotted to kill my father in one of the Catholic plots. Though he was executed, she had survived. But my lovely, lively guardian, whom I loved dearly and who held my young heart in her care as tenderly as a mother, was wrenched from my life for fear that I might catch treason from her like the plague. I learned then about the bloody struggle between Papists, who were still loyal to the Catholic Pope in Rome, and the newer Protestants, a struggle set off in England by the old queen's father, Henry VIII, my brother's namesake.

'Holy Mother, protect me!' my forest spirit had cried.

It was happening again.

If anyone learned of our meeting – or even of his intent – I was tainted by treason for a second time. And I knew enough from Mrs Hay to be afraid of more than Papists.

My father's demon enemies were here in England, like the supernatural *fanes* and *trowies* who are invisible until they show themselves. In the dreams I had after my nurse's stories, I saw devils riding on skeleton horses, the faces of dead men taking shape in the dust of the road. The sons of executed men clung to my father's back whispering vengeance in his ear. No River Jordan cut off his English Paradise to leave all his Scottish ghosts behind, shouting impotently and shaking their fists on the far bank. They rode south with him.

I knew from Mrs Hay that my father still searched his closet himself, every night before going to bed, for hidden assassins and still wore a doublet cross-quilted with thick padding to stop a knife. The fine embroidery over his chest and belly was laid with enough metal wire to dull any blade.

I don't know if Mrs Hay ever saw what else she was

teaching me along with respect for my father's youthful courage. I couldn't think what wires or quilted padding could armour him against knowing that he had accepted the English throne from the woman who signed his own mother's death warrant. My father had acquiesced to the death of my grandmother . . . his own mother. How could his children feel safe?

4

I tossed in the darkness. In spite of the poultice, my ankle throbbed. Having written the letter to Henry, I didn't know where to send it. At different times, I had heard that the king had lodged him at Oatlands, Windsor, Richmond and Whitehall.

When the sky began to lighten the next morning but before the sun rose, I struggled into a loose gown and cloak and limped out of the house to the Combe stables. They were still dark, although a few horses had begun to stamp and bump in their stalls. I tiptoed unevenly through the dusty air and smells of horse and hay to find my groom, Abel White, who had ridden with me from Scotland and with whom I had once played in the Dunfermline stables.

He was asleep in a cocoon of blankets in the box stall of one of my mares. I shook him awake.

He groaned, then peered. 'My lady!'

'I need you to serve me on a secret mission,' I whispered. My breath made a pale cloud in the chilly air.

His sleepy eyes widened. He scrambled to his feet. 'Gladly! Yes, your grace. Always!'

My mare, Wainscot, stamped her feet, whuffled and nuzzled hopefully at the side of my neck.

'It's too early for your breakfast,' I pushed her away and gave Abel my letter to Henry. 'No one but Prince Henry must see this. I'm trusting you with my life.'

He nodded seriously. 'I will protect it with my own.' He put the letter into his purse, then hooked his jacket tightly over the purse.

As if I were one of the sparrows perched on the beams above our heads, I saw the two of us, there in the shadows of the horse barn, barely grown, now echoing in deadly earnest the adventure games we had once played together as children.

'Take Clapper,' I said. 'He's strongest.' I gave him a purse holding most of my precious half-yearly allowance from Lord Harington. 'Use this to hire another horse if he grows too tired and to stable him well.'

I watched while he saddled up Clapper, a solid, roan Ardennais gelding strong enough to carry an armoured man. Then he led the horse out into the stable yard.

The sky had now committed itself to the day. I held the reins and leaned against Clapper's strong, warm neck to stop my shivering while Abel went to make his excuse to a fellow groom for missing the morning chores.

'There you are!' Wearing a cloak over her night-dress, my companion, Anne Dudley, picked her way towards me across the brick paving, looking both rumpled and alarmed. 'I woke up and saw that you were gone! Vanished! Nowhere in the room! I couldn't think where you had gone . . . my heart is still thumping! I thought perhaps your injuries had suddenly worsened and you had died in the night. Or else been kidnapped from the bed.'

I looked at her sharply but saw only worry in her blue eyes. 'Would you like to come with me for an early morning ride?' I asked. 'To watch the sun rise?'

Accustomed by now to my sudden fancies, she shivered. 'I'd rather go back to bed, your grace.'

Abel came out of the horse barn.

'I've said I'm going for an early ride,' I told him in Scots, with a glance over my shoulder at Anne retreating across the yard.

Abel looked worried and jerked his head back at the barn. 'I've told them I'm riding on an errand for you but not where or why.' He continued in Scots to confuse any curious Warwickshire ears inside the barn.

I nodded. I'd untangle our stories later. I stroked Clapper's muzzle until Anne had disappeared again through the stable yard gate.

'Go first to Windsor. If Prince Henry isn't there, go on to Richmond then on to Oatlands and last London and Whitehall. Don't rest till you find my brother and give him my letter.'

He mounted. I looked up at him. 'Let no one but my brother see that letter,' I repeated. With one hand on Clapper's neck, I walked beside them out of the stable yard.

Clapper's hoofs rang like gunshots in the cold morning air. I looked up at the house. No curious faces appeared at the windows. It made no difference now, in any case. The absence of man and horse could not be kept secret for long on this small estate.

From the gate of the main courtyard, I watched Abel trot away up the long tree-lined avenue burdened with treason, my life tucked inside his jacket. Even on Clapper, he seemed a frail vessel to carry so much weight.

I could not bear to go back into the dense vaulted shadows of Combe Manor, once an abbey, now turned private house. I felt that God had never quite loosed His chilly grip on the place, even though He had been turned out more than sixty years before. I limped around the brick-paved courtyard along the walls of the three wings of the house. Still not ready to fall back under God's stern eye, I turned right into the gardens lying in the elbow of the river Smite, where I soaked my shoes leaving a dark ragged trail through the dew on the grass. I was not good at waiting.

The Haringtons returned before sundown. They brought no news of disturbance abroad nor death in London. Lady Harington, short, wiry and as sharp-eyed as a sparrow hawk, at once spotted my wet shoes and sent me to change them. I waited for Lord Harington to ask me about Abel White and Clapper. But he said nothing about the absence of either horse or groom. We prayed as we always did before every meal. I would have begged to eat in my bed again but Lord Harington always fussed so much over my health that it seemed easier to brave the table than his concern.

Supper passed as quietly and tediously as always. The Haringtons, never talkative, chewed and sipped quietly as if a demon might not, at this very moment, be crashing about doing damage I could not bear to imagine.

I half-raised my spoon of onion and parsnip stew then set it back down on my plate. A pent-up force seemed to distend my chest. Any moment, it would burst upwards and escape like lightning flashing along my hair.

'What news?' I wanted to shout. 'What is happening in the world outside Combe?'

At Dunfermline and Linlithgow palaces, when I was merely the girl-child of a Scottish king who already had two surviving sons, I had stolen time for games in the stables with the grooms, including Abel, and with the waiting footmen, maids and messengers. I had known all the kitchen family and listened while they thought I played. I heard all their gossip, suitable for my ears, and otherwise. Now that I was at last old enough to understand what I heard, I had been elevated into an English princess, third in line to the joint crowns of England and Scotland. Who must be kept safely buried in this damp green place where everyone treated me with tedious and uninformative respect.

I knocked over my watered ale.

Lord Harington gazed at me in concern with his constantly anxious eyes. 'Are you certain that your injuries yesterday weren't more serious than you say, your grace?'

'Perhaps a little more shaken,' I muttered. Though I sometimes thought him a tiresome old man, Lord Harington was kind. I did not like lying to him. I didn't know what I would tell him when he at last asked why Clapper was gone.

Then it occurred to me that he might be pretending that all was well. He might have been instructed to lull me into false security until men-at-arms could arrive from London to arrest me. I caught my glass as it almost toppled a second time.

When we were preparing for bed, Anne gave a little cry. 'What did you do to your arm?'

I looked down at the line of fingertip bruises along the bone. I brushed at them as if they were smudges of ash. 'I must have done it yesterday while riding.'

I wondered suddenly if Anne had been set by her uncle to spy on me.

5

For a second sleepless night, I lay in my bed in the darkness, waiting, not knowing what I was waiting for. I closed my eyes so that I wouldn't see the ghostly abbot if he should decide to visit. Tonight, however, I didn't fear him. My head was too crowded to deal with one thing more. I lay thinking how past events, which seemed to have nothing at all to do with you, could shape your life.

I could hear again Mrs Hay's whispers of treason and danger as she readied me for bed.

Ruthven. Gowrie. Morton. The names thumped in my pulse.

Treachery and knives. Ruthven and Gowrie, kidnappers and possible murderers. The child king, my father, no older than I was, standing courageously against his attackers. Morton, the regent who betrayed him and died on the scaffold. My father signing execution warrants when only a child.

'Never listen to the gossip that calls him a coward,' Mrs Hay had warned me. 'His majesty had a terrible life for a wee bairn, royal or not. Being made king so young did him no favours. That Scotland you pine for is a fierce and wild place, ruled by unruly chiefs who call themselves "nobles" . . . I don't know what you do to make knots in your hair like this!'

I always wanted to tell her that if I were a boy, I would have liked to be one of those unruly chiefs.

But I was her golden girl, her royal pet, her child, her life. I was her Responsibility, she said, which was a fearful weighty thing, which she carried nevertheless with a whole heart. She had to prepare me for my future without making false promises of joy in this life, though she was generous on behalf of the Hereafter.

So I stopped telling her what I felt. When very young, I had tried to tell her what I truly thought about a good many things but soon learned that she would only look stricken, as if someone had accused her of failure, and tell me to remember who I was. And to be grateful that my father wanted me kept safe as he himself had never been.

Tediously safe, I had thought. Until today, when the demons had arrived at Combe.

Henry? Can you hear me? We are both in danger.

I pressed my thoughts out into the night. I often spoke to my brother as one spoke to God. Even though I loved Henry more than I loved God, I told myself that God could never be jealous. Jealousy was a mortal weakness. God knew that Henry deserved to be loved. He was God's perfect, shining knight.

I had seldom seen the king, my father. But, so far as I remembered him before he set off on his separate journey to London, he cut a poor figure beside his eldest son. Our father was thick-bodied and short-legged where Henry, though not over-tall, was slim, fair and well-formed. Our father was awkward and given to coarse wit, where Henry had a soldier's bearing and the seriousness of a full-grown man.

I knew that I was not alone in my high opinion of my brother. At all the great houses where we had stopped on our progress south, we were entertained by poetry and songs praising us both, but chiefly Henry, who would one day be king. At Althorpe one poet, Mr Jonson, wrote in his entertainment that Henry was:

The richest gem, without a paragon . . .
Bright and fixed as the Arctic Star . . .

The poets did no more than speak for the people. Everywhere we went on our journey south, the cheers swelled when Henry appeared, the noble, handsome heir to the throne of England. Every boy in England wanted to be like Henry. Surely, no girl ever had a finer brother.

Look over the strict ocean and think where
You may but lead us forth.

I needed my brother's level-headed advice. I needed him to lead me forth. I whispered the poet's words to myself now. *'You must not be extinguished.'*

Though some people were said to find him stand-offish, or even cold, I had seen at once, when we met at Holyrood, that Henry's supposed chilliness grew from a modest reserve that took little delight in trumpeting his virtues. He was far more modest than I (who made the most of little) even though he had many more virtues to be modest about.

I had seen him smile and wave for mile after mile at the cheering crowds that lined our route to London, even when his throat was dry and his eyelashes caked with the dust stirred up by so many feet. Once, as we prepared with our mother to meet yet another matched set of mayor and aldermen, he said to me over the basin of water and towels offered so that we could clean our hands and faces, 'I don't know why they cheer. I've done nothing to prove myself to them yet.'

'You've missed a streak of dirt, just there.' I pointed, testing our wonderful intimacy.

'I promise to reward their hopes,' his voice said through the towel. His face reappeared, shiny and damp. 'I must not disappoint them. Their hopes put me in their debt.'

'You could never disappoint.' I did not quite dare to push back a lock of hair, darkened with water, which had fallen over his brow.

He shook his head, but smiled with pleasure all the same at my vehemence. 'Oh, my Elizabella, our father disappoints them already, and he hasn't yet reached London.'

I shrugged. I still felt too shy to try to tell him how superior he was to our father in every way. Except perhaps in his reported indifference to his books. But then, that was a weakness I shared. I was also thinking how much Henry knew that I did not, and how he lived in a larger world than mine. A little startled by his disrespect towards our father, I was also thinking how much he must trust me to say such things to me. He was looking at me with his serious eyes, warming me, sharing his knowledge and candour with me, his younger sister, as an equal.

Henry?

In my bed, I turned and turned his ring on my finger, remembering how he had given it to me in Scotland, up on the crags above Edinburgh. We were breathless from riding. Henry had brought a young eagle he was training to hunt. He handed the bird to his falconer, then we perched on rocks on the Cat Nick. It was a rare moment of sunshine. The dark dragon island crouching in the Firth of Forth behind us had been brushed with light. The backs of a pair of gulls wheeling and screaming below our feet, flashed white in the sun.

'We don't know what waits for us, Elizabella,' he had said.

'In England?'

He nodded. Together we watched the neatly folded ears of my favourite greyhound bounce up into view from the long grass of the slope to our right, then disappear again.

'The king has been quick to send me instruction on how to conduct myself as a prince, but is less generous with information about our new country.' Henry tossed a pebble over the edge of the cliff. 'The English Secretary of State, Robert Cecil, has written to me offering – if I understand him right through his careful words – to help me learn what I need to know. But he's preoccupied at this moment with smoothing the accession of our father.'

'England will be an adventure,' I said. 'Won't you be grateful to escape from Stirling to see more of the world?'

'Of course.' He tossed another stone. 'But I feel the weight of it as well.'

I nodded, but in truth, I felt a pang. Of course, Henry would feel the weight of our new life. He would one day become king of England and Scotland, after our father. I, on the other hand, was merely a daughter, fit only for marrying off to some foreign prince or other. Mrs Hay had not put it so bluntly but that was what she meant about 'preparing me for my future'.

'We cannot know the future,' said Henry. 'We may hope, but we can't ever be certain.'

He shifted sideways and reached into the pocket hung inside his breeches. 'I had these made.' He showed me two rings, identical except in size, of twisted gold wires, each topped by a small, square gold seal engraved with a ship in full sail.

He put one of the rings on my finger. 'If ever you are truly afraid, send me this ring.'

He put the second ring on his own hand. 'And, if I am in need, I will send mine to you. "I am in danger," the ring will say. "Come at once! I need your help."'

'I will come!' I said.

Looking down at our two hands wearing identical rings, I felt myself grow until I was as vast and solid as one of the mountains marching into the distance beyond the city. I became a crouching dragon. I was as strong as the wind that blew at our backs and scoured the clouds from the blue sky.

My brother Henry had not only promised me his help if I ever needed it, he believed that I might be able to help him.

We kissed each other gravely to seal our pact.

I am trying, Henry, though you never sent your ring. You may not even know that you need my help.

In the shadows of my bed, I saw him dying under the knives of the friends of my man in the forest. I saw myself clawing at a locked prison door. Then turned into a headless chicken like the one I had seen in the farmyard at Combe, the broken-off head tossed onto the midden, the yellow eye still staring out sideways, the wings flapping as if flight were still possible. Chicken and head, too far apart. Nothing in its proper place. The outlines of the world had wavered like reflections on a pond struck by a stone. A curious dog wandered up to sniff at the head. I had imagined it crunching the head in its teeth and screamed at it to go away.

My golden brother, help me! Be warned, save yourself, but don't let anyone harm me neither. Lead me forth.

The next morning, breakfast followed prayers, as always. All day, from my high window, I listened to the usual daily sounds of the estate. No men-at-arms came marching down the avenue. No messenger arrived from London on a foam-flecked horse.

If I had imagined that my man in the forest was a spirit, perhaps I had imagined the man as well. Perhaps I was mad.

After supper, I looked into my glass. Pale, yes. A little red around the eyes from lack of sleep. But otherwise as usual.

'Do you think that mad people know that they are mad?' I asked Anne.

'Of course not,' she said. 'Well, perhaps . . . There's an old mad woman in the village. You could go ask her whether she knows if she's mad . . . or else my aunt would surely know. She knows everything.'

When the late, falling sun had shrunk to a small hot red coin just above the horizon, and I was pacing the muddy gardens with Anne trotting after me, I heard hoof beats on the avenue.

If they had come to arrest me, I would be ready. I was waiting in dry petticoat and clean shoes, still a little breathless, when Lord Harington sent for me a short time later, to come to his study.

I was not mad, after all.

6

'My neighbours had horses stolen from his stables last night.' My guardian's agitation was as great as my own. A moderate man of middling size, with a permanent air of mild anxiety, Lord Harington seemed swollen that evening with barely contained emotion. I watched his surprisingly lux-uriant moustaches heaving as they framed his words. The peak of curling, greying hair that rose from his square forehead quivered like a torch flame. 'It's possible that one of our horses was taken also . . . one of yours, in fact. We fear some great rebellion.'

His brows collided ferociously above the fear in his eyes. 'A groom is also missing,' he said. 'Perhaps dead, perhaps run off to join the rebels. No one can be trusted!'

Missing, I thought. Not yet caught. I felt guilt shouting from every muscle of my face.

I tried to listen to what my guardian was saying, but his words scrambled themselves into a confusion of devils and explosions, gunpowder, intended murder. Papists . . .

He paced as if running from his words, spilling them behind him in the air like a shower of live sparks.

Rebellion all around us. Murder and devastation in London. Thirty barrels of gunpowder . . . Opening of

Parliament . . . another Papist plot to kill the king. Deaths beyond number . . .

My own agitation seized onto 'Papist'. I was right. It was happening again.

He couldn't know what had happened to me in the forest, I tried to tell myself.

'. . . fires of hell to Westminster, and the death of all Members of Parliament,' he was saying. The hem of his heavy long gown swung as he turned. 'The king's infinite wisdom . . . midnight arrests . . . questioning in the Tower. There was still a great fear of popular uprisings . . .'

'Has my brother been harmed?'

Lord Harington looked startled by my interruption. 'The prince is well, your grace,' he assured me. 'Though Prince Henry was to have accompanied His Majesty to the opening of Parliament yesterday, he is as safe as your father. Both of them have been spared.' He looked relieved to have good news to give. 'A warning letter was brought to Cecil,' he went on. 'Praise be to God!'

A warning letter?

'Praise God,' I echoed weakly.

My letter had been intercepted, I thought. Henry had never received it. Or . . . dear God . . . he had received it and betrayed me to Cecil. And Harington knew. Or Abel had been caught and had surrendered it.

'Now, my dear . . .' Harington stopped in front of me and looked down. 'You must be brave, for the next news concerns you closely.'

Though my body seemed on fire, my fingertips made icy spots on the backs of my tightly folded hands. 'Would you please tell me once more, just what happened? I don't think I quite grasped . . .'

'Forgive me, your grace. It is momentous news for anyone to take in, let alone someone so young and so close to the subject.' He sat down opposite me and began again, more calmly.

'There has been a Papist plot to set off an explosion of gunpowder under the hall where Parliament was to meet.' His long square-edged face looked to see if I followed him.

I nodded, uncertain what to think. Surely, he would not be explaining with such mild patience if he believed me to be guilty of treasonable knowledge.

'His majesty and the prince were to have been present. If the plot had succeeded, they would both have been killed along with most of the Members of Parliament. Happily, one of these devils was arrested on the spot, with his slow match ready in his pouch. He is being questioned even now at the Tower, along with several of his confederates who were also taken.'

'But their plot has failed? No one was killed?' I made myself unclasp my clenched hands. Why would he tell me all this if he thought I already knew? 'But this is good news after all!'

'Not entirely, your grace. I come now to the part that concerns you.'

I went very still.

'These Papists traitors meant to kidnap you.'

I risked a small cry and widened my eyes in horrified surprise.

'Don't fear, your grace. Not to harm you, but, by means of civil uprisings, to make you queen of England.' He paused. When I said nothing, he added, 'After the deaths of your father and brother.' He watched keenly, waiting for me to respond.

He has been asked to report how I took the news, I suddenly thought. I was suspected after all.

'What sort of queen would I have been in those circumstances?' I burst into absolutely genuine tears.

'There, there. The devils haven't succeeded there yet, either.' My guardian stood up to lay an awkward hand on my shoulder. I imagined relief in his voice and absolution in that rare touch. But the mention of a warning letter still made a cold lump in my gullet. I could trust no one. Not even my kindly guardian and his seeming relief at my protested innocence.

He removed his hand. 'At least eight rebels have been arrested with their servants and families. Four more were killed resisting arrest at Holbeche. But we don't know how much wider the Papist rebellion has spread. Nor how many rebels remain at large. I hear that the arrests continue. England is in arms between London and Wales, and as far north as Leicester. There are fears about the loyalty of the Catholic lords, both in London and on their northern estates. I'm told that Northumberland is already in the Tower.' He began to pace again. I had never seen him so filled with vigour.

He looked out of the window. 'I sent this morning to the Chief Secretary for instructions on your safety and have been waiting for his reply. But I can't wait any longer. There was further trouble just now, this afternoon, not far away. I won't risk keeping you here at Combe.'

'Surely I'm safe enough here.' My voice rang false as I spoke. Fortunately, Harington was wiping his face with his handkerchief and seemed not to notice. I decided not to speak again.

'Alas, Combe is not a fortified house,' he said. 'And we seem to be at the centre of the troubles here. Still more horses were stolen at Warwick and Holbeche is too close for comfort. Other rebels were followed fleeing this way. Some may even now be hiding among our neighbours. You must move to more secure lodgings in Coventry.'

I nodded.

Before the dusk had fully turned to night, I was mounted on Wainscot, my right leg hooked tightly around the saddle head. I had been allowed to take only a single maid.

'All will be well, your grace.' Harington leaned closer from his own horse. 'I'm certain of that.' He sounded unsure. 'The Lord will protect you.'

He'd be even less certain if he knew what had already happened, I thought.

'All will be well, I'm sure,' he repeated. He wore his sword, which he seldom did at Combe. 'They will pray for us.' He nodded back at the house.

Our little cavalcade clattered off with a jingling of harness and squeak of leather on leather. Unfamiliar men-at-arms rode close around me on all sides. Their swords, saddle maces and faces told me what they were, but in place of identifying livery or badges, they wore plain leather jerkins and padded vests. No standard identified our party.

Skulking through the early dark of autumn with the hood of my plain wool cape pulled forward to hide my face, I felt like a fleeing criminal.

'Whose men are you?' I asked the rider on my right.

'We all serve the king, madam.' He turned his head away suddenly towards the shadows of the trees beside our muddy track.

'What do we fear?' I asked.

'Ambush.' No title, to hide my identity from any prying ears.

I fell silent inside my hood, which smelt of damp sheep.

The other horses closed more tightly around me as we passed through the village of Stoke and did not open out again until the lights of the last outlying farm were far behind. I wondered which they feared more – attack, or that I might tighten my leg around the horn of my side saddle and race away to join the rebels.

With less on my conscience, I might have enjoyed the ride. The carefree girl who had entered the forest yesterday might have pretended that she fled through the night like an escaping highwayman, triumphant at an audacious raid. But I felt a demon thrashing around us in the darkness, laying waste to my former life. In the dark gaps between trees, I saw the distorted face of the young man in the forest. His helpless rocking as I looked back. Twice I imagined that I heard hoof beats running beside us in the dark.

I had been to Coventry once before, the previous year. I remembered a bumpy carriage ride in the April sunlight, and the generosity of lengthening evenings. I had been accompanied by both Haringtons, and a troop of ladies from neighbouring estates. Lady Harington had sent one woman away for wearing her bodice cut too low. Then she had re-shaped the wire of my standing collar and changed the order in which we were to travel.

On our tour of the streets, cheering crowds and ranks of waving livery men – cappers, mercers, tailors and drapers – stood to watch us pass. I remembered catching a thrown cap and placing it on my own head amid a burst of laughing cheers.

This time, we rode almost unseen through the dark streets. Two watchmen raised their lanterns curiously but quickly lowered them again at a sign from my escort. This time, in spite of the warm welcome given me by a Mr Hopkins of Earle Street, a close friend of Lord Harington, I felt like a prisoner. The two men-at-arms stationed outside my door seemed more like warders than guardians.

'You can sleep at ease tonight, your grace,' Mr Hopkins told me. The citizens of Coventry had posted an army of guards around the house in case the Papist army attacked. No one, he said, could get in, or out.

Seeing my person secured, Lord Harington assured me one last time that all would be well. Free for the time of his great charge, he rode off in visible high spirits to confront the Popish army now rumoured to have gathered on Dunsmore Heath.

Again, I waited. Three days passed. I received no official visitors or delegations. I heard no news from Combe, London or anywhere else. I dined alone in my chamber. I tried to eavesdrop through my half-open door but heard nothing. I smiled at an endless string of different grooms and maids who found an excuse to have a look at me, but none could be induced to gossip. I read, I stitched, I walked in the small walled garden. I began to write a heroic poem but tore it up. I practised scales on my new lute though I could not find it in me to sing. At noon on the fourth day, I heard a disturbance in the stable yard, then men's voices on the floor below. Footsteps climbed the stairs. I left the door and sat on a chair by the fire.

My maid opened the door to a strange man-at-arms. Like my escort to Coventry, he wore no identifying livery badge.

'What news?' I demanded.

He stepped aside to escort me from the room.

7

A small lop-sided shape waited for me below in Mr Hopkins's great parlour. There was no mistaking him for anyone else. This was a far greater man than my temporary host.

'My Lady Elizabeth.' He sketched an off-kilter bow.

He should have been in London questioning traitors in the Tower.

Robert Cecil, now Lord Salisbury and the English Secretary of State. My father's chief advisor. Here in Mr Hopkins's large parlour, his sharp, intelligent eyes on my face. He cleared his throat.

If we were to stand side-by-side, he would reach no higher than the top of my ear. The fur collar of his loose gown did not quite disguise the uneven slope of his shoulders. Why then, did he cause such fear in me?

I struggled to hold his gaze.

Neither of us spoke. It was my part to speak. Unlike my conscience, my mind was blank.

'Has something more happened?' I asked at last.

'More than . . .?'

'About . . .?' I tried to wipe my thoughts clean, leaving only what Lord Harington had told me. But I could not remember clearly. 'About the fearful plot?' I was certain at least that Lord Harington had told me about a plot.

'And did your guardian tell you about the quick wit of the king, your father, in perceiving the threat?'

I could not remember.

'My father?' I echoed.

I had seen no attendants waiting in the hall. No secretary waited behind the little table below the window. Cecil was alone. I could think of no good reason why he had come here in apparent secrecy.

After another pause, Cecil pointed to a high-backed, unpadded chair-of-grace.

Flushed and angry with myself for needing his prompt, I sat. I noticed that he had slender, long-fingered hands, like a woman. Then I remembered to nod for him to sit as well.

'Thank you, your grace.' He perched at the front of a second chair-of-grace and smoothed the skirts of his robe over his knees. He cleared his throat again and spoke a little too loudly, as if I might be deaf. 'The king, your father was the agent of his own salvation. Praise God.'

'Praise God,' I echoed.

'A loyal subject had brought me an anonymous letter.' He looked away.

'A loyal subject?' I echoed again. Thank God, Harington had prepared me for the letter. I laid my hands on the arms of the chair and closed my fingers carefully around the oak grape leaves carved on the ends.

He nodded. 'A warning from a loyal Catholic lord.' He met my eye with a half-smile. His words rolled on smoothly. 'Which I showed to the king. His majesty saw at once what had escaped me – that it concerned the hidden intent to blow up the opening of Parliament.' He paused. 'The terrible plot was uncovered. Thanks be to God!'

I murmured an incoherent piety.

Not my letter after all! I felt my hands fly into the air like startled doves and quickly clasped them together in my lap.

His small lumpy bulk leaned forward. He braced his elbows on the chair arms, so that his long feminine fingers dangled from awkwardly suspended hands.

I looked away. I wished those eyes would stop looking at me and at my clasped hands. I wished the room were not so strange and close, nor hung with tapestries of bloody battle scenes. I ached to be back at tedious, familiar Combe. I had misplaced all my rehearsed lies. I was sick with waiting.

'Why are you here, my lord?'

He hesitated. My throat tightened. I tried to swallow but had forgotten how. I saw his eyes go to my throat. He watched me struggle. I managed to swallow on the third try.

'His majesty has instructed me to speak with you.' He looked back at my eyes. 'About these recent dreadful events.'

I stared back, afraid now to trust any sound that might come out of my throat. With effort, I unclenched my fists.

'Were you ever acquainted with Sir Everard Digby?'

I shook my head, cautiously truthful. To my knowledge, this was no lie.

'A traitor whom I have recently examined in the Tower, along with several of his companion devils.'

'Is he one of those who would have blown up Parliament?' The frog in my throat was quite natural, I told myself. In the circumstances.

Cecil smiled slightly, inviting me into complicity. 'This young knight, Digby, had a very different task – to take you prisoner.'

I met his invitation as blankly as I could. All I could see in my head was Digby – for that must be his name – standing with the coins of sunlight dancing on his shoulders and head.

Go away! I begged him. Get out of my thoughts! A treacherous heat began to bloom in my chest.

'A plausible young knight,' said Cecil. 'Well-formed and fair-haired. His family's estate is not far from Combe. Until he married, I'm told that many ladies had their eye on him.'

All at once, I saw the truth, Digby had confessed. He had confessed to our meeting in the forest. Cecil knew!

I shook my head, helpless to stop the red fire that stained my chest and flooded up my neck. Cecil knows everything, I thought.

'I never met a man who gave that name.' I frowned slightly, as if trying to recall. I understood very well. Digby had taken me down with him just as I feared. Had not taken my advice to flee, not in time. Good man or bad, he had turned out to be a *trowie* after all.

Cecil watched the telltale blush reach my cheeks and rise upwards until the roots of my hair felt ablaze. 'You might perhaps have smiled on him once?' he prompted gently. 'Perhaps not knowing who he was? He's held to be handsome and is only a few years older than your grace. Any young woman might smile on him.'

The Chief Secretary was toying with me. I could bear it no longer.

'Is this an examination, my lord?' I demanded.

'Should it be?' he asked mildly. He looked around the room. 'Do you see a clerk? Or witnesses to an examination? Should you be examined?'

'No,' I whispered.

On the far wall, one of the tapestries heaved. 'By God, it is an examination!'

I leapt to my feet and turned. I had heard that Scottish bellow before. In the corner of my eye, I saw Cecil wriggle off his chair.

With a flash of rings, my father knocked aside the edge

of a woven battle and stepped out of the alcove behind it. 'Anatomise her, man! Ye're too nice!' The king staggered in his excitement, his restless body made clumsy by the urgencies of his mind.

Cecil stared at the floor.

The king stopped in front of me, blocking my view of Cecil. 'Aye, Bessie! Y' know very well it's an examination! And you'd best thank God to be here in Coventry and not locked in the Tower with your friends!'

'"Friends"?' I repeated faintly.

'You'd be examined there, right enough! And not so gently, neither!' The king turned on Cecil. 'Why didn't you ask the questions I prepared? What have y'done with them?'

'I meant to come to them by degrees, your majesty.'

'There's no degree in being dead! And no degree in treason!' The king held out his hand. 'Give me my questions and act as my clerk. I will play Solomon. I'll examine this treacherous whelp of mine, who seems to have terrified you into degrees!' His over-large tongue dammed and slowed the flow of words pouring from his brain. His bright, hungry magpie eye probed at me.

From the table beneath a window Cecil took a densely written paper and gave it to the king. He returned to the table and sat on the stool behind it. Now I saw the waiting pen and ink.

'That devil Digby's in the Tower,' said my father. 'We know by his own confession that he and his fellow fiends meant to make you queen of England! After I . . . your king and father . . . had been blown sky-high, murdered, along with your precious brother.'

'Never, my lord father!' I whispered.

'What do ye have to say to that?'

'What sort of queen would I have been . . .?'

He jabbed a finger at me. 'A compliant one. Controlled by Papists, ruling at the will of Rome.'

'I had rather been murdered in Parliament with you than wear the Crown on such condition!' I spoke that truth with all my heart.

The small eyes skewered me. 'Fine words!' He pulled at his lower lip with finger and thumb. 'What are you?'

'I don't understand.' I glanced at Cecil but he was head-down at the table, recording our words.

'What . . . are . . . you?' the king repeated slowly and loudly, as if I were simple. 'Do I know you?'

'I'm your loyal daughter, sir.' I felt my own temper begin to rise.

'D'ye think me a fool?'

'I think you many things, sir, but never a fool!'

We both drew breath and stared at each other. Cecil's pen stopped scratching.

The king shook his list of questions in my face. I blinked but did not move. 'I ask you, just as your friends in the Tower were asked,' he said. 'Are you a Papist?'

Refusing to step back, I fixed my eyes on my father's thick padded jerkin, diamond hatched with stitching that held the thick lining in place to turn aside attacking knives. 'Never!'

'I know that you are a Papist!'

Like my mother? I wanted to ask but had just enough good sense not to say.

'Do you mean to accuse my guardian too?' I asked instead. 'Lord Harington hears me pray at his side five times a day.'

The close-set eyes studied me. The king scratched under his doublet. He tugged at his cuffs. He twitched his neck in his collar and seemed to chew on his tongue.

I had seen people ape those mannerisms, and then laugh. I did not find my father laughable. He terrified me.

I can make you obey where you ache to scorn, his behaviour seemed to say to those who aped him. That's real power!

The king bit at a fingernail. I felt the swift current of his

50

thought tugging at me. 'Why should I let you keep your head?' he asked.

'Because I've done nothing!'

We both pretended to listen to the scratching of Cecil's quill.

'Don't think, madam – you and your brother – that public acclaim is the same as power! From the common people it's worth nothing! It's a river that drowns all virtue.'

'I don't want acclaim!' I cried. 'I don't want power! What would I do with power?'

'Don't think I wasn't told how the people cried out in the streets,' he said, now just as agitated as I was. 'Singing out as you and your brother went by. "The golden pair!" "The golden boy, the golden girl!" "England's best hope!" Don't think you'll bury me, either one of you! Don't imagine you'll ever warm your arse on the English throne!'

'I don't want the English throne!'

'. . . because I shall marry you as far away from here as I can arrange. I'd marry you to the Great Cham, if I could, and send you to his queen in Tartary. I'd marry you to the Devil himself, if only he wanted a wife!'

He shoved his face close to mine. 'Listen to me, Bessie. If I choose to let you live, I mean to marry you off as soon as I can. Do y'hear me? Catholic, Protestant, doddering fool or dribbling babe – I'd give you this moment if your husband would take you and your ambitions away from England, out of my sight for ever!'

He folded the list of questions. 'We're not done with these yet. You don't deceive me. But first, I'll hear more of what your friends in the Tower have to tell us. Then I'll decide what's to be done with you.'

There's no point in lying further, I thought with despair. My father would make those prisoners say whatever he liked.

I opened my mouth to defend myself with the truth. Yes, I had met Digby, but not by my own will. I had refused to go with him, no matter what he might claim in his confession. I had threatened to kill myself rather than agree to do as the plotters intended.

Behind the king, Cecil gave a minute shake of his head.

I closed my mouth and stared past my father's shoulder in astonishment. Again, a tiny warning shake, no mistake. Then Cecil looked back down at his notes.

Then I saw how close I had been to disaster. My guilt or innocence in the treason plot did not matter. It had never mattered, once I had reported Digby's kidnap attempt to Henry alone. Not to the king or Cecil. That failure alone made me a traitor in the king's eyes. And if I had confessed, I would have dragged my brother down with me.

'My mother had friends like yours.' My father handed the folded questions back to Cecil. 'You should choose better acquaintance, lassie. With less taste for regicide. First your old governess Lady Kildare and her husband, now these Papist gallants. To be twice touched by treason is no accident.'

The king turned to Cecil. 'Come, Wee Bobby! Let's leave the "golden" lassie to her thoughts, while she still has a head to think them.' He struck the door with his fist. It opened. He left without looking back.

Cecil wiped his pen and inserted it into a leather roll. He gathered up his papers and tapped them to align the edges. 'Don't fear,' he said, so quietly that I might almost have imagined it.

'And lest her thoughts remain confused,' shouted my father from the corridor, 'I'll arrange a sight to clear them.'

'My lord . . .' I began.

Cecil held up his hand to silence me. 'As Lord Treasurer, among all else,' he continued, to the tabletop, 'I must advise the king that he can't afford to throw away even one of his two most valuable assets.'

When the door closed behind the two men and their

footsteps had faded, I finally let my knees dump me back into my chair.

Cecil would have warned me to keep silent only if he knew what I was about to confess. But if he knew, why was he protecting me?

8

Bonfires were lit across England to celebrate my father's deliverance from his brush with the fires of hell. From my window in Coventry, I saw arcs of glowing orange spring up against the night sky. No one invited me to attend any of the fires, nor the dancing, feasting and drinking that accompanied them. But even in the guarded household of Mr Hopkins, I felt a feverish exhilaration.

Something terrible had been averted, even if the details were blurred. The consuming darkness had been defeated. Demons had been slain. Those captured alive would soon be executed. The king declared that the anniversary of his deliverance would become a yearly holiday. Each year, on the fifth of November, the fires would burn. The threat to Henry and the Members of Parliament dropped from mention.

Once it was believed that all of the Gunpowder Plotters, as they became known, were either dead or in the Tower, I was returned to Combe. Lady Anne, left behind to avoid advertising my flight, was still agog with scraps of news. She lacked the discretion of Mr Hopkins, or perhaps his wariness, and eagerly poured her snippets into my ear.

The leader of the plot, Robert Catesby, had been killed at Holbeche House, not far beyond Coventry, with several others, including Thomas Percy, a cousin of the Duke of Northumberland.

Robert Catesby, I thought. 'Robin . . .'

'He was a known Papist trouble-maker,' said Anne. 'Even though he was a gentleman. A single bullet struck down both him and Thomas Percy, whose cousin the Duke of Northumberland lives at Syon and has been himself examined by Lord Salisbury and the king, your father.' I felt in her the same feverish excitement I had found in Coventry.

'My uncle had such a wondrous fire lit here,' she went on happily. 'He even permitted me to watch the dancing, though of course, I was not allowed to romp in a field with the tenant farmers.' She leaned closer. 'I did manage to snatch a mug of *eau de vie* distilled by our estate manager, but don't tell Uncle.' She looked at me for approval. She so seldom had daring to offer me.

'What of the other plotters?' I didn't want to mention Digby by name.

'You must ask Uncle. I know only what I hear on the estate.'

I went to ground, and waited. I wondered what my father had meant by 'a sight to clear her thoughts'.

Christmas passed with the social restraint and well-fed decorum you would expect in a household where the Papish word 'mass' caused unease. In a house that had once been a Catholic abbey, we marked the holiday merely by praying more often, to a Protestant God, in the chapel built for monks.

But although my Protestant guardian spoke only of 'Christ Tide', the old, forbidden word 'mass' lived on in the kitchen, gardens and stable yard. Other, even older spirits had their gifts too. Protecting holly springs hung in the horses' stalls. Mistletoe sprouted in the dairy. I left an appeasing plate of sweet, twisted anise-flavoured Jumbles in a corner of my bedchamber for the ghostly abbot, and found them half-eaten the next morning.

I used the more-frequent prayers to beg Henry to respond to my letter, if he had ever received it. Seven weeks had passed. Neither Abel nor Clapper had yet returned from London.

I sometimes caught Lord Harington studying me with a frown. Whether I imagined pity or coldness in his eyes, I felt the same quiver of terror. I tried to distract myself by playing with my monkey and my dogs. I rode whenever the bleak damp January weather allowed. I was never left alone again.

Like an animal, I felt a storm coming. I fell asleep at night with the fragment of granite from the Edinburgh crags in one hand, and Belle's furry warmth hugged close with my other, whenever I managed to smuggle her past Lady Harington and her fear that the little dog might soil the bed linen.

At the end of January, the king sent men-at-arms to take me to London.

9

LONDON, THURSDAY, 30 JANUARY 1606

From my chamber in the Bishop's house at Paul's, beside the Cathedral, I listened all day to the distant sound of the scaffold being built in the Churchyard. I had arrived in London by night, as furtively as I had fled to Coventry. Lord Harington sent me off from Combe professing ignorance of why the king had sent for me in secret. Besides the men-at-arms and the necessary grooms, only my old nurse, Alison Hay, had ridden beside me. Not even Anne was allowed to attend me.

As I rode away, I looked over my shoulder at my guardian. After more than two years, I still did not know whether I was merely a costly burden to him or whether true affection lurked in all his well-meaning severity.

Hammering, sawing. Faint and distant, but I knew what they meant. In the next two days, the Gunpowder Plotters were to die, some here at Paul's and some at the Tower. Listening to the sound of hammers, I tried to decide whether I had seen more than concern on Harington's face when I left Combe.

The hammering paused. In the brief silence, I understood why I had been brought to London. I was to be seized without warning and beheaded, along with the Plotters! That was why I had travelled in such secrecy, lest my fate raise a wake of protest among the common people who had cheered so loudly for Henry and me. Their cheers had meant nothing, just as my father said.

I saw now why not even my mother knew I was in London – for she had neither visited nor sent a greeting. I saw why I hadn't been allowed to go to Whitehall or to send a message to anyone. And why Anne had been kept behind, so she would not be tainted with my crimes. The king feared me, his oldest daughter, enough to kill me as his own mother had been killed, for the safety of the English crown.

I tried to tell myself that I was jumping to conclusions. But however much I fought it, the conviction that I was right twisted its roots deeper and deeper into my head.

Mrs Hay woke me in what felt like the middle of the night. 'You are sent for.'

The windows were still dark, with no hint yet of winter sunrise. The air was cold.

I gripped her hands. 'Do you know why? Tell me! I won't cry out, I swear.' My heart pounded. If I were to die, I needed time to ready myself. This wasn't fair! Not possible . . . 'Where must I go?' I could not imagine dying.

'To the Bishop's little study.'

'Not to the Churchyard?'

'I was told the study, here in the Bishop's house.'

'Only the Bishop's study?' I burst into tears.

'Oh . . .!' Mrs Hay stared, uncertain what to do. She hadn't held me for more than six years. Then she reached out and clutched my head to her breast. 'No. No! You mustn't think such things!' She smoothed my wild hair. 'How can you think it?'

I heard a pause while she did indeed think how the thought might have occurred. A new spasm of terror quivered through me.

'What does the king want with me?'

Mrs Hay sounded less confident than before. 'His majesty's at Whitehall, not here. And means to go hunting, or so I'm told.' She stroked my head again. 'Four of those Papist fiends are to die today. Grant, Digby, Wintour and Bates. No one else.'

Digby. I was here because of him. Digby must be the reason. I could not think straight.

She fingered a russet tangle at the back of my head, then began to unpick it, hair by hair. 'I'll attend you in the Bishop's study, if they let me.' As she lifted my heavy hair in both hands to shake it out, I felt a cold draft on my nape.

'I'll wear my hair loose today,' I said. I smelled fear in my armpits. I put my hands on my neck as if to hold my head in place.

A gentleman wearing the Bishop of London's livery led us to the study, a small room overlooking Paul's Churchyard on the far side of the Bishop's house from the chamber where I had slept. Apart from the bishop's man, Mrs Hay and myself, the room was empty. I had half-expected Cecil to be there. I felt him twined into my fate but did not yet know how.

The bishop's man gestured towards the window. With Mrs Hay beside me, I looked down through the diamonds of watery glass at the blurred bulk of the scaffold I had heard being built.

Outside, the sky was just beginning to lighten. Lanterns and torches still burned. A crowd already packed the space. I could hear it through the closed window, like the sea shuffling pebbles. The Bishop's man opened the window so that I could see more clearly.

The blades of halberds pricked the chilly air above the crowd, where men-at-arms stood stationed in every doorway, enough of them to stop a possible rescue attempt, which such a great crowd might allow. Or to put down a civil uprising, like those the plotters had believed would take place across England in support of the Catholic cause – and which the government still feared, to judge by that army in the courtyard.

Dignitaries stood crowded onto the scaffold close below me, talking amongst themselves as if in a waiting room in Whitehall. I was so close I could hear them coughing and clearing their throats. Cecil's small figure was first hidden, then discovered again, as the others shifted around him.

'Who is that man standing behind Lord Salisbury?' I asked Mrs Hay. 'There, the one with the thin face, who keeps smiling and nodding at the others.'

'That's his lordship's cousin,' said Mrs Hay. 'Sir Francis Bacon. Their mothers are sisters.' She tried to think what else to tell me. 'He writes a great deal.'

Though much taller and better formed, Bacon lacked his little cousin's authority. I watched him for a moment. He reminded me of an anxious dog, sniffing and wagging his tail at the other men on the scaffold. Then I forgot him.

The hangman was quietly and methodically testing his ropes and knots. It would begin soon. Soon they would be making me ready, pinning up my hair, removing my collar.

Then reason pulled me back from my leap to certainty. They were not preparing me, reason pointed out. I was here, looking down, buffered by staircases and corridors, not in a cell or a room more convenient to the Churchyard with a bishop praying over me and inviting me to repent.

I was not going to die today. Other traitors would die – real traitors, not an ugly troll of my father's imagination that pretended to be me. I was not here to die but to watch.

I felt the solid thump of truth. This was the clarifying sight that my father promised me in Coventry.

I stepped back from the window.

The Bishop's man gestured politely for me to return to my position.

With sudden clarity, I heard my father's avid voice in my

head, as he questioned the bishop's man. 'How did she bear it? Tell me, *mon*! Did she avert her eyes? At which death did she flinch the most? Did she seem to know any of them? Did she weep?'

I was still on trial.

I waved the man aside and noted that he took a position from which he could see my face.

Below me, the edgy crowd moved as one. Heads turned all in the same direction and craned to see over their neighbours. The dignitaries standing on the scaffold turned. Through the crowd, I saw the bobbing heads of three horses. Voices in the crowd shrieked curses at the prisoners. A fourth horse approached from the Gatehouse, where a woman was screaming. Then I heard a small boy's voice cry, 'Tata! Tata!' before a hand muffled him. The shouting of the crowd grew louder. A tussle broke out. Men-at-arms broke from the doorways.

Mrs Hay turned away from the window. 'I'm over here, if you need me, my lady.' She sat on a stool in the corner. After a moment, she gave our watcher a look and pulled out a defiant handkerchief.

Four horse-drawn hurdles broke out of the crowd, carrying the condemned men. They stopped at the foot of the scaffold. A woman struggled out of the crowd, threw herself down onto one of the prisoners and clung to him, weeping. Men-at-arms hauled her off and lifted the men up from the hurdles.

The reek of sweaty animal excitement rose from the crowd. The horses stamped and tossed their heads. A torch juddered below the window, sending up gusts of pine and burning pitch.

There was a moment of consultation and confusion. Then the first man to die climbed the steps onto the scaffold. I gripped the windowsill. I could not breathe.

Though Digby was changed, I recognised him clearly.

He still had golden hair, but no sunlight dappled his head and shoulders. He stood close enough to me that I could see beard stubble darkening his chin. In the strange dull light of early morning, he looked pale and heavy-eyed, as if he had not slept during his last night before eternal sleep. Even when about to die, he kept his air of amiability, lost only in our last desperate moments of struggle.

Then I realised that I could not hear the other man in the room breathing. His attention had fastened onto me so intently that his breathing echoed my own. Over my shoulder, I saw Mrs Hays's eyes on me. Surely, she did not doubt me, as well! Had the air at Combe hummed with suspicions about me that I never heard?

The small boy again cried out to his father. 'Ta ta!' Digby turned his head to the sound and smiled at his son's voice. His straight back and erect head reminded me of Henry. He opened his mouth to speak.

The crowd grew more silent than a playhouse.

Don't look up! I begged. I could not bear it, if he saw that I was there but dared not acknowledge him. The shame . . . Given what he had done and tried to do, I didn't understand why I should care, but I did.

In a strong clear voice, Digby admitted that he had broken the law. He apologised to the king. He asked forgiveness of God, the king, and of all the kingdom.

Heads nodded. There were murmurs of approval in the crowd.

But these were fatal admissions for me, if I had been mired in the plot by their confessions.

'. . . but Father Garnet knew nothing of our plot,' he was saying. 'The Jesuit priests knew nothing.' No one else knew what they had intended.

He lifted his head to my window. His eyes locked onto mine for an instant but moved on before I had time to respond.

In a clear voice he insisted that only the plotters themselves had known what they meant to do. No one else. No one!

He kept turning his face to include the whole crowd and all the people watching from all the windows, but I knew that he spoke to me and to any others who feared betrayal. He could not have known for certain that I was there, nor at which window. But he had guessed that perhaps I might be there, or had sent someone to report to me.

Relief unstrung my joints. I leaned harder on the sill.

Digby had not betrayed me in his confession, after all, whatever Cecil had implied. I was certain of it now. We shared a strange intimacy after our encounter in the forest. He was a good man, as I had told him. The wrong one for the task. As an abductor, he had tried not to alarm me. Even when about to die, he tried to console and reassure. I was certain of it. My relief was as intense as my earlier conviction that I was about to die.

Don't cry! Don't cry, with those eyes watching you, waiting to report every blink of eyelid and twitch of your lips. I felt myself growing older in a rush, like music played too fast or the riffled pages of a book.

Cecil had been testing me with his hints of confession, just as my father had been testing me, but with more subtlety. They didn't know what had happened in the forest at Combe after all. They had nothing more than suspicion to hold against me.

I pushed away the memory of Cecil's warning nod when I had been about to blab to the king. And the sharp-cornered question of my letter to Henry.

I watched Digby take his leave of the courtiers gathered on the scaffold. He took their hands with such friendly good will that he might have been setting out on a hopeful sea voyage to the Americas. A strong young man in his prime, sailing off on his next adventure.

Then he was climbing the ladder. He bent his head to accept

the noose. Was pushed off the ladder, jerked, kicked, swung only briefly before being cut down, choking but still alive, and delivered to the butchers' knives.

I closed my eyes, not caring who saw me. I wanted to stop my ears. The greatest courage in the world could not suppress his scream at disembowelment. Cries from the crowd beat at my ears, of fury mixed with grief. Women screeched and wailed. I imagined I still heard his reassuring voice above the crowd, but it wasn't possible, because, when I opened my eyes, a man was holding aloft his heart, shouting, 'Here is the heart of a traitor!'

I felt a heavy downward pull. All my weight was sinking into my feet. My eyes blurred and my head swam.

Don't fall! I was the First Daughter of England.

I leaned my elbows on the sill, as if to see better. Three more to go. God have mercy on them!

The First Daughter would not close her eyes again. Let that weasel-spy report that I watched without flinching. Though it was wicked for me even to imagine that I suffered. I locked my knees.

I tried to call up my wolf. Tried with her help to look through the scene under the Bishop's window into the vast scoured space below the crags, at the combs of rain scraping the distant mountains. The mist blowing in to cover the dragon crouching in the Firth.

A second prisoner was pushed up the steps of the scaffold.

Perched on the Cat Nick, I narrowed my eyes and tried to peer down into the chasm between Edinburgh and the crags, at Holyrood Palace at the bottom of the valley, like treasure sunk at the bottom of a lake. Where I had spent my last days of happy childhood, that short wonderful time with my mother and Henry. All three together for the first and last time, before I was hauled away from my true home and slammed down here in this damp green country where they tore out the hearts of golden young men.

'. . . Robert Wintour, will you renounce . . .?' a voice intoned below me.

The hearts of the best and most chivalrous men, I thought. The golden heroes. The near-perfect knights, Catholic or not. Henry's perfection was already turning the love of the people towards him and terrifying our father.

Wintour was climbing the ladder to the noose.

I tried to conjure up a wind off the northern sea to fill my ears. My eyes followed the long ascending spine of the Holy Mile up, up, clambering over hard, sharp grey rock to Edinburgh Castle itself, like a jagged outcrop of cliffs at the very top.

I heard another scream, then the thud of blades on a butcher's block. The next severed head was offered to the sight of the crowd. The next heart.

Wintour gone.

Strident voices from below me drowned out the rush of wind from the Firth. Though invisible through the cloud, the rising sun was warming the blanket of grey that pressed down on London. I must stand through two more deaths to show my father that I could not be broken. My forest sprite had died, but he had protected me. The reflection of a torch flared as a window swung closed. I could smell smoke and blood.

Another man forced up onto the scaffold.

The Loch. I tried to see the loch to the north just below the castle. A dark, brooding eye that seldom caught the light, where the *trowies* emerged at night from their underwater kingdom to steal babies or play eerie fiddles that drew you into fatal dances . . .

The third man shouted, 'It was no sin against God!'

I could not help looking down at this defiance. Not a demon, a blind man, his face terribly burnt.

I groped for the memory of the glint of the Firth . . .

Solicitously, the hangman helped the blind man onto the ladder. At the top, the prisoner crossed himself defiantly; was pushed off.

The noose may have killed him, in spite of the haste with which the hangman cut him down to suffer the rest of his punishment. I heard no scream this time, although I was braced for it. I clutched the sleeves of my crossed arms, hanging on. I forgot the man behind me and that he might, even now, be adding my white knuckles to his notes. I tried to remember my hand and Henry's side by side, two rings . . .

Scotland slipped away from me. The carnage below me was stronger than my imagination. My eyes saw with horrible clarity, a butcher's slab, dark blotches on the butchers' aprons. Severed joints. Another heart held aloft in bloody hands.

I've hunted, I told myself. I've seen blood before.

But these were men. And the cruellest huntsman did not quarter his prey while it was still alive.

My hands tightened until my knuckles almost split my skin. As I stared down at the scaffold, the faces of the witnesses changed until they grew so terrible that I could no longer look at them or else my soul would have run away and left my body a hollow shell for ever. I would never find my way out of this dark forest where I was suddenly lost. Would never see sunlight again, never smile, or feel joy. What I saw below me was too terrible. It would darken my mind forever.

Those men below me in their court robes served my father. With my father's permission, they had imagined these practices, and conjured them into life. They were *trowies*, crept out from cold dark unknowable depths of black opaque water. Destroying the young and brave . . . If this could happen to men like Digby, then who was safe . . .? And I was captive in their world, trying to swim in their cold black water, where everything lovely had drowned. Cecil. My father . . .

I'd seen blood before!

I shook my head to try to clear my sight. But the faces below me would not change back into men.

The last prisoner died, after long repentance and many

prayers for forgiveness. If my father wanted me to learn from this 'clarifying sight', I would. I watched now as if studying the actions of my enemy, in order to overcome him. Already older than my age, I now felt myself growing as ancient and cold as the waters of the loch.

It did not then occur to me, the First Daughter, the young she-wolf, that it might be safer to be seen as pliable and easy to rule than to challenge. It was not in my nature to understand the safety that lies in weakness. I was enough my father's daughter to understand his speed of thought, the urge to pounce-and-devour. I was still young enough to believe that you triumphed by proving yourself the stronger.

In Coventry, I had stared at that padded jacket without grasping its true message. I had listened to Mrs Hay's tales and learned courage from my father's childhood but never seen the deeper truth. That the greatest threat grows, not from confident power, but from fear and uncertainty. My father was dangerous, not because he was a king, but because he had once been a frightened, vulnerable boy at the mercy of guardians and violent, unruly nobles. In my ignorance, looking down into Paul's Churchyard, I determined to defy him.

10

I spoke to no one at Combe of what I had seen. Mrs Hay pretended that we had never left Combe. I would look at my lady guardian or at Anne as she chirped away about some small domestic adventure, and wonder if they saw no change in me, or if they merely feigned not to. Although Lord Harington must have known where I had been, he said nothing neither. The most that I could detect was the increased fuss Mrs Hay and the Haringtons now made about my health, asking unnecessarily often if I were chilled or overtired. Even Lord Harington's habitual civilities, like, 'How does your grace, this morning?' seemed to carry weighty hidden meaning.

'I am well,' I would reply fiercely. I was the First Daughter. I had survived a kidnap attempt and learned that I could be a fool. I had not weakened at the terrible death of my forest spirit. I must believe that I had the strength to deal with whatever waited for me.

A noble posture is all very well in the intent, and when you are standing face-to-face with a clearly seen terror. But the unknown catches at your feet and steals your breath. I no longer slept but lay all night fretting and fearful in the dark, imagining first this way, and then that way, how things might be, and how they might unroll.

Henry did not write to say, however guardedly, that he had received my warning letter. Abel White did not return with Clapper, nor send word of how he had fared. After what I had seen in London, I now had little doubt that I had sent my old playmate to his death. A cold worm of guilty knowledge and fear lay coiled in my thoughts, a bump I could always feel even when the surface of my day seemed to be running smoothly.

With gritty eyelids and the ache of sleeplessness thumping at my brow bones, I tried to bury myself in the gentle patterns of life at Combe, as if they were the last, precious warmth of my bed on a freezing winter morning. I startled Lady Harington by my sudden meek application to needlework, and my prompt appearances for Scripture reading and the endless cycle of meals and prayers five times a day. Though the king had forbidden me the diet of history, classics and philosophy prescribed for Henry, I was allowed languages and womanly arts. To the amazement of my tutors, I tried to forget myself in my lessons.

Sometimes, I surprised even myself and managed to forget the worm of fear and guilt when French words brought my whole mouth alive, or Italian rolled off my tongue. When singing, playing my lute, and practising on my virginal, I forgot all else.

Also, because a princess must dance when introduced at court, I had to learn. Against the grain of their own stern morality, the Haringtons hired a dancing master. Under his knowing eye, with Mrs Hay watching us all, I practised how to curtsey. I advanced and returned. I glided, stamped and dipped. And sometimes, swooping across the floor or reversing in a turn, I experienced an instant of free flight. How could I not feel pure joy when every muscle was alive, riding the pulse of a drum?

Even better, Anne had to learn too, so that I could practise dancing with a partner. Inevitably, as she was short, dainty and neat, while I was tall, long-limbed and wild-haired, I most often ended up dancing the man's part. When the dancing master at times insisted that Anne play the man so that I could practise my proper part, and she then tried to guide or to lift me, we would grow helpless with giggles.

I rode every day but Sunday, always under guard, chiefly on Wainscot, a little mare who was the lovely pale silvery brown of Russian oak, my favourite horse among the score stabled for me at Combe, now that Clapper was gone. Every day, I imagined Henry riding beside me, smiling at me across the space between us on the crags above Edinburgh, while the heads and haunches of our dogs bobbed up and down above the long silver-tasselled grass.

When Lady H was not watching, I helped the stable grooms with their combing and brushing and tried not to think about Clapper and Abel White. I never rode in the forest on the far side of the ford.

To fill any gaps in those quiet days, into which thoughts might otherwise rush, I wrote letters. I spent hours practising my signature in different sizes and coloured inks, including gold, to discover which self I should send out into the world.

Above a golden signature, I wrote in French to the Queen of France, whose son I might one day marry if my father had his way. With a chilly heart and in plain oak gall ink, I wrote formal, perfectly spelled and much re-copied letters of devotion to my father. In reply, I received stern admonitions drafted in a secretary's neat, official hand.

I wrote often to Henry, now at either Windsor or Richmond. He sent back loving letters to me, full of tilts, swords and horses. I read and re-read them, searching for secret meaning but still found no hint of my warning. My own letters to him grew harder to write. The brother in my mind was fading. I was wearing him out with overuse, rubbing him thin and ragged at the edges.

One day, after feeling out of sorts and shouting at Anne,

I discovered a pink stain on the back of my smock. A month later, the pink stain reappeared, a darker red this time, and my stomach ached dreadfully. I knew then that I must be dying. The worm of fear had gnawed away my vitals. The weight of guilty secrets had torn my innermost tissues. I was bleeding to death. My life would slowly seep away from that mysterious opening between my legs and no one but me would ever know why. I refused food for the rest of the day. It was best to get it over and done.

That night, one of my chamberers provided rags and explained that I would not die but had begun my monthly bleeding, which would continue forever, until I grew old. I didn't know whether to feel relieved or oppressed by her information. For reasons I did not understand, this messy, uncomfortable inconvenience also meant that I must now have Anne as my bed-fellow every night.

Though good-natured, Lady Anne Dudley was cursed by a sense of the obvious. 'Look, there's a butterfly,' she would announce. Or she might observe, 'It's raining today.' Or, 'Aren't those flowers red!'

I knew that she liked elderberries and disliked rhubarb, liked meat pies, disliked sauces made with ground almonds or wild garlic. I knew that she avoided melons for fear that they would make her belch. I also knew that she snored gently, just like Belle.

'I shall sew with red silk today,' she would say. 'No! The blue is far better for this flower . . . the centre of it, in any case. What do you think, my lady? Perhaps yellow for the petals? Or would blue be prettier for the petals and yellow for the centre, do you think?'

On the other hand, she was almost always cheerful and willing. 'Whatever you wish,' she would say. 'Shall I find Belle's other collar, then?' Or 'I shall go at once and change into my riding skirts . . .'

Soon after she arrived at Combe, we had become the angel

71

and the imp. I felt safe deciding that we should dig a secret cave in the hay barn where we might talk unheard. Or that we jump from an upper window to test whether our skirts would spread to slow our decent. Anne always agreed to whatever I proposed, but if she turned pale and silent when she trudged at my side, I would take pity and turn back – for her sake, I would tell myself, but with secret relief.

When we began to share a bed each night, I made the best of it, and entertained myself by whispering to her in the dark that the wind thrumming under the roof was the Death Drummer who always played before someone died. Or that *trowies* lived under the stones of the Smite ford and would reach up and pull her down if she tried to cross . . . I had seen one myself, I assured her.

Sometimes I frightened her with tales of a wild and unruly Scotland, where, I said, I was allowed to ride for miles by myself, seeing only the eagles and the seals on the rocks. 'And at dinner,' I would tell her, 'the nobles put their elbows on the same table as the king. And had such fierce debates that they leapt up and hacked at each other with their knives until blood flew through the air, and you didn't know whether you drank wine or blood from your glass.'

'You must find England very tame and tedious,' she said once.

Stricken by her look of misery, I continued to lie and assured her that she and I entertained ourselves so well that I hardly ever thought of Scotland at all, anymore.

My guardian, Lord Harington, continued to be kind enough to me and always respectful, never raising his voice in anger, and guiding me as if I had been his own daughter. In the absence of other parents, I might have loved him.

But one night, soon after I had first arrived at Combe, I had attempted to spy, to learn more about my new home. Hidden in the stairwell, I overheard him complaining to his cousin, who was also named John Harington, a godson of the old queen, and now, so I was told, one of my brother's gentlemen.

'Will you try to have a word when you're next at court? The king has ignored my last letter.' My guardian sighed. 'She's a heavy charge laid upon me by his majesty – and likely to prove a costly one.'

I flattened myself against the wall of the staircase, grateful to be wearing a soft gown. There was a long pause, during which I held my breath and felt my pulse begin to thump in my ears.

'I know that his majesty is concerned with weightier matters than a daughter,' Lord Harington went on. 'But perhaps, coz, you might think how to prod his memory on the subject of the promised allowance for keeping her. Or have a word with Cecil.'

My heart, already half on offer, had slunk back to its kennel with its tail between its legs. Now, since our return from the execution of the Gunpowder Traitors, I felt that his heavy charge weighed him down almost unbearably.

Just once, shortly after my return from London, our eyes locked over the supper table. His glance held so much concern that I had to glare down at my plate to prevent tears. The people in my life would keep changing. There was nothing I could do about it. When I was married, I would leave not only Combe, and England, but also my guardian. That night over supper, for the first time, I thought that I might miss him.

His wife, Lady Harington, on the other hand, had terrified me from our first meeting. My lady guardian was a woman of absolute certainties. Unlike her easy-going husband, she had a fearsome frown and strong views on how a young girl should be schooled. After my return from Coventry, she carried on her detailed instruction as if never interrupted. Whether her steady purpose grew from ignorance of what had happened or defiance, I could never decide.

73

Both Anne and I had already learned how to wipe our fingers at the table, to take the precious salt on the tips of our knives, and to count our linens against pilfering by our women. Teaching by her own example as well as by words, Lady Harington now marched on through the long list of other bad habits that we must learn to prevent in our servants.

No serving man ever dared to piss in the corners of her fireplaces. No scullery maid at Combe ever polished a glass on her sleeve or blew her nose in her apron. By constant example, Lady H showed us how to measure respect or insolence in others, to the very finest degree. And how to bring down with an acid word anyone who stepped over any of the invisible lines of rank and place that she taught us to see. She adjusted the angle of my head when I curtsied. For three months, I nodded meekly and accepted her instruction. Any moment, I thought, she might teach me how to make order out of the rest of the tumbling chaos of life.

Sometimes I tried to play again as I had once done, when I still felt like a child. I would make Belle sit up in a miniature gilded carriage in her blue velvet collar whilst Cherami, my most obliging small greyhound, pulled her across the floor, his nails clacking like tiny hoofs. While Anne laughed and clapped, I looked on as if from a great distance.

When the late winter weather allowed, I sometimes sat very still in the gardens and tempted the robins to eat crumbs from my hand. Once, while Anne made a dumb show of being ill, I tasted a worm to try to understand its attractions. I whistled back at the wild birds, trying to speak their language, but caused agitation in the bushes and trees.

'I think you've confused them,' said Anne.

In truth, birds, with their sharp little eyes and edgy flutter, troubled me.

On the journey south from Scotland, well-wishers had given me six caged birds to join my animal family – two larks, a finch and three paraquettos from the West Indies. I felt that the little creatures wished to be friendly but could not trust me, who had the power to thrust them back into their cages. Their fragility terrified me – those tiny bones and trembling heartbeats, so fast that my own heart would crash to a halt at such a speed, or else burst into flame. I feared that I might accidentally crush one of them in my hand. This terrible power alarmed me so much that I avoided handling them. Unobserved, I released a lark and a paraquetto and said that they had escaped.

Then I found the remains of the paraquetto left under a bush by a cat. Staring down at the sodden little bundle of bloody blue and green feathers, I wondered if, after all, even unhappy, they were not safer in their cages. I knew that I was the true assassin.

The paraquetto. Abel White. Clapper. Lord Harington burdened. Digby dead. Because of me.

'I am dangerous to know,' I whispered one night to Anne. 'Even for you.'

'Why?'

Could she not see why? I thought. She had heard Mrs Hay's tales.

'I just am,' I said.

'Don't be absurd!' She rolled onto her side away from me. 'Unless you mean the risk of tearing my best gown.'

11

Winter was clinging on into March, treading heavy-booted on the first green shoots of early spring. My large hunting greyhound, Trey, lifted his head and tested the damp grey air. Then Wainscot, too, lifted her head. Her ears swivelled towards the entrance avenue leading to the main house at Combe. Because Anne had chosen to stay inside by the fire, I was riding with only a groom and six of my hounds.

I held a small bunch of little wild daffodils to inhale their fresh odour while I rode, though I knew better than to curdle the milk by taking them into the house. Then I heard the hoof beats that my dog and horse had already heard. I shivered and threw down the daffodils. I pressed Wainscot forward through a haze of dark leaf buds, still as tight as fingertips while Trey and the other greyhounds sprinted ahead.

As we broke out into the avenue, a riderless horse was trotting down the track towards us. Riderless, like a horse in the tapestries of battlefield scenes, or at a king's funeral.

Wainscot gave a joyful whinny of welcome.

Clapper. Without Abel White.

I swung my right knee over the saddle head and slid to the ground. When he saw us, Clapper broke into a canter and nearly knocked me over as I ran to meet him. Surrounded by a mêlée of wriggling dog haunches and sniffing noses, I hugged him, rubbed his neck and kissed his nose and breathed in his smell. It really was Clapper, not the ghost horse I had imagined for an instant when I first saw that he had no rider. He was sleek and well fed. He still wore his old tack. I quieted Trey, pushed past Wainscot who had arrived close behind me, and began to search the saddle for a message or some other sign of who had returned him.

No pouch. No saddle bag. No sheathe for a sword nor a lance-holder where a paper might be hidden. No letter tied to the bridle. I flipped up the saddlecloth. Nothing there. Nothing under the quilted leather pad of the seat. Nor fastened to the back of the cantle, nor under the saddle flaps.

'Did you escape and find your own way back here alone?' I asked him.

Then, under the small buckle guard at the top of the girth straps, I found something. Not a letter, a small blue-grey spring of rue, threaded through the steel buckles. I extracted the sprig carefully and held it to my nose.

Clapper nudged me hard. I put a calming hand on his neck. I needed to think.

A fresh-cut evergreen herb, not dried, still sharply musky with its odd animal smell. It had to be a message. It had not found its way into the buckle by itself. It had been put there by someone who knew that I would search.

Evergreen. I looked at the sprig in my hand. Surely that was the message – evergreen. Perhaps Abel was still alive after all

But rue? My first surge of joy turned sour. Even in this wintry weather, there were other plant choices. He . . . whoever it was . . . I wanted the messenger to be Abel White but tried not jump to conclusions . . . might instead have chosen the evergreen bay to signify victory, honour and success. Bay protected. But he had not sent a victor's bay.

Or he could have sent protective rush. Or round-leafed

box, or a mottled heart leaf of the little sowbread cyclamen, to ward off evil spells. Or even a feathery stem of grey mugwort that is tucked into a traveller's shoes to give him strength for his journey. I could have read a happier story in any of those.

Rue spoke of repentance and sorrow. Rue spoke of regret. Rue could heal but also curse.

He dared not write but sent this vegetable messenger instead.

I could read only one conclusion. Abel had failed in his mission for me.

After supper that night, I sat beside my fire holding the sprig of rue between my palms willing it to tell me more.

The reappearance of Clapper cracked open the door holding back the future. It told me that, like the warmth of a morning bed, this life was going to end. Just as someone elsewhere had chosen to send back my horse, my true life elsewhere would begin whenever my father willed it. I could not let Combe and its people take root in my heart. I had merely borrowed this world and would soon have to give it back. I had no colours, or tastes, or smells for what awaited me.

I begged my tutors to tell me about Italy, France, Spain and the German states, in any of which I might, or might not, find myself living for the rest of my life.

I coaxed Mrs Hay to visit me at bedtime as she had once done. While Anne lay goggle-eyed beside me, my old nurse told me yet again the tales of my family's past, carrying the seeds of my future.

I watched the Haringtons together. I listened to the tone of their voices, watched what distances they kept between them, noted their exchange of glances, trying to sniff out the dark truth about this mysterious thing, marriage that made my father threaten me with it as the alternative to execution.

A perverse impatience began to press like a belch in my gullet. I hated my own helplessness and the false safety of Combe.

Knowing the worst would be better than knowing nothing. At least then, I could try to think what to do.

I would fall asleep each night holding the fragment of stone from the crags in one hand, cradling the smuggled Belle with my other arm. I was a creature of marsh and granite, temporarily asleep, buried in a green, green forest. But I could hear hoof beats in the distance, drawing closer.

12

'We might have been given more warning!' Lady Harington sawed at her roast meat so fiercely that her ear-drops flashed and her lace collar quivered. She gave up and slammed down her knife. Her small hands made fists on the table.

'One would think a shell had exploded in the forecourt,' said her husband mildly. 'It's only a summons to London for a short time.' He tugged unhappily at his moustaches, so hard that the end of his long bony nose was moved from side to side.

Lady Harington snorted. 'Do you imagine that duration makes any difference to her grace's needs? If she's to be presented to a king, it matters not one whit whether she stands there for an hour or for five days.'

'It might matter to her,' my guardian murmured

My Uncle Christian, who was my mother's brother and King of Denmark, was coming to England. I must join the English court in London to be presented to my visiting uncle.

'His majesty could land in England at any time,' said Lady Harington. 'We must all pray for contrary winds. Not tempests,' she added hastily. 'Merely winds from the wrong direction, and strong enough to delay his arrival until I can arrange what is needed.'

Her husband sighed and nodded.

Suddenly, I needed new gowns, embroidered smocks, standing collars, falling collars, and stomachers. To go on show before a foreign king, the First Daughter of England must have embroidered slippers, jewelled sleeves, silk stockings, gloves, purses, handkerchiefs. I overheard orders for pearls by the pound and silver lace by the bale and hoped that my guardian's cousin had managed to arrange extra money to repay Lord Harington for these expenses.

All at once, there was no time for riding, no escape to stables or garden. I had to stand still for measuring and fittings, while tailors and dress-makers from Coventry shook out stiff rustling taffetas and satins and cooed and knelt with their lips clamped tight on pins and turned me a half inch this way or that.

'She must take gifts to give to her new people,' I overheard Lord Harington say to his wife in despair. 'Surely, she will now be given a full household. Wherever shall I find the money to buy all those necessary scent bottles and pieces of gold and silver plate?'

'She must have them, all the same,' replied Lady Harington. 'We, and our care for her, will be under scrutiny at Whitehall just as much as she.'

As urgently as new gowns, I needed final instruction from Lady H, which she crammed into me like last-minute stockings into a travelling chest.

'You will become a magnet for the ambitious,' she warned. 'All wanting something from you. We've protected you from such people here at Combe. But in Whitehall . . .' She rolled her eyes just enough to make clear her doubts about the protection I would find in London. 'These climbers will try to turn your head with flattery, to win your favour. I hope you've learned here to be sensible enough to disbelieve them all.'

'Oh, yes, madam.'

'Distrust all compliments as flattery.'

'Yes, madam,' I said with less fervour. Was it not possible that an occasional compliment might be deserved?

'Take special care with your new ladies, for I'm certain you will have some, even for a short visit.' Her eyes narrowed as if assessing these distant figures. 'Every one of them will be someone's creature. They will report everything you do. Never forget. Beware, in particular of the rival noble families. The Howards will no doubt insert one of their bitches into the hunting pack. They can't bear not always to be at the centre. And Northumberland will also buy a place for one of his nieces . . . Serving you will be a sure step to a good marriage.'

She frowned at a rabbit embroidered in fine red wool on one of my new smocks. 'I may be only a countrywoman, but I know a thing or two about how things run there in London. And there's Lord Salisbury to fear, of course, Robert Cecil . . . the twisted little son of Burleigh. The Chief Secretary has an intelligencer placed in every noble house in England . . . and in France too, I've no doubt. One of your women or grooms will most certainly be reporting to him.'

Anne had been listening with open dismay. 'Will you not keep me as one of your ladies?'

'Anne!' said her aunt. 'Don't subject poor Lady Elizabeth to petitions already!'

I tried to imagine being without that placid, agreeable and slightly dull presence beside me, night and day. Warm, breathing, often less amusing than my monkey or dogs, but able to converse, to ask my opinion and able to understand my instructions.

'But I must have Anne with me!' I cried. I forgot how tedious I sometimes found her chattering.

Faced with Howards and all those other treacherous creatures described by Lady Harington, I could not imagine doing without Anne. 'You must be my Lady of Honour!'

'Yes!' cried Anne. 'Thank you, my lady!' She turned to

her aunt. 'Now I must have some new gowns too! May I have one with satin bows at the waist? I am so fond of bows!'

Lady Harington nodded. Though she had reproved Anne for asking, my lady guardian could not hide her gratification at my choice of her niece. 'You must keep each other steady,' she said. 'Whatever you do, don't either of you make an enemy of Lady Elizabeth's steward. You have no idea what petty tyranny that person can exercise over your daily life.'

At that moment, I wanted Lady Harington to come with me too, to guide me in a world that clearly would not be like Combe.

'I will dine with my mother again, as I did when I visited her at Holyrood Palace,' I told Anne that night. 'The two of us together, in her little closet, which had a beautiful red, blue and gold painted ceiling, and a fire, and with only one or two of her ladies.' Anne would fall asleep while I listed the delicacies we had eaten and the games we had played together after eating.

I did not tell Anne about the other scenes I imagined. In London my mother would take me in her arms again as she had at Holyrood. She would kiss my forehead, and look closely at me to see what sort of creature I had become, and say how much I had grown since she saw me last. I imagined how I might even, in time, tell her what had happened to me in the forest, so that she could tell me how brave I had been.

But in darker moments, I feared this London visit. I had not seen my mother for so long that I half-distrusted my memories of her. And I scarcely knew my younger brother, poor sickly Baby Charles, whom the queen had kept closer by her on the journey south than either Henry or me. I did not know where Charles was now, nor in whose care. I feared that Henry might no longer love me after being so long apart. The thought of my father stabbed my belly like a knife. Someone, somewhere, had my treasonous letter. In London,

I might learn who had it. At such moments, I did not want ever to leave Combe.

In the end, God did not dare to deny Lady Harington's prayers. Bad weather delayed my uncle for almost six weeks, even though it was already May. I arrived in London, panting for breath so to speak, just before the Danish ships arrived at Gravesend.

13

WHITEHALL PALACE, LONDON, 1606

At Holyrood, Henry had told me that our new people were good soldiers and successful merchants. He led me to believe that they were measured in temperament, being either wily or cheerful, and, when necessary, severe. The crowds I saw on the journey south had been clean, dressed in their finest clothes, and cheerful, made well-behaved by hope for their new monarch. At Combe, Lord Harington's example led me to believe that the English prayed even more than Scottish Kirk men. But in the bishop's little study overlooking the scaffold in Paul's Churchyard, my view of the English darkened.

Tonight, I could not tear my eyes from the alarming but educating spectacle around the royal dais in the Great Presence Chamber. Though Lord Harington had done his best to shield me, I had learned within a few days of coming to Whitehall that the English were not just cruel. They were wild men. They cursed, fought and drank too much, just for the sheer joy of it, not to a purpose like the Scottish lairds. They sweated over dancing as earnestly as they practised with their weapons, then claimed that neither activity made them turn a hair.

I had seen them tilt without horses, attacking each other on foot, and half-murder each other over a game of bowls. They came in all heights and colour of hair and skin. They believed that the rest of the world was theirs for the taking and, at full shout in any company, they resented the Spanish, Portuguese and Dutch as if these nations were other suitors daring to chase their women.

For the invading Scots, whom they openly called savages, they reserved their iciness. And their malice – drunk or sober.

And I had had other surprises, none of them good. My mother was not at Whitehall to greet me, but down river in her palace at Greenwich. To my consternation, I learned that she had recently been delivered of another baby, a girl, my sister Sophia, who died the day after she was born and whom I would never see. I had not known that my mother was pregnant again.

Because my Whitehall lodgings were still being carved out of the Small Closed Tennis Court, I had been bundled, with only Lady Anne, my chamberer, my single French maid, my sempstress, and two house grooms, into three rooms full of plaster dust in the old queen's lodgings overlooking the Thames, which were themselves still being finished to house my mother and her household. My two horse grooms were found sleeping corners in the stables. The rest of my small retinue, including Lady Harington who in the end had insisted on coming with me, were sent back to Combe.

The king's Lord Chamberlain, Thomas Howard, Earl of Suffolk, himself explained the difficulties to me. It seemed that the Lord Chamberlain, The King's Master of Works and other officials still scrambled to squeeze the new king and his family – all with their separate households – into the former palace of the unmarried, childless Queen Elizabeth.

Henry was at either Hampton Court or Windsor, but I had no time to seek him out before being told that he was gone again to Gravesend with the king, to welcome my uncle.

I was left behind with Baby Charles, to be loaded down with our finest clothes, and allowed to greet our uncle, the Danish king, on the Whitehall water steps.

Now six years old, Baby Charles had all the failings of the runt in a litter of dogs. While we waited on the steps, he allowed me to take his hand but avoided my eye. His weaknesses deserved my sisterly protection, I told myself. I wanted to love him and vowed to be both tender and patient with him. By surviving for even this long, he had confounded a general expectation of his early death. Still in the care of his nurse, he was small for his age and walked unsteadily on legs bowed by a softening of the bones. Pale patches of scalp showed through his fine, thin hair. When he dared to speak, he stammered and formed his words with difficulty. When silent, he wore a sulky expression. He showed no interest in riding or even playing. But he was my own, my brother.

His hand tightened in mine when sudden thunder began to shake the air. A loose roof tile smashed on the ground. The water of the Thames quivered.

'It's only the guns at the Tower,' I said. 'Saluting the royal barges. Listen! You can hear the people shouting. They're almost here!'

Distant cheers rolled slowly up the river towards us from crowds lining the banks.

The first boats appeared around the Lambeth bend, tiny spots of red and gold.

'Henry's c-coming!' Baby Charles exclaimed excitedly. I glanced down. He was smiling for the first time since I had arrived in London.

'Yes, Henry!' I smiled back and squeezed his hand. He and I were bound by our love for Henry, at the very least. 'Just listen to those cheers for two kings and a king-to-be.'

For a moment, I felt the glory of it all. I saw everything sharply and cleanly. The gilded boats catching the sunlight. Red and gold pennants sagging, then snapping back into life as if trying to jump from their poles. The hungry oars biting into the water and rising up to pounce again, trailing bright arcs of water through the air. The air itself pressed into my ears, thick with joyful shouting.

My skin prickled. I am a part of all of this, I thought. For the first time, I felt it. My life. I saw myself standing on the water stairs, all copper and gold, my hair tamed under a net of pearls, my high fine collar fluttering in the breeze, ripples breaking at my feet and spreading back out into the river. Who was also cheered. Who was even now being watched and had her own part to play. Who, like her older brother, had a duty not to disappoint. No longer a child. The First Daughter of England, who carried a secret she-wolf in her bones, waiting now to welcome a foreign king. Ready to face her father in their shared world.

I smiled and waved back at some young fishermen in a dinghy who had dared to row close enough to the steps to throw a posy of flowers at me. Their bouquet fell short and lay bobbing near the lowest step. While a boat of men-at-arms rushed to drive away the invaders, I sent a groom down into the water to retrieve the flowers. I held aloft the dripping bundle of iris and early roses and was rewarded by a chorus of delighted cheers from the retreating fishermen.

Baby Charles pulled his hand from mine, stepped away and frowned in disapproval. He wiped a water drop from his cheek.

The golden barges pulled in to the stairs. There was a flurry of securing, steadying, disembarking, bowing. There were more cheers from the steps, from the windows of the palace and from the turmoil of smaller boats following the royal progress up the Thames. My uncle, the king of Denmark, leapt up the water steps in three huge strides.

'What charming children!' he boomed. Hardly pausing, he pinched my cheek. Then the burly, ugly man was gone, one arm thrown across my father's somewhat lower shoulders.

My father had not seemed even to see me. With a wild look over his shoulder, Henry followed them.

Baby Charles was removed by his nurse. Dismissed as a 'charming child', the First Daughter of England skulked back to her dusty temporary lodgings and waited crossly in the smell of damp plaster and rotting water weed from the river under her window.

I would be summoned soon, I told myself. I had not come all this way nor had all those new clothes made just to have my cheek pinched in passing.

I ate dinner alone with Anne in my lodgings, trying not to drop crumbs or make grease spots on the copper-coloured silk of my taffeta gown. It had taken me more than an hour to be dressed. I dared not change in case I was suddenly called. If I were to be called.

After eating, I leaned on the windowsill and counted wherries on the river. I watched the sun set over the marshes. Then I had to ask my maid to brush the pink plaster dust from my gown. Briefly, I played my lute, then put it back in its case again.

'I don't know why we troubled to come to London!' I said.

'But I would never have had this gown otherwise.' Anne smoothed a blue silk flounce.

I need not have feared this visit, after all. The king had forgotten me.

Or he was slighting me. Teaching me yet again how little he valued me, and how easily I could be thrown aside. I listened to the faint sounds of music. Somewhere, other people were dancing. I had never seen courtiers dancing all together. I had never danced with anyone but Anne. I wanted to dance, here at court. I wondered what would happen if I were to present myself uninvited.

I rehearsed what I would say. Imagined the general amazement. My own dignity, as I walked fearlessly towards the king, head held high . . .

When my window began to grow opaque with darkness, I was at last summoned to the Great Presence Chamber. I gathered around me what was left of the first Daughter of England and set off.

I stopped just inside the door to stare like a gawk. I inhaled sharply and almost choked on the brew of civet, cinnamon, sandalwood, rose water and sweat. There were too many people jammed together even for such a vast space, all of them giving off a shimmering heat of urgency and importance. The air was thick with their voices and the rustling of silks and fine wools, the faint rasping of crusted gold and silver embroidery against jewelled buttons. Somewhere in the crowd, a lute and drum fought to be heard.

'Wait here, your grace,' whispered the page, who had accompanied me.

I looked about me.

In Scotland, even in the palaces, our ceilings were often built low to conserve the heat in the long, fierce, damp winters. We did not try to emulate God's own space between mountains, above the sea. Here at Whitehall, the roof was so high that it vanished into the shadows above the torches, making me feel as small as an ant. At the far end of this hall, my father sat raised above his courtiers as if on an altar, with my uncle beside him holding a glass of wine.

Even while he spoke to my uncle, the king's bright jackdaw eyes leapt and darted, searching for something of interest, pretending not to see me waiting at the door. His fingers explored the arm of his chair, his sleeves, his buttons. Dark and heavy against the surrounding finery, he wore one of his plain quilted velvet doublets, as if scorning the extravagant efforts of the courtiers to deck themselves for him.

The jackdaw eyes chose to see me. Though his doublet was plain, I saw the flash of unfamiliar gems on his fingers when he lifted his hand to summon me. When he angled his head, a white sun flared just above the brim of his hat.

I moved towards him, half-terrified, half-enraged. I kept my eyes down, not from modesty but from fear of having my thoughts and senses overwhelmed.

Life in Scotland had been all polished wood and leather, and the comfortable smells of wood smoke, dogs, damp, mice and horses. Even at Holyrood, everyone had lived bundled together, separated only by invisible lines of the respect owed to my parents. I had not altogether lied to Anne. My mother ate with her ladies, and then with Henry and me when we were there, in a cosy closet off her bed chamber. My father's nobles leaned their elbows on the same table as he did. The king of Scotland was the chief among the other clan chiefs. He did not sit apart on an altar like an image of God.

I advanced through a parting sea of courtiers, feeling the stares hammer at me. Voices grew sibilant with 'she' and 'princess' and my name, 'Elizabeth'. I heard a murmur, '. . . one of the Scottish brats.'

A lock of twisting red-gold hair had escaped from its pins. I would have blown it out of my eyes but refused to give that mocking English voice further reason to laugh at my uncouth Scottish behaviour.

Musk and candle smoke caught at the back of my throat. A miasma of sweat and oil of roses swirled around my head.

'She . . .' 'She . . .' hissed the sea.

The curve of my skirt met the line of my father's altar plinth. The air was sickly sweet with wine vapours. I looked up. A young man sat on the dais at my father's feet, with his arm draped over the king's right knee.

Tonight, unlike the fearsome man who had brushed aside the wall-hanging in Coventry, my father overflowed with satisfaction and drunken arrogance. He seemed to tremble on the edge of bad behaviour, like a child overwrought by too many fine gifts.

'Here's my little Bessie!' he shouted. 'My country mouse has ventured out of her hole at last!'

A red flush began to climb my chest. I curtsied faultlessly.

'Would she not make any father proud?' he demanded at large. The rings on his fingers flashed. A knife blade of light from the diamond on his hat sliced across my vision. Another gust of wine fumes reached me on his breath.

Burning with humiliation, I put on my chilliest face and let the crudely exacted compliments rain down on me.

'Is she not a pearl beyond price, monsewer?' My father leaned forward and aimed this question past Wee Bobby Cecil, squarely between the eyes of a French-dressed envoy standing in the front rank of attending courtiers and foreign visitors.

The sight of the Secretary of State made my heart thump with guilty memories of Coventry.

'No longer a child, after all!' said my uncle, looking me up and down. 'Not in the least.'

'Come up here and sit by me, Bessie!' The king waved a flashing hand. 'Fetch the lassie a stool!' he shouted. 'Come on, Bessie! Don't be shy. Come up and give your father a kiss!' His voice hardened. 'It may be your only chance to look down from up here! Come make the most of it!'

I climbed the steps and kissed him without recoiling from the wine fumes. I sat and held the glass of wine he forced into my hands, over the head of the young man lounging between us.

Straight-backed, I pretended to ignore the stares, so many eyes on me at the same time. A quick sideways glance met the considering hazel gaze of a dark-haired, narrow-jawed man with a thin mouth pulled down by discontent – Sir Francis Bacon, last seen nodding and smiling among the dignitaries on the scaffold in Paul's Churchyard. I looked away and met the eyes of the young man at my father's feet. Enemies everywhere.

Henry, the next king of England, should have been sitting with his father and uncle, in place of that smirking stranger. Henry who was not there at all.

I snatched a look at the 'monsewer' who had been challenged by my father. He was now studying me, his head tilted to the man beside him. Then he leaned to the other side and murmured to Cecil.

My father was watching him. 'But can France afford her?' he called. 'No one else can!'

My humiliation was complete. I was not here to meet my uncle. My father had called me here to be inspected like a market heifer. A gangling, red-haired, freckled heifer, I thought savagely. 'A Scots brat'. Exposed to the ridicule of the English court as crudely as if he had set me in the stocks.

The faces below me began to bob in a dance. My head felt like a net full of jumping fish. I no longer wanted to dance. I needed to escape from all those eyes and sort my thoughts. Trapped up there on my stool I looked again for Henry but could not find him. I imagined standing up and walking out. But in my imagination, the sea refused to part to let me escape. I would be trapped in a cage of bodies.

In a gap between dancers, I spied my guardian sitting with folded arms against one wall, now joined by Wee Bobby Cecil. From their gestures and Lord Harington's frown, they appeared to be arguing about me. Bacon leaned on a pillar watching them while dancers jogged around him. I caught my guardian's eye, then a gaggle of dancers hopped between us.

What use was a guardian, I thought, if he didn't guard you?

The racket of voices and music grew louder until I heard only a blur of sound. The young man at my father's feet tilted his head back while the royal hand toyed with his curls. My father leaned forward and whispered in his ear.

I stared down into my wineglass. I knew that I had just learned something else momentous but did not yet know what to make of it.

The king of Denmark hauled a woman onto his lap and

began to play the clown with the hoops of her farthingale, threatening to put them over his head. Neither of them seemed to notice that her legs were exposed to the knee.

Lord Harington appeared at the foot of the dais, pinched and resolute. 'Your majesty, with your permission . . .' When he saw that my father still whispered into the young man's ear, Lord H held out his hand to me.

'Who is that man who was earlier standing beside Lord Salisbury?' I murmured as he steadied me down the steps.

'The French envoy.'

'And the other, who didn't speak? The one who still keeps staring at me?'

'The Duc de Bouillon, envoy from the German Palatine, chief state of the Protestant Union in Europe.'

I didn't ask about the young man leaning on my father's knees.

I curtsied to my oblivious father.

Lord Harington mouthed words about my recent journey and the dangers of too much excitement. As we turned to leave, three of my father's Scottish gentlemen began to lay loud wagers on how much more of the woman on my uncle's lap would be seen before the night was done.

'Depends on how oiled she is,' said one.

'*Nae*! *Nae*! S'nowt to do w'drink!' another shouted back, as Lord Harington hustled me away. 'A good bush need no wine!' My father and uncle laughed loudly.

Lord Harington forgot himself far enough to give me a little push towards the door.

'Where is Prince Henry?' I asked, when we reached the corridor. 'Why is he not here?'

Lord Harington pinched his lips. 'Best if you had not been here neither.'

'Can we go back to Combe now?'

Harington hesitated. 'I will ask permission, but I fear that his majesty has not done with you yet.'

I walked a few feet in silence. 'Are you still my guardian?'

I heard him breathe in sharply. 'Yes, your grace. I will be your guardian until you marry. But I cannot remove you without the king's permission.'

I nodded, but could not stop the unworthy, childish feeling that he was abandoning me in the monster's lair.

14

Henry and I found each other at last, the following day, in the gardens. My brother was just as handsome as I remembered, but taller, and beginning to fill out into a man. He had been on his way to the tiltyard and carried a sword. It was our first time together in private since I had arrived from Combe.

'I knew that you would be here,' he said with delight.

'I knew that you would be.'

We kissed each other gravely and stood looking into each other's eyes, both of us a little shy after so long apart but buoyed up by the miracle of a shared impulse that had brought us both to the same place at the same time.

Henry in the flesh seemed very like the Henry in my head, apart from a faint new, darker smell that came off him when he kissed me. In Edinburgh, he had smelled of fresh cut grass.

'What do you read in my face?' asked Henry. 'After studying it so earnestly?'

'I wonder if you still love me,' I blurted. 'And I see that you have a red-gold fuzz on your upper lip and chin, just the same colour as my hair.'

'You're taller but are still my Elizabella,' he said. 'Quick as a squirrel, always darting and leaping, looking for a new nut.'

We ordered our attendants to stay by the fountain. Since most of them had sore heads, they were happy to comply. Over my shoulder, I saw Anne settle on a stone bench with one of Henry's gentlemen. We set off together without them down the long central gravel path that divided the pattern of box-edged formal beds.

'Where were you last night?' I asked, instead of all the other questions I wanted to ask him.

'I had to sit with them through dinner.' My brother flushed and looked down at his feet crunching on the gravel path. 'When I couldn't tolerate their coarseness and drinking any longer, I excused myself.'

'I lacked your courage,' I said. 'I stayed.'

'It needed more courage to stay than to flee.' He swung his sword in a fierce downward arc. 'I never dreamed that our father meant to summon you last night. I would have stayed. I should have been there to protect you.'

'Do you still wear your oath ring?' I asked. 'Like the one you gave me on Cat Nick?' I held out my hand wearing his golden ship.

'See for yourself.' Henry held out his left hand with the matching golden ship on the middle finger. 'Our hands are the same shape,' he observed. 'Even if mine are a little larger. In Scotland, we were so innocent of the true dangers. We should swear again.'

We stopped walking. A robin landed on the wooden obelisk in the centre of the nearest bed and trilled encouragement. Solemnly, with the robin as witness, looking into each other's eyes, we again pledged ourselves to rescue if the other sent for help.

Even against our father? I wondered if that was what Henry meant by 'true dangers'. Having now had a little time to observe him, I felt a new weight pressing down on him. Like Atlas, he seemed to have shouldered the world.

The robin gave a final trill and jumped away into the air.

We smiled at each other. His presence still created that familiar circle of warmth that I wanted to step inside.

As we began to walk again, I thought how there was something bright and pure in him, of which he seemed unaware, that made crowds shout out his name and press forward to touch him. Today in the gardens, I saw how the women pushed out their bosoms at him. His grooms and gentlemen followed him with their eyes. Unlike our father, he was patient with attention and wore his golden manacles of duty as if they delighted him.

'You might have needed protecting last night, too,' I ventured.

'From the king, you mean?' He pinched his lips and turned his head away. 'He would have been happy enough if I had stayed away altogether. But the people expect my presence.'

Even at my most hopeful, I had not thought this meeting would be so easy. Very soon, I would confess how I had once talked to him at night. And why.

'We must both be strong,' he said. 'There will be more nights like last night while our uncle is here. The Danes are notorious for their drinking and carousing.'

'That's what Lord Harington said.'

There was a moment of silence, in which I felt our thoughts pulling back from the same uneasy terrain.

Henry balanced his sword at the end of an outstretched arm. 'This sword was a gift from Spain.'

'It's very fine,' I said.

He shrugged. 'Not as fine as the suit of golden armour given to me by my spiritual father, who is the model for all kings.'

'And who is that?' I asked obediently.

'Henri IV of France. A true warrior king. Unlike our father.'

I said nothing. Ever since I was six years old, Mrs Hay had whispered that the king wanted me to marry Henri's son, the infant Dauphin of France. That was the future for which she had to prepare me, she had said. The closest I had come to imagining this future was the image of living with someone like my younger brother, Baby Charles, who lay somewhere between a nuisance and a pet.

'Our father hopes I might marry the Spanish Infanta,' Henry said. 'He seems to believe that if I accept a sword, I might accept a bride.'

He stretched his arm over the low box hedge and began to tickle a daisy with tiny circles of the sword tip. I watched the tendons working in his wrist.

'I cannot marry a Papist.' He glanced up at me. 'I don't want you to marry a Papist, neither.'

'I don't much want to marry at all,' I said. 'But I must. Just as you must one day be king.'

Henry lunged with the sword. Silently, I admired the line of his leg and the steadiness of his blade. 'We could run away together to the Americas.' He straightened again and lowered his voice. 'This is not idle dreaming, Elizabella. You won't have heard of my interest in the London Company and its enterprise in the new Virginia colony, because I must hide it to avoid stirring up the commercial rivalry among the different English joint stock companies – the East Indies Company, the West Indies Company, and the Virginia Company. And it's also better that Spain and France, who already have an eager foothold in the Caribbean, don't know that the future king of England has a keen interest in the Americas.'

He lowered his voice even though we could not possibly have been overheard, except by the robin, which seemed to be following us. 'I have invested money in the new Virginia colony, Elizabella. Even the king doesn't know how much. His interests lie all in Europe. I am helping to shape a new British kingdom, which I will one day rule. The first expedition named their first landfall at Chesapeake Bay after me – Cape Henry. We could rule together there as brother and sister, as I believe happened in ancient times.'

'I could marry a handsome savage prince,' I said. 'And you would marry his long-haired golden sister.'

'Queen Elizabella,' he said.

'King Henry the Ninth of England, Scotland and the Americas!' I made a deep reverence. 'But how could you leave England?'

'England would forgive my absence because I would send back so many riches from this other kingdom. Gold and silver. Coral. Beaver pelts, *tabacco* . . .'

'. . . live bears and beavers for the royal menagerie . . .'

We stared at each other with excited surmise, even knowing that we spoke nonsense. The Americas might be real. Henry's eventual rule there might be real. But Queen Elizabella of the Americas was idle dreaming.

Henry whacked the head off a daisy. 'Meanwhile, we both must go wherever we're summoned.'

'But if you're there, too, I won't mind. We can suffer together.'

'They wallow in beastly delights. It's not right for a young girl to see and hear such things.'

'But surely, I must learn the ways of the world before I'm sent out into it.' I rolled my eyes and pretended to stagger.

Henry glanced back at our attendants. Then my earnest, well-behaved brother fixed me with a cold heavy-lidded stare. His eyes darted suspiciously around the garden then stared at me again. His fingers began to pick at his sleeve, then at his buttons. He tapped his foot. He chewed on his tongue. He took one graceless step then leaned an elbow on my shoulder

He had caught our father so exactly that I could not help giggling. Then I remembered the father I had seen in Coventry.

'No more!' I said. 'Someone might see you!'

'Our father dislikes me already. But like me or not, I'm his heir. He knows the value of both of us, you and me.'

He sounded so certain that he half-convinced me.

'I must go practise swordplay now in the tiltyard with my friends,' he said. 'My trained band of gentlemen. Would you like to come watch us?'

'Of course.' I trotted to keep up with his quick stride, still bubbling with pleasure that he had shown me a hidden part of himself. 'Perhaps one day, you'll let me try.'

He looked amused. 'If you wish, though I don't know why you would.'

'I wish,' I said.

'It will spoil your hands,' he warned. He stopped and held out his own for me to see the roughened palm. I reached out across my skirt flounce and laid my hand palm down on his. We looked at our two hands in silence.

'Wherever you are, I want to be,' I said. 'No matter how beastly.'

'Would you truly tolerate being a witness to immorality like last night's to be with me?' asked Henry.

'Yes,'

He nodded. 'Then we will suffer together, as you say. And I will look after you.'

'As far as my guardian permits.' I wanted to hug him. Because my skirts made that impossible, I settled for a smile. Tomorrow I would ask if he had ever received my warning letter. Not today. Today was just right as it was.

15

But the right time to ask eluded me. Henry and I saw each other again several times after our meeting in the gardens and took pleasure from each other's company. But we were always surrounded by a court racing in full cry after the pleasures of my uncle's continued visit. Treason was not a subject for a snatched moment on the way to a banquet or tilt. Sooner or later, I would confront my fear of knowing the worst. But not yet.

Because I was not made for fear and gloom, I began to thread the bewildering events of my temporary new life together, to order them like a string of bright beads. Rashly, after the bad beginning of that first evening, I began to believe that I needed less protection than Henry and I had feared.

Though still an object of curiosity, I was only one of many entertainments on offer during my uncle's visit. Courtiers vied to present the most lavish banquets and masques. Members of every noble family in England displayed their looks and skills as dancers and singers in these shows. So many spectators, supporters and enemies alike, crowded to see and discuss the performances that the women were forbidden to wear their wide-hooped farthingales in order to make more room.

Dressed in one or another of the new gowns that had put Lady H into a fever and emptied my guardian's purse, I sat on the royal dais at as many of these masques as I could. There, I learned how much delight the stern-living Haringtons had denied me at Combe. I saw the true purpose of my lute lessons and my dancing master. Here was magic made real. A safe ecstasy. The perfect marriage of wonder and glue.

'Did you ever see such things before?' Anne would murmur close behind me. 'Oh, just look at that!'

Transported out of my everyday self, I watched the sun rise behind wood and canvas mountains. I saw ladies of the court transformed into musical nymphs. Earthquakes destroyed temples. Monstrous lions roared out fire. Gods descended from the roof or sprang from cloven rock. A sky full of candles burned, and red, green and blue lanterns, and other mysterious lights that I could not name but which stirred unnamed memories and elusive wisps of lost dreams. The jewels that flashed in the folds of my gowns looked suddenly like fallen stars and my thoughts felt opened as wide as the night sky.

'I didn't know such things existed!' I told Henry under my breath, when we met once at the door of the Royal Chapel before evening prayers. 'Please tell me that you don't think all the ways of the world are wicked!'

Sometimes the king was present with my uncle at these performances, though he would often fidget violently, then spring up in the middle of a song and leave before the final dance. Sometimes he stayed away altogether, reportedly locked in debate with his attendant wits or drinking in his lodgings, with or without my uncle. Sometimes, he vanished altogether to hunt at Newmarket or Royston, or at Theobald's, Cecil's great estate in Hertfordshire. I heard whispers that he disliked crowds and found excuse to avoid them, fearing a sudden assassin.

Whatever the reason for them, I rejoiced in his absences,

which let me forget fear. With whole-hearted pleasure I could then attend tilts and applaud my brother fighting in the lists. I could marvel at fireworks where dragons spat flames at each other, Catherine Wheels blossomed on trees and rockets briefly imitated the stars. I could listen to music that made me want to weep with joy, as if the vibrating strings of the viols were the strings of my own heart. My body would lie singing under those bows.

'Was that not fine music tonight?' Anne would ask as we bedded down for sleep. 'You could almost sing the tune along with the players. I do prefer the old songs, don't you?'

One night, freed from my father's heavy-lidded gaze, I danced for the first time with a man, in the general dancing that followed the masque. None of Lady H's warning words had armoured me against his smiling gallantry nor against the disturbing yet exciting smell of a heated adult male body so close to mine. As we turned around each other, carried shoulder-to-shoulder on the music, face looking into face, I felt my future quiver with sudden, unexpected brightness.

We danced again. His blue eyes pressed into mine but shifted away just before I could grow awkward with self-consciousness. I glanced at his mouth, under his fair, curly moustache. He bowed over my hand and delivered me back to my chair. I danced with other men. Smiled at Anne as I passed her in a figure. Then I danced with my first partner again. And again. Whenever the drums began, I flew.

'Elizabella.' Henry arrived at my side when I sat down to catch my breath. He looked magnificent in cream-coloured silk embroidered with pearls. His russet hair gleamed. He studied the heaving mass of dancers below us. Nodding and smiling at acquaintances, he said under his breath, 'It's fitter exercise for women than for men.'

I scarcely heard him. I was watching the slim lean shape of my first partner as he danced with a fair-haired young woman. She had full breasts, I noted, trapped quivering behind her bodice top. And a knowing look in her eyes that I envied.

Henry followed my gaze. 'A Seymour,' he said, meaning the man. 'William, has a brother, Thomas. Distant cousins who carry royal Tudor blood.' He stared at the girl, but did not name her.

We watched William Seymour duck his neatly barbered head to lead his partner under the arched arms of another couple.

'I'm told that he has hopes of marrying you,' said Henry.

'If marriage means nothing but dancing,' I said, 'he would suit me very well.'

Henry shook his head earnestly. 'Our father will never let an ambitious English noble get so close to true power.'

'Then I must be content to dance with him.' But in truth, I was sobered by the cold purpose I now knew lay behind that smiling gallantry. I felt foolish, out of my depth. I could never lower my guard.

After that night, I lost much of my taste for masques and dancing and began to take refuge whenever I could in a more familiar haven, the royal stables in Scotland Yard. They held wonders never seen at Combe. Rows and rows of shining flanks. An entire barn full of saddles and tack. War saddles with sheaths for weapons. Ceremonial saddles set with gold. Ladies' side-saddles with curved heads and X-shaped heads. Embroidered saddlecloths and jewelled cushions.

Wearing an old gown, with my farthingale left off, I persuaded the grooms to let me curry and brush my own horses several times a week. When finished in the stables, I wandered into the royal kennels where a greyhound bitch had just whelped, to watch the pups clamber over each other and nose for the teat. The King's Master of the Hounds welcomed me and let me select a pup to have when it was weaned.

I chose one of the two dogs. I watched him wriggle to the

top of the squirming pile, latch on to a teat and hang on undeterred even when another pup stepped on his face. 'Mars,' I said.

The Master of the Hounds also told me that the lioness in the menagerie at the Tower, named Elizabeth after me, had whelped. Poor Anne had to come with me from Whitehall and attend me for hours as I sat by the stacked-up cages, on a chair carried there for me, watching the infant lions suckling and learning to play.

'I can't think why you like it so much here,' muttered Anne in a rare moment of rebellion. 'It stinks.'

'You just want to go back to Whitehall so you can flirt,' I said. I had spoken lightly and was startled to see my old playmate's cheeks burn as red-hot as a sunset.

Then, I saw my first play, performed by the king's own company of players in the temporary Banqueting Hall, built when the old one burned down. Not a mix of songs, dances and poetic declamations like the masques. Just bald, unadorned words, spoken as we speak ourselves, if a little more loudly. With the exception only of the murderous queen in the story, who struck me as strange until I finally saw that she was played by a boy, the players seemed to live as we did, progressing through time, breathing, loving, loathing, fighting, scheming, suffering, murdering.

But what braced me upright in my chair was the whiff of truth that drifted down from the trestle stage of the King's Men. Not all men at court were flatterers after all, even when they wore flatterers' clothes. This play had been written for my father, to be presented before him and my Danish uncle. It was tricked out in the usual flowery dedication. And yet it spoke terrible truths, more truth than any of the flattering poetry of the masques I had seen.

I looked around the Banqueting Hall. I could not believe that no one else noticed. An ambitious, Scottish would-be king.

From a place described as 'too cold for hell.' A king who killed his rivals for the throne. A man with a vast and fearful imagination that showed him vividly what horrors might await him. A man of foreboding. Of changeable purpose.

'Faith, here's an equivocator,' complained the player Porter. '. . . that could swear in both scales against either scale . . .'

I could not look at my father, seated at the centre, on my left. In the side of my eye, I saw his foot jiggling impatiently.

'He means that traitor Jesuit, Garnet,' a voice murmured behind me. 'Who was complicit in the Gunpowder Treason and equivocated his way to the scaffold.'

'No doubt,' another low voice replied, unconvinced. 'No doubt.'

I did not turn my head to see who spoke. Sideways, I watched my father drink, and lean to speak to the young man sitting at his side, a different youth from the night my uncle arrived. I watched the king smile and nod, and pick at his buttons, and drink again, and sometimes watch the stage where blood dripped from royal Scottish hands.

Vengeful enemies attacked. The ghost of a murdered man returned. My father's demons walked and spoke on that stage. It was disguised. It was cleverly confused, with witches, different names and a wicked queen, but I felt the hard dark core of the piece. My family's history, perceived and related for what it was.

I looked at the other spectators around me with new eyes.

Not simply a clumping of ambitious, powerful men and women around the central power of my father. For the first time I saw the court as an animal with its own independent life and strengths. My father . . . our family . . . merely rode it for the time. Like a well-schooled horse, it colluded, allowing the rider to rule it. Though larger and stronger, it permitted the rider to determine when to go, to stop. To choose direction and speed. Like a horse, it was more powerful than its rider and might choose at any time to disobey.

Even though a forest began to advance across the stage and a climax of some sort seemed to be near, I could no longer listen to what the players were saying. My thoughts grew treasonous. Directly opposed to all that my father said and wrote. Opposed to his will, and to God's. They were thoughts to be slammed behind heavy doors.

The Scottish king was being killed, out of sight behind the central curtain. The killer returned with the king's head and saluted another man. 'Hail, King of Scotland!'

Order, said the play, was being restored to the world. The king was dead. Long live the new king.

How did they dare? Who gave them this licence? How could they survive?

Until seeing that play, even after all of Mrs Hay's tales, I had not truly understood that my father could be unseated. I glanced at him again, still drinking, still smiling and talking over the voices of the players as if he had failed to notice this terrifying reality.

You've drunk too much, I told myself. You're wine-addled.

'So thanks to all at once,' said the new player king, 'and to each one, whom we invite to see us crowned at Scone.'

My father was applauding before the last trumpet flourish died. Then he was on his feet, cutting through the spectators, demanding a piss pot and another glass of wine.

Standing by my chair, I clapped the bowing players until my hands burned, a secret new recruit to treason.

16

THEOBALD'S, HERTFORDSHIRE, 1606

A few days later, on a clear spring afternoon, I rode with the royal party to attend what was to be the climax of my uncle's visit, Cecil's own entertainment for the two kings. We arrived at dusk at Theobald's, the vast, golden brick and stone house in Hertfordshire that Cecil's father, Lord Burleigh, had built for entertaining Queen Elizabeth.

'Everyone says that the Chief Secretary means to outdo the grandeur of anything seen so far during your uncle's visit,' Anne whispered to me, as we rode through the entrance gate at the top of the long drive. 'Look at those lights up in the trees! However did they get them all the way up there?'

Lanterns sparkled in the branches of the beech avenue leading to the house. As we rode behind the two kings down the double river of lights, hidden musicians played in the bushes on either side. Inside the big gatehouse, decorated with twisting double chimneys and arched niches filled with classical busts, more musicians played in the first of the huge courtyards. Sweet-smelling fires of apple wood and herbs burned in braziers. Grooms rushed forward to seize our horses and lead them away to the stables.

In the great hall of the house itself, grew a tall oak rustling with silk leaves. On each leaf was written 'WELCOME'. Clockwork birds sang in its branches.

'Look,' whispered Anne. 'Musical birds. Don't they look real!'

'The place is far too fine for a king!' my father proclaimed loudly, gazing up at the intricate, lace-like plaster ceiling. 'I suppose it might just about do for a Chief Secretary.' Without looking, he threw his cloak into a pair of waiting hands.

There was a subdued titter among his followers. A few people glanced at Cecil, who stood waiting to welcome his monarch.

'Enough gawping. I need wine.' Without glancing at the marvellous tree, my father steered the Danish king out of the hall by the arm, with Cecil scurrying behind them. 'We'll help ourselves,' I heard him say over his shoulder as he disappeared. 'I ought to know by now where to find it.'

The arriving courtiers hummed around us. Servants ran everywhere instead of walking, balancing platters or burdened under heaps of cloaks like ants with over-sized crumbs. Women tugged at their gowns and turned suddenly to go back to their lodgings to change their jewels. The air inside the house was rich with perfumes, herbs, wood smoke, sweat, dog, and roasting meats.

The usual feast preceded the masque. Wine fountains bubbled on the tables. The diners stretched to thrust their glasses under the transparent red sheets of falling claret. Serving men stood at every elbow with flagons of ale. I had seen this greedy, abandoned drinking before, but never with such a wild edge. A last chance to indulge, at the Chief Secretary's expense. Even before the arrival of the roast meats, Cecil's ambitious hospitality was beginning to unbuckle the evening.

'Where's the prince, your son?' my uncle boomed, waving

his glass at the packed tables. 'I've scarce seen him since Gravesend!'

'He'll be off somewhere losing his voice with hallooing and singing of anthems,' my father replied sourly, not caring who heard. 'And praying for our souls, I don't doubt. And rattling coins into his penance box against all the foul language he fears we'll use tonight.' He shot a malevolent look at Cecil, sitting at a lower table. 'He needs better instruction!'

Seated with the women who were to be the chief maskers that evening, I heard one of them murmur that the Danish king had cast a vile spell over my father, just as the witch Circe once turned Ulysses and his men into swine.

'Perhaps no spell was needed.' Sly glances slid in my direction.

'Hush,' said another young woman. 'You forget yourself.' I recognised her as the fair-haired girl who had been dancing with William Seymour. This evening I could see her nipples peeking above the line of her bodice. I could have sworn that they were rouged.

'The Danes are all drunkards. Everyone knows that!' the first woman insisted. 'All of them! I accuse only the Danes. It's their long cold nights.'

Other voices joined in. 'They're not so bad as the Scots!' 'As you say, those cold, cold nights.'

'English women . . .!' The dancing girl with the rouged nipples rose to her feet and hoisted her glass. 'Our honour is at stake.'

I saw now that she was only a little older than I in years though she seemed at least a decade more in experience.

'Women, of all kingdoms and ages,' she cried. 'To the barricades! We must not lag behind the men in revelry.' She saluted me with her glass. 'Will you join us, your grace? I hear that you have a pretty singing voice and a neat foot for a figure.'

I met her cat-like blue eye. The countess of something . . .

Suffolk? Derby, perhaps. 'I still study the ways of the court,' I said. 'I'm a mere apprentice. Let me sharpen my battle skills a little more before I join you at the barricades.'

She shook her head and smiled but her eyes were assessing and cold. 'Quite sharp enough already, I think. We must all take care when you decide at last to enter the lists.' Her mocking curtsy was a little marred by a sideways stagger.

A Howard, I decided.

'Faith! Hope! Charity!' Yet another woman rose to her feet. 'Come! The Queen of Sheba has already withdrawn. We must follow her to prepare.'

'But you yourself are Charity,' cried the woman who had called the Scots drunkards.

'So I am!' said the first in astonishment. 'So I am! But I never begin at home . . . nor finish, neither.' She knocked over her stool with her farthingale as she turned to go.

'Courage! To the field!' cried the young Howard woman. She marched away with her glass held high like a standard over her head. Faith, Hope and Charity followed tipsily, laughing, together with several others.

No one summoned me to sit on the royal dais, so I found a place by the wall from which I could watch but not be widely seen. I saw the Chief Secretary standing in the shadows below the two kings. Though he had arranged this ambitious evening to flatter the king, Cecil was keeping himself in the background.

Take note, I told myself. Ambition and power wear many guises, including modesty.

A trumpet fanfare set the audience jostling for position. Then an opening solo announced the coming of the Queen of Sheba to the Temple of Solomon. For the first two verses, I eyed the young man who sat at my father's feet, gazing at my father in adoration even though the king ignored him. My father now sat on a stool on the royal dais, elbows on his knees, head hanging forward over his wine glass, staring at the floor.

The noblewoman playing the Queen of Sheba emerged from the golden temple, carrying an ornate basket filled with gifts of a jelly castle, cakes and wine for the two kings. Her ladies, scantily clad in veils, pantaloons and turned-up slippers, danced on behind her. The Queen of Sheba staggered and almost dropped her basket. Out of step with the accompanying trumpet fanfare, she wove unsteadily across the floor towards my father and uncle under their canopy.

She reached the dais, attempted to climb onto it, tripped, fell headlong, and flung her gifts into my uncle's lap. The jelly castle shattered and slithered down his legs in glistening, jewel-like blobs. The cakes and wine made a red porridge on his lap and in the crevices of his cut-out sleeves.

Servants rushed forward with napkins. The Queen waved away an offered hand and pushed herself back to her feet, haunches first like a cow. She smiled at the two kings. With great care, she revolved, walked away, and attempted to join her ladies in their dance. When they raised their arms above their heads to begin a turn, two of these ladies fell over backwards onto the floor, as drunk as owls.

'Come back here, madam!' shouted the king. My father stood up unsteadily, negotiated the steps, and began to dance with the Queen. But he managed only a few steps before he, too, fell to the floor. Flat on his back, he then spewed the contents of his stomach over his coat.

The young man at my father's side leapt from his stool to help three grooms, instructed by Cecil, to carry the king into an inner room to lay him on a bed to recover.

I watched them go, the man who so terrified me, now helpless, stinking and ridiculous. Temporarily unseated, although no one seemed to notice. Across Lord Salisbury's great hall, I saw Lord Harington searching the dense noisy crowd, as purposeful as a tracking hound in a mêlée of drunken peacocks. I was certain that he was looking for me. This time, I was not ready to be rescued. I was studying the court and king with my new eyes, remembering what Henry had once told me, that there are two places where a sword thrust will always kill an armoured man – the armpit and groin – but you must know them. I thought of my monster father made slave to his own shameful weakness. The evening had still more to teach me. I stepped behind a pillar of the Temple of Solomon.

Now Faith, Hope and Charity entered from the golden temple, bearing their gifts for the two kings. They stood uncertainly at the foot of the royal dais, staring at my father's empty stool.

Hope curtsied first and opened her mouth to speak. Then she closed it again. She peered up at the ceiling as if seeking her missing words. With a 'Pray forgive me, your majesty,' she staggered off again. Faith had already disappeared. I heard her being noisily sick behind the temple.

Through the press of bodies and fog of smoke and wine fumes, I spied the feather on Lord Harington's hat, still moving purposefully, drawing closer. I moved farther from the wall-mounted torches, deeper into the shadows. His face crossed a gap in the crowd, wearing a comical look of horrified distaste.

I ducked around a couple locked together at the mouth, out of Harington's line of sight into the lee of a statue. With one eye alert for my guardian's questing feather, I stepped up onto the wide plinth of a marble Roman general, with a red silk scarf thrown over his head and a feathered hat on his sword.

Clinging to a marble knee, I watched Charity wobble up the steps of the dais to my uncle's feet. She presented him with a jewelled casket then spewed her supper across his knees, on top of the remaining jelly, cake and wine.

She drew herself up and studied her handiwork. 'I shall go home now,' she announced loudly. 'There is no gift left which Heaven has not already given Your Majesty.'

Other revellers now threw themselves into hauling down the setting to take away parts of it to keep. A pillar of the Temple crashed down. I heard wood crack. Canvas tore. Men began to pull the costumes from the female dancers. Bare breasts flashed and jiggled.

I turned in alarm towards the sound of screaming. Then I saw that both men and women were laughing. I looked away from the tangle of bodies.

Its rider unseated, the court horse had now bolted.

'Your grace,' said Lord Harington behind me. 'There you are!' White around the mouth, he offered his hand to help me down. 'Please come with me!'

I took his hand. I had seen enough now.

'This is no place for you,' he said. 'In the morning, whether his majesty likes it or not, I take you back to Combe.'

'I like it,' I said. 'Whether the king does or not.'

Harington gave me a startled look. Then his gaze turned thoughtful.

'I thank you,' I said, and let him lead me for the moment to a safer place.

The thought came to me, as clear and definite as an icicle, that happiness belonged to childhood, and that, when I wasn't looking, my childhood had ended.

PART TWO

The Bride Market

For there is no question, but a just fear of an imminent danger, though there be no blow given, is a lawful cause for war.

'Of Empire', Francis Bacon

Envy worketh subtilly and in the darke, and to the prejudice of good things....

'Of Envie', Francis Bacon

17

How dare my own son despise me? He scarcely troubles himself to hide his scorn. I can read the set of that prim mouth while he seems to obey. I've heard how the people shout, 'The golden prince!' He soaks up the love of the commons as if he means to leave none for me. He swaggers in front of me on those lovely long legs, so unlike these scraggy shanks of mine. Perhaps he's someone else's get, after all . . . As for my Bessie – twice marked by treason. Hell-cat . . . hell-kit . . . If you allow it, an infant viper can still sting you to death.

   Henry must be mine – who else would have been willing to roger his mother? A silly whore, or would-be whore, if she could. A whore like my mother. Whore, whore, whore! That's the truth my tutor once beat into me. 'Say it!' he ordered me. 'Your mother is a whore!' Mulier portentosae libinis! *'Say it!' My blood is tainted. My stock is dangerous. Whores and traitors are my heritage and my legacy. My own children carry the taint of treason.*

   I did not ask to replace my mother on the throne. I was a babe! But a dangerous one all the same. A babe with bloody hands. With such cunning subtlety, my own King's Men dared to accuse me in their play! Yet I dare not accuse them for fear of condemning myself.

Again and again, it's proved. I can trust no one! Not even my own blood, my own seed. I allow Wee Bobby power because he's hated by the people. England would never tolerate another crook-back on the throne, not after Crooked Dick . . . I like that . . . 'Crooked dick' . . . even in the darkest truths, I find little gleams of wit . . . or a crude jest. Be honest. I lodge my affection only in the beautiful and stupid, where I can control. Even when infatuated by a perfect line of lip, the shell of an ear, a wrist, a thigh, a promising codpiece, a fresh healthy young prick, I'm alert. I know I can think faster than any of my lovely boys.

I dare them to sneer. I rampage through the gardens of their delicacy. That's true power – to command obedience from those who want to scorn. I pick my nose and scratch my groin, just to watch them force smiles and pretend to see nothing amiss. If I were God, I could pick their noses for them, and scratch their groins . . . I could strip off their clothes and ride on their backs naked, and they would not dare protest. God would not have to bow to his twisted little Treasurer and meekly agree to cut his costs. God would not be reproved like a naughty school boy for neglecting his work.

Our Father Which art . . . where's the cushion for my knees? Father, tell Your son on earth how he must speak for You. Hold him firm in the place You have ordained for him, a mortal Prince of Peace. Without Your Will, there is only sad comedy.

. . . Beauty. Oh, my sweet Robert! I can drown in you. In your company, I too become beautiful. Beauty softens my sinews . . . thaws the frozen rivers of my veins. Even pans of hot coals can't warm this bed as beauty can.

My whelps, Henry and Elizabeth, at least give pleasure to the eye. If not, I'd have them put down like the dangerous cubs they are . . . I jest, of course. No one could fear Baby Charles, who jumps in terror if you speak to him and can't get his words out past his teeth. 'Fa . . . fa . . . fa . . . father . . .' Alas, he's no beauty.

I must teach Henry not to trust his power. Teach him not to trust anyone – least of all that flattering little dwarf who thinks I don't see how he battens on my power. A leech like all of them, but a necessary leech.

... No one hides here behind this hanging. Nor here ... But they will come again at night with their knives and lock me in my chamber, again, with the breathing, and the rustling. Blind, deaf, I'll feel them around me.

What was that? Listen! Do they come? ... LIGHT THE CANDLE AGAIN! DEAR GOD! COME! LIGHT, HERE! PLEASE, LIGHT AGAIN!

I made peace between England and Spain. Where is peace for me?

Elöi, Elöi Elöi, läma sabachthani? My God, My God, why hast thou forsaken me? The candle must not go out again. Fill my bedchamber with lights!

18

Reluctantly, in the next years, the Haringtons were forced more and more often, on the king's orders, to return me to Sodom and Gomorrah to be viewed by the foreign marriage brokers.

'You can't sell a horse unseen,' I overheard Lady H say briskly to her husband on one occasion. 'If you fear so much for her soul, don't loosen your protective grip until the king orders it. We must take a house closer to London.'

So they set up a household in Kew, little more than an hour's journey by river from Whitehall. I acquired my own barge, with eight rowers and a fine, sonorous drum to keep the strokes in unison, so that I could continue to live with them but still travel easily to Whitehall when summoned. Even better, I could also visit my brother Henry, who now had his own household at St James's, diagonally across the park from Whitehall.

Although I continued to find the Haringtons' stern faith and endless prayers as tedious as ever, I always returned from Whitehall with secret relief. Lady H's brusque questions were a purge for my glutted senses. Lord H's pinched lips and raised brows settled my slight giddiness after supping of a court that tasted both rich and a little rotten, like a lustrous, overripe fruit.

On the other hand, continuing to live with them slowed my own learning about court ways.

My father wanted me kept ignorant, in any case. 'You should no more educate a woman than tame a fox,' he once told me. 'It makes them both dangerous.'

Though he summoned me to stand on show for envoys from a prospective husbands, he denied me all information and had ordered that no one answer my questions. I was to be protected from all 'signs of love' from my suitors as if from a contagion. I was not allowed even to see their portraits.

In those years at Kew, I saw the court only in bursts when attending state events. I tried to string together the beads of these events into a coherent tale. Like a magpie, I collected every other bead of information that I could, by keeping my eyes and ears open. In trying to keep me ignorant, my father had forgotten rumour and poets.

Poets, essayists, letter writers and pamphleteers drained barrels of ink as they detailed the extravagant masques and feasts of dreamlike richness, where sugar flowers bloomed on tables and silver fountains bubbled with wine, some of which I had seen for myself. They spent their ink on the heroic tilts and prize-givings, the king's lavish gifts to his favourites, the royal opening of grand new shops, the hunting, the launching of ships. They described the fire-works and the processions on the Thames of gilded barges accompanied by golden dolphins and whales. They evoked the coronet fanfares that ushered in the king. Made their readers smell the perfumes, and squint at glittering acres of cloth of gold and silver. They eulogised the royal family – king, queen, two surviving princes and a princess, the living image of the new stability of the Crown in this glorious 'New English Age'.

And there I was, from time to time, trapped in all those words, described as 'spirited', 'witty' and 'beautiful' (or 'handsome', depending on the writer).

Some of what they wrote was even true. My difficulty lay in knowing which parts to believe. I could judge the lies about what I had myself experienced. Much of the rest belonged to a world I did not yet understand, the affairs of men and of state.

The king was reported to spend most of his time away from Whitehall, hunting at Theobald's, Royston, or Newmarket. Whatever the reasons for his frequent absences, I was deeply grateful.

Henry, on the other hand, could often be found in the brick and stone palace at St James's that had been built by the last King Henry for his children. The busy pens told, truthfully, how my brother and I rode together and sometimes dined quietly at St James's with the growing band of young Protestant noblemen who gathered round him. These young knights were, as reported, chiefly English but included Huguenot French and Germans among them, most of these young men as earnest and sober as my brother.

The occasional reports of my high spirits may have reflected the fact that one or two delightful flirts in this band were happy to let me practise my upward glances and sideways looks, whose power I was just discovering.

My presence was noted, watching these young men practise swordplay or tilting. Nowhere, however, did I read of the hours I spent listening to them talk of art and religious wars, while all the time I was comparing their different mouths and the smoothness of their cheeks. No one wrote that I fell in love with three of them at the same time, or that I became breathless at the way their slim legs cut the air and their strong young male hands gripped a sword hilt. To my grief, none of these men was suitable for a royal husband. A princess cannot marry her brother's master of horse, even when he is a French seigneur.

In any case, Lady Harington's voice always whispered in my head, even as I – 'The Pearl of England', the 'Second

Gloriana' – tossed back pleasantries, and smiled at the extravagant compliments.

'They all want something from you,' Lady Harington had said. 'Dismiss all compliments as hopeful flattery.'

I did not need Lady H to point out the flattering lies in what the poets and other chroniclers scribbled. Of my own accord, I could see their ignorance. And sometimes their malice. In my father's new Age of Peace, I soon saw for myself that men not only flattered but also drew blood with their pens.

Almost the very first time I had been rowed from Kew to London after we moved there from Combe, Henry had taken me into his pale-plastered study and shown me the copy of a secret letter that had fallen into his hands. This writer, intending his words only for the eyes of a trusted friend, described how the king took pains never to let the prince make progresses nor arrive alone on state occasions. His majesty would always arrive first, to receive the first wave of cheers, and let Henry follow.

'Lest I gather the love of the people to myself,' said Henry bitterly. 'There are many more letters like this. If my father ever knew half of what is written or said about him, he would leave a trail of bloody footprints.' He locked the copied letter into a chest. 'But the flattery of his courtiers, the protection of Cecil and his own armour of self-satisfaction protect him.'

'Not entirely,' I said, thinking of the padded doublet and that scene in Coventry. 'Sweet Hal, take care!'

'Don't fear, Elizabella.' He picked up a paper from his table and began to read it.

'It's so hard to know all the dangers.' I swallowed. This was the moment to ask him about my warning letter. If I didn't take it now, I never would.

'Our mother is not spared neither,' said Henry. 'She's charged, by tittle-tattle and pen-pushers alike, with frivolity and wilful extravagance at her household, which she insists on keeping in Greenwich – charges that the king does not trouble to deny.'

'Hal,' I began.

'Perhaps he believes that her extravagance distracts from his own,' said Henry.

'Surely, the charges are false,' I managed to reply. 'Hal . . .'

'You'll learn the truth for yourself when you are more at Whitehall,' said my brother. 'I've seen the reports by Cecil's accountants, detailing in dry columns of figures the royal extravagance, both hers and the king's, and noting the absence of money in the Exchequer to pay for it all.'

'Hal,' I said. 'Did you ever get my letter?'

'What letter?' he asked.

'From Combe,' I said. 'When I still lived there. I sent my groom, Abel White, to find you.'

Henry shook his head. 'Never saw the man. What did you write?'

'Never mind,' I said. 'I don't remember now.'

My letter was lost! Floating with other dangerous letters, like those Henry had locked away, in a deeper, secret layer of words, bald, unadorned and brutal, flowing through England in a hidden current. Someone, very likely a man who bowed to me and murmured compliments, knew that I was a traitor.

Then, I found that I had to sit down on the nearest stool. Perhaps my father had my letter, after all.

I had assumed that he would confront me with my treason at once. A false assumption, I saw now. For all his outward coarseness, my father had a subtle turn of mind. He would enjoy playing cat-and-mouse with me.

'I will tell you something in confidence.' Henry settled onto the stool beside me and leaned his head close to mine. 'Now that I'm here at St James's, Cecil has begun to groom me secretly for kingship, just as he once tutored our father on how to gain the English throne.'

'Our father doesn't know?'

'Of course not. He would believe that we were weaving his winding sheets. But Cecil says that it is always best to be prepared for any great change. That preparing is not the same as wishing for it.'

I should warn him, I thought. That I may already have drawn him into treason. On the other hand, if my letter had never reached Henry, then he could not be blamed. Until I knew more, I decided, I would leave my brother unmarked by my crime.

19

At Holyrood, before we left for England, I heard a terrible story told in whispers like cold drafts from a cellar. The Countess of Mar had refused to hand Henry over to travel south with my mother, who had had him torn from her arms at birth to be given to these severe strangers to raise. Confronting the implacable countess, my mother had beaten her fists on her pregnant belly in despair and rage (the whispers said) and thereby killed the first of my two lost sisters.

I could almost have disbelieved it if I had not seen my sister's tiny coffin for myself when I kissed my mother goodbye. I had clung to her hand to stop her mounting into her seat beside the little gilded box. But the tiny body had ridden south with my mother in the royal coach while Henry and I were left behind to catch up later.

After we arrived in England, she and I never met alone. I saw her only on state occasions. I curtsied to her and exchanged formal greetings. I walked in her train, in her progress through the court. Sometimes I was allowed to sit with both my parents on the royal dais during masques or other entertainments. But we had not exchanged two words that were not formal, let alone repeated the delicious intimacy of our last days at Holyrood. I told myself that her life was always too busy with court affairs, and that I always vanished back to Kew just when she might have found time to see me in private.

Then, after three years of increasingly frequent travel by barge from Kew, I was instructed to move to Whitehall, where my lodgings in the Small Closed Tennis Court were now ready. When I arrived, I learned that my mother had also moved to Whitehall from Greenwich.

I wrote to her at once.

'I am near to you again at last,' I wrote. *'My heart overflows with joy at the thought of seeing you once more as soon as your high- ness wills it.'*

I reminded her of our suppers together in her little closet at Holyrood. I asked my tutor to see that my grammar and spelling were perfect. I signed in gold, *'Your most hopeful, loving daughter, Elizabeth.'*

I prepared a gift to take her, an engraved silver box to be filled with sweetmeats.

I told myself that I was not disappointed when she did not reply at once, that same day. That night, I polished the last finger marks off the silver box with the hem of my shift.

The next day while I waited for her reply, I explored my new lodgings, as eager and restless as a cat. The tennis courts, which were near the Cockpit and Tiltyard, had been floored and divided into a suite of rooms to accommodate me and my new household. Behind the tapestries, the drying plaster walls still smelled of damp earth. The frescos of Greek gods and goddesses in my big receiving chamber still gave off the sulphurous taint of egg. The flesh of freshly-painted infant angels on the Tennis Court Gallery ceiling still glowed a lurid pink.

But my familiar enclosed, four-posted bed which had followed me from Dunfermline to Combe, had been waiting for me, with its faded red silk coverlet and plump down-filled pillows. My velvet-covered box of combs, a New Year gift from my parents, lay on a table.

I stroked my old friends, the four upright Scottish lions that served as stout oak bedposts. I smiled back at my new chamberer, who looked as uncertain as I felt. I dared to ask her to lay a folded blanket across the foot of the bed, so that my dogs could sleep on my feet, as Lady Harington had never allowed. She obeyed at once.

Watching the unfamiliar young woman . . . Jane, I reminded myself . . . as she smoothed out every last wrinkle so that my dogs could sleep in perfect comfort, I felt something shift under my heart.

Suddenly, my life seemed to be rushing me on. I tumbled forward, all arsvy-varsy, struggling to find my footing. I already inhabited a new unfamiliar body with breasts and startling hair that turned my armpits and the fork of my legs into strange, small animals. Like Henry, I gave off new smells that I sometimes sniffed secretly at night. Sometimes, like now, watching an unfamiliar serving maid obey an order I had never before dared to give, I did not know where to put myself.

I called for Belle but she did not come. I paced the length of the tennis court gallery and back again. I wandered from room to room in my new lodgings.

Why had my mother not yet answered me?

'Belle! Cherami! Bichette!' Then I saw the little dogs through a window, below me in the orchard with Anne and my French maid. They were waiting for me, but suddenly I did not want to join them.

Alone, I fled like a thief through a high closed gallery that crossed the public thoroughfare of Whitehall itself. From the Parkside, where my lodgings lay, I arrived on the Riverside of Whitehall, where my parents lodged and the state apartments lay.

For a time, I wandered, lost in the maze of courts, alleys and random jumble of buildings. I entered state chambers and quickly left them again before I was noticed. I found the royal chapel. I looked into a presence chamber filled with petitioners to the king. I crossed and re-crossed a large open courtyard. A few times, I was recognised and received startled curtsies and bows. The rest of the time, a single, purposeful, cross-looking girl – I saw my reflection in a hanging glass – reminded no one of the distant doll in silks seen from time to time on the royal dais or on horseback in processions.

It was clear that Whitehall Palace had grown in bits and pieces, sprouting a room here, an alleyway there. Mysterious gateways, open-roofed passages that might have been inside or out, sudden spiral stairs in unexpected towers, were all packed together with no respect for the rectangular order and French reason of Dunfermline Palace, where I had lived in Scotland.

Feeling foolish at being so lost, I began to make a map in my head. King's lodgings on the river, upstream, towards Richmond. Queen's lodgings on the river, downstream, towards Westminster and the City of London. Court offices behind the state apartments, Chapel and Banqueting Hall. Beyond the offices, my goal, Scotland Yard and the royal stables.

Wainscot, Clapper and my other horses were comfortably settled after being brought from Kew. I spoke to each horse, and stroked and scratched. Then I lingered, feeling more like my old self, walking past endless lines of glossy tails and cocked hoofs, of the horses belonging to the king and queen. I found the quarters for foreign horses. Their grooms spoke French and Spanish.

On my way back, I paused to take note of a room that bridged a busy public thoroughfare. From a window, I looked down curiously onto the tops of passing heads.

The street below me led from the Whitehall Stairs on the river, which were used by the public, to the wide right of way of Whitehall itself that split the Palace into separate halves. I added this information to my growing, imagined map of the palace.

By trial and error, I found my way through the state chambers and the king's lodgings to an enclosed jetty upriver from Whitehall Stairs, which I had seen from the window that bridged the public street.

Suddenly, I knew where I was again. My barge from Kew had landed here. The privy water stairs, for the private use of the Palace residents.

I stood at the end of the privy stairs and gazed out across the silver running of the Thames at the low line of the Surrey shore. For a time, I watched the wherries and barges slide past, and listened to their wakes lapping at the palace walls. Fish jumped close below my feet.

'A pleasing sight, is it not?' I asked the guard.

'Indeed, your grace. I always volunteer for this post, even on rainy nights. A man can breathe out here.'

'And a woman too.'

We exchanged quick glances.

'Your brother often comes here to swim at night,' he said.

I wondered how far Henry ventured on these private swims when the water was black instead of silver.

I imagined calling my boatmen and setting off on a voyage. If I travelled far enough to my left, I would reach the sea. And if I then turned left again and followed the coast to the north, I would reach the Firth of Forth and Edinburgh.

It could be done. The possibility both startled and comforted me.

If, on the other hand, I travelled upstream to my right, I would wind deeper and deeper into the heart of England. And if I set off directly across the Thames, I would come to the Lambeth marshes and the last houses, fields and inns of Southwark.

I stared curiously at the distant line of trees and rooftops. Many gentlemen of the court, even some of Henry's earnest knights nudged each other and traded stories of having pockets picked and purses stolen among the lawless dangers of the London Ward Without. I had heard that even my father went to Southwark for the bear-baiting.

'Have you been to Southwark?' I asked the guard.

'I have, your grace.' As I watched, his face went red.

'I should like to see it for myself one day,' I said.

'It's no place for you!' He looked horrified. 'Your grace,' he added.

I decided not to ask if he had ever accompanied the king across the river and turned back to study the dangerous forbidden territory. If Henry had not been so strait-laced, I could have asked him to take me.

Then I looked into the flatness beyond Southwark. Even farther in that direction, lay the southern edge of England which I had never seen.

I shall come stand here, I decided, whenever I need to know where I am.

When I returned to my lodgings, there was still no word from my mother. But the afternoon offered some distraction. I met some of my new ladies-in-waiting. I would still have to appoint them formally, but the choice had been made for me. Alone with Anne afterwards, I remembered chiefly smiles, curtsies and assessing eyes filled with private thoughts.

'I know the fair-haired one with the cat eyes,' I said. With a twinge of alarm, I had recognised the young woman with the cold assessing stare, who had cried, 'Courage! To the field!' and led her army of drunken Amazons into battle at Theobald's.

Frances, born a Howard, now Countess of Essex, Anne told

me. Already married, but living apart from her young husband, who had been sent abroad to grow into manhood. Anne looked away and blushed.

I wondered whether or not Frances Howard had been too far gone in drink at Theobald's to remember her challenge to me. Ready or not, I had now entered the lists.

It made me a little queasy to think that these young women were now under my authority, where once I had ruled only my pets. I knew how to talk to Anne, to stable grooms, to my old nurse, and to my brother Henry, not to gentlewomen, most of whom were older than I.

'Tell me their names once more.'

'Another Frances,' Anne prompted. 'The one with the dark hair and long nose. A Northumberland, this one, not so pretty as the Howard one. The "Other Frances" we must call her.' She laughed. 'And the shortest one is Elizabeth Apsley. The "Other Elizabeth" I suppose. I did like her green gown . . .'

Lady Harington's voice rang in my head as clear if she had been standing in the room with me. I remembered every word like a catechism.

'Every one of them will be someone's creature,' she had warned. 'They will report everything you do . . . Beware, in particular of the rival families. The Howards and Northumberlands . . .'

'You remember Frances Tyrrell from Scotland?' continued Anne. 'Freckles and won't smile because of her bad teeth. Perhaps that explains her blunt manner. Now that I think of it, I remember my aunt telling me . . . And you know Philadelphia Carey, who is much plumper now than when she was your playmate. And there's me, of course!'

'Thank God!'

That same night, returning from relieving myself in my *garde-robe* after supper, I paused just inside the door of my sleeping chamber. I did not intend to eavesdrop, but my ladies in the outer room were speaking in those irresistible lowered voices that signal private gossip.

'. . . a long-legged Scottish dobbin.' I could not be certain but thought the self-assured voice belonged to Frances Howard.

'She's tall, for sure,' another voice agreed with a hint of Scots. Perhaps Frances Tyrrell. 'And I hear she's wilful.'

'I think she's rather pretty,' said someone else, almost certainly Philadelphia, whom I had first met at the age of six and a half and seemed to have forgiven me for soaking her skirts at the Smite ford.

'She's very kind!' protested Anne's voice, with a heat that astonished me.

They fell silent when I entered the room. Then all of them began to chatter at the same time.

There was still no word from my mother.

I decided to chance a ride across the park to visit Henry. Though he now lived closer, he seemed in many ways more difficult to reach. As heir to the throne, he had a much grander household than mine and far more to do. Every morning, crowds of petitioners and suitors waited for him, hoping to be allowed into his presence. Painters, woodcarvers, plasterers, brick-makers and all other sorts of craftsmen petitioned him for commissions.

As well as my brother's band of young warriors, I had already met one of his new favourites, a Master Jones, who was his surveyor. There were other builders, too – my brother's newest passion was for buildings. And poets. And there were men who wanted to be his officers, his gentlemen, his glove-maker, his chaplain. Courtiers swarmed around him, hoping to win the good will of the future king. Statesmen already jostled towards positions of influence in his government.

Henry welcomed me at St James's but was engrossed in conference with a messenger recently arrived by ship from the infant colony at Jamestown, Virginia, in the Americas. Among the others attending on my brother that evening, was Sir Francis Bacon, lean, sharp-eyed, dissatisfied – the man I had noticed during my uncle's visit, watching Robert Cecil and my guardian, the man I had seen smiling on the scaffold in Paul's Churchyard. Unlike his cousin Cecil, Bacon seemed willing to risk our father's jealousy by openly wooing Henry.

While I flirted harmlessly with the Seigneur de St Antoine, I watched Bacon. I did not like the man, I decided. His manner did not fit his position. Even though he was a Burleigh cousin, an esteemed scholar, and said to be one of the few men at court who could match my father for sharpness of wit, he filled me with the unease.

He stood always on guard, a little apart, watching, his eyes eating up everything they touched. In particular, I did not like the way he studied my brother, as if noting what made him smile or frown. In that entire evening, I never once saw him unguarded nor laugh from good-humour, but only because my brother, or some other person of influence had laughed.

He reminded me of a bad-tempered dog – suspicious, watchful, wagging its tail even while its lips drew back in the beginning of a snarl. Already elevated, he reeked of further striving and ambition.

Two days earlier, a petitioner had given Henry a toy greyhound that delighted him and which he held on his lap while he conversed. Not to be outdone, Sir Francis this evening presented him with a full-sized hunting greyhound.

Unfortunately, the larger dog bared its teeth and lunged for the smaller hound in the prince's lap. A dog groom controlled the hunting hound at once and no harm was done. Henry thanked Bacon and sent his gift to join the other dogs in the royal kennels.

I saw something angry and tight in Bacon's eyes as he bowed and professed his delighted gratification in giving his highness even the smallest pleasure.

What the man made of anything eluded me. All that he sucked in through those hungry, acquisitive eyes turned into thoughts I could not imagine. Except that all other men seemed to strike him as slow-plodding fools. Even Henry brought that edge of silent scorn into Bacon's eyes, though it was quickly veiled again with false admiration.

I caught my brother in a quiet moment. I leaned close to scratch his new miniature hound behind the ears. 'Don't trust Bacon.'

Henry smiled at me 'But I'm not going to marry him to my Elizabella. To rule, I will need men about me with intellect like his. I don't need to like them so long as they serve me. Sir Francis has a good mind for strategy. Which, as you know, I do not.'

Henry never minded making such admissions. He knew his own strengths, which were those of a true ruler. He had honesty, decision and courage. People wished to warm themselves at him.

I could not think how to say that while Bacon might have intellect, he did not seem to me to be wise.

'You already have Wee Bobby,' I said, remembering what Henry had told me about Cecil's private instruction for the heir to the throne.

'England has Wee Bobby, not I. He's no more loyal to me than he is to our father. Salisbury will always choose his own devious way to achieve the best for England. I trust him because I know what he wants. And I trust Sir Francis for the same reason – and it's far simpler to understand. He wants to be Attorney General.'

'I think he wants to become his cousin, Cecil,' I said.

'Don't be fanciful. He wants to rise, as all men do. You

mustn't hold ambition against a man, Elizabella, or you'll like none of us.' He flashed his smile at me. 'And if I couldn't forgive flattery, I'd have no one left to like but you . . . and my horse.'

20

BACON

I do not understand. Yet my understanding is quicker and more profound than that of most other men – who are fools, with very few exceptions. Surely, the truth must be clear to those other than myself!

The king is repulsive. Nevertheless, power and position make him lovely to those beautiful boys. At least, insofar as outward effect over-rules inward emotion. If you're the king and the hand of Carr is on your cock, you need not care what lies in the boy's brazen, greedy little heart. I'm sure that the boy truly loves you, your majesty, just as a babe loves the teat that flows with milk.

I flow with wisdom, scholarship and readiness to serve. Why then does the king frown and pull his lip when I speak, and look away as if I weren't there? I'm well-enough formed, not too old. I have a lively hazel eye, and, God knows, a quick wit. I can discourse on any subject the king pleases. I entertain him as well as any other of the court wits, yet I take care not to best him in debate. I lick his arse as sincerely as any man. I bow as deep. I study and imitate every courtier trick. Why, then, does he seem to find me repulsive?

If I say a thing is true, he knows that I am right. I am rated – by more than my own vanity – one of the most able men in England, the most suited to help steer the ship of state, yet I stand at the side, overlooked, humiliated.

My little cousin keeps me down. Drip, drip, drip, into the royal ear trickles the Little Toad's poison, along with all his wise counsel. Drip, drip, drip. The constant noise of my cousin's voice leaves no silence for wiser counsel to penetrate.

I dislike myself in this petty humour. But it infects me like a rheum. When I should be reaching for larger thoughts, I find myself watching little cousin Cecil and inventing ways he might die. Or scheming how to cut off the roots of his favour with the king. I listen for a careless word of his that I can nurture into a viper to sting him. I'll find my weapon in time. We're too much alike, he and I, in spite of his virtuous pose. He has weaknesses. I have a sharp eye and inventive mind. I've had to learn patience.

The king will not live forever. His heir is made of more malleable stuff, imagining that he commands but always wanting to please. I have watched him. I know the prince better than he knows himself. I will give him cause to thank me. He will need me as his father needs both his favourites and Cecil.

21

After a week of polishing the silver box every night, I wrote to my mother again. Each day, I woke up certain that she would call for me that day. I filled the silver box with cherries, which were as beautiful as jewels. Then I polished each fruit until it reflected a tiny star of light. Each day, I chose a different gown – my dark blue silk taffeta, my copper-coloured shot silk, and stood patiently while my French maid tamed my hair into an orderly halo pinned high off my neck so that I could wear a wired lace collar. I spent each day trying to keep my skirt hems clean and my hair in order. I stopped visiting the stables to stroke Wainscot lest I carry back too strong a whiff of horse and stable dung.

My mother did not send for me.

One morning after breakfast, I gathered my courage and asked the Herd, as I now privately called my ladies to make them less fearsome, to tell me who attended the queen. I was startled by the rush of gossip I provoked. I saw that if I winnowed out the chaff from the malice the Herd could become unwitting intelligencers in my war on ignorance.

In one voice, they all agreed. The lady to petition was Lucy, Countess of Bedford. Another Harington, Lord Harington's daughter, though seldom seen at Combe.

She had killed two horses, they said, in her race to Edinburgh to get to the new Scottish queen before any other English gentlewoman. She had since become a lady of the queen's privy chamber and my mother's closest companion, thus proving the truth of the old saw about early birds.

That same afternoon, I lay in wait in the great court of the palace, just inside the Court Gate.

'There she is,' murmured Anne, who waited with me.

I thought the Countess of Bedford very beautiful with her fine fair hair, oval face and porcelain skin, but perhaps a little over-pleased with herself. And her nose might have been the least bit too long.

'Your grace!' she exclaimed when she saw me, no doubt startled by the wild-haired, red-faced apparition that leapt into her way. She exchanged glances with her attending gentlewoman and sketched a curtsy.

I decided that I loathed her. I wished that I had taken as much trouble to dress that day as I had the day before.

'I beg you, be kind enough to tell the queen that I am eager to see her now that I'm here in Whitehall,' I blurted. I thought I detected slyness in her self-satisfaction. It suddenly occurred to me that the countess herself might have intercepted my letters.

'Her majesty knows your desires.'

'When may I see her?'

Lady Bedford smiled in gentle reproof. I knew how I must look to her hatefully long-lashed eyes. An overgrown hoyden wearing a country gown, with freckles and flyaway hair.

'Her Majesty is not well.' Her sweet voice made me want to pull out that lustrous hair. 'She's still melancholy after the loss of three babes – the boy Robert in Scotland, and then the two girls. And you must understand that she is also pre-occupied with the health of the young duke.'

I raised my eyebrows in disbelief.

I knew that Baby Charles, now ten years old, was much

improved. When I had met him again only the day before, formally, in the care of his new English guardian, Lady Carey, I had noted the changes since I last saw him at our Danish uncle's visit. The bald patch on the back of his head, where he had once rubbed it against his pillow, was now overgrown with fair, curling hair. Though still very small and with legs that still bowed, he could walk unaided, without braces to straighten his bones. Though he stuttered, he was talking at last.

He had clearly forgiven me for splashing him on the water stairs with water from my posy. He asked the names of all my dogs and their breeds, the names of the stones in my rings, whether I was to have my portrait painted too, like him, and what gown would I wear, if I did sit for the famous Flemish painter who was to paint him, and had I seen our brother Henry triumph in the tilt yet? He talked, hardly drawing breath, not heeding my replies.

Not only did Baby Charles not seem cause for continuing concern, I also knew that my mother was no longer completely drowned in melancholy at the loss of her babes. All the court ladies of honour, including my own, were atwitter with her plans to stage a new masque. In it, the queen was to play the principle part herself and would choose a dozen fortunate ladies to play her nymphs.

After parting from Lady Bedford, I returned to my lodgings and waited. I tried to do my needlework but kept stabbing my finger with the needle. My ladies invited me to join them in a game of *Cent*, but I could not settle to cards or to their talk of flirtations and gowns. Supper served in my lodgings offered a distraction, but I had no appetite.

Just after supper, there was a knock on the door. One of the queen's running footmen. At last.

I leapt to my feet. 'Come help me change to a finer gown!' I said to Anne.

The footman bowed. 'Her majesty has sent you a gift of

welcome, your grace.' He stepped aside and waved forward the person standing outside the door. 'Here it is.'

My mother's gift entered and stood staring at me in open disbelief.

22

'There's no letter?' I stared back at the new arrival.

My ladies gawped over their cards.

'What am I to do with her?' I wanted my mother. Not this strange girl who looked as startled to see me as I was to see her, and not much happier about it.

'The queen sent no letter, your grace.'

No word of welcome. No invitation. No explanation.

'I don't want her,' I said at last, fighting desolation.

'That is for your grace to say.' He bowed again and backed out of the room.

'You may go, too,' I told the girl. 'I thank you, but I have no use for you.'

She stood frozen, clutching a painted leather lute case in front of her like a shield. She wore what had once been a fine black silk gown, now re-cut many times and faded to dusty grey.

She was perhaps a little older than I was and much the same height. But she was more delicate, like a tall wading bird. A cloud of black hair stood out around her neat round head that balanced atilt on a long slender neck. The hair framed large eyes, a full mouth, a firm pointed chin, and a nose that was a little shorter than mine but wider and flatter.

Her skin was almost black and shone with purplish lights on her cheeks and forehead, like a plum.

She didn't deceive me, who was the mistress of that same false stillness, which I recognised as a mask for intense feeling, like anger or fear.

'You may go,' I said again. And take your anger or your fear with you, I thought. I have enough of my own.

She bobbed a tight serving maid's curtsy and went, holding her lute case against her breast.

But when I headed later towards the privy garden for an after-supper stroll, I saw her again – the sop my mother had thrown me while withholding herself. The girl was standing at the far end of the long gallery near the door of my sleeping chamber, a shadow cut out of the evening glow that fell through the high narrow windows. In the late light, her skin and dark gown looked almost the same colour. The open lute case sat on the floor by her feet. The alternating light and dark stripes on the back of the lute in her hand stood out clearly against her skirt.

I pretended I did not notice her.

An hour later, when we returned from the privy garden, she was still there, the lute now re-cased. This time, I approached her.

'Not gone yet?' I asked. 'I told you to go.'

My ladies murmured behind me. My gift glanced at them, then at me but did not reply.

I was certain that Lady H would have found her insolent. But my lady guardian had never taught me how to deal with a human gift. I felt the possibility of undefined social disaster.

'Go lay out the cards again,' I told the Herd over my shoulder. I wanted no witnesses. 'I'll come join you shortly.' They rustled away into my main receiving chamber.

'Why are you still here?'

'To serve you, madam.' Her voice was unexpectedly low

146

and husky coming from her delicate frame. Her speech was pure rough Southwark. 'Or so I understand.'

'You sound more English than I do!' I exclaimed.

'Yes.'

Again, I considered her tone. I could detect only the flatness of blunt truth.

'But I've no use for you,' I said. 'I told you before. My mother has a taste for exotic maids and grooms, not I. Go back and offer your services to her.'

'I can't.'

'Why not?'

She looked me in the eye again. 'If I leave here, I risk being hanged as a thief.'

'For stealing what?'

'Myself.'

I stared back at her for a moment. 'Come walk with me here in the gallery.'

'Thank you, madam.'

I gazed at her sideways as our skirts swung in unison like a pair of bells. In the failing light, she was beautiful. And mysterious in a way that made me feel earthbound and ordinary. I would not have been surprised to see her perched high up like a dryad among the leaves of a forest tree, or looking up from under the water of the Thames. Her dark, gleaming skin made me feel pasty and pale.

I looked down at our hands. In the dusk, hers were solid shapes of darkness. Mine swam like pale fish just under the surface of the water. Her lithe elegance and long bones made me think again of a graceful wading bird, while I felt like a half-grown hound or yearling deer still awkward with its new length of leg. I should have hated her, as I hated the Countess of Bedford. But she felt like another kind of creature altogether. I might as well envy Wainscot.

Wainscot was beautiful, yet I loved her. And it seemed that this girl was mine, just as much as Wainscot was.

147

'You were bought?' I did not add, 'like a dog or horse,' but felt the unspoken words shake themselves loose into the air and racket around both our heads.

She nodded. There was a tiny jolt in the air between us. I looked more closely at her. But the air had turned smooth again.

'I must call you something,' I said awkwardly. 'Do you have a name?'

'Thalia Bristo.'

I don't know what I had expected, but it was not 'Thalia Bristo'.

'Thalia . . . one of the nine Muses,' she began to explain.

'I know the names of the Muses!' My father might not wish to have me educated like Henry, but I could read. 'She's the muse of either Comedy or Pastoral Poetry. Which are you?'

'She's also one of the Three Graces, if you prefer.'

I wished again for Lady H to guide me in this odd, uneasy conversation. I sat on a bench in a window bay and motioned for the girl to sit beside me.

Thalia Bristo folded herself down onto the bench, arriving exactly where she intended, with no shuffling or rearranging of farthingale and skirts.

'How do you do that? I asked. More often than not, I felt like a long-legged dog that had to turn around and around in its basket to find the right fit.

'Sit, do you mean?' She gave the tiniest shrug. 'Like everyone else, I imagine.'

I decided to leave it. 'Did the queen buy you?'

'I don't know who it was, madam.'

'Are you a slave?' I had never thought much about slaves before. There were slaves in plays and masques, of course, and heroic poems, most often captives of war, like Queen Tamora and Aaron the Moor in *Titus Andronicus*. And Henry's beloved Ralegh had made at least one slaving voyage between

Africa and the West Indies. But real living slaves were rare in England.

She shrugged as if tossing off a foolish question.

Nothing of what I thought I knew fitted this girl with her worn black silk dress, lute and speech more English than my own Scots roll.

People's services could be bought. Apprentices sold themselves at mops and market fairs. Labourers sold their sweat to planters in exchange for money or land at the end of their term. The guardianship of a wealthy orphan could be bought. Even wives.

'Not indenture?' I ventured.

She gave another shrug. I felt that she was learning more from our exchange than I was.

'Where were you bought?'

She hesitated. 'In Southwark.'

A chink in her self-possession at last, I thought. I tried again. 'But where are you from?'

'Southwark.' She returned to flat civility.

'No,' I said impatiently. 'Where are you really from?'

'Southwark.'

She could not look like that and still be less strange here in London then I was. I squelched my rising irritation. 'Surely, you weren't born in Southwark!'

'No,' she agreed. 'I was born in Bristol, madam. That's why my name is "Bristo".'

I breathed in sharply. I was certain now that she was mocking me.

'Or so I've been told,' she added.

'But you don't know?'

She shook her head.

'What do you know, then?' I asked. 'Do you know what you're for?'

I felt her quiver, like a tree hit by a sudden blast of wind. 'That's for you to say, madam.'

'God's teeth! Please, give me one straight answer! Can you play that lute?'

'Oh, yes, if you wish.'

We were sliding across each other in this conversation like a pair of greased planks. I couldn't fault her tone, which was civil beyond reproach. And yet. 'You can begin by telling me why your civility irritates me so much.'

'Forgive me.' She sounded startled. 'I was trying to be agreeable.'

I turned on the bench. Our glances locked. 'Not entirely,' I said.

'You don't find being agreeable to be agreeable?' she asked with real curiosity, looking at me properly for the first time.

'I find it agreeable to have my questions answered,' I said. 'I'm surrounded by civil lies and flattery and secrets that aren't my business to know. Sometimes I think ignorance will drive me mad. Or else kill me.' I pressed my fingers against my mouth, startled to hear myself say these words to someone so strange, whom I had just met. Whom I owned.

She nodded with feeling, then looked down at her hands. Her palms were ashy pink, divided by a clean boundary line from the dark brown, almost black, of the backs of her hands. Her nails gleamed in the dusk like pink oval moons. The set of her shoulders warded off further questions.

I studied her neat blunt profile. She was not the first blackamoor I had seen. My brother Henry had one in his household, a youth named Peter Blank, though his skin was much lighter. He was a freeborn running footman, who was the great-great-grandson of Henry VII's court trumpeter, John Blank. There were two African grooms in my mother's stables, one of whom she dressed in red and gold and took with her everywhere. African merchants and sailors were seen in the London streets, though less often than before the old queen had ordered them sent away. But I had never sat so close to one, nor paid such close attention.

From so close, even in the failing light, I could see that her hair stood out by itself, held up by its own tight zig-zag curls without the aid of any horsehair, puffs or wires, as mine tried to do but fell just short of achieving.

'Are you the same colour all over?' I asked, determined to make her answer at least one question.

She pinched her lips tightly then sighed with what sounded like resignation. She held out her hands, paler palms up. 'My feet are like my hands. Pale soles.' She opened her mouth and showed white teeth and a pink tongue.

I nodded. There was a small silence.

'I can sing in three languages, dance, and pick at a lute,' she said at last. 'I can play *Cent* and bowls, throw dice, peel you an apple and make a posset.'

'Why didn't you say so at once?'

'I didn't know what you wanted.'

'What I don't want is for people to be all slithery and courtier-like! I want them to tell me the truth at once, so I don't have to dig and guess and try to pick apart their cipher.'

She raised her eyebrows.

'Truly,' I said.

'Then you must give them time to learn to trust you,' she said. 'Telling the truth to those with power over you can be dangerous.' She half-smiled. 'Is that more agreeable?'

I blinked. I had never talked like this before in my life. Not even with Henry, nor with Anne though we slept in the same bed. I wasn't even certain what 'like this' was. The voice of Lady Harington remained surprisingly silent. Thalia's strangeness put her outside the place where the usual rules of conduct might apply.

'You can trust me,' I said.

She weighed me up openly now. 'Not yet,' she said at last. Her eyes met mine defiantly. 'Am I still being agreeable?'

'A little more than before.' I felt an unexplained stirring of

151

exhilaration. I wanted her to trust me so that our conversation could continue.

Now I was the one being studied. She sucked in both her lips, which gave her the comical look of a toothless old woman. I sat in the steady beams of those large dark eyes wanting to ask her what she saw. After a time, just as I began to grow irritated again, she suddenly observed, 'You have beautiful hair.'

'So everyone tells me. It's safe to compliment my hair.'

'No. Truly. I know women who stain their hands and faces orange trying to achieve that amber-gold colour. Or else fry their ears with irons trying for those curls.'

I smiled to cover my confusion at her evident sincerity. 'To avoid offending the queen, I suppose I must try to find a use for you,' I said. 'Will you come show me how you sing and pick at your lute?'

'If you wish.'

'Surely, there's no danger in plain "yes"?'

'If you say so, madam,' she said, with a tiny smile.

Our eyes met.

I offered a half-smile in return.

23

'What music do you play?' I asked. We settled a little way from my ladies on a pair of stools.

'What music do you . . .? Her eyes flicked from her lute to my face. 'Whoops!' she said. 'I nearly was disagreeable again.'

My ladies were pretending to look at their cards.

Thalia held up the lute close to her ear and listened intently as she plucked the strings. 'Let me think . . .' She tightened a string and listened again. Her fingers rippled out a gentle cascade of notes. 'I can be doleful with Master Dowland . . .'

At the first notes, my ladies stopped pretending to be interested in their cards. 'We shall have wondrous heathen music now,' Frances Howard murmured.

I watched the pink moons of Thalia's nails dancing on the strings.

'. . . or martial . . .' She slapped the belly of the lute – one, two, three, four. In the firelight, her lute was more visible than her face. Her eyes, fingernails, and the white edging on her smock stood out against the rest of her.

'Where is she from?' asked Frances Tyrrell.

'She's an Ethiop!' Anne announced, as if that fact had escaped the others.

Thalia bent her head to her lute as if she had not heard any of them.

'Perhaps she's from the Menagerie at the Tower.' Frances Howard again.

'Mistress Bristo is from Southwark,' I said.

The ladies at the gaming table exclaimed in surprise.

'I don't know why you're all so astonished,' cried Anne. 'Prince Henry's blackamoor footman was born at Richmond.'

'But he's not truly a blackamoor!' retorted Elizabeth Apsley. 'His mother's as white as you are and comes from York.'

'Play anything you like,' I said.

Thalia cleared her throat. 'Sleep, wayward thoughts . . .' An air by Dowland, who had been court musician to my uncle in Denmark and was now my father's musician. Who had followed the queen, some said, when she came here from Denmark.

Like her speaking voice, Thalia's singing was strong and husky, deep for a woman and a rich sound to come from such a slender frame. Her tongue was pink like her palms and nails. Against her dark mouth, her teeth looked bright.

My ladies abandoned their cards and gathered around us to listen.

'I am astonished . . .!' murmured one.

'Where ever did a savage learn to sing Dowland?' Frances Howard demanded at large.

'*Queen Elizabeth's Galliard,*' Thalia announced, drumming a dance rhythm on the body of the lute.

Now she grew intent, frowning down at the lute cradled against her body, forgetting the rest of us. Her fingers leaped and attacked the strings. Her whole body rocked with the fierce triple beat. Her shoulders lifted a little with each suspended pause. Her elbows marked the leaps and the landings. Her head sketched the flow of the runs, so that she herself seemed to be dancing on her stool.

In my lap, my hands twitched and mirrored hers, as if touching strings. My feet jiggled. My bones hummed. Behind me, I heard the rhythmic rustle of skirts, and tapping fans.

'Hoop! La!' cried Thalia, playing even faster.

'Yes!' My feet insisted. I stood and danced a few steps.

She struck a fierce final chord and looked up. My ladies clapped and exclaimed.

'Who'd have thought it?' cried Anne.

'The creature plays wonderfully well,' said Frances Tyrrell.

'I don't know why you're all so astonished.' Frances Howard imitated to perfection Anne's earlier earnestness. 'Monkeys can be trained to do wondrous clever tricks.' She spoke just loudly enough for me to hear and just quietly enough so that, if I chose, I could pretend that I had not.

There was the tiniest of pauses while they all waited for my response. Thalia's face became a dark blank oval, as she looked at the floor. I was not certain whom Frances had most insulted, Thalia, Anne or myself.

'Fetch me my lute,' I ordered. 'Let's see what tricks this Scots dobbin has learned.' Frances Howard did not meet my eye.

You invited me to enter the lists, I reminded her silently.

While Lady Anne went into my bedchamber in search of the lute, I listened to our breathing in the silence. Stays creaked. Lace scratched against silk as someone fidgeted. The floor creaked under shifting weight. Someone cleared her throat. I could almost hear the glances colliding behind my back. The two chamber grooms who came to light the candles both blushed dark red when they realised how intently they were being watched by a group of silent young women.

'Do you know the parts for the *Seven Passionate Pavanes*?' I asked, when my instrument was in my hand.

Thalia nodded.

I pulled my stool closer to hers. I lagged behind in the duet, but Thalia was kind and waited each time for our notes to meet and marry again. At the end, my ladies clapped politely.

'Now follow me,' Thalia ordered.

She played a phrase and stopped expectantly. After a moment, I responded with a phrase of my own. She nodded then questioned again.

Again, I answered. She asked; I replied, gaining courage. Faster and faster, into a country dance now, playing together, fingers slipping, mistaking, recovering, galloping, until we were both laughing too hard to play the right notes at all.

'Now I know what to do with you!' I blew a loose strand of hair out of my face. 'I must make you my music mistress so you can teach me to play as well as you do.' I felt as light as after a morning gallop, ready to do exactly the same again.

There was more polite applause, followed by a silence as thick as porridge. I handed my lute to Anne. I stood up and shook out my skirts.

Thalia leapt to her feet.

'Well!' I looked at the paler faces around us. The candle-light showed speculation in one or two pairs of eyes, curiosity in another, naked animosity in another. Poor loyal Anne looked wary.

'That's all,' I said. 'Time for bed.' My ladies swirled and rustled as they put away the cards and set their chairs against the walls again.

'Good night, your grace.' 'Good night.' One by one they curtsied and left, with backward looks over their shoulders at Thalia. None of them spoke to her.

My gift watched them taking their leave, frowning.

'What are you thinking?' I asked.

'Nothing, madam.'

'But I saw a thought in your eyes.'

She looked around to see that we were alone. 'Perhaps it was my own thought.'

Insolence! whispered the voice of Lady Harington in my head. No doubt about it this time.

'I can't bear to see it and not know,' I said.

She shook her head stubbornly.

'You can't imagine how I long for people to be open!'

After another moment, she nodded. 'I was thinking that you'd best take care, madam.'

I inhaled sharply. 'What do you mean?'

A pale palm flashed to ward off more questions. 'I may be new here, but I know about women living all together like this, even you ladies . . .' She hesitated. 'You'll make enemies for both of us.'

'Your grace?' Anne's voice called from my bedchamber.

'"Your grace"?' repeated Thalia. 'What does that make you, then?'

'A princess or duchess,' I said a little sharply to this exotic creature from Southwark, who presumed to advise me how to behave with my own ladies. One Lady Harington was enough. 'Or a bishop.'

As soon as I entered my sleeping chamber, I realised that I had just refused to answer a perfectly reasonable question. It had not occurred to me that she might not know who I was. I ran back to the door, but she had gone, perversely, when I had wanted her to stay.

At the very least, the arrival of Thalia Bristo required me to thank my mother for her gift. In my letter, which I began to write at once before going to bed, I would ask to do this in person.

'You torture me with my impatience to see you, madam,' I wrote. *'I beg you . . .'*

I stopped. What if something was wrong with my mother that no one would tell me about? Perhaps my father had secretly put her into the Tower. Perhaps she was fatally ill. Perhaps my father had ordered her not to see me, just as he had stolen Henry from her. Whatever it might be, some force that she could not overcome was keeping us apart.

I would not write after all, I decided. I knew a surer way to learn why my mother was being kept from me.

24

THALIA

Fool! Fool! Don't make that mistake again! You had the world's finest tutors in deceit, but would you learn? You pushed her too far, should never have believed her when she said she wanted the truth.

Madam doesn't know what she really wants. She'd send you back fast enough if she knew the truth about you.

She's trying to trick you, girl, whoever she is. Trying to trap you with seeming friendship. I read what she really thought, in her eyes at the end. 'Presumption.' She asks for openness but wouldn't give away so much as her own name. Now she's angry. I feared she was going to send me back.

'Princess or duchess . . .' she said, mocking me for my ignorance. No bishop, for sure. Forgive me, madam, but I can't read minds. You may be richly dressed but you're lodged near horses and fighting cocks – I have a nose, can smell them both. God's Blood! Will no one be civil enough to explain the simplest things? If they don't mock me like she did, they gape and sidle away.

'I don't want her,' she said. The way she'd refuse a cake. I'm handed about like a parcel. If I were a dog, someone would feed me at least, and give me a basket to sleep in.

But I won't be sent back!

Hide for now. Keep your head down. Try to get some sleep so you can think straight tomorrow . . . then decide what to do next. Too much for one day. Lost. This cursed palace is a city in itself. Lucky chance, finding this gallery.

Here's just the place, in the corner, out of the torchlight, out of the way. Blend with the other shadows. If no one claims this pallet . . . I might have the devil's luck and not have to sleep on stone. No food, but sleep at least. If no one notices me . . . but what's the chance of that?

You'd never think that we're sleeping in a palace – more like homeless people in an alley than maids and serving women. Well, I can tell them, their farts stink like anywhere else.

Even tucked here in the corner where I can't see my own hand, I can still see the whites of eyes out there, staring at me over blanket tops. Even in the dark, I can't turn invisible. How they all keep at a safe distance! Do they fear I'll eat them in the night? All the better for me. Gives me room to stretch out my legs.

So, Tallie. You're not where you feared to find yourself, but where are you instead?

On a pallet in a gallery somewhere in Whitehall, I know! But will no one tell me what my situation is? What are my circumstances now? Oh, Lord! I'm going to cry! Hunger, that's all it is. You need sleep, girl, if you hope to keep your wits about you on an empty belly.

Should be used to stares by now, but sometimes they wear me out. Make it hard to think straight. Even with my eyes closed, I can still hear the breathing. And belching, and sighing and scratching. Now that one's snoring . . . more like farting through her nose. Packed bodies reek just as much here in Whitehall as they do in Southwark . . . there's something alive in this straw . . . Even with my eyes closed, I can feel the stares. Pushing at me. Push. Push!

You, there . . . yes, you. Let's see if you're so bold when I stare back. Ha! Got you!

. . . No, Tallie, don't do that! Danger. Danger! You swore you wouldn't. Please God! Don't let her get a bellyache or cut her thumb

*for the next fortnight, or else she'll cry, 'Black witch!' and swear
that I put the evil eye on her.*

*Don't get rattled. You don't know exactly where you are, but just
think where you might be instead . . . If she sends me back, I'll jump
from the boat, this time, even if my skirts pull me under.*

I'll make her keep me.

*I thought I had hooked her with the music. But she slipped off
again. Is that wooden angel above me playing a viol? I think so. It's
a sign. Don't get sent back!*

*Who'd have thought I'd end up sleeping under angels! Ha! Not
funny.*

If I can ever sleep!

Crying from hunger, nothing more.

*More angels on the ceiling . . . can't see clearly. Their wings look
like they're moving in the torch light. The ceiling is flapping its wings
and flying away. Feel sure that real angels must be more like winged
dragons, hot and quivering with light like the heart of a charcoal
fire. They might even be black, like me . . . the real ones, not all those
little pink and gold babies on her ceiling, with their useless wing
stubs and baby nut-cocks. I'd wager that painter had a little baby's
nut and never saw a real cock.*

*Truth! Her grace . . . madam . . . tempting me to be honest. She
lives with painted lies but wants me to tell her the truth, does she?
What can she know of truth, standing there in her silks and jewels,
surrounded by her yes-madam-no-madam ladies? Does she think
truth is some novel form of entertainment? Doesn't she know –
princess, duchess, whoever she is – that telling the truth is like
springing a leak? Hard to control once it starts. And a truth like
mine can sink you. She'll get no more truth from me. I don't owe
her truth. Truth isn't dangerous to her.*

No one bought my truth.

*I feel like a coiled spring . . . a serpent coiled at the bottom of the
sea. Lying low. I'm protecting the bones of my mother, no face . . .
memory of warm. Don't know yet what the serpent can do. There
are ships to swallow, sailors to terrify. Ladies to chew up into little*

161

pieces and spit out again . . . that gristly bitch with the slanting eyes
and loud voice, speaking nice and slow to be certain I understood.
Keep an eye on her. I can wait. I know what always happens to the
serpent in the stories. Or to the dragon. I won't go the same way, I
promise! I'll wait and watch and work out another ending, if I live
long enough . . . Sleepy at last. May sleep after all . . .

Uncoiling. I'm a long, brown sinuous shape sliding out of my
cavern in the rocks, with needle teeth and eyes like shining green
glass. Fanned by living lace, I drift in a warm turquoise sea, steering
with the tiniest flick of my tail, wings tucked to my sides like fins.
Overhead, a mirror reflects back my undulating image. Can't see
what lies above. I pierce the mirror and soar up with a great clap,
trailing the glitter of broken waves from the edges of my wings . . .

25

The cherries had begun to soften. Their plump skins were dented with brown spots. I tipped them out of the silver box and ordered fresh ones.

I stood still in the morning light for Lady Anne and my maid to dress my hair and pin the side of my stomacher firmly to the bodice of my gown. I put on my amber necklace with diamond clasps to hold it in position on my shoulders. I washed my hands carefully in a basin and rubbed them with the linen towel to remove any last scent of monkey, dog and horse.

'Will you attend me?' I asked Anne.

She nodded, as pale and silent as if I had again suggested jumping off the roof.

Leaving the Herd looking curiously after us, I took only Anne and a footman to carry the silver box and headed for the long gallery that crossed Whitehall. I was grateful for my imagined map. I saw my route clearly. From the Parkside, where I lodged tucked in with the cockpit, tiltyard and large tennis court, by way of the gallery on the upper floor of the Holbein Gate, across Whitehall to the Riverside, where my parents lived. The two parts of the palace were like halves of a leaf divided by a central vein. Outside the Holbein Gate, the vein of Whitehall continued like a stem, as the Street. Inside the gate, on the Riverside, the king's lodgings lay on the Thames to the south, upstream. The queen's apartments lay to the north.

When I reached the queen's lodgings, I ran out of map. I had not entered them before.

Anne saw me hesitate. 'Would it not be better to wait?' she asked. 'If no one knows that you're coming, her majesty might be away.'

'But I want to catch them all unawares.'

I prepared myself to outface my mother's guardians. I had learned enough in the last months to know that they might look as much like gentlewomen as soldiers, but guardians they would be.

I would find her. 'I know,' I would say. 'You have no need to say anything.' And I would cross the space between us and slide into her arms again.

We would talk and laugh as we had done at supper at Holyrood. I might even dare to tell her what had happened to me in the forest at Combe. Looking back, it seemed to me now that I had been very brave for such a young girl. My mother would never betray me. At last, someone who cared for me could tell me that I had shown great courage. I needed to hear it confirmed before it would be true.

I advanced our little party into a small reception chamber and met myself looking back from a hanging glass. I stopped again, scarcely aware of the stir I was causing in the room.

I was thinking like the child I had left behind. I wore a stiff-hooped farthingale like a grown woman. My mother would likely be wearing one too. Rather than embrace, we would clasp hands across our ledges of pleated silk and look into each other's eyes. We might both be a little shy and uncertain. She might need a quiet moment to take in how I was grown almost to full womanhood. But, seeing me, she would then be eased in her grief for the loss of my two infant sisters and a short-lived infant brother left buried in Scotland, about whose birth I had not known at the time.

First, I would thank her for her gift, though I still didn't know what the devil to do with it. Then I would say how happy I was to be with her alone at last. I would tell her that I enjoyed watching the games she sometimes played with her ladies in the privy garden and hoped one day to be allowed to join them.

Though she must surely know already, I would remind her that I could sing and dance, that I played the lute and virginal tolerably well, and dared to hope that I might soon be invited to take part in one of her masques. I would give her all the reasons she could possibly need for taking me back into her life.

Then we passed the open door of an ante-room where I saw the queen's ladies sitting. Startled faces looked at me. My heart began to rush.

I took the silver box. 'Stay here.'

I went through the door alone. Lucy, Countess of Bedford, raised her eyebrows but led me to the closed door of an inner room.

A tall thin woman in white stood staring our of the window at the river.

Lucy withdrew back to the ante-chamber and closed the door behind her.

This long-nosed woman at the window, with her slightly protruding teeth, looked very little like her youthful wedding portrait, which I had once seen. Or like the splendidly dressed, slightly feverish woman of court celebrations to whom I had curtsied on state occasions or watched from the gallery of the Banqueting Hall, whose extravagance was deplored in Cecil's accounts. She looked even less like the smiling, swollen-bellied mother I remembered from Edinburgh.

After a moment, I turned my head to see what held her

attention on the water. But I saw only the little wherries and rowing shallops that constantly crossed from one shore to the other and ferried passengers up and down stream. In the silence, the shadow of a bird dipped across the window and disappeared. In her plain dress of pale grey silk, she looked like a ghost.

I shifted my weight to make the wooden floor creak.

She didn't move. The reflected light from the water wavered across her cheek and nose.

'Madam?' I said cautiously. I remembered Holyrood and how she had sung to Baby Charles and me in French. '*Maman?*'

'Who are you?' she asked.

26

'I'm your loving daughter, madam,' I stammered. 'I wrote . . .'

The queen turned to me at last. Her eyes glinted as she studied my face, my hair, my bitten nails, my clothes. 'Is this wild girl the babe I bore?' She shook her head and turned back to the river. 'Not mine any longer. Never mine.' She closed her lips tightly across her teeth as if to hide them.

I slithered wildly on the ice of her words. Was I not, then, a princess? Not a Stuart? Was I my father's bastard by another woman? Or merely not good enough to acknowledge?

At last, I asked, 'Did you not bear me then, madam?'

'I cried for you, sure enough.'

'Then I am your true child.'

The teeth slipped into view again. The pretty girl of her wedding portrait was long gone. 'I have no children.'

'Who are we then . . . Henry and me and Baby Charles?' I asked desperately. My body still yearned to run to her, to embrace her as I had done in Edinburgh, to feel her hand on my hair. It occurred to me that she was mad.

She raised her hands between us, as if warding off an invisible evil. Gems flashed and burned on her taut fingers.

'You're the king's children. Not mine. His majesty stole all my babes . . . the ones that God didn't take. "The bairns", he called you, as if that made you some other sort of creature that a mother could not love.'

She turned back to the window and leaned on the windowsill. In her long limbs and sudden awkward movements, I felt a terrible echo of my own still-growing, unwieldy limbs 'I thank you for coming,' she said. 'God speed you, mistress . . .'

Look at me! I wanted to shout. If you look at me, you will see how I am your child.

We stood in silence. I wanted to scream, or tear off one of my sleeves, or hurl a stool crashing through the diamond panes into the river.

My mother looked at me sideways, without turning her face from the window. 'How is the other one? The boy? That was once *my* boy?'

'Henry?'

'That dangerous heir who must be kept locked away like a wolf or bear.' She glanced at me again. 'As you have been too, for that matter, caged somewhere in Warwickshire, and then at Kew. My husband may have toppled his own mother from her throne while he was still in swaddling cloths . . . but a girl? What harm does he think you might do him?'

I could never tell her now about the young man in the forest who had turned out to be a devil. Nor about this devil's terrible, gallant death, and my own certainty that I was next on the scaffold. I should have kept my mouth shut, but her words stung me.

'I think he fears me as he fears Henry, madam.'

'No.' She shook her head. 'Don't flatter yourself. You're a female and will soon be a woman. We offend his eyes, the likes of us. We don't wear breeches or show our legs in silk stockings, and swagger and swear that we love our dear, sweet "kingy-wingy" better than we love God . . . No! I lie!' Her voice rose. 'We must swear that our dear, darling, and ever-generous "kingy-wingy" is God Himself . . .' She clapped her hands in mock astonishment. 'La! Listen to me prattle. But I'm only a woman – what else would you expect?'

My mouth had opened as I listened. I closed it.

'Why did you ask to see me?' The queen seemed suddenly calm again.

I swallowed. 'To thank you, your highness, for your gift.'

'My gift?' She sounded genuinely puzzled. 'Oh, the black-amoor, do you mean?' She waved a dismissive hand. 'A title-seeking petitioner brought me two, a boy and a girl. I kept the boy for a groom. He looks very well with my grey gelding . . . at the banquet for Henry's christening, we had the chariot of Ceres drawn by a noble blackamoor instead of a lion, for fear of frightening the ladies. He was a former soldier. My groom is not such a noble moor as that one, but like Titania . . . like the goddess Diana . . . I will have my changeling boy.'

Our conversation seemed ended. Still, I could not move. Not until she ordered me. The silence grew.

The glittering eyes suddenly turned full on me for the second time. 'Are you happy, child?'

I inhaled. 'No.'

'Good.' She nodded as if I had given the correct answer to a catechism. 'You begin well. Learn never to expect happiness. You're female. You will be married. Learn duty, and how to smile, and to pass the time tolerably, but learn never to expect happiness.'

I shook my head dumbly.

'Make yourself what happiness you can but be prepared to see it taken from you.'

'Yes, madam,' I whispered. Now I wanted to run.

'Let me tell you all that you need to know.' She pulled her lips across her teeth again and curved them in a taut smile. 'May I give you a mother's advice?'

I nodded but my hands lifted as if to push her away.

'When you breed – as you must – don't ever attach your heart to that little piece of your own flesh that pats your bosom with tiny hands. Don't give in to loving it, as charming as it may be . . . as delicious as its head smells, and though it looks into your eyes and lies close and warm against you as if you were all the world . . . Are you listening closely?'

I nodded again, but she was no longer looking at me.

'It will try to charm you with smiles and comic gestures and miniature hiccoughs.' Words now overflowed from her. 'Never let yourself kiss its tiny toes nor brush your cheek against its soft, round little belly, as I did with your brother, before I learned better. The child will be taken from you. You cannot fight the king's will. I tried. I know. You must hand your babe over to someone else at once before it's too late. Or you will feel a darkness enter your soul and think never to see the light again.'

'But you stole Henry back!' I cried. 'From the Earl of Mar! Everyone said so! Mrs Hay told me.'

'I took Henry from the earl's servants, and from his lady. But I was no longer his mother. He was already grown and treated me as civilly as he would any other gentlewoman. I would not have had him even then if the king, my husband, had not used him to bribe me into behaving well on the way south to London.'

'I'm here now!' I had to make her see me. 'You don't have to steal me!'

She shook her head. 'What use would it be to either of us to speak and grow familiar again? You'll be married soon. Your father wills it. Then you will be sent much farther away than Warwickshire. Please go. I can't bear your presence a moment longer!'

27

I will not! My feet drummed out the words as I marched back towards my lodgings in the little closed tennis court. I blundered blindly past the great presence chamber and across the large open court.

I will not end up like my mother! That will not be my life! Never! Never!

I would have to marry. I did not imagine that I could escape that fate. Like it or not, it was my part and my duty. But . . .

I veered into a narrow, open alley between two walls striped black and white with bands of flint and chalk. Suddenly, I found myself in the privy garden, staring at a large sundial set at the junction of four gravel paths.

At last, I understood my father's threat in Coventry. The choice between marriage and execution. How marriage could kill as surely as the sword.

He would have to lock me in the Tower first. Kill me. I would not let misery warp me as it had my mother. I would not, like my mother, be destroyed by acceptance. I should have understood the pity in the Countess of Bedford's eyes, instead of hating her for being close to my mother when I was not.

The gravel was sharp under my thin-soled shoes. I fled

from the garden and its straight lines and geometric male authority. I turned left, had to turn right, then left again, found myself back in the great court. Then I saw that Anne and my footman had been panting after me and that we stood at the entrance to the public thoroughfare of Whitehall. At this moment, in my agitation, I did not recognise any of the buildings opposite. My imagined map had turned to mist.

When I stopped, my footman took back the silver box, which I had forgotten to give to the queen, and offered to lead the way to my lodgings. I nodded and followed blindly.

I had gone for my mother's blessing and returned with a curse laid on me.

We climbed some stairs, crossed Whitehall through the Holbein Gate. My feet clicked out the rhythm on the polished plaster of the gallery floor. I will not! I will not!

28

Thalia Bristo was sitting on a stool against the wall in my study with her lute case on her lap. When she saw me, she stood and made an unsteady curtsy that reminded me of Faith and Hope trying to dance after too much wine. Here was another drunk like my father.

'What are you doing here?' I waved for Anne and the footman to leave me. I needed to be alone to think about what had just happened. I almost felt sick, but not quite. 'Has no one given you anything to do yet?'

'No.'

'Why not?' My head ached.

'Waiting for an instruction from you, I imagine.'

'Well, they can stop waiting! I don't know what to do with you, for sure!'

'I am not to be your music mistress, after all?'

'I don't know! Did I say that?' Just now, I could not remember anything I had told her last night.

'I see.' She tightened her grip on the lute case. 'Will you send me back, then?'

'God's Teeth! I don't know where to send you, do I?' I looked around to tell someone to take her away and give her work. But I had sent everyone away. Only Cherami and Belle remained, heaped one on top of the other in their basket by the study fireplace.

'How can I send you back?' I asked. 'Rejecting her gift would offend the queen even more than I've offended her already!'

Thalia narrowed her eyes. 'Why are you in such a temper?'

'I'm not in a temper!'

'Why not have a good bawl instead of shouting at me?'

'I don't want a good bawl!'

I closed my eyes and inhaled hard. I wanted to slap her. But tears escaped and ran down my cheeks. I inhaled again, raggedly. More tears escaped. I made a noise between my teeth like a low growl. Gasped for air again. My nose began to run. 'God's wounds!' I said between clenched teeth.

She waited silently until I began to breathe more steadily.

'Here.' She offered a handkerchief.

I snatched it and rubbed at my cheeks.

'You'll wear off the skin if you go on like that,' she said. 'And you've got your hair all into a bird's nest. If you have a comb or brush, I can sort it out for you.'

'That's work for my maid.'

'I've done it before.' Crossing the floor to me, she was definitely unsteady. I sniffed but could not smell wine on her, just a sharp fruit odour like ripe apples.

I sat on a stool by the window in my sleeping chamber and let her unpin my hair. She shook it out without any of the remarks my maids usually made about the tangles in my curls, as if I had somehow willed them. Then, before using the brush, she combed my hair with her fingers. As she worked silently, I began to feel calmer. The steady, gentle tugging of her fingers slowed my thoughts.

'I see why my dogs sit so still when I stroke them,' I observed after a while. 'They're praying that I won't stop . . .'

Her hands suddenly faltered. 'I'm a gift from the queen, you said?'

'Yes.' I squeezed my eyes against a new threat of tears.

She picked up the brush and set to work again.

But after a few strokes, her hands dropped heavily onto my hair. Then she braced herself with one hand on my shoulder, as Henry had done when imitating our father. I felt the shock of her weight pressing me down.

'What's wrong?' Startled, I twisted my head to see her face. She looked very odd. 'I can't tell whether or not you've gone pale. Are you drunk?'

She shook her head.

'Ill, then?'

'I think I need a moment to . . .' She made a small vague motion with her hand. Touched her head. 'It has all been . . . You can't imagine . . .'

'Yes, I can!' I said fiercely. After a moment, I asked, 'Are you giddy?'

She nodded.

'Sit down on my stool.' I rose and poured us both a glass of *eau de vie* from the bottle on my big dresser. Her fingers were icy when they brushed mine.

She swallowed the brandy in a single gulp. 'Thank you . . . Oh, Lord, straight to my head!'

'You haven't brought the plague from Southwark, have you?'

She shook her head. 'Just hungry.'

'Hungry? When did you last eat?'

'Yesterday morning . . . bread and beer.'

'You didn't eat breakfast today?' I asked.

She shook her head and made helpless circles in the air with her hand.

'Nor dinner yesterday, nor supper last night?

She shook her head again.

'Why not?'

'Where would I eat?'

'No one found you a place?'

Another shake.

Now that I thought about it, it seemed obvious. I felt a twinge of guilt.

'No wonder you're giddy.' I gave her another glass of *eau de vie* and pulled up a second stool. 'I'll have my steward find you a seat for meals in my household mess.' I called my chamberer and ordered bread and cheese.

Thalia rested her head in her hands until the chamberer returned. I watched her try not to gobble the bread and cheese. She ate even the cheese rind. Then she licked the pink tip of a finger, touched it to a last crumb on her lap, and popped it into her mouth.

'Do you feel better now?'

'Are you truly the Princess Elizabeth?'

I stiffened. 'Who else would I be?' Then I remembered how I had intended to apologise the previous night for not answering her question. 'Yes, I am.'

'Do you know who that tall, thin plain woman was, who came and looked at me yesterday, before I was brought to you?'

I touched my front teeth in question.

She nodded.

'The queen, most likely,' I said.

'The queen of England?'

'Yes. My mother.' I couldn't keep a bitter edge out of my voice.

'You are truly the Princess Elizabeth?'

'I just said that I am.'

She started to shake her head. 'Hey ho,' she said. Her voice wobbled. 'Hey ho! Hey ho!' She kept shaking her head so that her cloud of hair swayed, trying to keep up. 'Oh, my! Oh, my!'

'Are you going to bawl now?' I asked. 'If you are, I'll give you back your handkerchief.'

29

THALIA

Wrong again, girl. She does know, silks and jewels notwithstanding. Poor girl. Even if I don't know what caused it, I know misery when I see it.

Whoops, Tallie! Danger! Get your feet back under you. You let her foist your tender feelings like a silk handkerchief out of your pocket. She condescended to take care of you that day when it amused her. Nothing more. Why shouldn't she take as much care for me as for her poxy dogs? I saw how much gold changed hands for me there in Southwark. Of course she'll feed me, water me, keep me free of moth like a costly gown . . . the king's daughter. How was I to know? A great noble woman, clearly. But she didn't behave like a princess . . . how do they behave? Ambitious as my training was, I was never tutored in princesses.

But no fatal mistakes yet. And still here now, after most of two weeks, though the ground shifts yet again. Having given me away, the queen of England has now called me back. Sent for me direct. I don't think the princess knows yet. Slippery ice!

30

At last, a bead for me to grasp, solid, inarguable, seen with my own eyes. Early that spring, Frederick Ulrich of Brunswick, son of my mother's sister and the duke of Brunswick, arrived at Gravesend. Everyone said that the German prince was merely including England in an educational tour before he came to power. Henry sent him an invitation to dine at St. James's Palace and asked me to join them.

'I hope you will like him, Elizabella,' said Henry, the day before Frederick Ulrich sailed upriver to London.

'Is that the true purpose of his visit?' I asked. 'Liking? Did the king order you to arrange this dinner?'

Henry flushed, then nodded. 'But Elizabella, I believe that it's for the best. I would choose to entertain him in any case. From all that he writes, this Frederick is everything a Protestant warrior prince should be. He will be one of my strongest allies on the Continent when I am king. A true brother-in-arms, if he pleases you.'

At last, I was to be touched by those forbidden signs of love. I would be able to form an opinion. It felt like a victory.

'How far is Brunswick?' I asked.

'Not much farther than France.'

Because Henry spoke so well of him and called him a

brother-in-arms, I felt certain that this German, Frederick Ulrich, would be very like my brother. Tall and fair, with long legs, like Henry's and mine, legs of a familiar shape. I would confound my father by finding joy, even in a political marriage.

'. . . if he pleases you,' Henry had said. My brother, if not my father, cared for my feelings in the matter.

'What if I don't please him?'

Henry laughed. 'How can you not?'

That night, I sent for a German sempstress who worked in my wardrobe and, in exchange for a pair of amethyst ear drops, asked her to begin to teach me her language. *Ja.'* Yes. *'Nein.'* No. *'Danke.'* Thank you.

'Ja,' I repeated after her. Yes. *'Liebe Frederick. Mein mann.'* My husband.

I saw myself escaping from my father forever, with a young man who would always remind me of Henry. Whom Henry would always be happy to see when he visited his beloved sister, living just across the German Sea. Only a few days away, with following winds.

I asked Tallie to sing me to sleep with German lullabyes.

'Guten abend,' I murmured sleepily. *'Gute nacht.'* Good evening. Good night.

'What if you don't like him?' she asked between songs.

'I feel certain that I will.'

The next day, I changed my mind twice about which gown to wear to Henry's dinner. I put on my amber necklace but found it too earnest and old. I replaced it with my lighter-hearted necklace of enamelled gold flowers. I ordered a chair to carry me across the park, rather than ride to St James's and arrive windblown and smelling of horse.

Frederick Ulrich would be judicious, I reflected, while my maid pinned my bodice to my jewelled stomacher . . . like Henry, and serious of mind, but with the same sudden smiles when something amused him. He would laugh like Henry, at my attempts to amuse him. He would find me a good listener, to whom he could unburden his soul, just as Henry did. I would know him before we ever spoke. He would know me as the sister of his heart. In short, he would be another Henry. But he would be able to become my husband, which Henry could never be. I could imagine no better fate. I was already half in love with Frederick Ulrich before he bowed and kissed my hem to greet me when he arrived.

Alas, my brother's standards were not those of a possible bride.

Under lowered lids, I eyed this great lump of a newcomer with dismay. His hair lay flat on his head and hung over his ears like dark, damp straw. His long red face and neck erupted in small boils. His French was appalling, his English coarse. I would have forgiven his lack of languages if what English he did speak had not been so full of oaths and blasphemies.

And I didn't like the way he kept eyeing me.

'God's Body, Henry!' he exclaimed over dinner. 'Your sister is handsome!'

'His sister is sitting right here and capable of being addressed directly,' I said.

Frederick emptied his wineglass and held it out for more. I saw baffled irritation in his eyes. I felt certain that he wanted to make a sharp reply but could not form a suitable one in English.

'Here in St. James's, you must pay a shilling fine each time you swear,' said Henry. He pointed at a small iron money chest with a slit in the lid, sitting on a sideboard. 'In the swearing box.'

Frederick Ulrich grinned. 'You want to be a soldier, and you never swear?'

Henry jerked his thumb at the money chest. 'St James's is not Whitehall.'

'God's Cock! You are in earnest!'

'And again,' said my brother. 'Your second fine.'

180

Frederick stared at him. Then he swore in German and called for one of his attendants, eating at the serving-men's mess in the next chamber. He gave the man a heavy purse and waved at the fine box. 'Put in all,' he ordered. 'Save time.' He turned to Henry. 'By God . . .'

'Third,' said Henry doggedly.

I hid my smile in my glass. Frederick had misjudged my brother if he thought Henry could be laughed out of anything he thought to be right.

'A good strategy for when you command your army!' Frederick threw up his hands in mock amazement. 'You don't pay your soldiers to fight. You make them pay you!'

I smiled again, with him this time. For an instant, I almost liked him.

Then, after supper, while Henry had gone to relieve himself, Frederick rose from his chair, grabbed me like a lout and tried to kiss me.

He was sweaty and smelled rank. Sour gusts rose from his clothing. His breath reeked like my father's when he was drunk. He cut my lip against my teeth.

'What's wrong?' he asked. 'I saw you smiling at me at supper.'

So that's what kissing a man is like! I thought. I wiped my mouth with my hand.

'You'll learn to like it soon enough! And more.'

'Not with you!' I could not imagine spending the rest of my life exiled to Brunswick with this self-satisfied boor. Under his rod, obedient to him as my lawful husband. I heard Belle yelp under the table as he returned to his chair.

'Did you just kick my dog?'

Even Henry felt the ice in the air when he returned.

'You can't always expect gentle behaviour from a soldier,' Henry said to me later, uncertainly. 'Frederick Ulrich is a very good soldier.'

'Does the king like him?'

'Well enough.'

With an icy reserve, I attended the official festivities planned for the German prince's entertainment. Jointly and severally my ladies whispered how, before the end of his first week in England, Frederick Ulrich had put his hand down the bosom of a laundress, then up the skirts of a sewing woman, a chamberer and two ladies' maids. Tallie reported that at last, he succeeded in taking one of the maids into his bed.

I detected hesitation in her voice. 'Did he try to fumble you as well?'

She looked at the floor.

'Tallie . . .'

She rolled her eyes. 'Yes, of course. A man like that will grope anything with tits, so long as it moves. And then give her the pox.'

Nein! Nie! Never! I didn't wish to expose my ignorance by asking her if you might catch the pox from a slobbering kiss.

I sent my excuses to St. James's Palace for supper that night, then sat down and wrote a letter to my father.

31

'Learn not to expect happiness,' my mother had said. But there were limits to the misery I was prepared to accept. When I thought of that flash of irritation in Frederick Ulrich's eyes, I felt uneasy. The thought of having to let him touch me or kiss me made me feel sick. Even being forced to be civil to him for the rest of my life was beyond imagining.

A lifetime spent stumbling in German, being closed out by rapid murmurs in a foreign tongue. Watching the court ladies and all the serving women, wondering which of them my husband was fumbling. Or worse, meeting a pair of knowing, triumphant eyes, like Robert Carr's when he looked at my mother. I knew that my wits would turn even wilder than hers had done. I did not imagine that I could avoid a political marriage, but I knew I would not survive marriage to Frederick Ulrich of Brunswick.

At the end of the following day, one of my father's secretaries replied to my letter. The king was away hunting. It was not known when he meant to return.

I set off at once through the Whitehall maze to the offices beyond the Great Court which were used by the Chief Secretary.

*   *   *

Wee Bobby gave me a tired smile. 'I'd like to speak to the king myself, your grace. He is needed here. There's work for him to do, and he ignores all my letters and messengers.'

'Is he hunting at Theobald's?' I asked.

'So far as I know.'

'I must speak with him.'

Cecil cocked his head, inviting me to say more.

Friend or foe?

'In person?' he asked.

I nodded. Any letter I wrote to the king would burst into flames from the heat of my words. Or else he would throw my letter aside unread, as he had thrown Cecil's letters. 'I must go to Theobald's at once,' I said. In truth, I was so swollen with fury and fear that I would explode unless I could take action myself, at once, any action, so long as I did not have to wait, yet again, for someone, somewhere else, to make a decision.

'You will need an escort,' Cecil said.

'I'll manage without.'

'I think not.'

'I know the way,' I protested. 'I'll take a lady and a groom.'

'Is your memory so short, your grace?'

I stared, trying to think how to answer. Then it was too late to pretend innocence. Our gazes met and held.

'The third in line to the throne can't trot about the country-side unguarded,' he said. His high, wide forehead contracted in thought. 'Would you like to carry out a secret mission for me?'

'A secret mission, my lord?' I stammered, confused by this unexpected shift in direction.

He gave me a sudden smile. I realised that I had never before seen him smile. A civil upward twitch of the lips, yes, many time. But never this open grin that narrowed his eyes and showed small square, yellowish teeth. His odd, high-browed, slipped-down face grew bright like a naughty child's. His smile invited me to collude.

'What mission?' I asked suspiciously. But I rather liked the thought of acting as a secret agent.

'Delivering a personal letter. A small matter of estate management. I will organise an escort for you.' He searched his desk for a clean sheet of paper and began to write. 'You haven't accepted. Surely, there's no harm in a letter?' His voice was light with private amusement.

The next afternoon, I set off for Hertfordshire with an escort of men-at arms arranged by Cecil. Anne rode with me. I had to leave Tallie in London because she said she had never learned to ride a horse.

'Why such secrecy about a small matter of estate management?' I had finally dared to ask Cecil before I left him. In my purse, I carried a sealed letter addressed to his Master of Hounds at Theobald's.

'If all goes well, you will soon learn,' was all he would say.

As I rode, trying to rehearse my speech to my father, I kept hearing Cecil say, 'Surely, there's no harm in a letter.'

At Theobald's, the steward told me that the king had just ridden back from a good kill. Through a gateway, I saw the body of a stag still lying on the courtyard stone. I asked to see the Master of Hounds and delivered Cecil's letter. Then I asked to see the king, at once. And, no, I could not wait until the following day.

My father was in his bedchamber with Robert Carr when I was announced. Both men were in shirtsleeves. Their doublets lay thrown over chairs. The king sprawled in a chair by the fire while the Golden Weasel dried his bare feet. A basin of water steamed on the floor beside him.

'What the devil is she doing here?' My father glared at the steward as if the poor man were to blame for my interruption. 'Who let you in?' He turned his glare onto me. 'Make an appointment like everyone else.'

'I did! With your Chief Secretary.' I had meant to be calm,

formal and reasonable, but my voice climbed before I had spoken four words. I forgot my prepared speech.

'I won't marry him! I'll kill myself first!'

'Who's that? . . . Don't stop, laddie.' He turned back to Carr as if I weren't there 'Feels good.'

'Frederick Ulrich!'

'The German princeling?' he asked. 'The young Lutheran warrior who stirred a bit of life into that monastery your brother keeps at St James's? . . . Aye, that's the spot,' he added to Carr.

'He drinks too much and he stinks!' I said. 'His hair is lank, his nose is already going red with booze. He has a foul, blasphemous mouth and can't keep his hands off the waiting women!' I drew a breath. 'And he kicked my dog and laughed.'

'Am I to gather that y'don't like the lad?' My father's amused smile infuriated me out of all caution.

'I won't end up like you and my mother!' I warned him in a shaking voice. 'Not speaking, pretending to be civil on the rare occasions that you are forced to meet!'

I thought, but had the sense not to say, that I would never let myself be driven so mad that I hated the sight of my own children.

'She's done her breeding,' he said. 'Why should the two of us speak any longer? Only dead babies come out of her now. But I still respect her as the mother of the next king. And that's what you must pray to become, lassie – a "mother of kings".'

'Not with him, I won't! Not with that great, stinking, red-faced hulk who everyone says will give me the pox as soon as a son!'

My father withdrew his left foot from Carr's lap and replaced it with his right. 'Aye, rub just there above the ankle. Do you remember how I eased your leg with my hands like that, after you broke it?'

'I won't do it!' I shouted. 'Do you hear me?'

He gazed into the fire as if I hadn't spoken.

My hand acted without my will. I seized a squat glass wine bottle from the nearby table and hurled it. He threw up an arm to protect his head.

The good angels guided my flung bottle away from the king's head. It smashed instead with a satisfying explosion of wet glistening shards on the hearth beside the Golden Weasel. My father's *privado* leapt up, shaking off broken glass, his white shirt blotched with red, his pretty, stupid face both fearful and outraged. My father lowered his arm.

'You can see why I wish to avoid the inconvenience of your opinion,' he said.

'I won't!' I said into the silence. 'You can't force me!' I saw myself in the forest, pressing the point of my dirk against my throat. 'Not even you!' Tears of rage filled my eyes.

'I can, and I will.' My father picked up his tankard, drank, looking at me over the rim. 'But why are you in such a lather, Bessie? The lad was sent back to Brunswick yesterday, with a broken heart. Did no one think to tell you?'

32

Ouff!

When I regained my breath, I saw how my father had shifted the war. I could defy him all I liked. He would still out-manoeuvre me. I rode back from Theobald's with my escort, feeling like a prisoner again, fighting melancholy and exhaustion. I had let myself be lured out of cover and had been shot down.

Wrapped in the last of my tattered defiance and still badly out of humour, I went uninvited to a rehearsal of my mother' new masque. I had a right to go. Thalia Bristo was my musician, taken back by the queen without my permission.

My mother must have seen me on my stool at the side of the hall but she said nothing. No one else dared ask me to leave, not even the queen's Master of Revels.

I ignored my mother just as she ignored me. I sat on my stool and glowered, feeling worse than if I had moped alone in my rooms. I should have learned my lesson the last time I presented myself to her uninvited.

'These things are but toys,' Sir Francis Bacon had written of masques. But he saw only the surface show and missed the deeper meanings. The jostlings for power and preference. The coiling and uncoiling of connections. The coded messages in the assignment of roles and relative richness of costume. In who was made beautiful and who was condemned to be grotesque. Even in where people stood and by whom they chose to stand.

This particular complex 'toy' was my fault, it seemed. First, I had reminded my mother about her gift. Then one of my ladies must have blabbed that the princess's new blackamoor could sing and play the lute.

Heeding Thalia's first warning, I had appointed her as merely of my musicians not my mistress of music. Once they grew accustomed to her strangeness, my ladies, including Anne, could now ignore her, as no more than an unusual chair or wall-hanging, adding to the pleasantness of life without needing to be greeted or otherwise spoken to. The rest of my musicians were men, who did not expect to play in my bedchamber after I had settled for the night. Therefore they could not envy her.

Now I was the one feeling jealousy.

When Thalia had returned after her first summons from the queen, I called her into my bedchamber. I waited until Anne left the room to make me a soothing posset.

'So?' I demanded, holding out my arms so that my maid could untie my sleeves from my bodice. 'Has my mother taken back her gift?'

'She wants me to perform.' Thalia released a ripple of notes from the strings. 'Her majesty has a fancy to turn poet and write a masque.' She offered me this confidence as if to salve her forced betrayal. 'We've all been sworn to secrecy. The true author will be revealed only after the final triumph.'

I flinched at that 'we'. I was not among them. I waved away my maid and tied the ribbons of my night-dress myself as I had always done in Scotland and at Combe.

'Why does she risk making a fool of herself?' I tried to think of the pale woman at the window dancing in a masque, let alone writing one.

Thalia looked down at her lute.

'What are you thinking?' I asked.

'Wondering which of you I serve now.'

'Would it change your answer?'

'Of course!' Her eyes told me that I had asked a foolish question.

I climbed into the bed turned back by my chamberer and pulled the covers up to my chin. 'Then you had best decide.'

She shook her head. 'Don't mock me. You know it's not my choice.'

'At this moment, here in this room, it is.'

She gave me a long look. 'In truth?'

'Do you call me a liar?'

She smiled thinly and avoided my question. 'The queen has not assigned me a place to eat in her household mess. If I want to eat, I believe I'm still yours.'

I leaned back into the shadows of the bed so that she could not see my secret gratification.

Her fingers now began the melody of an old French lullaby while she spoke over the music. 'We must all pretend that a Mr Daniels is the author, who seems to be her majesty's tame poetaster.'

'You never answered my question,' I said. 'Why does the queen take this risk?'

'I believe,' said Thalia carefully, 'that no poet would agree to write what her majesty wants.'

Anne returned with my posset. 'Do you speak of the queen's new masque?' she asked eagerly. 'I have been asked to sing in it, as well as Mistress Bristo. And Frances Howard, and the Other Elizabeth.' She offered me the warm, foam-topped mug of milk, egg, sugar and sherry. 'My aunt is pleased with me. It's an unexpected honour!'

I bent my face to my drink. I understood. My mother meant to act as if I were already gone from England.

'This new masque is to be a reply to the masque we missed

while we were still at Combe,' Anne went on happily. 'Do you remember, your grace? All that excitement about the Gunpowder Treason and the marvellous bonfires that followed it? It was that same year, but much earlier.'

I did remember. For Twelfth Night, 1605, the beginning of the year that ended so badly for me, my mother had commissioned her first masque at the English court.

'On Twelfth Night.' Anne rambled on, undressing for bed in her turn. 'Her majesty's first court masque in London. *The Masque of Blackness*, it was called. The queen and all her ladies blacked their faces and bosoms and arms with soot.'

Thalia stopped playing.

In *The Masque of Blackness*, my mother, six months pregnant, had played the chief Nymph and Daughter of Niger.

'But the transformation scene, when they were all to be washed white and cleansed of their sins by the power of the king of Albion . . . Albion meaning "white" of course' – Anne's head reappeared through the neck of her sleeping smock – 'as well as "England" . . . it failed disastrously. Frances says that the greasy blacking paste would not wash off on stage. It clung to their faces and came off only when scrubbed hard with soap and warm water. Master Jones had to rewrite the ending without the happy transformation. Now her majesty has been inspired by the arrival of Mistress Bristo to try again.'

'She means to call it, *The Return of Niger to Albion*,' said Thalia in a flat voice.

'Lucy, Countess of Bedford, says that the queen has six apothecaries working day and night to make a blackening paste that will easily rinse away.' Anne climbed into bed beside me.

I now attended the rehearsal when the Daughters of Niger were to try the new blacking paste for their skins. The ladies had stripped to their smocks and under-petticoats baring their shoulders and arms.

My mother, Lucy, Countess of Bedford, Lady Arbella Stuart,

and two others retired to a neighbouring antechamber to black themselves in private. I watched them leave.

My quiet, older, distant-cousin Arbella always made me uneasy. She had attended my mother for as long as I could remember. Her father had been the younger brother of my grandfather, Lord Darnley and her hand had often been offered by my father in his political manoeuvring, but never given. I had heard rumours that he once intended to marry her himself instead of my mother, to strengthen his dynastic claim in England. I sometimes wondered if she ever dreamed of being queen in place of the woman whose train she carried on state occasions.

When the queen was gone, the rest of the ladies laughed and jostled at the three watery looking glasses hung on the wall for the occasion, as they began to sponge onto their faces, bare arms and bosoms the queen's new paste of soot, borage oil and water.

'Mistress Music!' Frances Howard called to Thalia, who waited quietly on a stool with her lute in her lap. 'We all try to look like you today. What do you think?'

She did not reply. But I thought that she shone more strange and mysteriously beautiful as the others grew blacker and more like clowns.

'Are we not lovely?' The ladies shrieked with laughter and rolled their eyes. There was a mock fight to look in the mirrors. Bare blackened shoulders and knees gleamed like obsidian.

'I might paint myself up like this for dinner and give them all a fright!'

'I swear that my soul feels more wild and savage already,' said Frances Howard. 'May I have a bite of your arm please? I begin to feel hungry.'

'How do I look, your grace?' Anne stood shyly in front of me. Or I believed that it was Anne. Her face was a comical mask of thick black paste around the white rimmed patches of her eyes.

The rehearsal itself began with the now-black Nymphs of Niger singing their music while they walked through the more-or-less correct positions.

'Great Albion, again we come.
Once more we beg your healing powers . . .'

As was usual in a court masque, the chief parts were sung by the court ladies, while the court musicians filled out the sound and anchored the tune.

I watched Thalia, now waiting on a wood and canvas rock while the black-faced queen and her ladies, half-clothed in fragments of their eventual costumes, went over and over the more difficult passages of their opening song. Though a mere musician, Thalia had been given a solo.

When her turn came to sing, I understood why she was the reported inspiration for the new masque. The hall fell silent when she began her lament. In her husky voice, she expressed, most movingly, her deep sorrow at having to remain behind, black and still impure, while her sisters sailed for Albion to try again for the purification that had eluded them before.

Unlike that of her sisters, her blackness would never be washed away.

There was a hush when she finished, then applause.

If I had not been so unhappy at being left out, I might have wondered how she felt about her role. At that moment, however, I hated her for being the one in the masque, for singing so beautifully, and even more, for earning a 'well-sung' from the queen.

I was not the only one to notice the queen's praise. I saw Frances Howard exchange looks with another young gentlewoman above a fixed smile.

The queen, Lady Arbella, and two of the other older ladies again retired to wash in private. Only Lucy, Countess of Bedford, who was closest to the rest of us in age, remained.

'Ladies . . .!' The Master of Revels tried to call them to order. 'We will now attempt the libation scene – that troublesome transformation. In the performance, of course, your chosen gallant will help to wash you, but today, these grooms will assist.' He pointed to a group of red-faced boys standing-by with water jugs. 'Please go now to your positions beside your seashell ship on the shore of Albion.'

Dash not our hope but let us bloom
As snow-drop white as vernal flowers . . .

They held out beseeching soot-blackened hands. The grooms poured water from the jugs. There was a burst of hilarity and shrieks. 'That's too cold! I freeze!' Water splattered and spread in puddles on the stone floor. More shrieks.

'My ladies!' cried the Master of Revels. 'Please attempt the lines again.'

With shameful satisfaction I watched the song dissolve into chaos. The new blackening paste did not appear to rinse off much more easily than the original one had done. The Daughters of Niger were soon streaked black and white, their gowns sodden and smeared with the soot. Fabric clung to wet skin. The odd breast was exposed. A string of pearls broke and bounced across the floor. I leaned sideways and picked up one that rolled as far as my skirt hem.

'Back to the beginning, I beg you,' prompted the Master of Revels. '*Great Albion . . .*' He was wasting his breath.

'Whoops!' High-heeled shoes skidded. Grooms frantically wiped up water from the floor and ran to fetch more jugs of water. With helpless dismay, a tailor watched the ruin of his silk shawls and sashes.

'I vow, Frances, the more pure you become, the more lewd you look!' I could no longer recognise the speaker.

194

'All the better to attract a man!' cried Frances Howard. 'I know who I want to wash me clean.'

'But you're already married, you wicked creature!'

Frances ignored her. 'It's not coming off this time, either! It's like the old saying. "As soon wash white the Ethiop".' She glanced up at Thalia.

Thalia sat unmoving, as if she had not heard. I felt the first quiver of apprehension invade my misery.

'Who has ever tried to wash an Ethiop?' someone demanded.

'Not I!'

'Nor I.'

'We must seize the chance!' cried Frances.

Dripping and laughing, they all turned to Thalia.

I opened my mouth, then closed it again.

'Your turn, Mistress Music,' said Frances. She took a jug of water from a groom. 'Yes, you! Come down here. Don't be shy!'

After a moment, Thalia climbed down from her rock, leaving her lute behind.

I looked away. In truth, I was still a little afraid of Frances Howard.

'Hold out your hands.'

Thalia cupped her hands as the others had done. Frances poured. Thalia rubbed her hands with the offered towel.

'It's no good. You must rub harder.' Frances glanced at the other young women, then at me. 'Try again.'

'My skin is black all through,' said Thalia. 'You won't find white no matter how hard you wash!'

'Then you're a sinful she-devil who can't be washed clean!' Frances glanced around at the others. I felt Lucy look at me.

This is my mother's doing, I thought. Nothing to do with me.

'We can't leave her soul to black damnation! To the field, ladies! We must try to save her!'

'It's no use,' protested Thalia. She put both arms behind her back.

'Are you confessing to resolute wickedness then?' demanded another dripping black mask. 'See how she stares like a witch!'

'Surely not!' said Frances. 'We won't tolerate a determined sinner in our midst! Hold her whilst I save her soul!' She seized Thalia's wrist. The others pressed close around, pinning Thalia with their bodies in wet, skimpy clothing, netting her with their hands. They forced her left arm out in front of her. Only Lucy held back.

I wanted to tell them to leave her alone, but part of me muttered that she should not have been there in the first place.

'I don't find this amusing,' said Lucy. When the others ignored her, she went off after the queen. After a moment, a figure that I thought was Anne also stepped back from the mêlée.

'Don't loose her!' Frances Howard tore a flap of canvas from the corner of a rock and began to scrub at the back of Thalia's hand.

Thalia set her teeth. Then she began to struggle. She made no sound.

'Harder! You must go deeper. She's still black!'

Her head began to twist wildly from side to side. I stood up.

'Now she's black and red.'

Thalia pinched her lips against a scream. Silently, she twisted and heaved, but the nymphs held her tightly with their own bodies.

'Scrub a little harder. Her sins must surely wash away!'

'Look! She bleeds like an Englishwoman . . .'

'Stop!' I shouted.

'But, your grace, we're just having a game.' The women fell back, even as Frances Howard protested.

'. . . all in fun,' added another.

Thalia hid her arms behind her. I heard her panting.

I seized her elbow and pulled her arm from behind her back. 'This is not in fun!'

'But they don't feel pain as we do,' someone murmured. 'See! She doesn't turn pale at the sight of her own blood!' There was an uneasy giggle.

'Rehearsal is done!' I said. 'Go! Now!'

'But your grace . . .' A male voice spoke behind me.

I rounded on the Master of Revels. 'They've learned all they need to know today!'

He turned to look for help from the queen then remembered that she had gone.

I led Thalia back to my lodgings and into my little closet, where I made her sit down. I examined her injury. Seven inches of skin on her wrist and hand had been rubbed away, exposing the raw flesh beneath. Tiny deep red wells of blood rose in the dark pink flesh. When I wiped, I saw the white of an exposed tendon. A violent tremor shook her arm.

She tried to pull away. 'It will heal.'

'How can you not cry?'

'And give them the satisfaction?'

I reared back at the cold fury in her eyes. 'But doesn't it hurt?' Perhaps that woman was right, and she didn't feel pain in the same way.

'Of course it hurts, you fool!' Thalia clapped her other hand over her mouth.

There was a long silence.

'I don't think you're meant to speak to me like that,' I said.

Thalia stared mutely at the floor, her mouth tight. 'Are fine ladies meant to behave like beasts?' she asked at last.

'No.' In silence, I found a clean handkerchief in my cupboard. 'This will hurt.' I wiped gently at the worst of the blood. Then I took a small stoneware jar from a chest my chamberer kept. 'Marigold, beeswax and other things. I believe it will ease the pain.' Gently, I applied the unguent to the raw skin of her wrist and hand. She squeezed her eyes shut in pain but stopped trying to pull away.

'Will your playing be affected?'

She shrugged. 'You're not a fool,' she said between gritted teeth. 'I apologise.'

We both watched my finger gently smoothing the salve onto her wrist.

'I'm sorry I didn't stop them sooner,' I said.

She nodded.

I fetched another clean handkerchief and wrapped it around her wrist. I could have called someone else to tend to her but found that I was enjoying it. I so seldom touched another person, or was touched, except when I was being dressed.

I spent longer than I needed over tying the bandage just right. I felt towards Thalia the same warmth that filled me when I was looking after one of my pets, or being kind to Baby Charles. A fondness grew in me for the one I was being kind to. I knew that I had betrayed her with my hesitation. Tending her let me begin to think better of myself again.

'Sometimes it's safer if others think you a fool,' she said.

'Do you mean me, or you?'

'Both.'

'We should know but not seem to know?'

'Yes.'

'Is that how you are with me?'

She pulled away her hand, which I realised that I had been clutching. 'What do you truly want from me, your grace?' Her voice shook. 'I no longer know where I am! When I first arrived, I tried to be courtier-like and agreeable and keep a respectful distance, but that wasn't what you wanted. Then I tried to tell you the truth, as you asked but you didn't like that, either. Now you tempt me out of cover into greater and greater danger. How am I to keep myself safe while giving you true answers? I'm now confused out of all good behaviour!'

The moment teetered, unbalanced and fragile. But a door was cracking open. I had no idea what lay beyond. I gave it a push.

I drew a long breath. 'I'm not angry that you called me a fool, because it's true. I was being one.' I stood up. 'Wait.'

I felt under my pillow for the little piece of Scottish granite and held it over my heart. 'I vow to you that I won't grow angry if you tell me I'm a fool, or anything else, so long it's true. Here . . .!'

With my free hand, I lifted a gold chain over my head. On it hung an enamelled gold medallion bearing the profile of the goddess Diana, carved in white sardonyx and framed in diamonds and pearls. 'I mean to say, I can't promise not to be angry for a time, but I swear not to punish you. Please take this and wear it. And if you ever think that I've forgotten my promise, just touch the medallion to remind me.'

'I can't take that. It's too costly for me.'

'Its value lies only in the meaning. That goddess punished truth-seekers in terrible ways. I vow never to do the same.'

After a moment, she opened her fingers and let me drop the chain and medallion into her palm.

'Vow or no vow, you still own me,' she said. 'That's the only truth that matters. You have no right to demand truth from a slave.'

My warmth cooled. I put the wax stopper back onto the little stoneware jar. 'Do you think I begged for a blackamoor maid to carry my handkerchief, until my mother indulged me by buying you?' I slammed the jar back into its chest. '. . . that I wanted to flaunt you like an egret feather or a locket made from the hair of the Great Cham's beard and a dragon's tooth?'

'No one asked my opinion in the matter, neither.'

'Well!' I was uncertain what to say next. 'I can't apologise nor make an excuse for owning you, because no one asked me. I didn't want you bought. It's no good being angry with me!'

She weighed the chain in her hand while she studied me with her large eyes.

'You're a slave too,' she said.

'What?' My jaw trembled as I tried to form words. I raised my hand to slap her.

'Though your price is a little higher.' She raised her fore-fingers in a mocking cross to ward off my slap.

I looked at the handkerchief around her wrist and dropped my hand.

'You see!' she said. 'You don't want to hear the truth. Only the part of it that you choose.' She held up my chain and jiggled it in my face. 'I've just done what you ordered me to do and you don't like it. Now you want to punish me for obeying you.' She dropped her eyes to my still half-raised hand. 'A slave can never trust the master.'

She sank into a curtsy of such exaggerated reverence that my cheeks burned. 'I beg you, your grace, to release me from honesty.'

'I'll release you from everything, if that's what it takes!' I cried. 'I give you back to yourself! See how you like it! You'll see how easy it is to be your own mistress without help from anyone! And good cess to you!'

Trying to straighten again, she stepped on her hem and staggered. 'That's a cruel temper!'

'Cruel?' I was now filled by an unreasoning fury. 'I call it generous!'

'And when it amuses you, you'll forget your generosity.'

'How dare you?' I ran to my writing chest, flung it open, fumbled for a pen. I sharpened the tip of the quill as if beheading it. Spat into the ink to moisten it and scribbled. 'There!' I shook the paper under her nose. My voice shook almost as much. 'Your manumission! D'ye want it or not?'

I heard the Scots leaking back into my voice, a sign even to me of my fury.

'I don't toy.' I tried to sound calmer, dignified. 'How dare you call me a changeable flibbertigibbet? Go on, take it!'

She looked at the paper and back at me. 'You're in earnest?'

'Don't stare at me so!'

Thalia took the paper and read it. With satisfaction, I saw it begin to rattle in her hands.

'So?' I asked. 'Are you content now?'

She folded the letter carefully into four and tucked it into her bodice. She stood for a long time with one hand pressed flat and rigid against her breastbone over the paper, staring into the corner of the room. 'Do you want me to be grateful now?'

'Aren't you?'

She gave me another of her opaque looks. 'You mean well.'

'I'll have it witnessed!' I managed not to shout. 'Tied up in ribbons and seals, if y' like. But there's your proof of my intention. With my signature!'

She nodded.

'Aren't you even a little grateful?'

'Oh, aye,' she said, imitating me perfectly. 'That I am, among much else.'

'Well then?'

'And now that I'm free, you'll send me away?'

'Why would I do that? Why d'you think I wrote that if I didn't want you to stay here and talk to me?' I understood my own words only as I heard them come out of my mouth.

'Are you in earnest?'

'God in Heaven, why can't you believe me? You'll make me angry again.'

'And now, you're not?'

'Yes!' I shouted. 'I am angry! Show me that damned necklace before I . . .'

She seemed not to hear me. She stood looking down at

her hand pressed against her breast. 'Please, your grace . . .' She shook her head then looked down at her hand again. 'With your permission . . . I need . . .' She made a vague flapping motion with her free hand and ran from the room.

'And I'm not a slave, neither!' I called after her, and burst into tears.

When I calmed down, I saw how she had tested me. The door had opened although I did not yet see what lay beyond it. I sent my chamberer to the gallery where Thalia still slept, with a draught to help her endure the pain that night.

I felt calm as I slid into sleep, without knowing why. The next morning, I woke early, filled with unexplained joy. I lay listening to Anne's gentle snores, trying to decide why I looked forward to the day with such expectation. I could not say that I had gained a friend. The relationship into which Thalia and I seemed to have launched ourselves was far too spiky and complex to be called friendship. All the same, I was eager to see her again and ask how her arm was healing.

My first task of the day was also clear.

33

Through my secretary, I dismissed Frances Howard. She could go wait for the return of her young husband somewhere else. Then I appointed Thalia Bristo as my Lady Musician of the Bedchamber, her salary to be paid by my steward and properly recorded in my household rolls. I told my chamberer to bring a new pallet bed to my lodgings and a locked chest for Mistress Bristo's belongings.

Then I sent for Thalia and waited happily to tell her what I had done.

She took a very long time to appear. When she did present herself, her renewed wariness felt like a slap.

'Walk with me,' I said. Silently, she followed me down into the orchard away from curious ears.

'Where's my chain?' I asked, without breaking step. 'I told you to wear it.'

She paced steadily beside me. 'Your chain? Then it's not truly mine now? You also told me that I was my own mistress, did you not?'

I walked on several more paces, breathing hard. I recognised a crossroads. It was now my choice which way to go. I noted the angry heat of my forehead and cheeks. I remembered the easy joy with which I had slid up into the day.

'Mistress Bristo,' I began, not entirely certain what was going to come out of my mouth.

'Tallie,' she said. 'I'm easier with Tallie.'

I stopped dead and looked at her. I knew suddenly what I felt when I was with her, even when I was angry with her, or confused, even amongst all the strangeness, false steps and mutual misunderstandings. She made me feel not alone. Just as I had felt not alone on the Cat Nick with Henry, looking down on Edinburgh. As I had not felt since coming south with any creature, except my dogs and horses, and Henry, when we could meet. Not even with loyal Anne. Henry was still my other soul and I was his. But we were two different halves of a single nut. Unlikely as it seemed, Tallie felt like the same half that I was.

I thought of every way in which we differed. Including the fact that she clearly did not feel as much kinship for me as I suddenly felt for her.

'What took you so long to come when I sent for you?' I asked.

'I got lost . . . why do you laugh?'

'Come with me. And remember the way, this time. Whitehall is a labyrinth.' I took her to the Privy Stairs.

We stood side by side looking out over the water. 'This is where I come to start from, when I don't know where I am,' I said.

'So here we are?'

'Yes.' I thought she seemed as relieved as I was by our recaptured accord.

We continued to stare out at the glinting water. After a time, I saw that she was very far away in her thoughts, looking across the river towards Southwark.

'Are you homesick?' I asked.

'No!'

'I'd like to visit over there.'

'I promise you, you would not.'

'Why not?'

She shrugged, closing me out again.

I took her arm and lifted the bandage. 'At least it's not infected.' I replaced the handkerchief again. 'Tallie, I need your help. I am at war. You must . . .' I caught myself. 'I ask you to be my intelligencer.'

'I feared as much.' She shook her head wryly. 'Hey ho! Hey ho.' She did not ask with whom I was at war.

'I need you to be my eyes and ears where I cannot go.' I hesitated. 'The king's orders are to keep me uninformed, most of all about my marriage. He has found a slower way to kill me than the axe or sword – torturing me with my ignorance.

'There may be risks,' I added.

'Oh, yes,' she agreed. 'There's risk.'

I narrowed my eyes. 'Do we speak of the same dangers?'

'Of course, your grace.'

34

TALLIE

There it is still, just across the water. Waiting for you to slip and be sent back.

Must lose my memories or else they might leak out. She listens too well for me to be safe. Like just now. She can't possibly see what I see when I look over there – the house, the women, the base coin of counterfeit delight. The babe I saw smothered at birth and taken away to be thrown into the Thames. And yet she makes me feel that she can.

'So here we are,' I just said to her. And where the devil is that?

I'm dependent on the favour of a girl younger than I am, who seems to find a kindred spirit in me. If she only knew what unfit company I make.

I forget that I may be free. Can't think what that means yet. My head won't . . . The world is suddenly grown too big for my thoughts to compass. Don't trust it yet.

I can think for myself. Only myself . . . makes me giddy. Decide soon what to do. Free, but not safe.

Where can I go?

Don't ever let yourself feel safe. You're too visible everywhere. Every move watched and judged. If I even belch, I'm proved a savage. I've heard the ladies whispering, 'black witch'.

Damn the queen and her masque, hanging me out for all to see. Elizabeth still doesn't believe the danger. She's never been in my place . . .

. . . But I don't think she can hide neither.

She means well. At least, she doesn't speak slowly in that false tone like the others, to be certain that I can understand their drivel. As if court ladies with minds like lame cart horses and the morals of weasels spoke some great wisdom denied to a savage.

'Pray, where are you from?'

'Southwark,' I say.

That shuts them up, though their mouths hang open with astonishment. I don't belong to land or to water. Born at anchor in Bristol harbour, Mrs Taft told me. Bobbing about on the current, ready to float away. Or sink. Wet or dry, it's down to chance.

I think I may have just been given a chance to land dry. Mistress Thalia Bristo, free-woman. Seeker-after-truth. Truth-teller to a princess.

Don't know whether to laugh or cry.

There was a princess in Ancient times – I heard a student visiting Fish Pool House tell about her once – who always saw the truth of the future but the gods cursed her so that no one believed her. I must learn to keep my mouth shut.

But I think she sees it too, that everyone is doubled. One self walks just beside the other – the one they think they are beside the other one. Sometimes I think she sees both of me.

That's reality over there across the river . . . Sweet Lord, I'd love to show them where I've fetched up! In a palace! That would make them goggle!

But I fear that it's like one of those spun-sugar palaces at a banquet, ready to crack under the first spoon. It will all disappear again, no matter how well I behave.

I'm already weary with trying to think what is true, in order to please her, instead of mouthing some platitude. Speaking the truth is hard work. Not as exhilarating as I once thought it would be, when all I had to do was repeat obedient nonsense and keep my head down. Now I have to watch all the time in case the wrong truth slips out. How long can I live as what I am not?

But what am I now?

Remember. It's her truth she wants, not yours. Yours is no affair of hers.

I must hold my nerve.

Don't even look over there or it will suck you back. Wherever you end up, it must not be there.

35

The following day, to my surprise, the Countess of Bedford presented herself and asked to speak to me alone. We went to stand in one of the window niches of the gallery, over-looking the orchard.

There would be no further rehearsals for *Niger in Albion,* Lucy told me.

I thanked her for taking the trouble to bring this news to me herself. I had no doubt that the queen's intended masque would never be mentioned again.

'There is another matter,' she said. 'Even more delicate.'

I gestured for her to continue.

'Has your blackamoor musician recovered?' She cleared her throat. 'What happened was unfortunate.'

'It was beastly,' I said. 'I credit you with being the first to see as much. I have apologised to her for taking so long to cry halt.'

She nodded. 'When even wise men debate the natural character of the different races, I suppose we must try to tolerate the beliefs of the ignorant.' She straightened as if to go. 'You dismissed Frances Howard.'

'Word travels fast.'

'She's doing what damage she can before she's sent home

209

to wait for her husband to claim her. Forgive me, your grace, and try not to detest the messenger . . .'

'I'm happy to place the entire blame on Mistress Frances,' I said, feeling suddenly chilled. 'Please continue.'

'She's saying that her dismissal is unfair. That Thalia Bristo is a witch, who charmed you into preferring her and giving her rich gifts. That perhaps, she also charmed the queen.'

For a terrible instant, I hung over the gulf of doubt.

'She cites the king's own investigations into witchcraft blames the girl herself for what happened to her – claiming that she set a spell even on the unsuspecting ladies to turn them into wild Maenads. As proof, she claims that Mistress Bristo felt no pain, having remained silent even though she bled.'

'Has she complained to the king?'

'Not yet directly. But I'm sure she counts on rumour reaching him.'

My doubt about Tallie vanished as quickly as it had come. Lucy raised a calming hand against my surge of rage. 'I think you'll find that most people would agree with me that Frances is a false, dangerous little cunny.' The fine pink lips smiled demurely.

Yes, said her amused eyes. You heard me right.

Then I remembered that this was the young woman said to have killed two horses under her, racing to be first to meet the new queen.

'I thought you should know.' She dropped me a graceful curtsy. 'And while I'm making you hate me, you should be aware that she's following her family's tradition of seducing monarchs. As she can't seduce the king, she has set her cap at your brother.'

I watched the fair hair and slim back of my mother's chief lady as it dwindled down the gallery and glided through the door. I could not decide whether her embassy had been an act of friendship, or not.

No act of friendship for Frances Howard, for sure.

I prayed that my father's restless mind had left the subject of witchcraft behind. On the other hand, he would be flattered to hear his authority cited. As for Henry . . . I remembered how he had watched Frances Howard dancing. A married woman. My poor brother could easily find himself enmeshed in a scandal that he would not know how to handle. I tried to think how to warn him against those knowing cat-eyes and that insinuating smile. But I could not think how to rescue him without either angering or humiliating him.

Protecting Tallie was a little easier. Here, I could use my position. I was not the only person at court who was alert to the tiniest signs. I ordered a new gown to be made for her, of deer-coloured satin with a brocade panel let into the front of the petticoat.

My ladies had begun to complain, on behalf of fathers, brothers and husbands, that my father's favourite, Robert Carr, was already controlling who gained access to the king and who did not. Although I had no real power in Whitehall, people would recognise my chain and the gown as marks of royal favour from the third in line to the throne. It was the best armour I could give Tallie against the malice of Frances Howard.

I lay awake considering how to protect her from the king and his past interest in the legal prosecution of witches. Being careful not to disturb the dogs sleeping on my feet, I turned restlessly, listening to Anne's gentle snores. In spite of my care, Belle woke and crept up to nestle against my chest. As I drifted towards sleep at last, soothed by the softness of her fur against my chin, the answer slipped into that fertile gap between reason and dream. A way to protect Tallie and also alert Henry to his danger.

For the next two days, I wrote at the table in my little closet, cursing my ignorance of how such things were properly done.

211

I had to rely on my own ability to think clearly and use reason. Carefully and coolly, I recorded exactly what had happened during the rehearsal for *Niger in Albion*. When it was done, I rode across the park and showed my work to Henry.

'"*A True Account of the Happenings*",' he read aloud. '"*Set down by her grace, the Princess Elizabeth* . . ."' What is this, Elizabella?'

'A precaution.' I explained what the Countess of Bedford had told me of Frances Howard's threats to Tallie, leaving out the rest. 'I need you to read it and tell me whether it could serve as evidence, should an open accusation ever be made against my musician. It would be an account set down while memory was fresh, against old hearsay. I want to show that Mistress Bristo behaved in every way like an ordinary woman, never as a witch.'

I saw his face colour as he read it. 'If you truly fear for your woman, it's just as well to have this account,' he said when he had finished. 'The Howards are powerful, even now.'

'But would it help?' I asked.

He returned the paper to me. 'It might be wise to have the signature of another witness.'

He said nothing about the behaviour of Frances Howard. I could only hope that he had been a little warned against the 'false, dangerous little cunny' who might be setting her cap at him.

A week after I gave Tallie her letter of manumission, she came into my little closet, where I was reading by the window, to show me the new gown I had ordered to be made for her.

'So?' she asked, holding her arms stiffly out to the side in their heavy embroidered sleeves. 'I confess, I don't feel like myself any longer.'

I set aside my book. Looking at her standing defiantly in

the deer-coloured silk, with the gold chain of the Diana medallion around her neck, and her cloud of black hair, I wondered how someone so strange could be so familiar at the same time. Although the clothes fitted her perfectly, they looked to my eyes like a masque costume, turning her into something she was not.

She should be dressed in silk slippers with curled toes, I thought. And veils, like an exotic princess living in a distant land where turquoise-tailed peacocks shrieked, red and gold birds hung in trees like singing fruit, and people rode about on lions and elephants.

'Forgive me,' I said.

'I'm used to stares. Yours is friendly, at least.'

'I'm sorry you feel uncomfortable in your new gown,' I said.

'Don't mistake me. It's just that I've never before had one so fine.' She curtsied. 'Just listen to that sound of new silk. No old gown sounds so crisp.'

She straightened with a rustle and hiss like falling sand. In reply, I curtsied in a sigh of velvet. She grinned in acknowledgement and sank rustling down again while I straightened.

'A duet for taffeta and velvet,' she said.

Laughing, we see-sawed up and down, listening to the delicate music of our clothes.

'If I called Lady Anne to put on her best satin, we could play a concerto for gowns,' I said with delight. Our eyes met in shared pleasure. 'Where are you really from, Tallie? There's no danger in telling me now.'

'You don't give up, do you?' She stopped smiling and gave me a look with eyes suddenly turned as opaque as burnt-out coals. 'Like I told you. Southwark.' She laid her pink palm over Diana's fierce sardonyx face on her breast. 'The truth, whether you like it or not.'

Curbing my impatient curiosity, I pushed her no farther. I did not want to risk closing off the new space beyond the opening door. We would grow to know each other once we were safely there.

'Tell me something I don't know, that only you can tell me,' I challenged her. 'Not too safe.'

I stood still under her scrutiny and watched her decide to let me win this time. 'White-skinned people,' she said at last. 'Use their hands differently. More closed. Not opened up like flowers. Not letting go.' She raised both hands with her fingers extended, as if releasing a bird.

I looked down at my own hands nesting curled inside each other, then back at hers.

'Their hands are always balled up into fists,' she said. 'Holding on. To themselves. To power.' She looked away for a moment. 'To the belief that they're always right.'

She slapped her palm onto Diana again and waited. Perhaps I hadn't won after all.

I had asked for it, however. I opened my fists. 'Here's a more dangerous question. What do you hear being said about Sir Robert Carr?'

'Oh Lord!'

'Eyes and ears,' I reminded her. I waited to see how much more she would risk for me.

She glanced out into my sleeping chamber and dropped her voice. 'Carr has already been given Sir Walter Ralegh's manor of Sherborne and profits from traffic in honours and commissions . . .'

I nodded impatiently. I knew about Sherborne from Henry, who continued his close friendship with Ralegh even after the king imprisoned the former adventurer in the Tower.

'Carr's knighthood may be followed soon by viscount . . . Do you want more?'

I nodded.

'I hear that he's the king's he-whore.'

My ears filled with pounding blood. The dark landscape she had opened up was vast and terrifying, filled with monstrous, hungry, prowling shapes. But she had been willing to go there with me.

'Did I survive your test?' Tallie asked.

I ignored her question, not wanting to admit the hit. 'I've something else to give you.'

'Another way to command my obedience? Like this goddess?'

I held out a small ring of keys on a ribbon. 'For my lodgings,' I said. 'Including my bedchamber door and this closet. Your lute will be safe in here. None of the other women has this key, not even Lady Anne.'

She put out her hand slowly. 'Your grace is trusting,' she said. 'How do you know that a girl from Southwark is not a thief?'

I put the keys into her pink palm. 'I hope that you are an accomplished thief,' I said. 'Thieving is very much what I have in mind for you.'

Her hand jerked back and her eyes hardened.

'Don't be a fool,' I said. 'I'm jesting. I know you're not a thief.'

'How can you be sure?' I heard a new coldness in her voice.

'God's wounds! I just know! How does a dog know at whom to bark? How does a cat choose a lap to sit on? Don't ask me to give you a reason – I just know! Please take the damned keys without a catechism.'

She wiped her palm across her mouth. 'Forgive me,' she said. 'I've learned the habit of self-defence.'

'With good reason, I'm sure. But I beg you, not with me. Not any longer. Always having to be so careful of your feelings is wearing me out.'

'What?' Tallie looked astonished.

'When you first arrived, you claimed you were trying to be agreeable,' I said. 'But I promise you, it was like conversing with a hedgehog. And sometimes, it is still. I never know what will upset you and what won't. We'll be in perfect accord, or so I think, then suddenly I'm faced with all these bristling spines warning me to keep my distance. Like just now. It makes me feel like weeping.'

'Well,' she said. She looked down at the keys for a long moment. 'I see.' She still did not look at me while she carefully tied the ribbon on the key ring to her girdle. Then she tucked the keys out of sight somewhere in the depths of her gown. She nodded to herself to conclude some internal debate. 'No more hedgehog, then.'

Then she looked at me directly, her large eyes no longer cold. 'I thank you for the keys, your grace . . . my Lady Elizabeth. And for the gift of your trust.' She sank into a grave curtsy. 'I shall try to be as generous with mine.'

The door was open at last, I thought. I felt my breath grow unsteady.

Then she straightened. 'Whose pocket shall I pick for you first?'

36

We became accomplices in crime.

'Sweet Lord!' she exclaimed when I told her my first task. 'So long as we're hanged together.'

'Copies of letters,' I said. 'Even reading and reporting the contents will serve. I shall lend you to the king's musicians . . .' I had a sudden thought. 'Forgive me,' I said carefully. 'I must risk arousing the hedgehog.'

'I'll do my best to control the beast.'

'You can read and write?'

'You saw me read my manumission.' She kept her indignation in check, but I felt it.

'But people sometimes pretend.'

'That's true,' she said quietly. 'They do indeed.'

I studied her for a moment, wondering where in Southwark she had learned, not only to read and write, but to play the lute and sing in three languages.

'I must also see a portrait of the Dauphin of France,' I said. 'How large is it?'

'I don't know even that much.'

With stolen words, written or remembered, overheard or secretly read, Tallie helped me begin to track down the knowledge my father had forbidden me. At her suggestion, I gave

217

her a purse of gold coins to help loosen further any indiscreet tongues and to pay for the work of secret scribes. Though I trusted her with the money, she insisted on giving me a detailed list in her nightly report, of exactly where each coin had gone and what it had bought us.

She accepted my praise with composure. 'Once they stop gawping at me,' she said, 'or asking to touch me, or to finger my hair, they pay me no more attention than if I were a dog or cat.'

Every night, as I prepared for bed, she came into my chamber, to sing me to sleep and report on anything she might have learned.

Together, we made a list of my proposed suitors.

The Dauphin of France. Becomes Louis XIII of France, after the death of his father. Catholic.

Even I already knew that France was my father's greatest ambition for me. When I was six, I had eavesdropped on the Harington's discussing my marriage to the Dauphin, the son of French king, Henri IV, and his queen, Marie de Medici. Union with one of the two great powers of Europe. Negotiations with France had begun in 1603, as soon as my father took the English throne.

Frederick Ulrich of Brunswick. Protestant.

I was forced to include Frederick Ulrich. After befriending the wife of the clerk of one of Cecil's secretaries, Tallie reported that the German prince's spring visit had been unofficial. In spite of any overtures he may have made, there had never been a formal proposal. Therefore, his proposal had never been rejected. His mother continued to pursue the match. My father continued to consider her overtures.

Along with Brunswick, my father also flirted with every

crowned head of Europe, as well as an assortment of lesser rulers and a few English nobles. In the next months, Tallie smuggled letters, overheard talk or bought information, sometimes no more than unverified gossip or hints. Our list grew:

Victor Amadeus, Duke of Piedmont, son of the Duke of Savoy.
His sister offered to Henry. Both Catholic.
Felipe, Crown Prince of Spain, son of King Philip III. Sister, the
Infanta Ana offered to Henry. Both Catholic.
Frederick, The Elector Palatine. Protestant. Rumour only. No
letter seen.
Edward Seymour. Protestant.
William Seymour, his brother. Protestant.
The Earl of Northampton. Uncertain.
Lord Howard de Walden. Uncertain.
The Great Cham of Tartary.
The Devil.

'Don't trouble yourself trying to find letters or other signs of love from the last two,' I told Tallie. 'My father speaks for them himself.'

I had expected her to be a good listener when I lent her to other companies of musicians to widen her freedom to roam Whitehall. I had guessed that she might have dog-sharp ears for gossip. But I wondered where she had learned her astonishing skill at smuggling portraits, borrowing documents and stealing copies of official letters. I ached to learn more about her than she was willing to tell. Questions quivered on the tip of my tongue every time she slipped another filched paper from her sleeve or fished a clandestinely borrowed miniature out of her bodice. But, remembering her anger when I had jested about thievery, I never quite dared to ask. Even with the hedgehog subdued.

In the early triumph of a successful hunt, I confused the

capture of names with a grasp on reality. As if he knew what I was trying to do, my father constantly changed his stated intentions, blowing hot, blowing cold, rejecting, pursuing, until the growing list of my suitors swam under my eyes.

Prince Otto of Hesse. Protestant.
Prince Gustavus Adolphus of Sweden. Protestant . . .

All of them possible. None yet certain. I began to feel more confused than when I had known nothing. Through Henry, I learned that even those closest to the king had difficulty keeping up with his ever-changing thoughts on my marriage. Even the subtleties of influence on him were elusive.

Cecil might or might not have influence. Carr very likely carried weight though he would undoubtedly echo his master's choice. My Catholic convert mother, when asked, quite naturally favoured a Catholic match. I knew from Henry that several of the militantly Protestant German princes, including Brunswick, Hesse and the Palsgrave, or castle-holder, of the Palatine, were already pressing him, in secret communications, to become an ally in the threatened religious war on the Continent. My brother had entered into a war of wills with the king, threatening the king's purpose in Europe by his vigorous opposition to a Catholic match for either of us.

Hot with satisfaction at having made peace between England and Spain in 1604 after forty years of war, my father had taken to calling himself 'The Peacemaker King' and announced his intention of mediating like another Solomon between the Catholic and Protestant states on the Continent. He would marry one of his two older children to a Catholic, the other to a Protestant. And until he decided how to arrange this even-handedness, he meant to keep me hanging in the balance.

I didn't know even what language to pray in.

*   *   *

'I've seen the Dauphin's portrait,' Tally reported one night. 'It's kept in full sight in the king's lodgings, in his small presence chamber, which is difficulty enough. And the frame is too large for me to smuggle, even if I could manage to foist it. You'll have to come see it for yourself.'

The king was away hunting at Theobald's. Even when he was at Whitehall, he would never permit me to enter as far as his small presence chamber. When he was away, I would have no reason to try.

'Only his close male friends are welcome there,' I said. 'How did you manage?'

'The same way you will. I'll tell you how when it's time.'

From the gallery of the bowling alley tucked behind my lodgings, I watched the Earl of Arundel cast his ball. I listened to his shouts, and those of his friends, urging the ball to roll straight, and heard the pleasing wooden clatter of his direct hit. Then I heard a burst of male laughter.

Near the door, still wearing his travel cloak, the Seigneur de St Antoine waved his arms and mimed tearing his hair. Arundel and the others gathered around him, still laughing. The Seigneur staggered as if in despair. He bayed like a hound, then fell to his knees before his delighted audience, threw his arms around an invisible neck and passionately kissed the air.

Sir John Harington, my guardian's nephew and close friend of my brother, broke away from the others. 'You should hear this tale, your grace!' he called up to me. 'The king's favourite hound Brutus disappeared last week from the hunting pack. His majesty was distraught, certain that the dog had been stolen. But then a few days later . . .' He met me on the little stairs and offered his hand. 'The Seigneur says that the beast suddenly reappeared in the pack as if it had never been gone.'

St Antoine leapt to his feet when he saw me, but I waved him back down to his knees to continue his antics.

'Och, my sweet Brutus!' he resumed in a fair imitation of my father's voice. 'Ye came back tae me! 'Wheer' ha'ye been sae lang?' Kiss. Kiss. Then he mimed discovery and astonishment. 'What's this? What can this be, tied to yer collar?'

He stood up and resumed his own voice. 'It was a stern letter to the king,' he said. 'Unsigned but reeking of Cecil . . . who else would have dared? "Come back to London, your majesty," it said. "You are needed here. There's work to be done."'

I clapped my hand to my mouth.

There was more laughter, but it had turned thoughtful.

'How did the king take it?' asked Harington.

'Evilly! He was out of temper for the rest of the day. But he obeyed the summons like a dutiful schoolboy and has returned to London.'

The men exchanged glances. If I had not been there, I'm certain they would have said more.

My father must never guess the part I had played, I thought. In a boil of terror and delight, I saw myself again, Cecil's clandestine agent, handing his secret instructions to the Master of Hounds. Then the delight faded. Once again, my father's gaze would weigh me down. And his return might make it impossible for me to see the Dauphin's portrait after all.

Two nights later, I sat in the Banqueting House at Whitehall, watching Henry dance with Frances Howard. She smiled shyly up at him, then looked down blushing, as if overcome by his nearness. When the set finished, he invited her to sit with him and watch the next dancers. As always, Henry was so civil and charming that it was impossible to tell what he truly thought.

I would not have recognised that demure, simpering crea-ture sitting beside him as the cold-eyed knowing young woman I had dismissed, if I had not seen her lean against his arm as if by accident, so that the side of her breasts pressed against him. My brother jumped and blushed.

I felt another body settle beside me.

'She has vowed publicly that she'll have his maidenhead.' When I turned my head to look into the Countess of Bedford's narrow, pretty face, I saw only the intent to inform. No malice.

'How widely is it known?'

'Wagers are being laid in the guard room,' she murmured.

'At what odds?' I felt sick with apprehension. Other eyes in the great hall were assessing my brother and his companion.

Lucy shook her head slightly, refusing my question. In silence, we watched my brother being urged on in conversation by wide blue fascinated Howard eyes. The breasts had retreated but hung provocatively, not far, promising another accidental touch.

I felt a tremor of excitement run through the big hall. My brother, widely thought to still be a virgin, had never been seen to favour a woman. I suspected that the same thought was in many heads, including Lucy's. I was certain that it was in the minds of the Howards. The Howard family had put two of their women on the throne as wives of the last King Henry. The first one, the old queen's mother, Anne, had almost wrecked England and paid for it by losing her head. The second one, too, soon lost her head.

As if reading my mind, Lucy leaned closer. 'I never believed the old saw about "third time lucky",' she murmured. 'I think this one will bring herself down, just like the first two.'

I almost trusted her with a reply but merely nodded instead. Then Sir John Harington asked me to dance and I lost track of Henry and Frances Howard as we took our places in a set, joking quietly about the adventures of Brutus the Mystery Hound. As I emerged from the bottom of the set after stripping the willow, I saw Tallie waiting in the shadows of one of the tall wooden pillars. She made urgent eyes at me. I excused myself to my partner and skipped out of the set.

'You go first,' I said. 'Then I have a new task for you.'

'Plead a megrim! Now!' She pushed me down onto a stool and laid a warm hand on my forehead. 'Poor lady!' she said loudly. 'To come on so sudden. No more dancing for you tonight. Shall I help you to your bedchamber?'

She led me out of the Banqueting Hall, but not back to my lodgings on the Parkside. Instead, we went into a cool room in the nearby pantries.

'Her grace needs quiet,' she told the serving groom asleep in one corner, supposedly guarding the cheeses.

'You may go,' I murmured, taking up my part at last. 'Mistress Bristo will tend me.' I was certain I saw Tallie wink and slip the boy a coin. She closed and barred the door.

'Now's your chance to see the Dauphin.' She shook out the bundle in her arms. A serving man's livery in my brother's red and gold.

'Why so urgent?'

'These clothes belong to Peter Blank. He's waiting half-naked in a cupboard just down the passageway till I return. Put them on. Quickly! He must go back soon to St James's with the prince . . . Pull the collar up!'

I could smell Peter's scent on his shirt. Putting on the smell of a man felt even odder than the clothes themselves. I tried to glimpse my strange new male self in my glass.

'No time for that.' Tallie pulled me away.

Stumbling after her towards the king's lodgings, in over-large boots and carrying a pair of candlesticks, I felt like a rustic clown in an anti-masque. I was certain my father would suddenly appear and yank off my cap.

'Go set the candlesticks on the tall sideboard,' said Tallie. 'The picture is there.'

'So are a great many people!'

'They won't see you, I promise, so long as you keep your eyes down and don't bump into anyone.'

Heart thumping, I obeyed. By the time I had walked half the length of the room, I saw that Tallie was right. People see what they expect to see. No one looked at me twice in my groom's livery. I felt my limbs loosen. I may even have swaggered a little in my over-sized boots.

I reached the sideboard, set down the candlesticks and snatched a hungry glimpse of the Dauphin's dark, trout-like profile. I moved the candlesticks a few inches to the left, to buy more time to look at my possible future. Not only was he much younger than I was, he looked both melancholy and arrogant. I remembered Mrs Hay's relish for the latest scandal from France.

'You must never say that I told you,' she had whispered. 'I have heard that he often throws up his shirt to show his cock to all the court ladies, and then asks the queen and her ladies to tickle it. "Please, *maman*, tickle my *pipi*!" he says.'

I wanted to stare longer but could not risk getting Peter Blank into trouble. Or being recognised.

'Did you enjoy being invisible?' asked Tallie when I met her again in the passage.

'Yes!' I said with surprise. 'I think I did.' Even if I might have to marry a melancholy baby trout. Who might ask me to tickle his *pipi*.

On balance, however, I thought I might survive him better than Frederick Ulrich. The Dauphin was a year younger than Baby Charles. I should be able to manage him. Marriage to Brunswick would warp me into a ghost, like my mother.

'I would like to be invisible forever,' I said.

I was almost asleep in my bed before I remembered to tell her to trawl for gossip about Frances Howard. I wanted to know what her husband and his family thought of her behaviour and what they meant to do about it. I could not bring myself to ask even Tallie if she thought that my brother had ever bedded a woman.

37

WHITEHALL, MAY – JUNE 1610

The stir had reached all the way to the stable yard. Throwing dignity to the wind, with my attendants puffing behind me, I trotted back from the stables after an early morning ride in St James's Park. There had been unfamiliar French grooms and strange horses still steaming in the yard. The stable hands had goggled at me wide-eyed until I wanted to shout 'What ails you? I don't know either, do I?'

As if I could explain anything yet. But I meant to learn.

As I crossed the Great Court, the hair lifted on my neck. My father's roar of unreasoning fury could be heard throughout the Riverside of Whitehall. I heard a distant crash. The maid scrubbing the floor of the passage lifted her head and froze. A groom paused as he replaced a burnt candle with a new one. Two more stood motionless with their chins hoiked up over armloads of firewood. They all scrambled to attention when they saw me, but no one spoke.

Was it possible that he had learned about my trespass to see the picture in his absence? I crept closer, into the next corridor, to try to hear what he said.

Hearing the shouts, a secretary paused, turned back, then

changed his mind twice more in a way that in other circumstances would have been comical. At last, reluctantly, seeming not to have noticed me, he continued onwards towards the source of the outcry.

I'm the First Daughter, I reminded myself. I couldn't run away to hide just because my father was enraged. I walked on into the great gallery of the king's lodgings.

'That Papist viper cunt!' His voice carried clearly along the gallery. 'So! Ma *bairn*'s no a fit match for the spawn of that great whore of France? Are ye tellin' me that? The royal widow's got her nose up the arse of Spain, has she?'

Not my trespass, after all. France.

I entered an antechamber filled with silent petitioners. Everyone listened, not daring to breathe.

'She'll marry her whelps with Spain now, will she? A double marriage, you say? She spits in the eye of the king of England, does she? Weel, you go tell her that I'll marry my daughter to . . .'

Someone closed the door of the room where the king was. I could still hear my father ranting, but his words would no longer be distinguished.

I rushed back to the stables and found the groom just leading Wainscot into her stall.

'Please saddle her up again,' I said.

Henry sat with his head on his arms. When he raised his face, I saw that he had recently been crying. Several of his gentlemen sat around him in postures of dejection. The Seigneur de St Antoine leaned against the wall, head down and red-eyed.

'My other father is dead,' said Henry. 'Cecil had word three days ago, but I refused to believe it until confirmation came today from France.'

I took off my cloak and slung it into a pair of waiting arms.

Henri IV of France had been assassinated.

I decided not to announce that our father was in a rage at Henri's widow. I sat down and let Henry pour out his grief to me.

'On the eve of setting off to make war against Germany,' said Henry. 'Oh, Elizabella, why does God allow the great men to die too soon? I had looked forward to having him as your father-in-law. He had every virtue our father lacks. He would have taught me how to be a king.'

I knew it was wicked of me to be secretly grateful that I might not now have to marry the great man's son. I should be grieving, not wondering who would replace the Dauphin in my father's ambitions.

How did you judge a man, anyway? I wondered. How could you guess, from the glimpse of a portrait, or the official language of a letter, whether he would make a tolerable husband or would wither you into an empty, half-mad shell, like the queen?

No matter how often I went to stand on the privy stairs, I could not see where I was. I visited the Haringtons at Kew. I received petitioners, even though they wanted only insignificant trifles from me – a place for their niece among my chamberers, or a commission to make me a new wired collar or saddle for one of my horses. Men offered to give me a puppy or silver goblet engraved with all the Muses, if I would ask Henry to hear their petitions for weightier favours than I could offer. They did not ask me for licences, military commissions, interventions or backing for founding settlements in the New World. Nor for my consent to marriage.

At Tallie's suggestion, I gave new jackets to my gentleman musicians. Remembering her very first warning, I also gave Anne a magnificent pair of velvet sleeves, closely cross-hatched with golden threads and a pearl set at every crossing. Also, a dainty chain of gold and enamel flowers very like my own.

My ladies were now wondering openly how soon I would make a match for Tallie with the free-born Peter Blank, great-great-grandson of the royal trumpeter.

'Do you like him?' I asked her. It would be easy enough to arrange. Though I could not bear the thought of her leaving to live with a husband in my brother's household.

'I believe that we share chiefly the colour of our skin,' she said. 'And even that's not as great a resemblance as it might seem. His mother's as white as you are. But I don't discourage him. He's pleasant enough company and more than happy to gossip with me about the prince's household.'

Tallie continued to play her lute and listen. She continued to widen her acquaintance among the palace serving people. She read people as I did and understood what I wanted to know, beyond the names of future husbands. Who attended on whom. Who quarrelled and passed each other in silence with averted eyes, or else smiled too civilly. Who exchanged quick secret smiles, or else looked away too quickly. Who waited to petition my father, who petitioned my mother, and who sought favours from Henry. And which men, like Sir Francis Bacon, petitioned all three.

She failed only in learning how Frances Howard progressed with setting her cap at my brother. My brother never spoke with his gentlemen about their relationship, or lack of one. His intimate servants deflected bribes. The Howards had built a wall of loyal retainers around themselves that even Tallie could not penetrate.

I listened to her evening reports when she came into my chamber with her lute, as if to sing me to sleep. Every time I added the name of a prospective husband to our list in dark oak gall ink, I waited for the pen to leap or twitch in my fingers as a sign. But each new name oozed from the nib and lay inert on the page, as lifeless as the others.

The murder of the French king by a crazed Catholic, and the newly proposed alliance through marriage of Bourbon

France and Hapsburg Spain continued to dominate concerns in Whitehall. For once, the king and prince were in agreement. For different reasons, they both saw the possible alliance of the two greatest Catholic powers of western Europe as a threat.

Though Henri IV had been a convert to Catholicism, he had nevertheless given French Protestants 'liberty of conscience and impartial justice'. Henry and his band of knights now talked of retaliatory war with the Catholic powers.

Our father, the Peacemaker King, took Marie de Medici's refusal to have me as a daughter-in-law as both a personal and a political insult. I could not have been the only person in Whitehall to suspect that a part of his fury was terror that a regicide had succeeded. A crazed French Papist had succeeded where the English Gunpowder Plotters had failed. All recusant Catholics in England were stripped of their arms and forbidden to come within ten miles of the court. I amended my list:

~~The Dauphin of France, now Louis XIII of France. Catholic~~
Edward Seymour. Protestant
William Seymour . . .

I asked Henry what he knew of these two brothers, now being discussed as serious candidates by the Privy Council after the withdrawal of the French marriage.

'Our Seymour cousins are too ambitious for the king's liking,' he told me. 'And too close to the throne in their own right. Our father will never let any of them get a grip on real power by marrying you.'

I was third in line to the English throne. The Seymours were descended from Henry VIII's sister, Mary Tudor, the line named in Henry's will as his heirs. Their claim had been set aside. My father's line were descended from the monarch's other sister, Margaret. I could see how some people might argue that we were usurpers.

'I hear that the Howard women are ambitious too,' I said wickedly.

'I don't know where you hear such things,' said my brother coldly.

So far as Tallie and I could learn, France had never, in fact, made me a firm offer of marriage. Nor, for that matter, had any of my other suitors. My portrait was painted, copied, sent abroad. Portraits of my possible husbands were sent back in return. From the documents that Tallie managed to read, copy or steal, I learned only that negotiations ebbed and flowed at a stately pace and resolved nothing. Then I sat for yet another requested portrait.

On the 5th of June, Henry was invested as Prince of Wales. The poets and other chroniclers suffered feverish transports over my brother's noble bearing, the feasts, the tilts, the fireworks. And I was invited at last to perform in one of my mother's masques. *Tethys's Festival*, with the queen herself as Tethys, Queen of the Ocean. I was to play the River Thames.

At last, I thought, I will be able to show that I can do more than stand to be gawped at by marriage-brokers. I would show my mother that I could sing, and dance any figure asked of me.

Throughout most of the masque, I reclined silent and unmoving on a shell. My cousin Arbella appeared, likewise shelled, as the Derbyshire Trent.

When I did speak, to pay homage as a tributary river to an Ocean Queen, she looked through me. Then I had to keep a smile on my face while Baby Charles played a much larger role, which included giving the new Prince of Wales a sword set with diamonds.

That should have been my part, I thought, behind my painful, fixed grin.

Then my younger brother stirred the court to cries of acclaim and delight when he danced prettily with a flock of noble girl-children.

I tried to rejoice for Henry, who played his part with all his accustomed grace and dignity. He triumphed in the tilts like a true warrior prince. He was cheered in the streets. Men threw their hats in the air as he passed on horseback. Women threw him flowers and kisses. He smiled and was kind to those who struggled out of the crowds to touch him. He danced with all the ladies, but most of all with Frances Howard.

I told myself that I must try to be more like him, to rise above my own petty concerns. Watching him smile and shine, you would never have guessed that only a month before, an assassin had broken out of a crowd to kill the king of France, for whom my brother still grieved. You would never have guessed his rage at our father, which he later confided to me in private. The king had cut the prince's budget for the celebrations, blaming the failure of parliament to agree relief from the royal debts.

'And his majesty's reasons for scanting me?' Henry was angrier than I had ever seen him. 'I am mounted too high in the people's love! And for that sin must be punished.'

I scolded myself. I knew I was ignoble. But this private confidence from my brother was my favourite part of the celebrations.

Then, suddenly, Henry cut himself off from me. Something happened to him shortly after his installation as Prince of Wales and I could not learn what it was. He became withdrawn and moody. He slipped away from questions. He no longer laughed at my attempts to amuse him. He even lost his temper unexpectedly when his friends teased him once, as they had always done.

'What ails him?' I begged Sir John Harington one night when he was escorting me back across the park after another glum evening at St James's.

He looked down at me, undecided whether to speak or not.

'Is is that Howard girl?' I demanded.

'Do you know about her, then?'

'I know only that she's dangerous. I fear that she'll either break my brother's heart or ruin his reputation.'

Sir John walked in thoughtful silence. 'His highness keeps his own counsel,' he said at last.

Except to me, I wanted to shout. Except to me. He talks to me. Always until now! I thought my heart would break. I wanted to kill Frances Howard for coming between us. I hated her for having those knowing eyes that suggested female weapons in her armoury that I could not even name.

Harington sighed. 'She did come to St James's several times, rode out with him twice, and went once with him on his barge to Greenwich. But she seems to have stopped coming.'

'Thank God!' I exclaimed before I could stop myself. 'Do you know why? Did my brother send her away, or did she change her mind about him?' Women did not reject an heir to the throne, but Frances Howard did not seem to heed any rules.

I stopped and seized his hand. 'I beg you, Sir John. You're almost kin. Don't try to protect my innocence like your uncle. Or are you obeying my father's orders to keep me ignorant?'

'I would tell you if I knew,' he said unhappily. 'I swear it, your grace. All of us are as perturbed as you. But I don't know.'

I did not dare ask Harington if he thought Frances Howard had taken Henry's maidenhead as she had promised.

I felt grief like that which I imagined would follow a death. I visited my brother at St James's several times but could not reach him. I might, even so, have abandoned all delicacy in my urgent need to make him respond to me, if a further piece of news had not warned me off.

One afternoon, during a picnic on the banks of the Thames, my ladies went into ecstasies of outrage. Frances Tyrrell had just learned from her cousin, who was one of his gentlemen, that Sir Robert Carr had fallen in love. With a married woman, Frances Howard, Countess of Essex.

Poor Henry, I thought. Now sure to be the subject of humiliating gossip, whether he cared for the woman or not.

Even I could recognise dangerously thin ice, cracking in so many different directions at once, with such cold dark currents rushing beneath it, that I dared not move at all.

I felt frozen likewise by the cold torpor that now infected the subject of my marriage. I was beginning to understand that putting royal urgency into action could take a very long time. Marriage negotiations were so protracted, with so many different prospects, and messages took so long to travel back and forth between countries, that I began to fear that I would share the fate of my royal cousin, Arbella Stuart.

Arbella was a plain, quiet, but sometimes erratic woman, who had been at Whitehall for as long as I could remember. Floating in and out of my notice, she trailed after my mother as her waiting woman, carrying her train, or kept to herself in her house at Blackfriars. She was distant royal kin, raised to be queen by an over-ambitious grandmother in Derbyshire. But she never stood as part of the family when we were on show, and her status at court was unclear. She would swallow an insult from the queen without blinking, then take offence at a trifle, like a server giving her the wrong slice of a roast.

My first friendly overtures several years earlier had fallen back at my feet as if I were tossing roses against a pane of glass. Once, provoked by her blandness, I dared to ask her if it were true that she had almost married my father and could therefore have been my mother. She had slammed the door of an empty pleasantry in my face, as I no doubt deserved.

Ever since I could remember, my ladies had whispered that my father kept her constantly on offer as a wife but refused to give her. I wondered if this were also to be a further torment for me that he had forgotten to mention in Coventry.

One night as Anne and I prepared for bed, Tallie told me what a clerk had told her of a letter written by the king to the widowed queen of France. It seemed that my father stubbornly refused to give up on marrying me to the former Dauphin, after all, in spite of the French rebuff.

I added the Melancholy Trout to my list again.

'I almost want to marry and be done with it,' I said dully. Even to the Melancholy Trout who might, at least, be manageable. To any husband so long as he was not Frederick Ulrich of Brunswick. 'It's like knowing that in the next day or two, you are sure to be beheaded. It would be better to end the fear.'

'Don't say such things!' cried Anne, who imagined that she was in love with one of Henry's gentlemen.

Tallie settled on her stool beside the bed and played the first bars of a Scottish folksong I had taught her.

> *'Stop, stop,'* (sang Tallie) *'My father is coming.*
> *Oh Father, hast brought my golden ball*
> *And come to set me free?'*
> *'I've neither brought thy golden ball*
> *Nor come to set thee free*
> *But I have come to see thee hung*
> *Upon this gallows-tree.'*

'How gloomy!' said Anne. 'You'll give us evil dreams.'

At a nod from me, Tallie continued.

'Stop, stop, I see my sweetheart coming!
Sweetheart, hast brought my golden ball
And come to set me free?'
'Aye, I have brought thy golden ball,
And come to set thee free.
I have not come to see thee hung
Upon the gallows-tree.'

'Once, I believed in such tales,' I said.

38

No copy of an old portrait was good enough. The king must have a new one for this suitor. Frederick, Elector Palatine, had confirmed the earlier rumour of his interest in marrying me. His envoy, the Duc de Bouillon, had recently arrived in London with a statement of firm intent. Perhaps. The marriage itself would depend on the negotiated terms.

No miniature portrait would do for Frederick. It seemed that the German state of the Palatine must have me life-size, standing, with the painted image of Richmond Palace behind me, flags flying from the turrets, wrapped in the distant gleam of the Thames. A whole kingdom implied in the image of a girl. The covering of so many square inches seemed to take a very long time.

Being almost exactly my height and shape, Tallie had stood for me for eight days, wearing my gem-encrusted blue satin gown and jewellery while each pearl, lace spider web and glittering, faceted proof of English wealth was recorded. Then the jewellery was removed from her. She was taken out of my clothes and I put them on, still warm from her body.

I stood in the light from a window in the Great Presence

Chamber, watched by ten pairs of male eyes. Once again, I was goods for sale, wrapped up in jewels, rich silken stuffs, military alliances and favourable trade terms with England.

My father watched me. With him were the Duc de Bouillon, the marriage-broker for the Palatine who had brought the news of the German prince's intentions, and Cecil. Among the rest were Sir Francis Bacon, now Solicitor-General, and Sir Robert Carr, who was still my father's chief favourite as he had been for the last three years.

I sniffed the smells of resin and oil, and thought about what I was wearing and whether it had meant something different when Tallie wore it. You didn't have to be a fool to read the message in this display of riches. But what would anyone looking at the picture learn about me?

One of the wires supporting my hair dug into my scalp behind my left ear. My nose itched. My eyes began to water from the itching. I wanted to scream with the effort of keeping still. I turned my head towards the shape of a bird on the window ledge outside.

I gave in and scratched my nose.

'Your grace . . .!' protested the artist. 'I must refine the details of your face. Will you be kind enough to look at the far wall again.'

I shot him with a fire-arrow glance but obeyed. He stared at my nose then touched his brush to the large wooden panel on his easel.

Even looking at the wall, I felt the pressure of eyes on me. Belle had nosed at the hem of my skirts and disappeared under them. I had nowhere to hide.

My father stood with his arms crossed, studying me. Close at his back, Carr, the Golden Weasel, fiddled with the point of his silly new yellow beard. The Duc de Bouillon stood beside the king. I forgot the artist's reprimand and turned my head to look at the little scene more clearly.

The small bent shape of Cecil stood a little aside from them

239

all, farther from the king than Bacon. As he talked to the German duke, my father pointedly ignored his Chief Secretary. Now that I looked, the scene was easy to read. Carr had taken Cecil's place at my father's side, whispering in his ear. Cecil was set at a distance, with Bacon baring his teeth in would-be smiles and shuffling his way forward as if playing a child's stealth game.

I rejected what I thought I saw.

It could not be possible that Wee Bobby had begun to fall from royal favour. The king needed him too much.

Cecil looked pale. A damp sheen glistened on his high fore-head.

The king said something under his breath so that only Carr and de Bouillon could hear. They both laughed loudly. Cecil seemed preoccupied by looking for a handkerchief. Bacon pinched his thin lips and pulled them into a smile, as if he, too, had heard.

I glanced again at Cecil and wondered what the Chief Secretary really thought about the royal children's marriages. I remembered how Henry had said that Cecil did not take sides, that he had his own private intentions for England and used people for that end. I knew that Cecil opposed the Savoy marriage for me but not what part he meant for me to play in his schemes.

Perhaps, like Henry, my father had seen that even he was a mere tool in Cecil's vision for the future of England. But because he lived only to be at the centre of his own world, my father, unlike Henry, would not forgive it.

The little man did look ill.

I tried to imagine Whitehall without Wee Bobby. It was impossible. Both his late father, Lord Burleigh, and then he himself had advised first Elizabeth and now my father. Father and son were both called the *de facto* rulers of England, by friends and enemies alike.

The king would recover from his fit of anger with Cecil, I

240

decided. With his love of constant hunting and his distaste for the details of governing, he needed the little man too much.

I tried to imagine gathering my courage at last and asking Cecil how much he knew about my letter to Henry, and why he had seemed to protect me in Coventry, and what his silence might still cost me.

I looked at the distance between the two cousins now and wondered if Cecil had seen the essay that Bacon had written, being secretly passed around the court. Tallie had brought me a copy. Reading it told me all I needed to know about their rivalry and mutual dislike. Bacon's essay, titled 'On Deformity' argued that outward deformity reflected a man's inward nature.

The Golden Weasel caught my eye as he bent to rest his handsome chin playfully on my father's padded shoulder.

I wish that bottle had scarred that smug, pretty face of yours, I thought. It was hard to believe that such a light brainless creature, with that girl's complexion and pink, petulant mouth, had stolen the love my father should have given Henry.

Does my father know that you love Frances Howard? I asked him silently.

Carr smirked at me across my father's shoulder. Lack of brains had not prevented him from taking on many of the powers that rightfully belonged to the Prince of Wales.

Last year, it was said, Carr had persuaded the king to dissolve Parliament for threatening to criticise my father's Scottish favourites. I had no doubt that Carr dripped poison about my brother into my father's ear.

I held his pale blue eye until he looked away. Soon to be viscount, indeed! Viscount Legs! I thought scornfully. Viscount Oil! Did he pretend secretly to be a prince in my brother's place, just as he begins to advise in place of Cecil?

241

Wee Bobby and I might share a common enemy.

I glanced sideways at the dark awkward shape of my father. I had learned a great deal about him in the past months as I studied him for the gaps in his armour. He was unpredictable, restless and wilful. He showed open disregard for my mother along with a taste for beautiful young men. He gave extravagant gifts to his favourites but borrowed from his courtiers to pay a gaming debt. He had an unshakeable belief in his own wisdom and goodness. He found the details of governing tedious and much preferred to hunt.

Having seen him ride, I suspected that he felt most like a king when mounted on a horse. On horseback, he became a centaur – part man, part noble beast, powerful and graceful, as he could never be on those two awkward legs of his.

'Your grace . . .' said the painter unhappily.

I returned my eyes to the wall.

My father was also a man of hungry scholarship and prolific, if changeable, enthusiasms. Uneasily, I remembered how Henry had once said that I was like a squirrel, always dashing off after some new nut. I did not wish to resemble my father in any way, but he too seemed to have a taste for new nuts.

While we were still in Scotland, it was witchcraft. Wide-eyed and frightened out of my wits, I had read his *Daemonology*, a detailed study of witches and demons.

Then came the proper conduct of princes. Still in Scotland Henry had shown me a copy of the *Basilkon Doron*, the king's admonitory treatise written for his oldest son on the correct behaviour of princes.

'He must think me a fool,' Henry had said unhappily. 'To tell me to keep my clothes neat and my nails short . . . And, listen. ". . . select loyal gentlemen . . ." Does he think me such a gowk that I would seek to be served by traitors?'

Henry turned to another page. 'And here . . . Hunting on horse-back, he permits. But not football or tumbling. I am to use "(although but moderately) running, leaping, wrestling, fencing, dancing and tennis." He even tells me how to rhyme my poetry, should I write it, being sure to choose a worthy subject – nothing that is full of vanity . . . And he warns me to behave with piety and to give thanks to God!'

He shoved the pamphlet at me. 'Not content with giving me this private counsel, he must publish it so that everyone may know how he fears my short-comings! And I must make public show of filial gratitude.'

I detected some good sense in the work as well as condescension but thought it best not to say so. To study the laws of the country, to invite in foreign merchants and to study history for foreign policy, all seemed to me like sound advice for a future king. And in those days, in Scotland, I was still in awe of our father, just as Henry still sought his praise.

'At least he thinks to advise you,' I had said. 'I await similar instructions for a princess.'

Shortly after his accession to the English throne, our father had taken a passion against the smoking of *tabacco*, Walter Ralegh's gift to England from the New World, and published his *Counterblaste to Tabacco*. Even now, six years later, Ralegh was still out of royal favour, and Whitehall courtiers still slipped out into the alleys and gardens to smoke their pipes in secret.

Then, after the Gunpowder Treason, the king turned the force of his mind onto Jesuits and treason. As if his restless wits needed yet more exercise, he also set some two score of scholars to work on a new version of the Bible and began to lecture the Commons on the God-given authority of kingship. But his chief game since the Spanish treaty of 1604 had been to play 'The Peacemaker King' in Europe, and I was a mere piece on his board.

'A handsome lass, is she not?' My father's voice cut through my thoughts. 'Perhaps too costly for your master to maintain?'

I risked a glance.

He nudged de Bouillon and nodded at me. 'She's my paving stone. In my *via media*.' His middle way as he sidled between embattled Catholic emperors and Protestant princes.

'A handsome paving stone,' replied the duke. His eyes were noting every jewel, gold thread, military treaty and trade alliance hanging on my body, lingering on the inventory.

'Worthy of the greatest monarch of Europe,' my father said.

'Yes, she's handsome enough,' the duke answered at last.

I stiffened, suddenly alert to something in his tone.

'She will do very well,' he added. His voice carried more meaning than his words.

I looked him in the eye.

'His highness will be pleased with her face,' said the duke.

'Your grace!' protested the painter.

I looked away. Heat rose from my bodice towards my neck. I was not too innocent to know that the duke's eyes had moved on from my face and were now undressing me. My thoughts began to flap like hens at the sight of a fox.

Trying to keep my head still, I swivelled my glance away from the watching men to the rare, glorious afternoon outside the window.

I tried to think of something else . . . Wainscot needed exercise . . . Distraction wasn't working. I felt coated in slime by the duke's insinuating eyes.

'Do sit down, man!' I heard my father say impatiently.

I watched a servant bring Cecil a stool.

'I beg you, your grace!' cried the painter. 'I am addressing your eyebrows. When you turn your head in the least . . .' With the handle of his brush held between his teeth, he scraped at his panel with a small knife.

'But you re-invent me in any case!' I protested. 'Why must I be still, whilst you do it?'

'A hit!' said my father. Today, he was all noisy good-humour.

'A very pretty hit,' echoed the Golden Weasel.

'On the contrary, your grace.' The painter held his ground. Brush in hand again, he stared hard at a point between my eyes. 'I struggle to do justice to your true loveliness.'

I snorted. For this portrait, my hair had been tortured upward into a great domed sugar loaf in an attempt to make me appear regal. I thought it made me look like a startled acorn.

My bodice stays dug into the top of my belly. I straightened my back and heard the painter sigh.

'Forgive me, sir,' I said. 'I do see your difficulty. I have only to sit still – whereas you must strike the exact balance between telling the truth and flattery.' I wished at once that I had kept my mouth shut.

'*Brava*!' said the duke.

'Expound, Bessie!' my father ordered.

My skirts bulged and heaved as Belle woke and turned around under my petticoats. I shifted my feet to give her room, ignoring the artist, who flicked his eyes towards Heaven.

'Expound,' prompted my father. 'Display for the duke your wit as well as your face!'

Instantly, my mind became a blank.

'Tell, tell!' cried the Golden Weasel.

I thought I detected sympathy in Cecil's eyes.

The painter laid down his brush in resignation.

'At this moment,' I said stiffly, 'the artist is far more important than I am . . .'

'That's your proposition,' my father interrupted. 'Get to the argument!'

Belle flopped across my feet again. I groped for coherent thought. All the time, I could see the duke watching me avidly. Amused. Curious. Judging.

'My portraits are sent abroad to foreign princes or dukes, to influence negotiations for my marriage,' I said. 'By shaping the image in the portrait, the artist's brush therefore shapes the negotiations.'

'Yet another unproved proposition,' said the king. 'Give us an instance. We wait!'

I unclenched my teeth. 'A blob of paint on the tip of my chin might lower my worth in Heidelberg.'

The duke laughed.

'An over-sensuous curve to my upper lip could raise questions about the diplomatic honesty of the English in Savoy.' I stared at the far wall.

'Conclude,' said my father.

I thought that I had concluded. 'If a man can be burnt at the stake for misrepresenting an angel,' I ventured wildly, 'as I have heard can happen in Italy, what might the penalty be for smudging a princess?'

'Nay, that's mere rhetorical flourish, not a conclusion.' But my father looked at the duke in triumph.

'Both handsome and spirited,' said the duke. 'She will serve very well indeed. The Palsgrave is young and will need every encouragement.'

I felt myself go still.

My father and the Weasel laughed loudly as men do when more is meant than is said. Cecil looked at the floor.

For the last three years, I had been wilfully blind.

With another laugh, they were gone. I looked after them.

It was like looking for the first time at the truth of my own death. Under my skirt, Belle sighed and shifted her warm weight on my feet again, a small hot point on my cold body.

'. . . will serve very well.'

Serve. To render service. To be used.

I saw what I had managed, somehow, not to see, just as I had not seen danger when Digby stepped into my way. I understood what Frederick Ulrich had meant by 'more', which I had refused then to understand even when I felt it in his clumsy urgency, smelled it rising from his clothes and tasted it on my cut lip. The voice and eyes of the Duc de Bouillon had finally cracked my shell of wilful ignorance.

Every brush stroke recording my face, my bosom, or my waist was a message in obscene code, expressing my suitability, or lack of it, for that thing that must happen to me in marriage, whether I wished it or not.

What I was really for. The reason for that over-loud male laugh. The adult secret that I would soon be forced to share. For the first time, I asked myself what exactly marriage would mean for me beyond exile and loneliness. For the first time, I thought that the raw brutal facts, learned from watching animals in fields and stable yards, might apply to me, as well as to beasts.

But surely, it must be different for people! I thought. Not violent like the breeding of horses, filled with huge dark shapes beneath the stallions' bellies, and biting and squealing so that you feared the mares would be killed. Nor almost comical like the vacant-eyed pumping of a dog mounting a bitch. There must be more to learn, that would allow room for the human soul, a way for this soft flesh in its jewel-crusted gown and this bundle of fragile thoughts that was me to survive the dreadful invasion.

Liking, or not liking, my future husband took on urgent new meaning. My certainty that I would not survive marriage to Frederick Ulrich had been right.

Belle yelped and emerged from under my skirts.

'Forgive me!' I bent to scoop her up. I pressed her stepped-on paw to my lips, then buried my face against her curly back.

Just as urgent was the question of why some women failed at what they were good for, being wives. Why some, but not others, were humiliated and cast off. Even queens could fail, like Anne of Cleves. It was suddenly clear from what I had just heard that such women had not provided the necessary 'encouragement'. They had not done 'very well'. They had not served. I could already imagine my father's rage and scalding mockery if I were to be rejected and returned. Frances Howard would no doubt know all the answers, but I was not Frances Howard.

A strong smell of resin reached me. When I looked up, the painter was cleaning his brushes with turpentine-soaked rags.

'I can't stand any longer today,' I said.

'I had gathered as much, your grace.' Although I was certain that he would have liked to throw one of his stone pestles at me, the painter managed a thin smile and deep bow as I left.

Outside the Presence Chamber, I stopped, with Belle in my arms, uncertain where to go next. I felt awash with ignorance again. It was intolerable. I turned into the long river gallery that led away from the king's chambers.

Most of all, I was angry with myself. My only true talent was lying to myself. I had been a child playing at learning about the world, spying and prying with Tallie's help, in order to defy my father. Flattering myself that I was suited to be the First Daughter of England, while, in truth, I was only an ignorant girl who knew nothing and had nothing at all to say about her own life. I didn't know the first thing about my chief duty, the only thing I was good for. My maid most likely knew more than I did.

I climbed a stone staircase up onto the open walk on the gallery roof, where I stood looking out over the Thames. For a long while, I watched shards of broken sunlight jittering on the wind-stirred water. I breathed in the balmy air. Once again, I was calmed by the river and the great open space beyond it. I watched the criss-crossing wherries filled with people going busily about their own lives, lives just as important to them as mine was to me.

I might be the First Daughter of England, whose life had never been her own to choose. I could, however, choose what to make of the life I had.

'No more of feeling sorry for myself,' I told Belle after a time. 'No more wolf crouched with its leg caught in a trap, waiting helplessly for the hunter.' I thought of my mother, and her helplessness, and the losses that had made her refuse to love.

I won't end up like her! I vowed again. I had let myself forget my secret, learned from my meeting with Digby in the forest. Though I was young, I was not powerless.

The more I learned, the more I could control. And what I could not control, I could at least be prepared for. Willing or unwilling, my heart would be ready.

Thoughtfully, I continued to watch the distant people in the wherries. My eyes followed the waving red feather of one man's hat all the way across the river, from the Whitehall water steps below me to the far shore.

I need to talk to a man, I decided. For a start. One whom I could trust to tell me the secrets of men's minds and what they expected, but without laughing at me and making me feel a fool. He might even be able to tell me – if I ever found one of my suitors tolerable – how I should go about making the man want me urgently enough to override my father's wilful indecision.

Briefly, I considered asking John Harington. But, in or out of humour, Henry was the only male I could wholly trust.

39

I found him after supper in the Privy Garden, marching briskly around the perimeter as he often did. Two of his hounds trotted at his heels. Some evenings, one or more of his gentlemen marched with him. But tonight both his attendants and mine were content to sit gossiping on benches in the last of the sun, to wander pensively along the water rill, or flirt in the deepening shadows of the big sundial.

He did not look at me but did slow his pace when I dropped in beside him. Even so, I had to hold my farthingale firmly to keep it from swinging as I trotted to keep up.

'Please speak to me,' I begged. 'I need you to answer some questions.'

Henry raised his eyebrows but did not reply. We rounded the corner at the farthest end of the garden.

'Questions about men,' I said, breathing hard. 'And marriage.'

Henry stopped marching and stared at me. 'What?'

'You're the only man I dare ask. What really happens in marriage, for example?'

His face reddened.

'I know that you're bedded,' I said quickly. 'But what does that mean, exactly? Consummation? For humans, I mean, not in the stable yard. I can't believe that it's the same.' I felt hot. Blood drummed in my ears. 'Does it hurt terribly when a maidenhead is broken? How exactly does that happen? What will be expected of me?'

'We shouldn't speak of such things.'

'If we can't, then who else can I speak to?' I made my face as miserable and desperate as I could manage.

He scowled. 'Ask one of your ladies.'

'And expose my ignorance?'

Not even to Tallie, not on this question. Tallie knew so much about me while I knew so little about her. I might be the princess, but the power of knowledge was entirely hers. From time to time the voice of Lady Harington still muttered that I should keep Tallie in her place, that nothing good could come of upsetting the natural order.

'I scarcely rule my ladies as it is,' I said, 'without giving them one more reason to laugh at me behind their hands.'

He knelt down and busied himself scratching the ears of his hound. The other hound licked his ear.

'You already know the worst about me,' I said. 'And have sworn that you loved me all the same. If you love me still, help me!' I stooped down in a pool of skirts and stroked the dog's back so that our hands moved in unison.

'Dearest Hal, please! You always say that knowledge underpins true power. And you have Wee Bobby as your tutor.' I watched our rings, moving together. 'Even I can see how he's building your power with all his letters and news from his intelligencers.'

Absently, I felt the second hound push its nose under my other hand. 'I don't have a Cecil,' I said. 'You must be my teacher.' I took Henry's hand from the dog's head and held it in both of mine. 'I fear what I don't know. Please, dearest brother! Is fearful ignorance what you wish for your sister? Should the Queen of the Americas not know all that she can?'

251

Henry pulled away his hand. 'You already know the sad truth from the stable yard,' he said stiffly. 'I fear that men are no better than the beasts, however much they deceive themselves with talk of love, and however much the poets may dress it up with fine words.'

Like the beasts after all, I thought. Like dogs and horses. But this unwelcome information still left me confused and fearful. What dreadful reality needed deceit and fine words to dress it up? And, however beastly, man could not be like both a stallion and a miniature greyhound at the same time. In body or soul.

I knew that I should not ask. I knew what Henry would say. I swallowed. 'May I see your cock?'

'No!' Henry drew a deep breath and stood up. 'Of course not!'

'Where is the sin?' I asked, scrambling to my feet. 'We are the same flesh, brother and sister, two halves of a single soul. Babes from the same womb.'

He turned away from me.

'Look!' I pulled at the ring that he had given me in Edinburgh. 'I am giving this to you now!'

'Don't be a fool!'

We walked on a few paces in silence.

'Please, Hal! Your beloved little sister is so afraid – more afraid than you could ever be, of anything.'

We walked a little farther. Then he exhaled sharply. He stopped walking, wavered. Exhaled again. Then, scarlet-faced, he turned his back on the garden and motioned me to stand in front of him. Reluctantly, with another look over his shoulder, he untied the placket of his trousers and fished inside his underclothes. 'There,' he said. 'Not much to fear, is it? I hope your anxiety is settled now.'

I stared. 'But how on earth do you insert that inside anything?' Let alone break anything. I thought.

'If the woman is desired, it stiffens.'

'But what if the woman's not desired?' I couldn't imagine

the Melancholy Trout desiring anyone. 'Why did the duke say that the Palatine would need every encouragement? What did he mean?'

Henry fumbled in his haste to tuck himself away. 'That's enough! I can't tell you any more!' He finished lacing his placket.

I knew my brother too well to push him any further. Had he done it with Frances Howard as rumour would have it? I suddenly wasn't so certain.

'Have you . . .?' I began, in spite of myself.

'I said, that's enough!' He set off so fast that I had to let him go alone. I sank down onto a bench and pretended to study the night sky. My brother had raised as many questions as he had answered.

40

After several hours of tossing in the dark and listening to Anne's snores, I got out of bed and shook Tallie's shoulder gently. I felt her flinch and freeze before coming fully awake.

'It's only me,' I whispered. 'I have questions.'

'In the middle of the night?'

'Please.'

We huddled with coverlets around our shoulders, in front of the banked fire in my little closet. Tallie knelt to prod the coals and light a candle.

'How does a man stiffen if he doesn't desire the woman?' I burst out.

Tallie stopped lighting a second candle. Her shoulders tightened. 'Why do you think I'd know that?'

'I don't think it. I tried talking to Henry. You're the only one left whom I can ask.' I watched her light the candle.

She looked up at me with narrowed eyes. 'That's the only reason?'

'God's Body! If you won't answer my questions, who will?'

The pale tent of her coverlet rocked slightly, forward and back in front of the fire. I heard her suck the air in past her teeth and blow it out again. 'I can't,' she said. 'Ask anyone else.'

'I'm to be married to a stranger,' I said. 'How do I know he'll like me? What if he rejects me as King Henry did the princess from Cleves?' I pulled my coverlet tightly around me.

'He'll like you.' She continued to stare at the fire. I watched her absently rubbing the pale ovals of the nails of her left hand with her right thumb. In the orange firelight, the scars on the back of her hand stood out against their black shadows.

'You can't know that!' I said. 'And even if he likes me, I'm afraid of being ignorant of my part. I know almost nothing of the world, or those who live in it.'

She still said nothing. Her thumb still rubbed.

'Please, Tallie! Why won't you answer? How much do you know?' I heard her give a little snort.

'Hey, ho,' she said to herself. She turned her head and looked at me for a long time across her tented shoulder. She looked away again. 'Yes. I do know. More than you may imagine. You don't know what you're asking.'

She shook her head to herself. 'I'm not certain I can bring myself to be your teacher.' She dropped her forehead onto her hands and rocked again.

I stayed silent. Her argument was with herself, not me.

'If you truly want to banish all ignorance,' she said at last. 'You can have your wish to visit Southwark . . . I can't teach you but I can take you to the oracles, who will tell you more than you'll ever wish to know about playing your part. Give me a few days to prepare our visit. I'll tell you when all is ready.'

She wrapped her arms around her knees and dropped her head onto them.

41

Tallie shook me awake. She was still in her nightshift and robe. 'The king has sent for you.'

'Now?' I asked in sleepy alarm. 'Before breaking my fast?'

'At once, his footman says.'

I swung my legs out of bed. 'A footman, you say? Not a man-at-arms?'

Anne groaned and lifted a face creased with wrinkles from her pillow. 'What's happening?' She squinted through the parted bed curtains at the grey diamond-paned window. 'It's scarcely light yet.'

'Her grace must dress to see the king,' said Tallie.

'It's very early for his majesty to begin receiving.' Anne sat up, jolted wide awake. 'Aren't you alarmed?'

'Of course I am.'

'I'm sure all will be well.' She sounded very like her uncle, my guardian, as she mouthed this reassurance.

She and Tallie cobbled me into a gown while my maid tried to comb my hair. I washed my face, taking care not to spot my bodice with water, and wiped the crumbs of sleep from my eyes.

Tallie's hands were cold when they touched my skin. I saw again how many risks she had run for me.

'Is a reason given?' I asked.

She shook her head. 'No reason.'

The doors of my ladies' rooms were still closed when I rushed out of my lodgings behind the footman, into the gallery that led over the Holbein Gate towards the Riverside. Crossing a courtyard already buzzing with servants, I felt a chilly, early summer drizzle on my face and wished for my cloak. As I hurried through my father's presence chambers, I saw that the portrait of the Dauphin had been removed from the sideboard.

Perhaps I had been detected after all, in my livery and boots.

Perhaps, for a reason I did not yet understand, he had decided at last to confront me with my letter to Henry.

The king was half-dressed in stockings and breeches but with his night-shirt over them and a long gown slung on top of it all. His sound foot wore a boot, his gouty one a soft slipper. There were only four others present in the royal bedchamber: Sir Robert Carr, the Archbishop of London, the king's groom of the bedchamber, and a boy kneeling to coax the fire into warmth and light. The day was still too young for petitioners. In any case, my father disliked the ceremonial pomp of his Tudor predecessors as much as he feared assassins springing out of a crowd.

He did not let me finish my curtsey. 'Y'haven't done it too, have ye?'

'Sir?' My head jerked up. My curtsey wobbled.

'Don't think to imitate your cousin. You'll succeed no more than she did.'

I straightened and looked at Carr and the Archbishop, who both seemed to know what he was talking about.

'Which cousin?' I asked.

'That damned whore with that butter-wouldn't-melt face! That treacherous, would-be queen! Don't try to play the simpleton, you little polecat. You know very well that I mean your cousin Arbella.'

'I know nothing of the sort!' I said hotly. 'What has she done, that you fear I might imitate?'

'Marry behind my back!' my father shouted. 'And mind your tongue, lassie, or I'll have you whipped for insolence.'

The Archbishop took pity on my confusion and stepped in smoothly. 'The king's advisors in the Privy Council are outraged on his behalf. The Lady Arbella has married without royal permission. To William Seymour. There is concern that they might unite their followers against the king and make an attempt to claim the throne.'

'The Lady Arbella?' I repeated. Defiant marriage seemed an unlikely crime for that dumpy, slightly sour, moody woman.

'You haven't married another bloody Seymour, have ye?' demanded the king. 'Or a Howard? Your mother hasn't been plotting behind my back to marry you off to some Scottish duke? Don't think I'll let you ever again defy my choice of husband for you. Ye'll not ruin me in Europe by secretly hustling some upstart into your marriage bed.'

I stared silently at the floor. I could not deny my defiance over Brunswick, but the injustice of his second warning made my face and neck burn.

'At least this will put a stop to any talk of a Seymour marriage for you!' said my father.

'It was never my talk,' I raised my head and met his eye. 'My cousin is welcome to him! Perhaps she could be persuaded to marry the rest of my suitors as well!'

There was a long and dangerous silence.

'Let me make myself clear,' the king said at last. 'I know that none of you can be trusted. I've kept too light a hand on your rein.' The coldness of his heavy-lidded eyes withered my angry words like a winter blast. 'I've played Solomon long enough. I shall choose you a husband before the year is done. And, by God, you'll marry him!'

He limped closer and jabbed his finger at my face. 'Don't you ever again dare to defy me. If you ever again presume to tell me, as you did at Theobald's, that you refuse to obey me, I will clap you under arrest as fast as I have your cousin and her husband.'

I pinched my lips tight against a reply.

'And ye'll stay locked in the Tower,' he said. 'Even if the mobs seduced by all your smiles and waving come to bay for your release. I rule England, not wilful, whoreish women. Not Parliament. Not the mob. By the will of God, I rule. D'ye understand me?'

I nodded.

'Speak up! I cannae hear ye!'

'Yes, father. I understand.'

'Good.' He turned his back and stumped back to his chair. 'Now trot off before you enrage me again.'

As I curtsied again, to his back, I thought that my father sounded frightened as well as angry.

Now that my father had forced it to my attention, I saw how much Arbella and I were alike, in spite of our difference in age. Two unmarried royal females, both raised in isolation away from the sophistications of the court. Trying to find a place to put our feet, when our lives could be changed at any moment, without our consent. Both of us always on offer for marriage. Neither of us ever given.

I saw now that we shared the same blue eyes, that her dull reddish hair might once have been as bright as mine. I could feel my mouth and cheeks settle into the sour, sullen lines of her face. I did not want to end up like my mother. I did not want to become Arbella, neither.

But this new, reported Arbella was far more interesting

than the old one. This Arbella had dared to challenge her fate – and my father.

'If you want to be entertained,' whispered Tallie when I returned, 'spend this morning in the little presence chamber with your ladies. Everyone's in a furore of outrage, delight and political speculation, even before breakfast.'

'I'll eat in here alone, thank you.' I saw her face change when she caught my dark humour. She took the food from the chamberer, set it in front of me on the table in my little closet, and left me.

On reflection, and away from my father's alarming presence, I felt less surprise at what Arbella had done. Imagining myself in her place, I saw that she had been too quiet, too detached. I remembered that, under her bland surface, she sometimes seemed to give off a subterranean hum like a locked cellar full of wasps.

After I had toyed with my bread and watered ale, I went into my bedchamber and joined Tallie, who was on duty for me just inside the door, eavesdropping on the Herd gathered outside in my small presence chamber.

'But she's such an odd, secret creature.' Frances Tyrrell's voice pretended surprise.

'I don't believe it. She's almost thirty years old!' Philadelphia Carey, who was still only fifteen.

'You can still love at thirty,' said Lucy, Countess of Bedford, who had joined them.

'It's not love! Her ambition has burst out at last. Why else marry a . . .' The Other Frances stopped abruptly when I entered. The name 'Seymour' floated silently in the air.

'Have you heard the astonishing news, your grace?' asked Lucy, resigned to her repeated role as messenger.

'That someone once rumoured to be my suitor has married my cousin?' I heard the collective intake of breath. 'Why ever would she do such a mad thing as to marry?'

There was a moment of uncertainty while they assessed my tone.

'From ambition, your grace!' said Other Frances. 'Everyone knows that she's been scheming all these years, playing a deep waiting game.' There were murmurs of assent.

'That's unkind!' protested Anne, her pink cheeks hot with fervour. 'I'm sure that she fell in love and was overcome by reckless passion!'

'It's a pity then that they scarce had time to enjoy their wedding night before being arrested,' said Lucy. 'And doubly sad when she has at last found a flesh-and-blood husband instead of one born from her wishful imagination.'

'Perhaps she simply grew tired of doing nothing,' I said. Reaching the age of thirty and seeing nothing ahead but more of exactly the same life for the next thirty years. Unmarried, playing in masques, carrying my mother's train.

All eyes turned towards me.

'A dangerous impatience,' said Lucy. 'I hear she's under house arrest with Lord Parry in Lambeth, and her new husband is in the Tower.'

'They'll both lose their heads,' said Frances Tyrrell with suppressed relish. Her freckles stood out against a face white with excitement. 'Marrying without the sovereign's consent is a capital crime, if you're royal.'

I looked at her sharply.

'You can't be executed for love!' cried Anne.

'Love is dangerous,' said Lucy dryly.

'But she didn't act from love,' insisted Other Elizabeth, stepping in to support Frances Tyrrell.

As I listened to their gossip, I found myself secretly cheering on this new Arbella, this defiant, scheming, ambitious traitor. I wanted to ask her why she had been so eager to under-take the realities of marriage at such great risk to her freedom, if not her life.

'Love is dangerous,' Lucy, Countess of Bedford had said.

She seemed to be in the business of giving warnings. I wondered if she meant this as a warning to me.

But the lack of love can be just as dangerous, I thought, thinking of my mother.

After breakfast, with Arbella and her extraordinary act still racketing around in my head, I sat in my outer presence chamber and forced myself to be civil to a string of petitioners. Among them were five men who wanted to place their sons or daughters in my household, a man with a peacock and hen for sale and a young silversmith who begged a commission for buttons. Then Tallie arrived to say that we would go to Southwark the following night.

42

On her advice, I confided at once in Anne. Not the whole story, but enough that Anne knew to cover my absence the following evening.

'But what am I to say when someone sees that you are gone?' she asked

'No one must know.' I gave her a purse to encourage blindness in my chamberer and maid. After discussion, we decided that another attack of royal megrim would not over-stretch her mendacity.

'How exciting!' she said wistfully. 'I would like to come along.' She half-smiled. 'I always used to go with you when you set off on some mad venture or other.'

'You will play the most vital part here.' I leaned closer and whispered. 'Furthermore, you'll be free to flirt with you-know-who, without my hawk-eye watching you.'

I wasn't certain which of several 'you-know-whos' I meant, but my words had a gratifying effect.

'Oh,' she gasped. 'How did you know? Please don't say anything to anyone. My aunt would be furious.'

'Your secret is safe with me,' I said truthfully. 'Just as mine is with you.'

* * *

Tallie looked more and more grim as the wherry took us across the Thames.

'Oars!' shouted distant voices on the banks. 'Oars, here!'

Our wherry slid through the dark water with little surges, propelled by a single scull at the stern.

Giddy with sudden freedom, I watched the pulse of the bow waves and sniffed the smell of water, coal smoke, fish, damp wood and rotting water weed, with the occasional whiff of sewage. The sparks of boat lanterns on the river crossed and re-crossed, weaving a thick net of lights, doubled by their reflections in the water. As we moved away from the Whitehall Stairs, the stink of sewage receded and was replaced by a new, open smell that made me think of the sky.

I felt very odd and unexpectedly happy to be wearing Peter Blank's clothes again. I had even borrowed his name. Peter. No longer Elizabeth. Elizabeth was left behind in Whitehall with a terrible megrim. In spite of my apprehension about the exact nature of Tallie's oracle, I felt utterly content, suspended for a moment outside my life. On my way to entering the mysteries, at last. My Whitehall apprehension had become a slightly dreamy acceptance of whatever might come next.

I watched Tallie from under my hat. I did not want to ask what troubled her lest she change her mind about our venture. I looked past her at the growing lights of Southwark. Our wherry bumped gently against some water stairs.

She looked up at the crowds on the embankment above. I heard her exhale.

'Bankside,' she said flatly. 'Welcome to the company of other suburb sinners. I fear you'll most likely learn more here than you wish.'

She looked back across the river. Before she could decide to go back after all, I leapt from the boat onto the damp mossy steps.

She caught my arm as I slipped on some wet weed.

Behind us across the river, on the far side of the locked Bridge, the City, like Whitehall, was asleep. Its streets were silent except for the Watch and wakeful dogs, lit only by the lanterns hung by law outside each house. Anyone breaking the curfew moved swiftly and spoke in murmurs, as Tallie and I had done.

At the top of the stairs, I watched her look around the wide, cobbled waterside street. Here on Bankside, it was a fair at midnight. In its lawless Ward Without, London exploded with a shout and threw its hat into the air.

I stared about me, too, feeling a little dizzy. At court, the crowds and drunken revels always swirled around a single defined centre, the authority of the crown, even when the king was reeling drunk. Here, noise and motion were all hugger-mugger, racing in every direction at once, around us on all sides.

I wanted just to stand and look, feeling invisible and safe in Peter's trousers, hat and a cloak. Peter Blank could gobble up and remember all these new sights and sensations that the Princess Elizabeth would never be allowed to taste.

'I'm not certain . . .' Tallie began, looking back down at our wherry, now taking on passengers for the return crossing.

'I am,' I said.

Reluctantly, she turned away from the boat.

'Look at them all,' she said, as if to herself. She pressed her fingertips to her mouth and stared about her, just as I had done. But before she came to me, this had been her world, I thought.

I could not imagine how it might be to live here.

Beggars swarmed like gnats around us and other newcomers, mostly men, who climbed the stairs from other boats. Some already staggered with drink and breathed out fumes of wine and sack. But I also saw women in costly clothes stepping from wherries onto the river steps, wearing masks, offering their hands to the young men in frayed coats who skipped after them. Older men pushed past with avid mouths above fine linen collars and heavy loose gowns.

Tallie snarled at a grimy child beggar, waved away a vendor of white clay *tabacco* pipes and set off at a fierce pace upstream, away from the Bridge, with her hat pulled low over her face.

I had to run after her. I wanted to say something, to connect us again, but the gap between us felt too wide. What must she have thought of me when we first met, with my ladies and gowns, my careless indifference to everyone around me and my impertinent, invading questions? Small wonder that she had raised her hedgehog spines!

Men in silks and men in filthy leather sat drinking outside crowded taverns and inns. Women leaned on their shoulders. Other women, not so fine as the arrivals at the stairs, strolled beside the water with seeking glances. Men with watchful eyes leaned on walls. A gang of Flemings pushed past us, shouting and waving wine bottles, calling for a boat back to London. I heard Dutch, French, German and Italian, and tongues I didn't recognise. I saw white faces, pink faces, black faces and every shade in between.

I smelt the sweetness of burning *tabacco*. A forest of pale tendrils twisted up from the white clay pipes of waterside smokers perched on barrels. Inside the inns, smoke from still more pipes and from burning fires hung like a fog. Clearly, my father's *Counterblaste* against the terrible demon of *tabacco*, had had little effect here. I wondered what he thought of this disregard for his orders, when he came to Southwark for the bear-baiting.

I breathed in other smells of roasting meat, charred fat, piss and ale, coal smoke, wood smoke, and a dense reek of human ordure and sweat.

My ears throbbed at the din. Shouted greetings. Calls from the water, 'Oars! Oars here!' Bellows of rage and curses flung after a dog that slipped past our legs with a chop snatched from a plate. Fiddles warred discordantly from inside the different inns, largely drowned in any case by the shouting of filthy rounds and glees by those who sat drinking in the street.

The sound of curses mixed with thuds came from a piece of open ground to my left. There I saw a man standing balanced on one leg, his body twisted into an unlikely position, his eyes following his ball in a game of bowls. Then mocking shouts and the exchange of money began. Something familiar at last.

'Is there no curfew here?' I asked Tallie when I caught up with her.

'Yes.' She dodged around a seller of broken meats and rushed on. 'But no one cares to try to enforce it.'

I looked up at a small unexpected sound, fragile but insistent in the street-level din. Above my head, a finch fretted 'chip, chip' in a cage hanging outside an upper window.

Through it all wove the constant, bellowed orders of vendors to buy, buy, buy! Trays and baskets were shoved in my way. 'What d'ye lack?' 'What d'ye lack?' Drums? Little dogs? Birds for ladies?

I could have bought rat traps, love potions, meat pies, fresh water, or the services of a scribe. By the sign he wore, I learned that I could hire a former soldier, now without employment since my father's peace with Spain, to be my bailiff or watchman. Or I could buy a watch of the purest gold. Or fish hooks.

Or an assassin, I thought, dropping my eyes before one chilly gaze. I saw now why my father always took a pack of armed men when he left in his royal barge for the Southwark bear-baiting.

I eyed a man vomiting into the river. He wore ragged wool breeches. I thought of my father on his back at Theobald's, spewing puddles into his slashed silk velvet sleeves. Appetites did not change with wealth and power.

My eager curiosity began to darken. Passing alleys, I looked away from eyes that touched mine. I felt suddenly too costly in dress and too well-fed. I began to see that those who looked like me were the prey. They brought their appetites here to Bankside where hunger fed on hunger, thinking that they would feed. And became easy victims for every Southwark predator who offered to feed them.

Here on Bankside was all the dissolution I had ever seen at court, without any of the riches. Every corner and narrow alley was filled with bodies, some asleep, others arranging nests in piles of rags, nursing babies, picking at sores, staring into space.

Everywhere I looked, I began to see how sex ruled appetites, that thing I feared, the thing I had come to study. I saw it in the eyes of the leaning women and the strolling ones, and in the heaving shadows of the side streets.

I was still trying to imagine Tallie in this place before she came to Whitehall. I tried to see her among these women, and to fit the girl who must have lived here with the strange magical creature who had first entered my door.

Then I saw a pocket being picked. And remembered Tallie's skills with portraits and copied letters.

She must have felt something of my thoughts, because she paused in her march and gave me an odd smile over her shoulder. 'I escaped. Imagine that!'

Before she had gone four more strides, two women stepped in front of her, blocking her way. 'A black devil!' said one. She leaned closer to peer into Tallie's face. 'And, I do believe, a cross-threaded bitch as well!'

I walked up beside Tallie.

'A pair of 'em!' cried the first woman. 'We won't have doxy cheats here.' She pushed her face into mine. 'Gentry punks!' Her breath smelled like a dung hill.

'Trying to steal our livelihood,' said the second woman. 'This is our patch. Do you get what I say?'

Tallie raised her hands. No quarrel.

'Get out, or we'll tell our man to cut you.'

Tallie nodded curtly. She stepped forward, forcing the women to let us pass.

'Black witch!' muttered one of them. Glancing back, I saw her fork her fingers against the evil eye.

I found that my legs were shaking slightly but Tallie marched on without looking back. 'This may prove to be dangerous learning that we're after,' she muttered.

A little farther on, a deep rich bass voice, as fine as any I had heard at Whitehall, cut through the clamour. I stopped at the edge of a small crowd. A short, fat man stood on a barrel, singing the history of *'Clymme of the Clough'*. His voice steadied me and lifted my spirits again.

While I fumbled in my purse for a few pence to buy a copy of his ballad, a mangy cur sniffed at my boots. Looking down at its ragged pelt and its ribs, I could not help thinking of Belle and Cherami, plump and clean, and most likely asleep on the foot of my bed.

'What the devil are you doing?' Tallied hauled me roughly away by the arm. 'That's danger over there!'

I followed her eyes.

'Don't gawp, for God's sake!' She linked arms with me – two friends out for an evening stroll. 'Don't even look his way!'

At a table outside an inn, sat a tall, broad-shouldered man, ponderous with arrogant command. Once handsome, his face was now badly scarred. Before him stood a much smaller man, head down, hat in hand. Other petitioners waited their turn. I risked a snatched glimpse as we passed. He reminded me of my father receiving favour-seekers at court, or a judge delivering a sentence.

A pair of women, waiting their turn to speak to him, stared as we passed, then put their heads close and muttered.

Tallie kept her head down and tightened her grip on my arm. 'Dear God . . .' she murmured to herself. 'I've taken leave of my senses!'

'Who was . . .?'

She dragged me past two more taverns before she answered under her breath.

'That was "their man" . . . the one those whores threatened would cut us. The upright man of the ward. Takes whatever he wants . . . demands his share of all the thieves' takings.' She swallowed. 'He breaks all new whores. Those women back there, waiting to speak to him, knew us for female . . . I had forgot how sharp the eyes are here.'

She glanced back over her shoulder. 'What if he had spied us and decided that he wanted you? I should never have brought you here. I forgot too much.'

'He wouldn't dare harm us when he learned who I am,' I said, a little out of breath from keeping up with her.

'Oh, my poor chook,' she said. 'He'd enjoy you all the more – if he believed you, which he wouldn't.' She shook her head. 'I feared all the wrong things . . . Then he'd most likely cut your throat and throw you in the river. Who would you call to protect you?'

'I'd tell him what would happen to him.'

'And he'd howl with mirth. And call you mad. Here on Bankside, my boy, you're just a nameless footman from the wrong side of the river.'

She stopped and turned me to face her. I looked at her more closely. I had never seen fear in her eyes before and began to understand the enormity of what she had undertaken.

'My la . . . Peter . . . This is not Whitehall. And not a jape. I thought to lift your spirits. I've already let it go too far.' She took my arm to turn us back.

'Aren't we near?' I asked.

Reluctantly, she pointed ahead to a large, white house set inside its own high walls. I now saw the risk she was taking in bringing me here. If any mischance struck the first daughter of England and Scotland, Tallie would be responsible. And the upright man might have relished having her too. I had forgot that she could not easily refuse a request from me.

I didn't know what to say. 'You know better than I do,' I said at last. 'I'll do as you decide.'

She stood staring silently at the white house. 'You'd go back now, if I said?' she asked.

'Yes.' Hard as it was to say, I meant it.

She wavered, not looking at me now. 'I must make myself very clear. You do understand, don't you, the nature of the promised oracle? I'm taking you to a brothel.'

'I think that I guessed.'

She still stood, looking at the house, undecided. Then she snorted. She pulled her hat lower over her face and shook her head.

We walked on towards the white house hidden behind its wall.

We had left the worst noise of Bankside behind us. The twin towers of Lambeth Palace were a dark shadow ahead of us on the bend in the river, the inns were larger and set in their own gardens. The waterside here was dark, frequented mainly by strolling couples, foraging dogs and the occasional purposeful walker headed either upstream for Lambeth and beyond, or downstream towards Greenwich and the sea.

She stared up at the tall, white façade and stepped gables beyond the gated bridge.

'Hey ho,' she said. 'Fish Pool House. Here I am again.'

But she wasn't there with me at all.

43

TALLIE

I see the smouldering looks launched by the whores at the richly-dressed newcomer and the way he ignores them all. While Mrs Taft is still oozing welcome at him and all those looks bounce off him, I close my book, slip through the door into the gardens behind the former manor house, and crouch behind a rose hedge. I had seen his eyes pick me out from the others.

'Tallie? Little Tallie? Where are you, sweet?' Mrs Taft calls from the back terrace, terribly civil.

If I run, I'll never get away. Stand out too much in any crowd, even here in Southwark. His eyes would have picked me out, no matter what he had come for.

Feet crunch closed on the garden path.

'Where's that little black cow?' 'Sister' Meg who works in a wimple and robes, for the fervent Protestants who like to fight religious wars by pretending to ravish a Catholic nun. Now just the other side of the rose hedge. 'Puss?' she calls. 'Here, puss! You must put on your best gown and pack your things. Your time has come at last!'

I stand up.

'Got her,' Meg calls to Mrs Taft. 'Our priceless little Moorish virgin.'

She grabs me by the arm. 'It's you he wants. Time to earn back the cost of all those fancy singing lessons and dancing masters.'

I jerk my arm free and give Meg the Look. Don't mean to. It just happens. All the rage and fear swirling around in my chest twist together and rise up in a dark fierce beam, up through my throat and behind my cheek bones, and shoot out of my eyes. My eye beams feel like hot steel, like long pointed spears. I stand firm, like a swordsman, holding my blade poised at the enemy's throat.

Fear flickers in Meg's eyes. She lets go of my arm and wipes her hand on her skirt.

'Chook, you must be careful how you glare at people,' Mrs Taft once told me. 'Or you'll be taken for a witch.' Too late now.

No one told me where I'm going. Nor for how long. I glance at the man sitting beside me in the private wherry. He keeps space between us even when the boat rolls on a wave and he could easily let himself be thrown against me. He doesn't lay a hand on my leg, nor even touch my hand. He keeps his eyes averted, almost as if he wishes he weren't there. He does not behave as if he means to bed me. Perhaps he's only the agent for the man who's willing to pay a fortune to take a black maidenhead.

Either way, he bought me. I saw him put the gold coins into Mrs Taft's hand. Far too many for a single night, intact maidenhead or not. My lute lies in my lap and my small bundle of possessions at my feet.

I swallow down a sour trickle that rises into my throat. From the motion of the boat, I tell myself, not fear.

I glance sideways again. This time, the man is looking at me curiously. He keeps looking after I look back at him, but his glance does not connect with mine.

As if I'm a dog or horse he's just bought. I grip the gunwale when the boat rides up and over the wake of a barge, fighting down a wash of panic. I'm not certain I can bear to be bedded by a man who looks at me like that . . .

I look down at the distance between us on the seat.

Nothing feels right. The number of gold coins, far more than I've ever seen paid for the services of any of the other whores, even those schooled in music and dance like me. More than I've seen handed over for a prize-winning horse in the market.

That cool, curious assessment in his eyes. The hint of a shrug as he turns away to look out over the river again. That space between us, when I have been taught that he should be leaning on my shoulder, perhaps sliding his hand under my skirt . . .

Cold terror swamps me. I always imagined that when my moment came, it would happen in Fish Pool House with Mrs Taft on the other side of the door, most likely with her ear pressed against it. With the other women nearby, some of them perhaps even wondering how I was fadging. Each remembering her own first time.

I'm completely at this man's mercy. Alone, Lord knows where. No friendly women within earshot to hear me if I scream. No watch patrolling the Bankside . . . if not already inside drinking or tupping one of Mrs Taft's whores.

Can't swim. I look at the dark river water and imagine how it would pull down the weight of my skirts. But even on dry land . . . where could I go? With my skin, I can't hide for long. In my best skirt and bodice, and these silk shoes, I can't even run.

I press back against the seat, or I might fling myself from the boat. Why not? All that money might have bought my very life. How do I know that he isn't one of those men the whores whisper about, who liked to hurt women? Who need to hurt women in order to find satisfaction?

My bodice squeezes my ribs tighter and tighter.

You can never tell by looking at them, the other women said. Sometimes the mildest, weakest looking man can be the most vicious. Perhaps that smooth cheek of his, and cleanly barbered chin conceal inner foulness.

He must surely notice my agitation. Perhaps he enjoys my fear.

What if he hates me for the colour of my skin? Or secretly fears me? And means to bait me like a beast, to chain me like a bear and set his dogs on me, as I heard from a sailor visiting Fish Pool House

274

that the Spanish and French sometimes do with the natives in the West Indies?

What if he means to kill me?

Hiding in the garden, I feared losing my maidenhead. Now, I'd take the press and fumble of sexual interest that I've seen so often, rather than this chilly indifference that pricks the hair straight up on my arms.

We near the opposite shore. I stare up at what has always been a low distant cliff face of river walls. The wherry pulls up to the Whitehall Stairs.

The man leads me through a gate, a maze of streets and covered passages. I don't know if we are inside or out. Through more gates, guarded this time, then through more doors than I can count. I hug my lute in front of me like a shield.

Standing alone now in a small wood-panelled room watched only by a single silent man-at-arms. Why does he avoid my eye?

What happens next?

A tall, pale woman enters, stares at me, then leaves again without speaking. The man returns and leads me through more corridors, across open courtyards, up a flight of stairs and along a gallery. He opens yet another door. And there she is.

44

'What is it?' I asked.

'Do you still want to go on?' Her tone begged me to say 'no'.

'I must,' I said. I knew that if I wavered, we would both flee.

I looked back across the dark water at the few tiny lights of Whitehall stretched out along the other shore – my familiar world reduced to tiny orange spots of light and their broken reflections in the water. The windows of the Queen's lodgings to my right were almost all dark, but candles and torches still burned in the king's rooms. I was reminded of standing on the crags, looking down on Edinburgh Castle as if I were a bird, freed from the creature-self who lived down there.

'I must,' I repeated.

We had decided that I would keep answering to Peter, a young gentleman still with his maidenhead, who wanted to see how it was done before trying it himself.

'I shall tell them that you're a little simple. Remember not to speak. That Scots burr will give you away.' She chewed her lower lip for a moment, then took my arm. 'Here we go, Master Peter.'

I suddenly felt watery in the knees.

The watchman at the gate eyed us keenly. 'You two won't find what you want here,' he said. Then he looked more closely. 'Blessed fig! It's little Tallie!'

'Good even, Bull.' She shook his hand, then left him open-mouthed as she took my arm and hauled me briskly across the bridge over the little moat that surrounded the house. 'You'd best stay out of sight as much as you can,' she said. 'Anyone who's had a good look knows us for females. This is all complicated enough as it is without having to explain why I've brought a woman, let alone who you really are.'

I stood a little back from the main door and pulled my hat lower.

'Good even, Meg,' she said to the half-clothed woman who opened the door.

'Venus, bless me! Tallie! You came! And look at you!' The woman turned to call to someone behind her. 'Mrs Taft! It's Tallie, dressed like a young lord! We heard you'd landed at Whitehall?'

'That's true,' Tallie said shortly.

'And now you're bringing us wealthy custom.' She stepped aside for a short, handsome, authoritative woman wearing a fine gown of red silk taffeta.

'How now, Mrs Taft?' said Tallie coolly.

'Tallie!' The woman was of much the same age as Lady Harington and looked very much as my lady guardian might if she ever painted her cheeks and lips. She reached up, lifted off Tallie's hat and ran her fingers along the red-dyed feather. 'You've done well, my girl. I may have let you go too cheap.'

Tallie reached out and took back her hat.

'Are you broken yet?' asked an unseen woman.

'She must be broken,' said yet another woman's voice. 'Wearing such a doublet with those silver buttons . . . unless she stole it . . . did you foist it, pet, or earn it on your back?'

'Tallie! cried a new voice. 'How fine you look!'

'Will you bring your young gentleman in?' asked Mrs Taft. 'Your room is ready.'

'In truth, he's terrified.' Tallie stepped inside. She lowered her voice. The women all laughed at something she said. Then money clinked. The women laughed again.

'We'll see you right,' one of them shouted out to me. 'Don't fear! No need to be timid with us!'

'You're a lucky boy to be in her hands!' called another. 'I know a good few men who'd envy you!'

From a distance, I nodded curtly at the curious faces that appeared in the door.

'Does he prefer boys . . . is that why you're in that rig?' This question was meant for Tallie's ears, not mine.

'This way!' Tallie reappeared, grabbed my arm and hauled me away from the curious eyes, around the side of the house to a side door. 'They think you're the son of a nobleman who bought me.'

We climbed a flight of stairs that led to a narrow passage. Tallie opened one of a row of closed doors. I took off my hat and gazed uneasily but curiously around the brothel room.

It looked like any other fairly modest bedchamber. A bed, a high-backed chair and a table with a basin and ewer. A small fire burned in the fireplace. The air smelled sweetly of burning rosemary and something more musky. The bed hangings were silk, but the bed itself was covered with a simple linen quilt and held an excess of pillows. Then I saw the painting on the end wall.

Ignoring the picture, Tallie stood for a moment, grim-faced, with her arms crossed. Then she pulled back a hanging on another wall to reveal a cupboard niche large enough to hold us both. In the back wall was a wide, horizontal crack.

'A look-hole.' Tallie pointed. 'The oracle. Have a squinny.'

I went into the cupboard and put my eyes to the crack. I was looking at the bed in another room.

I realised that the painting on the wall was of the bed

I saw through the look-hole, but, in the painting, it was occupied.

'Men pay to watch?' I whispered.

She nodded, started to say more, decided against it.

'That's vile! Do the couple know?'

'There's no need to whisper yet. The woman knows, of course. The man?' She shrugged. 'Depends on whether or not he likes being watched on the job.'

Suddenly I wondered if my father had ever secretly watched Frances Howard and Carr.

The door of the other room opened. A young woman placed herself in front of the bed, wearing only a thin white smock over her naked body. She smiled straight at me.

I reared back.

'Stand at your post!' Tallie pushed me back to the peep-hole. 'You're the honoured mark here tonight. You must now choose your trull.'

The young woman turned her back and sent me, or the young man she imagined me to be, a smouldering look over her shoulder. She bent forward over the bed and pretended to straighten one of the pillows, displaying her generous haunches. With another smouldering look towards the look-hole, she left.

A slightly older woman replaced her beside the bed. She was tightly laced into a full bodice and overskirt made from frayed blue silk brocade, much like Tallie's dress when she had arrived at Whitehall. But the edges of her overskirt framed her naked legs, belly and dark wiry bush. She stood for a moment, hands resting lightly on her farthingale, then sat on the edge of the bed and opened her thighs so that I was staring at a strange flower of dark pink, fleshy petals.

I stepped back again. 'I can't do this!'

'You wished to know. Are you selecting which parts of the truth you want again?'

I returned to the look-hole.

The next young woman was very young, and black. I glanced at Tallie. Her jaw was clenched. The girl wore a long, fur-edged loose gown that fell open over her nakedness as if by mistake.

'"The savage virgin",' muttered Tallie. 'Who'd like to take her maidenhead . . . for the sixth time?'

I was afraid even to turn my head to her.

A woman in a nun's habit came next. Demure, downcast eyes gave me a chance to catch my breath. The nun lifted off her coif and shook down a head of bright red hair never given to her by God. She gazed into the look-hole with wide-eyed innocence.

It was like choosing a mare from a market parade ring.

I shook my head. 'What am I supposed to do? . . . I can't . . .'

'Just choose one, dammit!' Tallie clapped her hand to her mouth. Her eyes widened in the shadows. 'Forgive me, your grace!' she whispered.

'Tell them whatever you like,' I said. 'I can't.'

She left so abruptly that I wondered if she meant to return. I touched my purse to reassure myself that I had money and was just imagining how I would call, 'Oars! Oars, here!' when Tallie came back.

At almost the same time, Mrs Taft opened the door of the other room. She ushered in a youth wearing green silk velvet, kidskin boots and a terrified expression that attempted disdain. Mrs Taft poured him a glass of amber liquid from a jug and sat him on the side of the bed. Then she left him alone.

'He looks sick with fear!' I breathed.

'He is.' Tallie leaned her head close to mine. 'A virgin, sent here by his father for breaking after the father's own mistress failed. And he doesn't know we're here.'

'Poor thing!' I remembered the duke's eyes. 'I had never thought that the man might be frightened . . .'

'The more they bluster, the more they fear.'

His narrow head turned to the door. His mouth opened a little. He did not stand up for the woman who entered.

I didn't know whether I was relieved or frightened by Tallie's choice – the first young woman in the smock. The one who was the most like me.

The girl sat on the bed beside the young man, who now looked ready to leap up and run.

'Now it begins,' said Tallie. 'Not too fast, or he might bolt. See how first she chatters, as if they had no business in hand – Mrs Taft will have primed her with latest gossip. Now . . . just touches him as if by chance. And leans her breasts on his arm when she reaches for the wine jug.'

Like Frances Howard with my brother, I thought.

'And she now rests her hand, as if to steady herself, on his thigh. There! She made him laugh. A good beginning. Not too much wine, or he'll stay limp as a shoelace. Now she laughs as if he were the wittiest man alive . . . See how she licks the wine from her finger? Now she will invite him to do the same . . . and now she licks his finger . . . and again, slowly, with the tip of her tongue, looking into his eyes. I'll vow he's beginning to stir.'

'It's degrading!' I whispered. 'Like training a dog.'

'It's a kindness,' replied Tallie between her teeth. 'He'll be grateful enough when he finally thrusts home, triumphant. And leaves feeling that he's now a man and can swagger at last in front of his father.'

Then I realised that the young woman, like a player on a stage, was making certain that whoever was behind the look-hole had a clear view of everything she did. The young man, on the other hand, clearly had no idea that anyone was spying on him.

'Now she begins to niggle him in earnest.' Tallied sucked in her lips in the way I had come to recognise as retreat into thought.

I watched the girl's hand teasingly explore the young man's

codpiece. She probed deeper, exclaimed in delight. Untied the laces and produced the cousin of Henry's pink worm, slightly swollen. She brushed it lightly with her fingers.

'Now she'll lift him on.' Tallie now sounded matter-of-fact, as if reciting a catechism or the course of a tennis match.

I watched the young woman's hand move up and down the slowly-growing cock. She raised her head and flicked a glance at the look-hole. This could be your tool in my hand, said her eyes.

Tallie herself must have been taught these things, I thought. Perhaps at this very look-hole. If she had not been bought as a gift for my mother, she might well have been in there on her knees now.

I glanced sideways at her shadowy profile. That thought must have occurred to her, too. I felt slow-witted and clumsy. I felt fearful, as I had feared when holding a caged bird, that I might damage it.

The girl in the other room slid down onto her knees between the young man's legs. She braced one hand on the bed. Her head bobbed up and down.

'She has him in her mouth,' whispered Tallie. 'Alas, she can't show you more without giving the game away.' She leaned back against the wall, arms folded.

Chilled and repelled, I stared through the look-hole. Please, God, I would never need to practise what I was learning!

'But she'll be sure to stop before he's satisfied.' Abruptly, Tallie left the cupboard.

I watched the lifting of the smock, the placing of his hand. I watched the girl push him back a little and straddle his lap. I tried to imagine Tallie still here, in that girl's place.

I followed Tallie out into the bed chamber. 'I can't watch any longer. They've reached the part I already know.'

Tallie was sitting in the upright chair, staring down at her knees. She did not look up. I turned back and pulled the hanging back over the cupboard, even though, to judge by

282

my last sight of him, the young man in the next room would not have heard us if we had started to bellow a marching song.

Without looking up, she said, 'One of the whores training me advised me, "Whilst it's happening, go somewhere else. The country of your mind is as vast as the world . . . as the Heavens . . . plenty of places in there to run and hide".'

'Why are some people so hungry for it?' I asked. Even some of my ladies. 'I don't understand.'

She seemed not to hear.

'Tallie,' I said. 'I thank you.'

She looked up at that, and nodded. 'Have you learnt enough?'

I tried to imagine myself doing those things with German Frederick. 'More than enough.'

'Shall we go back, then?' She waited for my reply, as if she had asked a real question. Then I understood that it was.

'I'm not leaving you here!' I said. 'Did you think I would?'

She unhooked her hat from the corner of the chair back and opened the door.

As we crossed the river back to Whitehall, Tallie asked quietly, 'And what do you think of me now?' We were alone in the wherry ordered for us by Mrs Taft.

I could not let her know that my mouth was still dry and my stomach still clenched at what I had just seen. 'I know now why you were so afraid of being sent back.'

She nodded, frowning.

'Well, you're safe now. You've left the place for good,' I said.

'Do you still want a would-have-been whore as your companion?'

There was a long silence, filled only by the splashing of the oars and forward surge of the boat.

'You yourself told me that I was for sale too.' I stopped her protest with a lifted hand. 'And don't say now that you merely spoke in anger. We both know that it's true. Even if my price is higher.' I swayed with three more surges. 'And I fear that I will need a whore's skills.'

'You may be lucky. There are some good men in the world. If not . . .' She looked past me, back at the receding Southwark shore. '. . . the country of your mind is as vast as the world. Wide as the Heavens . . . plenty of places in there to run and hide.'

'You don't need to hide now.'

'It's not so simple as that,' she said. 'I learned something tonight. I hated every moment we were back there, but I also felt relief that I could stop pretending. While I was there with the whores, and now with you.'

'You're not the same Tallie who arrived at Whitehall.'

'But I'll never settle as a fine English lady, neither. I can't spend the whole of my life pretending to be what I'm not and hiding what I am, whatever that is now . . . or was raised to be. Fearing exposure.'

After a long silence I asked, 'Does that mean that you can't spend the whole of your life with me?'

'I don't know what it means.' But she couldn't take her words back. 'Your life will change,' she said. 'Just as mine did. Perhaps just as much. When I still lived at Fish Pool House, those women were all my world and I couldn't imagine life without them. Even the ones I feared or despised. Now I can't imagine life with them again.' She looked back at the shrinking lights of Bankside. 'You may not want me in your new life.'

An evening already so strange made me reckless. 'You may not want me in yours,' I said.

She blew out a sharp breath, as if I had winded her and turned to look at me. Her face was a steady darkness against the dancing sparks on the black water. 'What if I said you were right?'

I swallowed a belch of sour desolation. 'I would let you go.'

And then I would have no one. Tallie gone. Henry left behind. My mother had been right. I must guard my heart against everyone, even Tallie.

'"Let"?' she repeated to herself. '"Let you . . ."' She had the advantage of the lantern light from the bow of our wherry and leaned closer to see my face. 'I could live very well without the princess,' she said after a moment. 'But never without Elizabeth. Not unless forced by events neither of us can control.' She reached out and picked up my fist from my knee. 'I promise to stay while we try to find you a good man.'

I turned my face away and caught a tear with my tongue.

45

The next day we were both quiet. Exhausted, I sat numbly listening to petitioners. When the last of them left, I put on a thick wool cloak against the rain, even though it was June, and walked across the park in search of Henry, hoping that he too had finished his public duties for the morning. Rather than go all the way around to the big northern gatehouse, I slipped into the palace by the kitchens on the south side, which opened onto the park.

I found my brother in his pale-walled study, just off his bedchamber with windows overlooking the park, in the shadow of King Henry's Tower. As the door opened, I saw him cover his work. He had no clerk or secretary with him. There was ink on his fingers. When he saw that it was only me, and that I was alone, he uncovered his papers again.

I shook my cloak carefully and gave it to a groom who took it away to dry in front of a kitchen fire. I had a question for him that he might, this time, be willing to answer.

'Letters from Virginia,' Henry explained when the door had closed. 'A ship has arrived from my third kingdom in the Americas . . . our third kingdom.' He smiled at me and selected a letter from the pile. 'I'm almost done. Then you must come let me show you what else has arrived with these letters.'

Oddly enough, ever since our meeting in the garden, we were friends again, as if Frances Howard had never come between us.

He waved a letter. 'George Percy writes here to me about his explorations. The land, he says, *"is flowing over with fair flowers of sundry colours and kinds, as though it had been in any garden or orchard in England. There be many strawberries and other fruits unknown . . ."* Ah, Elizabella, it is those *"fruits unknown"* that we seek. He calls the place *"this Paradise"*. With the *"woods full of cedar and cypress"*. There's even talk of silver. And I've just been sent treasure of a different kind.' He dropped his already-quiet voice. 'I've now written promising to send more money, ships and guns. The Spanish are taking an interest again.'

He signed his name at the bottom of a letter and blotted it with sand.

'Our cousin Arbella,' I said. 'Why do I feel that our father is afraid as well as offended by her marriage?' Under Cecil's tutoring, my brother had begun to gain a firmer grasp on the 'whys' as well as the 'whats'.

Very seriously, Henry began to fold his letter so that the contents could not be read once it was sealed. 'Because you're right. Above all, our father is afraid. He sees the marriage as a direct challenge to his authority.' He fell silent while he concentrated on melting a stick of sealing wax and dripping a small red puddle onto the letter. Then he imprinted the puddle with his signet, worn on a gold chain around his neck.

He sends money ships and guns to a new colony, I thought. I use my signet to seal the contract of sale for silver buttons and peacocks.

Henry stood up, shook his right hand to loosen his ink-stained fingers and began to pace, stretching his muscles, shaking out his shoulders, which were now as broad as those

287

of a full-grown man. I noticed a new, coarser golden stubble glistening on his chin.

'You might wonder at the absence of a clerk,' he said. 'Wee Bobby has taught me to write my own letters – like these – when there's need for secrecy. Can you think what the king would say if he knew I was playing a part in a venture begun by the discredited Ralegh? He's so fixed on saving Europe that he overlooks the best future interest of England, in the New World.'

He gathered up the Virginia papers and locked them into his painted leather and walnut writing chest. 'Cecil trusts no one with his true secrets. "Never trust your secretaries," he says.' He put the key to the writing chest into a pouch inside his breeches, then locked the door of his study with a second key. 'Now, come see my new American treasures.'

As we trotted down the wooden staircase in King Henry's Tower, Henry turned his mind to my last question. 'Our father is afraid,' he said, 'because, in some eyes, our cousin Arbella has far more right to the English throne than our foreign-born father. A right strengthened when she chose to marry another royal cousin, William Seymour, with his own rightful claim to the throne.'

He rounded a carved newel post topped by a bowl of sturdy oak fruit. Our feet drummed down another short flight of stairs between the landings.

'All the same,' he said, 'Cecil doesn't think we need fear a popular uprising or other political disturbances on her behalf.'

'Popular uprising? Is she so dangerous?'

Henry shrugged. 'Our father believes she is, and that's what matters. Don't be deceived by his swaggering. Our family's on sufferance here, Elizabella. And Arbella is the queen *manqué.*'

'Does Cecil tell you that?'

'Not in so many words, but he has made me understand

that our chief strength as Stuarts lies in the promise of a stable dynasty.' He paused with his hand on the crowning apple of another bowl of wooden fruit. 'Our weakness,' he said, '. . . is that the king is foreign-born. And all his surviving heirs are foreign-born – me, Baby Charles, you. The English may swear that they love us, but to many of them, we're still foreign Scots!'

'And Lady Arbella is English.'

He nodded. 'Our father is terrified of her, and even more terrified that she might bear a royal English child.'

We emerged from King Henry's Tower and followed a narrow passage towards the mews and stables. We stepped out into a brick-paved courtyard and sunshine. A pair of dog grooms bowed to us and moved on with their pails of meat scraps from the kitchens. Above our heads, a maid shook a pillow out of a window.

Henry led me into his pheasant yard, where birds of different ages waited in pens to be released for hunting. On the far side of the yard stood a low wall of stacked willow basket cages.

'My American treasures,' said Henry excitedly. 'A new breed of chicken . . .' He opened a cage, reached into a furore of cackling and fished out an indignant brick-red rooster with a black tail. He tucked it under his arm and soothed it with his finger. 'Said to be very hardy and the hens are generous with their eggs, laying through the winter.' He returned the chicken to its cage and showed me another cage of American doves. Then led on to a third cage. 'And here is a turkey. The settlers hunt them for meat.'

I stooped down to peer at the strange creature in the cage, with the body of a bird, head of a beaked lizard, and strange long strand of grey-pink flesh dangling beside its beak.

'I'm building an enlarged aviary to house them all,' he said. 'Together with my West Indian parrots and the ostrich which the Venetian ambassador has promised to send me.'

Then he opened the slatted front of a solid wooden box cage. 'Come,' he said to the cage's occupant. 'I won't hurt you. Good girl.' Carefully, he lifted out what might have been a fluffy grey fox kit, except for its black-banded tail. 'Would you like to hold it? I don't think she'll bite, but take care.'

The little creature wrapped itself around my hand, clinging on. I cradled it and looked down. It had pricked ears and a pointed snout like a fox but wore a comical black mask of fur across bright eyes that looked up at me warily. It clung to me with paws almost like hands, which emerged from its soft, warm fur like wrists from a bulky jacket.

'A raccoon kit. I have a pair of them,' said Henry. 'They will grow to the size of small spaniels.'

Still clinging on with one paw, the raccoon began to pull at my buttons with the other. I felt a rush of the same warmth I felt when cradling Belle, a moment of peace when I forgot all other concerns. Then the little raccoon began to squirm and twist to escape. Reluctantly, I handed it back to Henry, who returned it to the cage.

I remembered why I had come looking for him. 'Are you afraid of Arbella, too?' I asked.

Henry squatted down and gazed intently at the turkey. 'Not afraid. She claims to want only a husband, not the English throne. She's only a woman, without an army. And Cecil says that the English have had enough of petticoat rule. But I can see the threat this marriage poses. Our father is not entirely wrong. She was a fool to provoke him in that way. What was Seymour thinking of?'

'Was she never to marry at all?' I asked. 'She's almost thirty and a husband has never been found.'

'And Cecil says that our father never meant to find her one. Unlike you, she's safe only when unmarried.'

'One marriage is safe but another is unsafe?' I asked.

'It was a close and crowded race for the throne after the old queen died. You may have been too young to understand how close it was. Without the help of Lord Salisbury, our father might still be in Scotland.'

Henry led me to the centre of the pheasant yard, away from all windows, doors and gates.

'That's why Wee Bobby is already preparing me for kingship,' he said quietly. 'Not to set my father in his winding sheet before time, as the king would have it, if he knew. Cecil merely wants me to be ready to move decisively when the time comes. To forge my own Protestant alliances on the Continent in advance of the need and make my political intentions known. To be a step ahead of any rivals for the throne.'

His words made good sense as he said them, but a shimmer of fear spread under my ribs. 'Be careful, dearest brother.'

'For what reason? I do not threaten the king. I'm a loyal, dutiful son. I wait my turn in patience. Our father chastises me for idleness and being too fond of the arts of war. He should approve of my earnest labour, not fear it.'

Then why do you hide it from him? I wanted to ask. Instead, I nodded, but my fear did not go away.

'. . . Arbella,' I prompted after a moment.

'The king hates this marriage for the same reason he refused the Seymours for you.' He flicked me a glance to judge the effect of the name, Seymour. Apparently satisfied that my heart was unbroken, he continued. 'The union of royal cousins, both carrying the blood of Henry VII.'

A sudden burst of cackling from the cage of American chickens set off the pheasants in echoing alarm.

Henry rotated his shoulders, then cracked his knuckles. 'If Cousin Arbella ever had a child by a Seymour, the babe could claim the throne through both its bloodlines. Unlike any of us, it would be English-born. It could threaten to dislodge us.'

He gave me one of those uncertain glances that tore at my heart. 'That's why I must work hard now to show my own fitness to rule when the time comes. Most of all, I must prove it to Cecil.'

I wanted to shake him and weep at the same time. How could he not see how much he was already loved? How could he not see that Cecil had already embraced him as the future king?

'Tennis?' he asked abruptly.

'Of course.'

We left the pheasant yard and went to his small closed tennis court, where he turned his back while I put off my farthingale and heavy outer petticoat. As I chose my racket, I ventured another warning.

Henry's handsome face set stubbornly. 'Do you fear that our father might have me locked in the Tower, like Arbella's husband? He wouldn't dare! If I were to challenge him for the throne today – if it were between the two of us – I dare to believe that the people would support me.'

'Don't say that!'

'But is it not true, Elizabella? If it came to it?'

I imagined ears pressed to the flimsy wooden walls, behind doors. I shook my head in silent protest. Suddenly, I found myself up to my neck in treason. With Henry, of all people. The buried subject was suddenly in the open. His words gave hard reality to the unspoken currents that surrounded his troupe of young knights. To the dark thoughts I saw passing through our father's eyes as he pulled at his lower lip and watched my brother. His words gave reality to the murmurs of factions. To the fulsome dedications, like those written by Sir Francis Bacon and his pleas for my brother's patronage.

'But I would never allow a rebellion,' he said. 'You know it. The king must know it. Cecil knows. Apart from all else, he knows that I'm not ready. If his tutorials are ever discovered, he can reassure the king of my dutiful patience and industry in the unending battle to overcome my many faults.'

He flung his racket into the air. I caught it and we climbed fist over fist to the end of the handle. My serve.

I lost every point of our first game and handed over to the Seigneur de St Antoine, who had heard the thumps of the hard, hair-filled ball against wood and wandered in to watch us play. As I smiled at him and asked after his favourite horse which had gone lame from a bad stop in the last tilt, I wondered how much he had heard of my conversation with Henry.

The king ordered Arbella moved from London to more secure and distant imprisonment in Durham. Court gossip avidly tracked every detail of the lady's resistance to this move north. First, she swore that she was ill and could not be moved from Lambeth. Then she failed to recover. The king again ordered her to be moved, regardless of her health. He sent doctors who declared her fit to travel. Her doctors vowed that travel might kill her. In the end, it was said, she clung to the sheets and had to be carried out of the house still in her bed.

They got her no farther than Barnet before her claims of ill-health forced them to stop again. It was still a long way to Durham.

With suppressed delight, I waited for the next chapter of her story. In the next months, I watched my father's anger at his defiant Stuart cousin grow, the more she mounted in the people's love.

Oh, how they loved her! She was no longer an uneasy political loose end but a star-crossed lover, denied her true love by a cruel king. There was even a play about it, the most popular play in London. I never dared to attend a performance, but I sent Tallie in my place.

'It does indeed treat a pair of lovers imprisoned by a Tyrant,' she reported. 'Just as rumoured. The crowd cheered the lovers and booed the Tyrant. Feelings ran so high at the end that he was hit hard in the eye by a well-aimed hazelnut from the gallery and forced to play his death scene with one eye squinnied shut, like this.' She grimaced and pretended to fall off her stool.

I carried on with the routines of my life but Arbella's situation left me both thoughtful and uneasy, as if it might throw light on my own future, if only I could only read with the right eyes.

Then one morning, I received an unexpected petitioner. Waiting for the future – Arbella's and mine – I had forgotten the dangers of the past.

46

He was a pleasant-looking young man, a year or two my senior, with a fair, neatly-trimmed beard and eyebrows bleached white by the sun. He had presented himself as an ordinary petitioner and stood with a letter in his hand. He seemed to be waiting for me to speak.

'Your grace.' He smiled uncertainly. 'You don't know me, I see.'

'I won't pretend,' I said. Then I saw the front tooth chipped in a riding fall. 'Abel!' To my horror, I felt a lump come into my throat. I blinked. I wanted to grab his hand but saw Anne and the others looking at us curiously. Anne seemed not to know him yet. My other ladies were watching us intently.

I reached for the letter that he held forgotten in his hand. I opened the letter and held it out as if to read. 'Will you walk with me, sir?' I strolled slowly, as if reading whilst I walked. Abel followed at a respectful distance. When we reached a window alcove and I judged that we were out of earshot of the eager Herd, I asked under my breath, 'Where the devil have you been?'

'Did Clapper come home safe?'

'With an evergreen message. For which, I thank you . . . It was from you, was it not?'

He nodded.

'I was certain I had sent you to your death.'

'And I feared I might have been the cause of yours.' He turned to look down into the orchard below the window. 'I failed in my mission for you.'

He has darkened, I thought. From the cheerful youth who leapt up offering to risk death in my service.

'The bitter rue,' I said. I wondered suddenly if he had been in the crowd at Paul's when the traitors had died. 'Failed, how?'

He smiled and gestured at the orderly grid of trees below us. 'You'll have a fine apple crop this year.' With a glance towards the Herd, he moved away from the window and placed himself between me and their avid eyes, with his back to them. 'My purse was taken from me at Hampton Court.'

'Did you ever learn what was in it?'

The new, darker Abel lifted one side of his mouth. 'I'm as curious as any man, your grace, but not such a fool as to risk knowledge. Not any more than I must.'

Now I turned away to the window. Tallie could read lips. Other ladies might have the same skill. 'Do you know who took your purse?' I realised that I had caught his care in speaking.

He shook his head. 'A pair of thugs jumped me, thumped me and left me sitting on the cobbles beside Clapper with a bloody nose and a much reduced opinion of myself. I never heard of the purse again.' He smiled. 'At the time, I was chiefly relieved that they hadn't stolen your horse.'

I gripped the sill. Still on tenterhooks as to who had my letter. It had not been lost and destroyed by accident, in a river crossing or accidental fire, after all. I now knew for certain that someone had taken it, knowingly, and kept it for a purpose.

'On the other hand,' Abel said, 'one of Lord Salisbury's men dug me out of the stables and took me to his master.

Cecil offered me the post of messenger. Because, he said, I already had experience.'

'Ah.' We looked at each other.

'I have taken several packets to France for him. And some books to the English ambassador in Venice, where I stayed long enough to learn Italian. He advised me to stay away from Combe.'

'Why come today? After all this time?'

'I'm back in England for a short time. And asked Lord Salisbury if I might visit, to tell you that I was still alive. He trusts my discretion.'

'I'm grateful to see you. You've been on my conscience these past years.'

He gave me a quick look. 'I'm very pleased to see you well, too, your grace.'

'It's a miracle,' I said lightly. 'We're both alive in a uncertain world.' I re-folded his letter before it could start to rattle in my hand. At last, light illuminated one dark corner. Abel White had survived to become one of Cecil's agents. Cecil had intercepted my letter to Henry. The Chief Secretary and Lord Treasurer held proof of my treason. He wanted me to know that he did.

47

SEPTEMBER 1610

Gustavus Adolphus, Crown Prince of Sweden. Protestant.

Tallie smuggled me the portrait of the Swedish crown prince, under a heavy satin loose gown she had worn for the purpose.

'Have a quick gawp,' she said. She handed me a small oval painting framed in ebony and pearls. 'I must return it straightaway. A firm proposal came with it, yesterday. The Swedes are in earnest.'

I stared at the tiny image, no larger than the palm of my hand. With his martial stance and serious air, the long-faced, fair-haired youth reminded me pleasantly of Henry.

I could see how they were alike. The Crown Prince Gustavus Adolphus of Sweden was sixteen years old, only a little younger than Henry. The painter had liked his subject, unlike the man who had painted the Melancholy Trout. His liking was there in the open, friendly smile, like Henry's, and the candid blue eyes. If the artist were to be trusted, the prince's legs were as fine as any in Henry's train. I felt a lightening under my heart.

I looked at the three dogs the prince had chosen to have painted by his feet, their heads raised to him expectantly, waiting to play.

I found myself standing with one hand on my ribs under my breasts as if cradling the sense of possibility that had unexpectedly arrived in my chest.

Tallie took back the picture. 'Peter borrowed this from the king's secretary in the name of your brother. I promised to return it at once. Don't want to make trouble for him.'

And I did not want to ask my brother to lie and say that he had taken the picture himself. He would do it, I was certain, but lying would cause him as much pain as swearing.

I caught Tallie's hands to see Gustavus Adolphus one more time before the loose gown swallowed him again. The more I gazed at this possible shape of my future, the better I liked it.

Sweden was not so very far away from Scotland.

'I must have a copy made of this picture,' I said.

Tallie rolled her eyes and said she would try. I set off to learn what Henry thought of the Swedish prince.

'I hear that he's a more eager scholar of Latin and Greek than I am.' My brother was in the small armoury at Whitehall, having the buckles adjusted on a bright new steel breastplate. 'But shares my taste for tilting, swordplay and military strategy. And he's a good Lutheran Protestant. He would be a good match, Elizabella.'

'That means that you would have to marry a Catholic,' I said.

'One battle at a time.'

I left Henry to the oiling of the wood-louse joints of his steel gauntlets.

Tallie reported that all the talk at dinner had been of how much the king liked the Swedish prince.

I asked my secretary to find a tutor to teach me to speak Swedish. Falling asleep that night, I let myself remember those fine long legs and serious blue eyes.

Three days later, Tallie brought me a pencil copy of Gustavus Adolphus's portrait.

'*Tank,*' I said, having completed my first Swedish lesson. 'How did you manage this miracle?'

'You'll have to remember the colour of his eyes,' she said. 'The artist had only an hour in which to work.'

'The prince is very handsome,' Anne agreed when I showed her the picture that night. 'He could be an Englishman.'

I tried out my new Swedish words on her. '*Man.*' Husband. '*Kärlek.*' Love.

For the next week, I kept his picture on my pillow. 'Gustavus,' I whispered. 'Goostaaaavooooos . . .' It was a beautiful name, echoing itself at the beginning and end, with that open 'aaaah' of wonder in between.

I asked Henry to let me study his maps of northern Europe. I imagined I was a gull, soaring over the coast of my new country, swooping down into the intricate folds of its painted coastline, circling the spires of golden domes. As I fell asleep, Gustavus Adolphus flew beside me. While I spiralled with the sun on my wings, he plummeted down to scythe the water with a beak the colour of coral. Then he beat his way back up again into the sky, carrying a glittering silver fish.

I was afraid to give words to the thought lest I frighten it away. I thought I could be happy with Gustavus Adolphus.

Fågel. Bird. *Hund.* Dog. Even his language felt familiar.

Alas, I had learned little more Swedish than '*ja*', yes, '*nje*', no, and '*God dag*', good day, when, one morning, my ladies fell suddenly silent as I entered the room.

I wagged my finger at them. 'I know that silence. What news do you not want me to hear?'

They exchanged looks.

Frances Tyrrell was boldest. 'The Swedish envoy has just left London, your grace, wearing a long face. The king didn't send a guard-of-honour to see him to his ship.'

'He's gone back to Sweden,' added Anne, to be certain that I understood.

I nodded. Tallie and I had missed the rumours of this one. *'Adïo'.* Goodbye.

'Why not Gustavus Adolphus?' I raged at Henry. 'He's royal. He's wealthy. One day he will rule a powerful kingdom.' I knew that my liking for him mattered not a jot, except to me.

'Sweden is at war with Denmark in a struggle to control the Baltic coast.' My brother sounded almost as upset as I was. 'I believe that the queen, our mother, balked at a son-in-law who was at war with her native country.'

'But the king entertained his suit all the same.'

'That was yesterday,' said Henry. 'Today, he has his sight trained on an alliance with the Netherlands.'

Maurits van Nassau, Stateholder of the Netherlands. Protestant, but not royalty . . .

And at least forty years old. 'He's older than our father!' I cried in dismay. I tried to imagine living with such an ancient man. I wondered if he smelled old, like so many of the courtiers, or like my poor Trey who now trembled in the haunches when climbing stairs and farted vilely.

I tried to live my daily life as usual. I received petitioners. I signed household budgets, approved wine orders and commissioned gifts for my ladies. I rode. I embroidered a curse of cushions. I walked in the gardens and stood while new gowns were fitted. I sat for still more portraits, ate meals, slept, watched entertainments. I visited the raccoons in the new aviary at St James's, which was slowly growing to include a menagerie as well. I attended the unhappy launching of my brother's new warship, *The Prince Royal*, when the king grew impatient and stormed out after the ship got stuck in the dock gates. I visited the Haringtons at Kew in my barge. I played cards, diced and gossiped with the Herd.

Each night in my sleeping chamber, while her fingers brought the strings alive, Tallie reported what she had learned that day. Sometimes, she even sang her reports in improvised couplets to make me smile. But all the time I felt that I was waiting in the dark for the Combe ghost to arrive.

We added names and details to the list of my suitors, as we learned them.

> *The Marquess of Hamilton. Third in line of Scottish succession. The Queen's choice. Therefore, unlikely.*
>
> *Prince Frederick, Count Palatine of the Rhine. Protestant. Also called the Palsgrave. Also known as the Elector Palatine because he will helps choose the next emperor of Holy Roman Empire. Protestant. Henry likes him. Says he matches me in lineage, has emperors in his bloodline, but the Privy Council worry about limited finances. The Queen of course against. Suit advancing.*

I remembered my father's gibe to de Bouillon when my portrait was being painted. 'Perhaps too costly for your master to maintain?'

Early in 1611, de Bouillon returned from delivering my portrait. In exchange, he brought my father a detailed description of Prince Frederick and proposed terms for the marriage. Tallie tried but failed to obtain a copy of this document.

'And if there's a portrait of the prince, I can't find it,' she said. 'As for gossip, the word is that he's your equal in years, superior in breeding, with influence in Europe but no money.'

'Then I might escape him yet,' I said.

The king publicly weighed this suitor's Protestantism against the likelihood of a balancing Catholic bride for my militantly anti-Catholic brother.

Henry petitioned the king on the Palatine's behalf. 'This

Frederick,' he assured me, 'even more than Frederick of Brunswick, would be a strong and reliable ally in any future war between Protestant Princes and the Catholic monarchs of Europe.'

Prince Otto of Hesse, firm proposal. Rejected.

I never learned why.

Victor Amadeus, Catholic. Prince of Piedmont, heir to Duke of Savoy who controls northern Italy. Portrait has mouth like a girl. Said to be lecherous and sly. Sister proposed for Henry.

The Count of Cartignana turned rumour to reality when he arrived in London with a commission from the Catholic Duke of Savoy, proposing a possible double marriage. Henry would marry the duke's daughter, the Infanta Maria of Savoy. I would marry his son.

The king set aside the Palatine proposal to me to parlay with Savoy on the double marriage.

'I will not marry a Catholic!'

My father and brother stood facing each other down the central aisle like champions in a list, preparing to charge. Neither had seen me. I retreated swiftly and silently towards the door of the royal chapel, where I had come to seek a few moments of solitude.

'I will never go to bed with the Church of Rome!' said my brother quietly. He stood with his back to the altar, as if interrupted at prayer.

I paused to listen, half-hidden behind one of the facing double rows of high-backed pews. Two choristers slipped past me out of the door. Near me, in the narrow aisle behind the pews, the sexton froze with a burnt-down stub in one hand and a clutch of fresh candles in the other.

'Ye'll do as yer told by yer king!' My father's bellow echoed back down from the painted, gilded ceiling.

'What will you do?' demanded Henry. 'Lock me in the Tower like Seymour? Do you imagine you'd be allowed?'

I listened to the long silence.

'I'll be allowed by a war-weary people to preserve the peace abroad that I've laboured so hard to achieve. You and your sword-waving love for the Protestant cause will destroy the balance and tilt us all into war again.'

From my hiding place, I could not see my father but I could hear his heavy breathing. I could just see my brother.

'Your *via media* will give the Papists a straight road back to power in England,' Henry said. 'My first care is for England, not Europe. We've already had Protestant martyrs burned in Smithfield and Lewes. Never again!'

'Are ye trying to say that I don't care for England?' Ice formed on my father's words. 'So spit it out like a man. Don't hide behind insinuation like a gossiping slut. D'ye say that I don't care about England? Take care how y'answer.'

Henry looked down. 'No, sir. I forget myself.'

'You're a dangerous fool,' said the king. 'The most dangerous. A simple mind that knows itself to be right. Leave me. Go play your soldier games. Leave me to rule England, and you.'

Henry rushed past me out of the chapel, head down, without seeing me.

'The prince imagines that he is already king!' our father shouted after my brother's retreating back. 'He would bury me before my time!'

I stepped deeper into shadow behind the pews and waited until the king, too, had left the chapel, while the sexton tried to pretend that he was not there.

For reasons that neither Tallie nor I ever managed to learn in spite of all our efforts, the king rejected the Savoy match for Henry but accepted Victor Amadeus for me. With the *provisos*, however, that I would not convert and that my children were to be raised, in Italy, as Protestants with English sympathies. Three different children of Henry VIII had ruled England in turn, the king argued. My children might well find themselves on the English throne. Cartignana left to take this reply back to Turin.

The king made Carr a viscount, and, therefore, the first Scotsman to be elevated to the Lords. Meanwhile my ladies fell in love and pined. They were betrothed, then married. One fortunate woman, the Other Elizabeth, loved and married the same man.

48

On the third of June, my cousin Arbella rode away from house arrest in Barnet, with a small party of attendants and dressed in men's clothes, headed for the Thames and a ship to the Continent. At the same time, her husband William Seymour escaped from the Tower. His reported means ranged from wearing a false beard to being bundled up in dirty linen. However he did it, he made it away safely to France.

Arbella reached her own ship safely. But she was overtaken on the sea, brought back, and locked in the Tower. My father claimed that she and her husband meant to shelter with one of the chief Catholic powers and mount a Papist attempt on the English throne. The tongues of rumour wagged. Here was a new Catholic threat, as great as the earlier Gunpowder Treason.

Arbella would never leave the Tower, the king promised. And should thank God that he let her keep her head.

The pressure of this Catholic threat brought into the open the battles between my brother and father over both Henry's marriage and mine. Henry now dropped his pose as a dutiful son, on this subject at least. He openly denounced the king's attempt to make balanced alliances with both Catholics and Protestants, and began to argue fiercely in public against my match in Savoy with Victor Amadeus.

He was said to be influenced in this by his friend Ralegh, who continued to write him long advisory letters from his imprisonment in the Tower. These rumours further enraged the king.

My heart had leapt so often from one possible husband to the next that I no longer knew what I felt. I spoke some Italian and so would not be completely adrift in Savoy. My excellent French was not now likely to be required. I had not progressed beyond the word 'love' in Swedish. I did not speak German and thought it a barbaric language. I was almost past caring.

Philip III of Spain. Catholic. Ruling monarch. Newly widowed. Very old. Father of my earlier suitor, Prince Felipe.

'I'd have the mighty monarch of Spain as my son-in-law!' the king crowed. 'Now there's a dutiful reverence from an old enemy that I'd be happy to accept!'

Both the Savoy and Palatine matches seemed forgotten.

'I won't let him send you to become a prisoner in a Catholic court!' Henry vowed to me privately. Publicly, he said that anyone who advised the king to marry me to Spain was a traitor to England.

'I begin to wonder if the devil would be so bad after all!' I said to Tallie. 'So far as I can learn, he's neither Catholic or Protestant.'

I had no strength left to speculate nor to prepare myself. The Herd began to drive me mad. I would eavesdrop and then wish that I hadn't, as they speculated about whether or not my heart had been broken, and which failed match had done it.

Though the details were blurred, I could see the broad

shape of my future clearly. I would do my duty. Leave England. Be miserable for the rest of my life. Grow to be like my mother, after all. I began to feel the truth in her instruction not to attach my heart to what I must lose.

I felt myself closing up, even with Tallie, like the mussels on the rocks in Scotland, which were sometimes torn loose in storms. I began to want my marriage over and done with, so I could get on with attaching myself to my new rock.

I hid from my father, excusing myself whenever I could from state occasions when he was likely to be present. I thanked God for his obsession with the hunt which kept him away for weeks at a time at Royston, Newmarket or Theobald's, which, two years earlier, Cecil had been forced to give to the king in exchange for an older, more modest house at Hatfield in Hertfordshire.

When he was in London, my father's humour had turned dangerous after his fight with Henry in the chapel. I was certain that others at court felt increased peril in his humours. He drank more, shouted, cursed. He took sudden frights and hid in his lodgings, then re-emerged to crash about the palace. He planted kisses on Robert Carr and didn't care who saw. Once, I was told, he turned to Frances Howard and asked her whether this was not indeed a bonny lad.

He would pull thoughtfully at his lower lip and stare with a new malevolence from under lowered brows at Henry, at me, at anyone who dared to contradict him or fail to laugh at one of his bawdy jests. At Cecil. Even Carr sometimes had a wary, uncertain look in his stupid, crafty eyes.

The king was already angry with Cecil, who had failed to raise 'the dark clouds of irreparable misery', as the king called his constantly increasing debts. The Chief Secretary, also Lord Treasurer since 1608, had in the last year undertaken to persuade Parliament to grant the crown a regular sum to meet the king's expenses, in place of a complicated system of *ad hoc* taxes, fees and grants. This sum would cover the king's extravagant gifts to his favourites of estates and jewels, as well as the king's own clothing and jewels, his horses, his hunting, his wine and feasting, and all the other costs of running large, luxurious royal households at Whitehall, Windsor and Greenwich. Parliament had refused even Cecil's most ingenious compromises.

'The penny-pinchin' dwarf', my father had taken to calling the man who had once been his own 'Little Beagle'.

I lay awake at night, even though Tallie sang and played quietly at the bedside until the fire died and the room grew cold. I woke once from an uneasy half-doze and heard Anne asleep beside me and Tallie asleep on her stool, both snoring gently.

I began to sleep later and later into the day and did not want to wake. Having an opinion about anything began to exhaust me. I could barely make myself stroke Belle and Cherami. I fed my birds only to keep them from starving and from sheer weariness lent Baby Charles my monkey, for which he had been begging. I lost my taste for riding or playing my virginal or lute. I no longer wanted to dance. Tallie and I no longer played duets together.

'You must practise more, your grace,' she once scolded me.

'Why?' I asked bleakly. 'For whose delight? My own is gone.' I heard how woefully pitiful I sounded and braced myself for the tart response I deserved.

'Hey-ho, my poor Lady Elizabeth.' She studied me, sucking in her lips as she did when thinking hard. 'Let me comb your hair, then.'

She unpinned it and began to comb with her fingers.

I almost told her to stop. I had not cried in a very long time, but the feel of her hands tugging gently at the tangles in my hair brought me dangerously close.

Henry seemed to work night and day, whenever he was not exercising.

'What letters do you write today?' I would ask. Then listen while he explained licences, possible trade alliances, the search to find the right stone for an architrave, good Flemish glass-makers, and the best horses for war.

One day I found him glumly reading a letter from the Jamestown settlement on Chesapeake Bay.

'Only now do I learn that the supply ship we sent with provisions was sunk in a *horricano*. Without those supplies, they went hungry.'

'Hungry in Eden?' I asked.

'I tell you this in confidence,' he said. 'The investors must not be discouraged. The difficulties will pass with continued investment and strong leadership. The settlers have lacked a strong leader since Captain Smith was injured.'

He folded the letter. 'I would like to sail to Chesapeake Bay to see for myself how this new Eden can best be made to flourish. Our other kingdom.'

'We will never be the King and Queen of the Americas.' I no longer believed that he and I would ever sail together to visit Cape Henry, named after him in the New World, nor the new English colony. 'Those were childish imaginings,' I said dully.

'They were not!' he protested. 'When I am king, I will visit my American subjects and invite you to accompany me. No husband could be cruel, or foolish, enough to forbid his wife to accept an invitation from the king of England, Scotland and the Americas.'

I shrugged. 'Who knows where I'll be by then?'

I could scarcely pretend interest in his outrage a few weeks later at the arrival from Florence of the portraits of two Catholic Medici princesses.

How could I ever before have imagined that I felt old?

One morning, a doctor was waiting among my petitioners. Cecil had sent him.

'I'm quite well!' I said angrily.

'Being not entirely well himself, Lord Salisbury is alert for signs of illness in others,' the man said tactfully. 'Perhaps you would allow me to reassure him?'

I was so startled by the news that Cecil himself was not well that I allowed the doctor to feel my pulse, examine my eyes and tongue and smell my breath. I had no doubt that the contents of my close stool had already been carried off and scrutinised. He said only that I might want to take more air and not to over-tire myself.

I was already taking that advice. More and more often, I went to sit on the Privy Stairs.

'You don't mean to swim like his highness, your brother, then?' one of the men-at-arms asked me the first few times.

I knew he wanted one of my pert replies to repeat in the guardroom, but I could only shake my head. The jest soon grew stale. The guards grew used to me and continued to talk quietly among themselves while I looked down into the water for an hour at a time and imagined sinking deeper and deeper until no one could ever find me. I wondered if Henry ever imagined the same. If I had ever had any secret strength, my father had now disarmed me with constant confusion and uncertainty.

49

I was taking refuge in my brother's company at St James's one rainy afternoon, pretending to leaf through a pile of architect's drawings on a window seat in the white-plastered small presence chamber, when Bacon arrived. A cool silence greeted him.

'Gentlemen,' said Bacon. 'Your highness.' He gave his tight-lipped smile that reminded me of a snarl. 'Nursing sore heads today, are we?' He bowed. Then bobbed his head again at me. His eyes made an inventory of who was there.

Sir John Harington and one or two others gave him polite smiles. However, Bacon's quarry was Henry.

'Your highness,' said Bacon. 'I beg leave to presume and speak to you as a true friend.'

Cecil must be very ill indeed, I thought. His cousin is already elbowing into his place.

'A true friend never needs to beg,' said Henry. 'May I hope that you mean to offer me another piece of writing?'

'Mere spoken words, this time, your grace.' Bacon jerked his head at the other gentlemen. 'In private, if it please your highness.'

Henry let Bacon draw him aside, to the side of the gallery where I was standing by a window now watching raindrops run down the diamond panes to join in little rivers along the lead joints. Henry's knights withdrew to the far end of the long gallery.

'I have been hoping to find you alone, your highness,' said Bacon. 'But you are always so densely surrounded by your many admirers that I began to despair, wondering how I was to unburden my heart of a matter that concerns me deeply.' He pressed one hand against his heart as if his concern could scarcely be contained except by force. 'I pray that you will not think me presumptuous if I say that some of my concern is for your royal self.'

Over Bacon's shoulder, Henry sent me a quick amused look. I know what you think of the man, said his eyes. But it's my duty to listen to him. And possibly, to learn. Then he turned onto Bacon the open, attentive and friendly regard that made both men and women love him. Only I knew how hard he worked to achieve that look and how tiring he often found it.

Sir Francis clearly found it encouraging. 'I have noted, your highness, that you have of late seemed cast down and I am willing to hazard that I . . .' He turned his back to me and leaned close to my brother, speaking so low that no one else could hear.

At first, I felt rather than saw the change in Henry.

As Sir Francis murmured into his ear, my brother reddened, then went white, not merely pale, but chalky, paler than the most slighting word from our father had ever bleached him. Even from my distance, I could see a white border form around his mouth like a welt.

I still pretended to watch the rain.

Sir Francis seemed to notice nothing amiss. Even when Henry stepped sideways as if trying to escape, Bacon merely turned with him, still murmuring, his eyebrows raised in expectation of some sign of agreement.

How could the man not see Henry's clenched fists? Even

313

from my window niche, I saw my brother's knuckle bones threatening to split the skin. Even from twenty feet away, I could feel the icy chill of his frozen stillness.

Oblivious, Sir Francis made smooth gestures with his well-manicured hands. He waved away an invisible thing, an unworthy thought. On one hand, we reject this, said his gestures. And then, on the other we have this, you and I, oh, how much, much better. He leaned even closer to my brother. And I offer it to you, said his hands.

Henry bowed his head, a gesture which Sir Francis seemed to read as acquiescence.

Sir Francis continued to murmur to my brother, both grovelling and condescending at the same time, as only he could manage. Henry raised his head again and stared fixedly past him, waiting for the man to finish. Sir Francis reached his conclusion. He touched my brother's arm with an insinuating intimacy and stepped back looking pleased with himself.

Henry's eyes dropped to his sleeve, where Bacon had touched him. His lips puckered as if he meant to spit out a gobbet of rotten meat. The silence grew. I heard boots shifting on the floor farther along the gallery. Bacon began to look puzzled.

'How do you dare?' The words escaped between Henry's clenched teeth, so quietly that I barely heard them. 'Men hang for that.'

'Your highness?' Bacon leaned closer again, as if he had either not heard or else disbelieved. He shook his head. 'Not kings.'

Henry stared past him. 'I forbid you ever to speak to me on this or any other subject. I do not want to see you again at St James's nor my lodgings here at Whitehall. I don't yet, alas, have the power to banish you from the court altogether, but I will do it when the power is mine, if you ever again dare show your face to me!'

I had never seen my brother so angry.

'Your highness, I never meant . . .!'

'Leave me!'

'But wherein did I speak false?' Bacon still looked startled and a little aggrieved, as if a previously friendly dog had just bitten his hand.

Henry raised his head and gave Bacon a look that stood the hairs up on my neck. Bacon staggered a step back, recovered his balance, bowed, and left.

His footsteps were the only sound in the room. When he passed me, puzzlement and disbelief were already giving way to calculation in his sharp dark eyes.

Henry flung himself to the nearest window and stared out.

'By Cock, that man leaves a bad taste in the mouth,' said Sir John.

'Fine in the box,' said Henry tightly without taking his eyes from the rain.

Silently, Sir John put his tuppence in the swearing box. We all listened to the tiny dull clink. I decided that he had sworn as a deliberate diversion. 'A good afternoon for tennis,' he observed after a moment. 'Henry?'

My brother waved for them all to go. I decided that I had not been included in his wave.

'Was he slandering Cecil again?' I ventured when the others had gone.

'Leave me alone! Don't you, of all people, start prying into my private life!' He turned and left the gallery, headed for his own lodgings.

I watched him go, feeling as if he had slapped me. I was also certain that he was crying. And that I had seen fear in his eyes as well as rage.

50

I had seen Henry angry. I had seen him downcast. I had seen him fretful and half-dead with tedium. But I had never before seen him lose his grip on himself, not even when our father snubbed him in public. My world wobbled. Like the shorn Samson, my ally and protector had lost his strength. Bacon had cast a dark spell on my brother. I didn't know how it might be lifted, but I knew that I must try. My turn to rescue him. It was an odd thought.

Henry ate supper in his rooms that night. After supper, I went to his bedchamber, where his chamberer told me that the prince had gone to sleep early with a megrim.

I found several of his gentlemen playing cards by the fire in the presence chamber. Lynn told me that the prince had not come to join the after-supper tennis. Filled with fear for him, I gave up for the moment and went back to my own lodgings.

The following day, the rain stopped. In the late morning, crossing the gallery over the Holbein Gate, I spied my brother in the tiltyard, practising on foot with two of his men-at-arms, thrusting at each other with tilting lances across a waist-high barrier. I knew him even at a distance by his fierce strength and the unicorn on his helmet. I ran down into the spectators' gallery.

Yesterday's rain had turned the dust to mud, which clumped onto the fighters' feet to give them pudding-bowl hoofs like plough horses. Henry thrust at his opponent again and again with the short lance used when they fought without horses, beating at the breast-plate of the half-armour they wore. I listened to the thud and clang and watched my brother beat ferociously at his opponent.

'A hit!' he cried. 'And again!'

The force of his thrust pushed the other man off-balance. As his enemy clattered to the ground, Henry turned and ran at the quintain, set to one side on its pivot, waiting to be used for mounted practice. He struck the dummy figure dead centre with the tip of his lance. Then he backed up and ran at it again. Then again. And again. Even twenty feet away, I could hear his harsh breathing.

'Henry,' I called.

He did not hear me. He charged the quintain once again, sucking at the air now like a man with the quinsy.

The man-at-arms climbed to his feet and brushed at the mud on his thighs and buttocks. He and his comrade watched their prince from the far side of the waist-high barrier as he kept running at the dummy. Though lighter than the arms and armour used for the mounted tilt, both the steel half-armour and lance were heavy, never meant for this repeated attack. Trying to use the unwieldy lance as a sword, Henry was beginning to tire.

He landed a blow off-centre. Ducked to avoid the spinning weight designed to punish any blow that missed the target point. He missed the centre again with his next attack. Then hit it. Then missed yet again and took the blow of the whirling sandbag on the side of his helmet. I felt the thud jolt my bones. Henry crumpled to his knees and stayed there, as if praying.

I started to run down into the yard, but his men vaulted the waist-high barrier and reached him first.

He waved them away, planted the grip of his lance in the mud and climbed it hand over hand until he was on his feet again. After a moment, he lifted his lance as if he meant to run at the quintain again. He took three steps, stopped, seemed to come to himself. He turned to hand his lance to one of the men-at-arms, then held out his arms so that they could undo the screws on his shoulders and unbuckle his breast-plate from the back-guard.

He lifted off his helmet. 'I was careless,' he said. 'Deserved that thump. Just as well we weren't in battle. Which of you will give me a game of tennis?'

He didn't look at me, but he didn't tell me not to follow and watch the game, neither. His gentlemen had divined his humour. They let him win all three games of tennis he played but made him work hard enough for his victories to satisfy whatever demon was driving him. At suppertime he vanished.

He did not appear among ladies and gentlemen who gathered after supper in one of the great parlours. Then Tallie learned from one of his chamber grooms that the prince had gone swimming in the Thames.

I went down to the Privy Stairs. Apart from the guards, the water steps were deserted. The wake from passing boats splashed gently against the pilings. There was a three-quarters moon. Out on the dark water, I saw a small rowing boat and the white shirt of the oarsman. Beyond the boat, I saw the indistinct bobbing head of my brother.

The head seemed to vanish. For a terrible moment, I thought he might mean to drown himself and opened my mouth to scream 'no!'. Then he surfaced from his dive.

I felt suddenly certain that I must not interrupt the thoughts he was chasing through the dark water.

51

HENRY

Swim.

   *Don't think about it. Smile. Continue to get through the days with
effort and sweat. You are watched. You are the ideal. You are the
model, the next king of England. You must be perfect in every way.
(. . . except in being a real man . . . no one must ever know. How did
Bacon guess? What is wrong with me? Am I to turn out like my
father, after all? A foolish gull who can be twisted about the slim
white fingers of any pretty boy? . . . Slim white fingers that will touch
him . . . Even the thought is intolerably wicked!)*

*Bacon lies! None of it is true! Cannot be true! I will not permit it
to be true! Duty will carry me. My father, for all his weaknesses,
understands that. And God understands. I have been chosen for this
uncomfortable part. I accept it. God wills it. England wills it.
Therefore, I will it.*

*I wish I could stop dreaming. I start each day by forgetting my
dreams. Too messy, too dangerous. Forest, where I hear howling and
strange animal grunts, close behind my heel, too dark to see them,
but they're there. Sniffing after me. If I can run fast enough, I will*

319

reach sunlight again – that clearing I see ahead, that open meadow, and leave those trackers snapping their jaws in the shadows.

Dive, down, down, colder and colder. Something brushes my leg. Back up! Back up! Dear God, please, where's the surface, and light! Moonlight.

Everything around me is too much. Men talk too much, smile too much. They bow too low. They stuff too much food into their mouths, drink too much, talk too loudly. There's a disgusting amount of food on our table at dinner. I would be happy with bread and a slice of cold meat. A few nuts. A single mug of small beer. There are too many female breasts on display, too many lips parting over white teeth, too much flesh, like the display on a butcher's stall. Meat for the taking. Being pushed at me, as if I were a Cannibal.

What is wrong with me? I smile knowingly when my men speak of Frances Howard . . . I can hardly bear to think of her. So far, she has seemed to keep her mouth shut, at least to the court at large. Secretly, I study her uncle and Carr for signs of mockery or derision. But the Howard clan want to put one of their women on the throne again – though I can't think why, given the fate of the last Howard queen. Until all her last hopes are gone of being my queen, she'll keep my failure as a man to herself. Given the family reputation, she'd likely manage to get a 'royal' babe planted, and dare me to damn myself by accusing her . . . who of her male acquaintance is ambitious enough, and daring enough to be her impregnating angel? Is that her game with Carr?

Reach, kick. Reach, kick. Feel each forward surge. No time to think . . . of anything . . . else . . . Who is that on the Privy Stairs?

My sister, my female self! She's there now, on the steps, looking for me. Fearing for me. Yes. I confess to needing that fear. I saw it in her eyes today. I would marry her, if I could . . . Mustn't even think such thoughts. But we could rule as brother and sister. I think such things were done in ancient times . . . must ask my tutor. He will know, and is endlessly patient with me . . . God knows, he needs to be! Everyone praises my 'wisdom' and my 'pleasant wit'. What lies they tell! But I must let them lie. It's their part, just as accepting their praise is mine. At least, I am truly courageous. At least, I think I am. I don't fear war, I almost wish we weren't at peace. I relish fighting. Never happier than when riding at the tilt, or playing tennis against a challenging opponent. My father is a conciliator, an equivocator. 'The Peacemaker King,' he calls himself. Promising all comers whatever they want. So why does he wear a padded doublet against a possible knife attack?

Via media? *How dare he preach his 'Middle Way'? My father is the worst of the excess around me here at Whitehall. His tongue is too large, his laugh too loud, his appetites so coarse and open. The bread crumbs and shreds of meat down the front of his coat. The vulgar size of his jewels, and his open delight in their sheer extravagance. He doesn't care what men think of him. Because he is king. Because, if he lets himself begin to think about what sort of man he is, he will never sleep easy again. This new Bible of his is mere religious posturing. He'll lose interest soon and be on to something else.*

He holds steady to nothing. The curious jackdaw, forever dropping whatever he hold in his beak to flap off after a new fragment of glass glinting in the mud. A new trinket. A new boy.

I neither mind nor don't mind that he is my enemy. It's a fact. He may ridicule me before his toadies. But I trust both God and honest men to make a true judgement between us. He's a fool to fear me, merely because his mother had cause to fear him. As a God-fearing Protestant prince, I am loyal to him as my anointed monarch. I would never wish to unseat him from his throne, even though I've heard the whispers and secret wishing. Virtue must wait its appointed time. But I vow that all honest men in England will be grateful when that time comes.

Elizabeth . . . my Elizabella . . . she's left the steps now . . . loves me truly and honestly and with all her heart. With the true loyalty of my hound. The only creature who loves me, besides my hound. And I love her in return. I confide in her things I barely know that I'm thinking, she seems so like another self. If she were a boy, we would truly be like the heavenly twins. Like Romulus and Remus, we would found another Rome.

Even now, we may yet make our new Rome in the New World. I will crown her the 'Queen of the Americas', just as I promised her. Empress of all that is new and unsullied. She will ship me back riches, some of them not yet discovered – pearls from Chesapeake Bay, beaver pelts, gold and silver from mines not governed by the Spanish. I'll have an army of dusky warriors with the same veiled fierceness as that Nymph of Niger our mother gave her ... But that will happen only if I become king very soon. Or else, she will be married and gone.

I can't bear to lose her. Who will I have left? Who will help me untangle my thoughts? Who will laugh at the snarls of the court? Who will get angrier than I do myself, at our father's slights and insults to me, and imagine terrible punishments for all those who laugh?

Our mother is nothing. A cipher. A silly woman. She gave up long ago and wants only to get through the days as painlessly as she can. She's a fool, but not a malicious one.

Sir Francis, on the other hand ... a devil but no fool. His sharp wit and snake eyes make me lose my words. Nothing stays clear in my mind when he begins to twist his words through it. He is evil! Dangerous. He says that he loves me, and claims to see the truth of my soul! I can't let any man live who can truly see such truth. Except that it isn't true, of course. Only the truth as he would have it. But his sharp wit carves other men's thoughts into new unwanted shapes. 'Ferret Eyes'! 'Ferret Eyes!' Elizabella made me laugh when she pulled faces at his back and called him names. What will I do without her when she is married and sent away? I can't bear it!

I'll be left with poor Baby Charles, who wants so much to be like me. Tongue-tied and blushing when he's with me. Unable even to lift my sword without staggering on his bowed little legs.

. . . Kick . . . reach . . . kick.

I find my only peace in exercise. Tilting. Tennis – innocent joy. The succulent perfection of hitting the ball in the exact sweet spot at the centre of the racket. My heart lifting in the arc with the ball, through the air. Then a blissful rush, no need to think. My body thinks for me. Whack! Whack! Another heart-lifting arc . . . a dive and save. Every muscle working together, a small piece of mind, like a single church candle, alight, guiding. The end known even before the other man misses. Truth at its most absolute and elegant. Standing, satisfied, breathing hard, no need to be any other thing than I am just at that moment.

Swimming. Sometimes, I really do swim. No words. Escape from words. As alone as I can ever be, even with that anxious watcher in the boat rowing after me. Here in the dark water, I remember that I am covered with living skin. I feel every inch of my bodily casing shiver with delight. I am golden, like my Spanish armour, as if my skin had turned to shimmering gold. I turn and float face upwards, looking up into the night sky. The water and sky are one. Broken light glitters on the water around me like stars. I imagine that my face is the moon looking up at its twin. I let myself urinate in the water, feel the fleeting warmth on my thigh. Like a baby. My secret sin. I think about putting my hand on my cock. I turn over and kick out hard, swimming fast against the current.

52

In the end, I simply marched past all my brother's guardians and gate-keepers, none of whom dared to restrain me by force, walked into Henry's closet and burst into tears. In his concern, he forgot that he did not want to speak to me.

'Bacon is your enemy now,' I sobbed. 'I saw it in his eyes when he left you yesterday. What did he say to you? I fear what he might do!'

Henry shook his head. 'Don't be so fearful, Elizabella. He's a clerk at heart, in spite of his sharp wits. He destroys with his pen, not a sword. And I don't think that, even with his pen, he'll dare attack the Prince of Wales. In any case, he's nothing while Wee Bobby is alive.'

'Why did he make you so angry? Was he attacking Wee Bobby again? . . . Thank you.' I wiped my eyes and blew my nose on Henry's offered handkerchief.

He shook his head. 'He wasn't . . .'

'You were very angry,' I insisted.

Henry moved his shoulders uneasily. 'He attacked our father.'

'Bacon attacked the king, to you? The king's son?'

The white line flared around his mouth again. 'He presumed to believe that I might agree with him.'

'Was he trying to trap you into treason?' I asked. 'You must report to our father if Bacon is speaking treason . . .'

'Worse than simple treason!' said Henry unhappily. 'And I can't complain to the king! Bacon knows very well that I'm already out of the king's favour. Am I to accuse our father to his face of the capital crime of being a sodomite? Bacon wanted to reassure me . . . that I need not . . . that the king's . . . behaviour . . .'

'You yourself often speak harshly of our father's "behaviour",' I said carefully. 'As do I.'

Henry searched the ceiling for words. 'Bacon wished to assure me that I must not think that all such . . . That there are other men, like himself, of greater refinement than the king, other ways to the same end . . .' His mouth twisted. 'Kindred spirits.'

I busied myself with the handkerchief.

'As a "kindred spirit", he assured me that I need not have to be like my father!' He snatched up his sword and slashed viciously at a curtain. 'How dare he claim me as a "kindred spirit"?'

As often happens, a person can tell you what you need to know while they think they have revealed nothing.

Poor, poor confused Henry, I thought. So much was expected of him, most of all by himself. For the first time in my life, I thought that perhaps his manacles were heavier than mine, and that I had the easier part to play.

53

From the window of the gallery over the King Street Gate, I watched the procession of men-at-arms, trumpeters and flag-bearers moving down Whitehall from the Strand. One of my running footmen had already reported that two German ships had sailed up river the day before to the Pool of London.

The king had returned from Theobald's to meet the new arrivals. He was waiting for me in his little presence chamber, seated on a low dais under a small scarlet canopy. The queen sat beside him, her mouth pinched to a tight line, her eyes fixed on a far corner of the room. She gave the impression that she had gone elsewhere and left behind only her physical husk.

'You sent for me, your majesty?'

'Bessie!' cried my father. The over-excited child again, this time relishing a delightful joke. 'Prepare to meet your new husband.'

'Which one?' I asked coolly though my heart started to race.

'The only one you're going to get! Study German.' My father

326

smiled. 'To please your Frederick.' He watched me keenly from under half-dropped lids.

He's daring me to defy him, I thought. So he can clap me into the Tower, like Arbella.

I shall run away, dressed as a boy, I thought. Tallie would help me sell my jewels. I would cut all the pearls from my gowns and yank off all the silver and amethyst buttons – enough there to live for . . . I will run to Scotland . . . Who might hide me there? No . . . not to Scotland, to the Countess Kildare if I could find her.

I would take Tallie with me, if she wanted to come. I would have to live as a boy . . . a stable groom . . . until the furore over my disappearance died . . . buried even deeper in the heart of England than I had been at Combe. Better buried than married to Brunswick.

'What d'you say to that?' demanded my father.

Better yet, I thought. I would flee to the Americas, where no one had ever seen me. I could live openly as a woman there . . . Henry would help me with secret passage on one of his ships. His friends there would shelter me.

'You might look better pleased.' My father was enjoying himself. And my apparent meekness. 'It's a good Protestant match!' He shot a glance at the queen.

'You aimed higher for her once,' she said to the far corner. 'France pleased us both.'

'France wouldn't have her!' The king glared at me as if the refusal was my fault.

'So now, you will turn our daughter into a huswife!' My mother still did not look at him. She clamped one fist over the other, as if holding it back from striking him. 'You will have her no better than a shop-keeper's wife in a coarse woollen apron! "Goody Palsgrave" they will call her. Where are your great ambitions now? Where are all your grand alliances?'

'Where is Sweden?' he countered. 'Who was it that would

not have mighty Sweden for a son-in-law?' He turned back to me. 'A hit! We have her there, do we not, lassie?'

'A goodwife!' said my mother bitterly. '"Goody Palsgrave", in her market apron and straw hat.'

'The Palsgrave?' I asked. 'The Elector Palatine?'

'Aye, Bessie,' said my father. 'As you're so fond of German Fredericks, I've found you another one.'

'The Duc de Bouillon has returned from the Palatine,' Tallie reported. 'A formal embassy this time, with a firm proposal from the Palsgrave.'

'What does the king say?'

'He hasn't delivered an opinion yet.'

'Did the duke bring a portrait?'

'Not that I've learned so far,' she said. 'But you will be able to see him in the flesh for yourself. He is coming to England in the autumn.'

I was summoned to dine in the great hall. I was too far from the king and his Palatine guest to hear their words, but the music of their voices was harmonious. I went to bed and wept.

I had escaped the first German Frederick, only to fall to the second. Another uncouth, drunken, swaggering haystack. Unable to sleep, I heard the duke's voice murmur insinuatingly, 'She's handsome enough. She'll do.'

I imagined the Elector's eyes probing like those of de Bouillon, weighing me up. In the shadows of the bed canopy, he grew less like a haystack and more like a pig, with a fat round, greasy face and little piggy eyes, snuffling as if I were a box of cakes.

I saw myself forced to open my legs to him. Entered, while I tried to close my nose to the smell of sour sweat and alcohol.

I rolled onto my side. Now, instead, I imagined his disdain for me, and how I would have to lift him on, as the girl at the

328

whorehouse had done with the terrified young man. The calculating caresses . . . bobbing head . . . in her mouth. The thought made me retch.

'Whilst it's happening, go somewhere else . . .' Tallie had quoted the whore who trained her. '. . . the country of your mind is as vast as the world . . . as the Heavens . . . plenty of places in there to run and hide.'

I feared that I would run so far inside my head, trying to hide, that I would lose my way and never find my way back to the real world.

I saw myself turned pale and cold-eyed, like my mother, a creature drained of all vital juices. A living ghost who could barely contain her thrumming of rage and grief and desperate longing.

My head grew thick and hot just imagining it. I would not fade like my mother. I would burst into flame and consume myself. Far better to be a heap of black ashes than the hollow shell that she had become.

I stared up into the shadows of the bed canopy. 'Why the devil does Sweden have to be at war with Denmark?' I demanded between clenched teeth.

'You might be in luck.' Tallie's voice startled me. I had forgotten that she was outside the curtains, sitting beside the bed. 'The queen hates this one, too.'

I pulled back the curtain. 'Do you think my father heeds her?'

Anne moaned and turned over in her sleep. Tallie and I waited until her breathing steadied.

'He must be seen to respect her wishes as your mother,' said Tallie.

I raised my eyes to the bed canopy again. 'I'll be good!' I promised God. 'Please save me from the Germans.'

Tallie snorted. 'I wouldn't ask a man to help me.' There was a pause. 'I have a suitor, too.'

'There's a swarm of them buzzing in Whitehall.' I swallowed. 'Who is he?'

'Master Simon Lynn.'

Not Peter Blank, as everyone expected, but a minor court gentleman attending my brother.

'You can stay with me if you marry,' I said. 'I'm not jealous like the old queen Elizabeth.'

'I don't mean to marry.' She picked up her lute and ended the conversation with a ripple of notes. 'You gave me my freedom. Why should I hand it back to a husband?'

If I had been a Papist, I would have turned nun.

'I can't lay my hands on a copy of the proposal,' said Tallie. 'My tame clerk says that he's under suspicion and dare not help me anymore. I'll try again with someone else.'

'Don't risk your neck.'

'Do you imagine that it's not already at risk? You did warn me at the start.'

'Any further, I mean.'

Anne came into the bedchamber to prepare for bed. 'Preparing to sing already?' She smiled brightly at Tallie as she always did, but could not hide her permanent air of being wounded.

'I'll ask Henry,' I said as if to myself.

Anne had begun to undo her hair. She took a hairpin from between her lips. 'Ask him what?'

'All the things that we women are never told,' I said.

'I have petitioned our father to permit the Palatine marriage,' said Henry. 'This Frederick is a fine fellow.'

'And a Protestant, of course,' I no longer trusted him on the subject of my marriage. 'But there's no sister for you.' I leapt for the ball and missed.

We were playing tennis in the great open court at Whitehall. I wore only a smock and simple, loosely laced linen over-dress. My hair was twisted into a bunch at the back. For a short time, I had felt gloriously light and very hot. Then Henry mentioned his petition.

330

He glanced at the score-keeper to see that his point was being noted. I was doing better than usual today and felt my brother growing a little flustered. My missed ball might help restore his good cheer. I didn't care whether I won or not.

'I hear good things of him,' Henry assured me.

'As you did with the other Frederick? And you haven't answered me about the lack of a sister.' I wiped my top lip on the back of my hand.

'We may have to marry separately if neither of us is to wed a Papist.' He sent me an unhappy glance and called for water.

I felt a chilly spasm in my gut at his words. While he drank, as seriously as he did everything else, I decided to lose.

Winning at tennis meant nothing to me and everything to Henry. The cold spasm gave way to a surge of my new compassion for him, who had always to seem faultless. He, too, would suffer if we were married separately. I was the only person alive whom he trusted with his secret fears.

I watched him wiping his brow with a towel and thought how dearly I loved him, imperfect even more than perfect. I had the odd feeling that I saw another, better self on the far side of the net. The same limbs, the same hair colour, the same set of the mouth. I was both here on my side of the net and there in him.

Tennis was one thing, however, my marriage another.

It was my turn to serve. I bounced the ball a couple of times first. 'Then you would favour this match for me?'

'More than anything.' He missed my serve.

I had forgotten that I meant to lose. But as I watched him chasing after the ball, I felt a jolt as if I had missed a stair. I didn't know why I hadn't seen it before. My brother was not well.

Henry not well. Cecil not well.

We played two more balls.

'I'm tired,' I said.

'We can stop if you like.' The relief on his face terrified me. Then it was replaced by a kindly smile. 'Women aren't strengthened as men are by military exercise.'

His cheek was cold and clammy when I kissed him goodbye.

Henry ill. Cecil ill and losing favour.

The river ice cracked under my feet. I was again alone in the forest.

Henry would be better soon, I told myself. I stopped at a high window to catch a glimpse of his distant figure, surrounded as always by his troupe of young knights when he emerged from the Park Gate on his way back to St. James's Palace. The plague in London was not bad this year. He hadn't cut himself that I could see, and developed a wound that would not heal. With any other young man his age, one might blame too much drink the night before, but not with Henry. It was very likely no more than a bad oyster at dinner.

I felt the old panic of not-knowing.

Tallie was not in my lodgings when I returned from the tennis court. Still in my tennis gown, and with Anne calling faintly after me, I ran unattended through the maze of the main palace to the stables in Scotland Yard. A startled groom handed over his brushes.

I buried my forehead in the soft warm groove behind Wainscot's jaw and felt the muscles move as she chewed her hay. Then I held her velvet muzzle and kissed the beautiful whorl of short hair, like a Catherine Wheel, between her eyes.

'Don't you dare get ill or go lame,' I told her. 'I need you to carry me!'

She nudged me gently and then stood, patient old lady that she had become, while I brushed her so fiercely that loose hairs from her coat made a cloud in the air.

What if my mother was wrong? I thought as I worked. And this marriage was the best for England? It then became my duty. Any ill feeling between me and my father became irrelevant. My feelings became irrelevant. Yet, the marriage might destroy me.

I could avoid it no longer. Though it frightened me, I needed to talk to Cecil.

54

'Why?' Henry demanded.

'God's Body! Why do you ever wish to talk with him? To learn, of course!' I dropped my coin into the swearing box before Henry could ask.

'I'm not sure that it's wise.'

'I've no patience left for wisdom,' I said. 'Is it not enough that I need to talk to the Chief Secretary? Look . . .!' I tugged at the ring he had placed on my finger. 'My need is so urgent . . .!'

He patted the air with a calming hand. 'Don't be a fool, Elizabella. Haven't I always tried to help you with your questions?'

'Generously,' I agreed. 'So why not now?'

'The risk,' he said. 'For everyone. You know that our father watches Cecil jealously.'

I also knew that I had won.

We together went that night to the Privy Stairs. The two men-at-arms saluted Henry but made no jests as they had done with me.

'Wait here. I will join you later.' My brother stepped into an unlit one-man rowing dinghy in the shadows at the foot of the steps. His boatman pulled away, leaving me alone gazing across at the lights of Southwark.

Then I saw a lantern bobbing towards the steps, pushed by the surge of the oars. The wherry was roofed with a canopy that hid the passengers from the world and would muffle their words, even for the oarsman. It bumped gently against the steps.

There was silence. The men-at-arms ignored the wherry as if it weren't there. No voice spoke from under the canopy. The canopy carried no livery device and the boat's lantern hanging on the bow blinded me to what lay inside.

I waited a little longer.

Still, no one spoke.

The strange silence and sense of secrecy kept me from calling out a name.

I went down the steps, lifted my skirts and climbed carefully over the side.

The dark shape of man was sitting under the canopy. 'Is this a kidnap?' I asked, only half in jest.

The wherry pulled away from the steps before I had an answer.

'A forced meeting, I believe,' said Cecil's voice. 'I am at your service, madam.'

My eyes adjusted to the darkness under the canopy roof. A little light from bow lantern fell over my shoulders. I peered again at the lop-sided shape facing me. Cecil seemed to be enclosed in a girdle of odd flat vertical bars tied around his middle.

'Cork,' he said dryly. 'I don't swim.'

'Nor I.' I looked at the dark water around us and remembered my thoughts of sinking out of reach.

'Why do you take the risk of meeting me like this?' Cecil dropped all pretence of pleasantries. And by 'risk' he did not mean drowning.

All the wrong questions crowded into my mouth, not what

I had planned to ask at all. They leapt out of the corners where I had kept them for the last six years.

'Why did you send Abel White away?' I gripped the gunwale and leaned closer to him. 'Why did you never tell Henry that I had written him a warning?'

'That's all in the past now.'

'I still want to know.'

'Why?'

'Because I know that I was in danger then. I need to understand the patterns of my life to be ready when danger comes again.'

'I suppose you do.' He sounded amused. He fell silent and shifted on his bench as if in pain. 'You know as well as I do the risk you took by sending that warning. What if the king had learned that you had guilty knowledge and never told him? I could not let the heir to the throne run that same risk. It was brave of you, but you didn't think it through.'

I nodded dumbly. Along with the rebuke, I heard the word 'brave'.

'The prince is too honourable,' said Cecil. 'He would have gone straight to the king, not thinking straight, neither. And where would that have left you?'

'Why did you protect me? Why didn't you let me speak in Coventry?'

'To what end?' He hesitated. 'Why waste your life or freedom? The plot was already known. Your father was already out of danger, as was your brother. I needed nothing more. Certainly not a brave, if foolish, self-sacrifice.'

'And my guardian conspired with you?'

'He believed in your innocence. And in your love for your brother.'

'Do you still have my letter now?' I knew before I asked that he did. A man like Cecil never destroyed a possible weapon.

He nodded. 'But secure.'

So long as you're alive, I thought. 'Am I in danger from my father?'

'No more than anyone else is. Unless you feel compelled to confess old sins.'

'You know the king's mind better than anyone,' I said. 'You shape his mind – everyone knows that to be true. What is he going to decide to do with me in the end? What do you want him to decide?'

Cecil shifted again. I saw a pale flash of teeth. It might have been either pain or a tight smile. 'You talk about what used to be. Things are much changed. I no longer know the king's secret mind. He no longer cares what I advise.'

'I can't believe that!' I exclaimed.

'You don't want to believe it, my dear. I'm the best father you and your brother ever had, but I can't protect you for much longer. Who wants to believe that their protector is failing?'

I gaped into the shadows. This was not where I had imagined our conversation going. 'I need your help, my lord. I care what you advise. I don't know what to do . . .'

There was a splashing in the water beside the boat. A sleek head broke out of the water. Hands grabbed the gunwale. I had recognised him by the time he pulled himself into the wherry.

'Henry!' I whispered

'No names, dear heart.' He reached for a blanket folded on the seat beside me and wrapped himself in it. When he sat next to me, I felt his body shaking with cold.

'You deign to join us, after all,' said Cecil.

'I knew I wouldn't get a word in edgewise before,' Henry said cheerfully. 'So I left you to it. Are you done?'

'Not yet!' I turned to my brother. 'Have all your swims been a cover for such meetings?'

'Not all,' said Henry. 'But a good many. How else could we hide from the king how often we speak together and that his chief adviser shares news and intelligence with the hated heir? What have you left to ask?'

'I want to know if the shifting and battling will ever end for me?' I said. 'Or is the king merely tormenting me? Does he mean to go through with this Palatine marriage, or will he change his mind yet again? Will I end up like the Lady Arbella, teased with possibilities until I snap. Does he want to drive me to take action, as she did, to give him an excuse to throw me into the Tower, or have me executed as a traitor? I want to know the truth. Instead, I must try to make sense of shreds of gossip and rumour and . . .' I almost said, 'stolen letters' but stopped myself in time.

There was a beat of silence in which I became absolutely certain that Cecil knew all about those filched copies and 'borrowed' paintings.

'You're safer innocent,' said Henry.

'You speak like our father!' I clapped my hand over my mouth the minute the words were out. 'Forgive me,' I said. 'But I have never found innocence to be a safe condition.'

'She speaks the truth,' said Cecil. 'Her grace will make as strong an ally for England as any husband, no matter where she goes. If she is kept informed.'

At these words, I felt an astonishing rush of almost-love for him.

We had crossed half way over the Thames, close enough to Southwark to hear the distant shouts for 'Oars' and cries of vendors. A pair of dogs barked excitedly at each other across the river from opposite shores.

'You can't imagine how much I need to learn,' I said. 'I hate the thought of this proposed Palatine marriage yet fear that it might be my duty, for the good of England. What must I do for England?'

Cecil sighed and shifted again.

'Savoy would swallow you up. You must resist Savoy. If the only bride offered to your brother by Spain is the third

338

daughter of the king, the six-year-old Infanta – and if, even so, Spain insists that the prince converts to Catholicism – I doubt whether Savoy, faced by the Bourbon-Hapsburg alliance, would honour your father's demands. You will never be allowed in the end to raise your children as Protestants in a Catholic country.'

'Which you will do in the Palatine,' said Henry, pretending that his teeth were not rattling.

'The Elector is the most important of the German princes,' said Cecil. 'But not so war-like as your brother.'

I felt Henry's shoulders jerk in a silent laugh. I surmised an old argument between them.

'The Elector is young,' continued Cecil. 'But if he shows that he can exercise power, he may be able to calm hostilities in Europe. He is the least likely of your suitors to draw England into the continental religious wars.'

'Why should England not be drawn in?' demanded Henry. 'I still don't see why you are so firm against war. Surely you don't still hold to our father's opinion that the Papists are no threat to England?'

'England can't afford another war when it can scarce afford a king.' Cecil leaned back and murmured something through the rear curtains. The wherry turned back towards the Privy Stairs.

'You must serve as a peace-offering,' said Cecil. 'Not a pointless sacrifice. I advise you to encourage the Palatine marriage. I fear that I no longer have the power to make it happen.'

Henry reached out and gripped my hand in his icy one. 'Promise me that you will marry this German Frederick. The king does not listen to me, but together Cecil and I might still have a small influence with Parliament and the people. We will help you.'

Cecil having small influence was unthinkable. But reasonable thought seemed to have deserted Whitehall.

I looked from one shadowed face to the other. At the very least, they cut through the confusion and offered me a clear purpose. I nodded.

'I'm afraid I have a poor thanks to give you in return for your advice,' I said. I fumbled in my hanging pouch for the folded paper Tallie had brought me some weeks before.

I held it out now to Cecil. 'Giving this to you feels like an unfriendly act,' I said. I leaned forward to put in within reach of the long-fingered hand on his short arm. An exchange of intelligence.

He took it.

'A work of your cousin, Bacon,' I said. 'In circulation but not yet published. I've no doubt that you've seen it already . . .'

Cecil tilted the paper to catch the lantern light. 'Ah, yes, *"Of Deformity"*. My cousin's faint praise. *"Certainly there is a consent between the body and the mind."* What a pleasing turn of phrase he has.'

Cecil could not possibly read in that near darkness. He knew the words by heart. '. . . *"persons that they think they can at pleasure despise"*. And again, here, we make *"good spials and good whisperers"*. At least he grants us the possibility of "Discipline and Virtue".'

He folded the paper and tucked it inside his cork girdle. 'No matter. I've had worse. But I thank you for your care in warning me. We all seem to be counting our enemies now.' He turned his head to look out over the water. 'An easier task than it used to be. They grow bolder and begin to come out of the trees.'

Cecil is dying, I thought suddenly. I didn't think he wanted to live. Henry was right. Our father's coldness was killing him.

Wee Bobby was not afraid of our father. He was afraid for England and was pouring his knowledge into Henry while he still could.

How fragile we all are, I thought. Henry shivering. Cecil beginning to withdraw his force from the world. I felt a surge of remembered fear, alone in the forest.

I was not happy, but I was clear.

'Are you ill, your grace?' Tallie asked me quietly, as I rose to go to bed that night.

'The world is ill,' I said. 'And I fear that it's beyond me to cure.'

'Is it the Palatine marriage?'

'No!' I said. 'Yes! . . . In part. I don't know!' I glanced at my ladies playing cards by the fire, joined tonight by several gentlemen. Fire glowed through a half-bottle of claret and made small bright pools in the bottoms of their glasses.

'I can't say . . . Which of those gallants is yours?'

'The fair one at the end of the table swears he loves me.'

With a lover's alertness, Lynn seemed to hear us and turned his head from his cards to nod gravely.

'Does he want to marry you?'

'Men swear a great many things they don't mean. Before they have you.'

I turned my head away. 'And after they have you?'

Oh, my poor, poor mother!

'Shall I call him over to us?' I asked. Even as I spoke, Lynn made his excuses to the table and stood up.

Tallie leapt to her feet. 'Pray excuse me, your grace.' By the time Lynn drew near, she had disappeared into my bedchamber.

I don't know what her problem is, I thought, watching his graceful bow. He might be a mere yeoman's son, but I'd have taken him before any man on offer to me. And for Tallie, a yeoman's son attending the Prince of Wales was a large step up from a footman.

I couldn't bear it if she were to leave me to live with a husband in my brother's household. But I would be married very soon, one way or another. My new husband might not want me to bring a blackamoor woman with me. Tallie might not want to go where he took me, and she was her own mistress now. I could not force her.

I followed his wistful glance. 'She can be a prickly cow,' I said. 'Have patience and persevere. At first, I had to be patient almost past enduring. Now I value her above any woman I know.'

He looked startled, then he grinned. 'I didn't think it possible, your grace, because my own opinion of her was already so high, but you have just added to her worth.'

I liked him. And not only because he knew how to turn a compliment back onto me. I resolved on the spot to make a good marriage for Tallie if I couldn't manage one for myself.

Then Tallie brought me the copy of a letter written by a court gentleman to the English ambassador at The Hague, about Cecil.

> . . . *it is on all hands concluded that his Lordship must shortly leave this World, or at least disburden himself of a great part of his Affairs, almost all our great Affairs are come to a Stand, and his Hand is already shrewdly missed.*

'Cecil has gone to Bath,' Henry said, when I showed it to him. 'To try for a cure in the waters.'

'A cure for what? How ill is he?'

'Fierce headaches and cold sweats.' Henry studied his hands for a moment. I thought that concern for Cecil was making him look drawn. 'His belly is grown even more distended than before.'

'I hear good reports of the waters in Bath,' I said, to try to cheer him.

'Our father's coldness is killing him,' said Henry again.

'Don't let it kill you, too. Perhaps the Golden Weasel is

having Wee Bobby poisoned! Bacon has already murdered him with his pen.' I stopped to consider my own suggestion. I ached to believe what I had just said, but unless Carr's apothecary knew a poison that caused the liver to distend and swell, Cecil was being eaten by a canker.

'How do I look?' Henry asked unexpectedly.

I looked at him and let myself see the dark half-moons under his eyes. 'As handsome as ever!' I slid the stolen letter safely inside my bodice. 'Like the future king of England, Scotland, Ireland, and the Americas.'

55

We stood in a row in front of the king, like guilty pupils being called to account. Cecil, looking white and ill, with damp standing on his forehead. Sir Thomas Lake, the Earl of Northampton, Shrewsbury, me. The king glared at us from his chair, wine glass in hand, Carr at his shoulder. From his loose limbs and the devil in his eye, it was clear that my father had been drinking for several hours.

'Who let this happen?' He scanned our faces for an answer. Then he turned to Cecil. 'I should have damned your advice and sent my Rochester, after all, to deal with that French bitch-queen.' He reached back and laid his hand on the arm of Carr, the viscount, as if steadying himself.

'And you!' He turned next to me. 'You're no use at all, Bessie!'

The public announcement had been made in Paris. France and Spain had now formalised their proposed alliance, through the same double-marriages our father still wanted for Henry and me.

'Why didn't your spies give us more warning?' Back to Cecil.

344

The Chief Secretary looked down wearily at the papers in his hand. 'We have known the French queen's plans for the marriage of her children ever since the death of the French king,' he said. 'I'm sure that your majesty will have read the letters from my agents in Paris.' He glanced at Carr, who for many months had been screening the king's papers as well as his petitioners.

Carr looked back unperturbed. His appointment to the Privy Council had just been announced.

'I hold to my advice, your majesty,' said Cecil quietly. 'You are still friends with Spain. "The Peacemaker King" will lose nothing, and England will gain, if the princess marries the German Palatine.'

The king turned away impatiently while his Chief Secretary was speaking. He held out his wine glass to the server to be refilled.

'That's what you advise, is it?' he asked, turning back. 'Have you perhaps been working secretly against the French marriage all along? Undermining me? Telling that royal French cunny to go ahead and ally herself with our old enemy, Spain? Perhaps you advised Spain and France to unite against me.'

'You know that I have always served both you and England loyally.' Cecil's voice was level.

'How do I know that?' shouted the king. 'You fail to secure the money I need from Parliament. You fail to arrange the marriage I most desire for the First Daughter of England. How do I know that you truly want to succeed? Who are you preparing behind my back, as you groomed me while Elizabeth still lived?'

He turned back to me. 'Word must have reached France how you dislike the Dauphin . . . laugh at him and call him names.'

The whole world called him names, I thought, furious at the injustice of his accusation. The whole world smirked at the former Dauphin and his reported antics.

'And all the while, she's in league with her brother, who wants to bury me alive.' He pointed at me. '"I will not marry him!," she says. "I would marry him instead." Letting the world know that she would not marry the Dauphin, who is now a king. Nor the Prince of Savoy. Nor any Catholic prince. "Oh, who could marry a melancholy trout?" she asks.'

One of my ladies, I thought wearily. Or one of Henry's gentlemen. Or a servant, or secretary, or a groom riding unnoticed at our side. One of the invisible people had blabbed.

Even so, my father must know that his accusation was unfair. The bride's dislike of the groom had never before determined a marriage of policy.

'Weel, one of you do something to put this right!'

'What does your majesty desire us to . . .' began Sir Thomas Lake.

'God's Body! Must I decide everything?' The king lunged to his feet and stormed out.

I met Henry in the great open court, freshly arrived from St James's.

'Is the news true, then?' he asked. 'Are the betrothals now confirmed?'

'We can both rejoice at our escape,' I said, still shaky with contained rage. 'But not within hearing of the king.'

'I heard him as I crossed the park,' said Henry with satisfaction. 'Eating his heart out at full bellow. So much for his Middle Way! The Papist enemy is lining up shoulder-to-shoulder against us. England's future role as a Protestant champion on the Continent grows more and more clear . . .'

Henry startled me by stopping and taking my hands. Both of his were cold. 'Promise me again that you will marry the Elector Palatine!'

'I promise,' I said, puzzled by his feverish intensity. Impossible, uneasy thoughts stirred at the back of my mind like the old dreams of my father's demons. I pushed them away again.

*   *   *

346

When my father appointed Robert Carr to the Privy Council, I should have read the sign. Cecil had always opposed Carr's advancement. I should have believed Cecil when he had told me in the boat that he had lost his power.

Just a few weeks later, in May, the impossible happened. Cecil died. After father and son had advised and guided the reigns of two successive monarchs, England no longer had a Cecil.

The death of the Chief Secretary set off an unseemly scramble. Unlike his father, Lord Burleigh, who had trained him, Cecil had not groomed a successor. He was more than 'shrewdly missed'. The governing of England seemed fallen into chaos. I did not need Henry or Tallie to tell me how the kites and wolves fell upon his titles and functions, tearing off gobbets of power here, and sources of income there.

Bacon became Lord-Treasurer. My father did not name a new Chief Secretary. All dispatches for him were received by Sir Thomas Lake, who passed them to Carr who passed them on as he pleased to the king, who may or may not have read them before he sent them back to his favourite to stamp with the royal seal.

Cecil's death also released a terrible flood of scurrilous popular attacks on him, quoted openly, encouraged by Carr.

> *'Here lies Robert Cicil*
> *Composed of back and Pisle'*

And,

> *'Here lies little Crookback*
> *Who justly was reckon'd*
> *Richard the Third and Judas the Second.'*

Sir Francis Bacon published his essay, *On Deformity*. I could not judge whether or not Cecil had ever taken bribes, or other men's wives, or done any of the dreadful things of which he was accused. But it seemed to me that much of the venom was the sort that is loosed upon those who have climbed high by those who remain below.

Now that Cecil was gone, I waited for one of his enemies to try to stop the Palatine marriage, which he had supported. It's possible that, in the confusion after Cecil's death, it was simply forgotten until it was too late.

56

Trumpets! The future was closing on me. There was a rustling and scraping of silks against fine wool, of sequins against jewelled embroidery and gold fringes. Bodices creaked like trees in a wind. Boot soles scraped. Voices surged and fell like water running over stones.

We waited on the royal dais in the Banqueting House, under the canopy, gazing down the long space between the two rows of carved wooden columns. The galleries on either side of the hall were packed.

Summoned to appear the moment he arrived in England, the Palsgrave, Frederick V, Elector Palatine, was arriving in person to present his case. This was the husband I had chosen. A real one. Not made up. Real. I dug the nails of my right hand into my left palm to feel the pain. The more I tried to grip onto the moment, the more it slipped away. I seemed to have a fever, to float uneasily outside my body.

Why does Henry look so pale? And why does he laugh so loudly? I know that forced cheer of his, when he's distracted by private thoughts.

What if the Elector doesn't find me 'handsome enough'? Will he refuse me in front of the court and my parents? I'm certain I will read his distaste in his eyes. What if he can't imagine getting stiff with me?

What if I hate him as much as I fear?

Why did Henry suddenly reach for his chair and sit down, just now? I would expect him to be pacing and turning on the ball of his foot, as if imagining a sword fight. To be sending me encouraging looks.

Why was Baby Charles sent to meet my new suitor at the water stairs? Was Henry feeling too ill? Or did my father want to keep this German in his place?

Tracked by the sound of trumpets, my likely future, still out of sight, was climbing from a boat, mounting the water stairs, entering the gate, striding across paving stones. It entered the Banqueting House and paused, looking uncertain.

Deafened by the internal roar of my own body in my ears, I flicked a quick look at the new arrival. The husband Henry wanted for me. The husband Cecil had advised.

Disappointment made me feel sick, as if I had eaten bad meat. Was this what Henry wanted for me? Was this his 'brother-in-arms'? The newcomer was as strange as the rough German tongue his representatives spoke among themselves. This was not another Frederick Ulrich hesitating just inside the door, but he wasn't another Henry neither. If anything, he was more like Baby Charles than Henry, but darker than either of my brothers, with long black curls and an almost swarthy skin. His plain, salt-stained clothing stood out against the waiting splendour of the court. His linen collar had rucked up at the back. His guttery boots needed polish.

He was small, my own height, perhaps a little less. His curls, and round, rosy cheeks made him look no more than twelve years old, at the most. Was it possible that he was fifteen? He had the large, dark, anxious eyes of a half-grown spaniel. Like a spaniel, he seemed wound-up and quivering with uncertainty.

I tried to imagine the reality of breeding with this boy.

Why didn't he look at me? You'd think his eyes would seek me out before all else.

I saw heads lean together behind him. Smiles, a snigger. Something had happened on the way here. The story, whatever it was, spread from bent head to bent head, behind hands. He heard them and blushed as dark as my old leather boots. He straightened his back but did not look around.

He walked towards us through the stares, braving a shower of eye-beams like thrown lances. He waded forward through the massed curiosity as if breasting his way through deep water.

I felt reluctant admiration for this disappointing stranger. His bearing reminded me that, young as he was, he was already a ruler in his own right. Baby Charles would have turned and fled in tears, then hidden under his bed and refused to come out.

I was still deaf from the pounding of my blood. A freezing terror gripped me unexpectedly. I saw Frederick bow deeply to my father. Their mouths moved in an exchange of civilities. I couldn't hear them through the roaring in my ears.

My father seemed friendly enough but was being the rough-cast version of himself, not the oily international peace-maker. I'm reserving judgement, his manner said.

Or that's what I would have read, in Frederick's place.

I looked at the new arrival's stained travel clothes and saw the subtle malice in the king's pretended eagerness that had summoned this visitor to come at once, before he had time to change into finer, cleaner clothing.

In his salt-stained clothing, Frederick now turned to my glaring mother and bowed so low that two of his dark curls brushed the floor.

The queen pulled her lips tight across her teeth and extended one hand absently, as if brushing away a fly. She left her hand lying in the air, looked up at one of the tall leaded windows, frowning with interest at the red, green, and blue glass geometry. Frederick had barely taken her hand before she withdrew it, rubbing her fingertips together as if to brush them clean of dirt.

The poor little German spaniel could not have turned one degree darker without keeling over with an apoplexy.

The English courtiers near the door smirked again. Some of the prince's German retinue frowned. Two of them exchanged glances. Henry flushed almost as dark as the new arrival.

Ignoring the smirks and whispers, Frederick bowed to the queen again and began a prepared speech to her majesty while she pretended that he wasn't there and half of his audience grinned at his discomfort. My father sat back, mouth moving as if he sucked on a sugar lump, with that assessing look of his that can lead to the gift of a jewel or title or house or else to sudden rage.

With dignity, my poor suitor laboured through to the end of his pious, formalised, favour-seeking oration and turned to Henry. By now, I had settled enough to hear that he was speaking French. With smiles and geniality, my brother tried to make amends for our mother's snub, but Frederick seemed uncertain whether or not to trust this apparent friendliness.

My anger rose at the smirking courtiers, at my mother.

Frederick came at last to me, the cause of this distasteful scene, the reason for his humiliation. I could not bear to think of what would be said in Heidelberg about the manners of the English court.

We looked at each other in a kind of terror. I felt a ridiculous impulse to burst into tears. Too much anticipation. Fury at my mother, at both of my parents for making this boy

352

suffer such humiliation. I was trembling with rage, quite certain that it was nothing else.

Frederick came so close that I could see a line of sweat on his downy upper lip, and a faint smudge of fine silky hair.

He began to bow, to take up my hem and kiss it, as the custom required. With a quick glance at Henry, I curtsied until I almost sat on my heels and snatched up the hand reaching for my hem. In my agitation, I almost fell as I stood up again, but Frederick steadied me. Before I could change my mind, I pulled him closer, leaned across the ledge of my farthingale and kissed him on the lips.

I felt many things at that instant. Satisfaction mingled with indignation, both of which gave me a fervour I had not intended. We collided in mutual surprise and awkwardness. I heard someone in the crowd murmur, '*Brava!*' I noted the unexpected warmth and softness of his full mouth.

I don't know which of us was more startled.

So that's what it's like, I found myself thinking.

I let go of his hand abruptly. Just because I was willing to rescue him from humiliation, he must not presume that I thereby accepted him as a husband-to-be.

Don't look at me like that! I thought. I can't bear it. What I saw in those large dark eyes was hope. Too much like what I was feeling.

Not to be trusted.

He kept staring at me, the churning stew of thoughts going on behind his eyes clear for anyone to read, nothing hidden.

Don't take that kiss so much in earnest, I warned him silently, though I didn't mind the approval I saw. Don't divine too much in it. I winked, the merest flicker of the eyelid, invisible unless you stood directly in front of me.

Frederick blinked. Then he grinned, a blazing flash of delight, gone before I was sure I'd seen it.

'*Princesse . . .*' He dipped his head to acknowledge my

gesture. His face was solemn again but his pupils stayed wide and dark.

They were as unlike my father's dangerous, hooded, pinpoint eyes as you can imagine, I thought. I felt us both now quivering with suppressed . . . not quite laughter. More like the bubbling of possibility.

I nodded my permission to proceed.

He struck an oratorical pose, one forefinger pointing upwards, his other hand clamped over his heart. He drew breath to begin his prepared speech to me. Then, with impeccable comic timing, he seemed to recall something he had forgotten. He rearranged himself to begin again.

This time, he made a double flourish with both hands and bowed so deeply that I thought he would stand on his head and kick his feet into the air like a clown.

I saw eyebrows raised behind him.

When he straightened again, although his face was stern, I imagined a glint of laughter in his eyes. I cocked my head like a listening dog.

The courtly but diffident manner with which he had approached the queen now changed. His voice deepened. The fulsome words required by the occasion grew round and full, inflated until they seemed to fill his mouth and stretch his lips as they ballooned outward into the air.

He looked at me to be certain that I understood what he was doing. I gave him a tiny smile and equally tiny nod.

Yes.

'*O, Reine des étoiles et des océans* . . .' he declaimed. Oh, queen of the heavens and the seas . . . '*Déesse de mon coeur* . . .' Goddess of my heart . . . He rolled out the words with such glorious mock pomposity that I forgot myself and grinned.

He expressed to me his overwhelmed humbleness, the infinite honour, *et cetera, et cetera,* filling the air around us with shiny, bulbous overblown words. He watched me as they floated upwards like a cloud of soap bubbles. I could almost hear them bursting high above all those rich robes and smirks. 'Pop!' 'Pop!' 'Pop!'.

'*Princesse sanspareille . . .*' Peerless princess . . . Up they floated, trembling, shining, absurd. Pop! Pop! '*Unique objet de mon espérance . . .*' Sole object of my hopes . . . Pop!

I was afraid to look at the king. He would know exactly what Frederick was doing.

With theatrical fervour, Frederick pressed both hands to his heart. He seemed fearless now, not caring what anyone thought but me.

Don't jump to conclusions this time, I warned myself. Don't believe just because you want. Perhaps he really is a fool and not just acting one.

I put on a glare like the queen and held out my hand, frowning as if thinking distant thoughts.

He took my hand and kissed it formally, but gave it a tiny squeeze. His hand was now very warm.

I had not mistaken his intent. He understood. He wanted to amuse me. I felt a stab of elation so sharp that it was painful. Who would have thought it could be so intensely delightful to be in collusion?

'. . . *la joie sublime,*' he concluded. He held the pause, waiting like a player for a flourish of unheard trumpets. Sublime joy, indeed.

When we left the Banqueting House, Frederick took my hand again, neither formally nor shyly but as if grabbing for safety, as if I were a lucky charm or an amulet. I should perhaps have objected to his familiarity before negotiations for our marriage had been advanced, let alone concluded, but I felt a rush of warmth at being able to give this feeling of safety.

'How did you dare risk angering both the king and the queen?' I asked.

'Because only your opinion matters,' he said. Then he blushed.

'I wish that were true.'

Then he was dragged away with Henry to wash and change his clothes in his own lodgings at St James's, though I felt that he would have preferred to go with me wherever I went, like a duckling following its mother.

From a high window, I watched him crossing the park with Henry. I felt startled but light. For some reason, I remembered my slight puzzlement at feeling the light blow on my head, alone in the forest long ago, before I saw that what had struck me was the golden leaf.

We both had to wait on the rhythms of state.

'Anatomise him, Tallie! I beg you,' I said. 'He must have faults.'

'If he's a man, he will.'

Knowing now how she had been raised, I forgave her.

I did not speak to him again until the following afternoon. Then, although his visit to my lodgings was formal and we were always surrounded by other people so that we could not speak freely, we laughed a great deal at not very much.

After supper, we met again, this time without the hindrance or buttressing of ceremony. Attended only by Tallie and Lady Anne in my small presence chamber, while my ladies gamed and flirted in the outer room, I waited for him to slip and reveal his true vile nature, like Brunswick. In truth, I was already almost past unfavourable judgement. If Tallie saw faults, I no longer wanted to hear them. I was sliding out of my own control.

His eyelashes were longer and darker than my own, I noted in the midst of my confusion. He gave off a fresh smell, like mountain air. In the firelight, his dark skin looked smooth and elegant beside my fair, freckled Scottish hide – not so dark as Tallie's but enough to make him a different creature from myself. He laughed happily when my dogs leapt up onto bench beside us and licked his ears and pawed at his legs.

Trey dropped onto his forepaws and stuck his rear haunches

in the air, offering to play. Frederick fell to his knees and slapped his hands on the floor to accept the offer.

I stopped laughing. He looked up. Suddenly we grew shy and still.

Trey barked to remind our visitor to pay attention to the game. Frederick smiled and slapped the floor again.

Apart from a slight shadow in his eyes, he now seemed perfect in every detail. I wanted to touch him. I felt sure that he wanted to touch me.

'You should rejoin your ladies,' Tallie murmured in my ear. 'They are all about to burst with curiosity.'

For the rest of the evening, we made somewhat tedious conversation as if marking time with no purpose but to know that we exchanged words and could listen to each other's voices.

A little before bedtime, he kissed me. It was only a forfeit in a game my ladies insisted on playing. But when he leaned over me and put his soft mouth against mine, I wanted him to go on and on kissing me. I could have leaned forever on the warmth of his mouth. I felt my life suffused by a warm, steady light. Happiness had not ended with my childhood, after all. If his kiss felt so good, I knew that I could tolerate the rest. A sudden warmth between my legs suggested that I might even enjoy it.

Then Belle growled from her place on my lap. My ladies laughed.

'She's jealous!' Frederick said with delight. 'Such a clever girl, to see the truth so fast.' He knelt beside me and offered Belle his hand to sniff. 'We must become friends, you and I,' he whispered to her. 'I'm sure we two love your mistress more than any other creatures alive.'

'I'll tell her to bite you if you insist on playing the fool,' I said.

'I'm not playing.' Our eyes met over Belle's head.

For the next few moments, we both scratched earnestly at

Belle's fluffy head, aware only of how our fingers chanced to brush against each other.

'I shall marry him,' I told Anne and Tallie that night.

Six weeks later, any chance of the marriage was gone. The reason was even more terrible than the result.

57

In the second week of Frederick's visit, Henry was forced by a fever to take to his bed. When I visited St James's in the afternoon, he greeted me happily and assured me that he merely had a bit of a chill. Only the day before, Frederick and I had watched him playing tennis, stripped to his shirt.

But Peter Blank told Tallie that the prince had been voiding both stomach and belly for most of the morning, then drinking thirstily between bouts of the flux and vomiting. When Tallie pressed him, Peter confessed that the prince had also been ill twice in the week before Frederick arrived but had sworn all his attendants to secrecy, so as not to spoil the occasion. Then I remembered how pale Henry had looked while we waited in the Banqueting Hall, and how he sat on a chair when I had expected him to stand.

The following day, my brother seemed recovered. Then four days later, on the twenty-ninth of October, he missed the banquet in Frederick's honour at the London Guild Hall. The next day, however, swearing that he was well again, he got up to play cards with Baby Charles and Prince Henry of

Nassau, who had come to England with Frederick. He did the same the next day.

Then even Henry could no longer pretend. His doctors sent reports to the king at Whitehall. The prince was pale and lethargic and could not rise from his bed. His head ached. He continued to spew up all that he ate.

The king ordered a visit to see for himself. My mother insisted on going as well. In the end, all of us – father, mother, Baby Charles, Frederick and I – crossed the park together to St. James's.

I scarcely recognised my brother. The doctors had shaved off his fair hair so that they could apply cupping glasses to his scalp to relieve his headaches. Newly-exposed knobs on his skull changed the shape of his head, making him into a stranger who looked something like my brother. The cupping glasses had burnt red circles into his scalp. His face, looking as raw and naked as a skinned rabbit, was pale and gaunt, stamped with dark half moons under his eyes.

'Your majesties . . .' Ill as he was, Henry tried to stand but had to lie back on his pillows again. He saw my horrified eyes on his hairless head. 'Don't fear, Elizabella,' he said cheerfully. 'It will grow out again before the wedding.'

Don't weep! I ordered myself. Henry must not know what I see!

Our father stood back from the bed. 'He'll recover,' he announced firmly. 'I'll send Mayerne.'

The four attending doctors exchanged glances. They understood very well. They had just been stripped of authority. Mayerne was the king's personal physician.

The king turned and left. The queen and Baby Charles followed him.

'Elizabella!' Henry lifted his hand to hold me back.

I ran to the bed, grasped his hand and stroked it. 'Dearest Hal! Mend! I beg you! You must!'

'Promise me again,' said my brother, 'that you will marry Frederick.'

'Duty and happiness join together,' I said. 'Can't you see how much he pleases me?'

Henry smiled. 'I'm happy for it. But that's mere liking. Promise me also resolve.'

'I swear it!' I said. 'On this hand.' I kissed his palm. Then kissed it again. 'Grow your hair back as fast as you can!'

'Elizabella . . .'

'Bessie!' my father shouted from the outer room. 'Come away at once! You'll tire the prince when he needs all his strength!'

'You don't tire me,' said Henry. 'Come back again, soon. I beg you.'

'I will.' I kissed his hand again. 'I promise.'

My father glared when I emerged from the bedchamber. 'You're not to visit again, d'ye hear? You'll catch the contagion.'

Contagion by illness, I wondered. Or contagion by Henry's power?

That night, I asked Tallie to borrow men's clothes for me again. She brought them, together with the first whispers of poison.

The Archbishop of Canterbury visited my brother.

Cold with terror and desperation, I set off to reach my brother disguised as a groom. I entered through the private gate that opened onto the park, using the key that Henry had given me. Then I slipped through the corridors and up the staircase in King Henry's Tower to the door of my brother's bedchamber.

Snatching a glimpse of the Dauphin's portrait had been easy. This time, people were watching for me, on the king's orders. This time, they saw me, not my livery.

'I'm sorry, your grace, I can't let you pass,' said the man-at-arms on Henry's door. 'His majesty fears the spread of contagion.'

I tried to peer past him into my brother's room. I could smell the sour stink of sickness and a fug of burning herbs.

'Bring me my sword and hat!' my brother was shouting. He struggled to rise from his bed. 'I must be gone! They wait for me in Jamestown!'

'Your highness, you rave.' The doctor placed his hands on Henry's shoulders.

Henry fell back onto his pillows. 'I promised them I would come! I will disappoint . . .'

'Henry!' I screamed. 'I'm here!'

Someone inside closed the door before I knew if he had heard me.

'Your grace,' said the man-at-arms. 'If you will not leave at once, I must escort you back to Whitehall.'

I smelled burning feathers.

I retreated into the park again. Faintly in the distance, I heard my brother screaming. When it grew darker, I tried again through the kitchens, which opened directly onto the park, stealing a flagon of wine to carry with me as a further disguise. This time, I was stopped even sooner, on the outer threshold of Henry's apartments. I tried once more, through the stables. They were alert for me everywhere.

The following day, I returned. I was stopped at the outer gate of the palace.

On the fifth of November, the king was told that his son was dying. 'Eight years!' he was heard to shout. 'Eight years after the plot to kill him along with me!' He fled to Theobald's.

On the same day, first word of the prince's illness reached the general populace. Prayers for his recovery rose in every church. Ralegh was said to have sent a sovereign cordial from his captivity in the Tower, claiming that his remedy was stronger than any poison known to man.

I paced the tennis court gallery and stared from the window across the park as if I could travel to St James's by the force of my will. Frederick stayed at St James's, to be near Henry and ready to bring me word of any change.

'You must try to go in my place!' I told Tallie. 'They might mistake you for Peter.'

Again, she borrowed clothes from Peter Blank. Late that night, she crept into my bed chamber and told me how she gained entry, taking a stinking close stool from a chamber groom doubled over with retching in the passage outside Henry's chamber.

'"I'll empty that," I said to him. And he was more than happy to let me.' She avoided my eyes. 'In the furore inside, no one noticed another groom coming and going with basins.'

Even a black one, I thought with terror. The doctors were blind with panic. 'What are the doctors doing to save him?'

'Their best,' she said, after the slightest hesitation. 'They're afraid, but doing their best.'

'Go back!' I said.

She took my hands briefly and went.

I lay awake on my bed. I must have dozed because I woke the next morning to the sound of shouting and weeping. I flung myself from my bed and ran to the door of my chamber. My maid sat weeping on a stool.

'What is it?'

'The Prince of Wales has died.'

In the corridor, people ran everywhere asking for news, to confirm the news.

'He's dead.'

I saw a groom sitting in a heap on the floor of the gallery, wiping his face with his sleeve. Then I heard Frederick's voice shouting, 'Where is her grace?'

Hatless and panting, he burst through the far door, followed by four breathless gentlemen. 'Your brother lives! I swear it! All this clamour lies. Henry is still alive! I saw him alive only a short time ago.'

He had run all the way from St James's to find me and reassure me.

I clung to him. His heat, even the smell of his sweat comforted me. We went together to pray in the Royal Chapel, then sat side by side in my presence chamber.

'Don't weep!' I shouted at Frances Tyrrell and The Other Elizabeth. 'There's no need to weep.' In one hand, I held my Scottish granite in one hand and with the other gripped Frederick's hand.

'Your brother is strong-willed,' Frederick reassured me. 'He believes that God has a purpose for him on earth. He will fight.'

I imagined Henry drawing himself up and refusing to go with Death, spurning the outstretched bony hand.

'England needs him to live,' I said. I needed him to live.

Frederick stayed with me through the day, saying very little. Holding my hand, touching some part of me while we waited.

'Go back to St James's,' I told him after supper time passed without eating. 'See that he still fights. Urge him on.'

After he left, I sat on Tallie's stool in my bedchamber, hugging her lute case as if holding her place in the universe while she filled mine at St James's.

Shortly before eight o'clock that night, Henry died.

Tallie ran into my room, still in her groom's clothing.

'I know already.' The last unreasoning shred of my hope waited for her to tell me I was wrong.

I heard a faraway howl like a beaten dog, from the King's Lodgings.

'How did it happen?' I asked.

'The doctors are already agreeing among themselves that he died of an ague brought on by swimming at night.'

'Of course they will all agree, to save their own necks! That's not what I mean.'

She looked away and pinched her lips tightly together. 'Your grace . . .'

I tried to take her arm but she pulled free. 'You were there! Tell me!'

'Please . . . You know enough,' she said. 'He's gone. That's more than enough!'

'Tell me what happened!' My wolf spoke, rising up through me from the soles of my feet. 'What did they do to him? Did he feel pain at the end? Was he afraid?'

I heard our breathing loud in the air. 'Which of us do you want to spare?' I demanded.

Her eyes searched mine. 'Though most often out of his wits, he had moments of clarity. I heard him speak once near the end, to ask a question.'

She seemed to hold me up on the beams of her eyes. 'He asked, "Where is my beloved sister?"'

I gasped as though struck in the belly. 'Did he know you?' I begged. 'Did he know that I had sent my other heart to him because I was forbidden to come?'

'There's more,' she said. Reluctantly she opened the hand she had been holding clenched against her breast. 'He gave me this ring for you.'

58

TALLIE

She stumbled and fell as if a hunter's arrow had pierced her heart. I caught her and called for help. This is the most terrible demand for truth she has ever made of me. God help me, I did not lie, but I did not tell all.

What good can it do her to know?

I have betrayed her trust in me. I have destroyed my own joy in being with her, because I must begin to guard my thoughts and tongue again. I am now the secret keeper of truths that properly belong to her, the prince's own flesh, sprung from a shared womb. Hiding them, even from kindness, I must begin to be false again. Everything between us will now be false again. As false as it was until I showed her Southwark and my true self. I had been afraid of the truth, of springing a fatal leak. I had feared the effort of truth-telling, but it was so simple in the end. I opened my mouth and allowed truth to be born. The hard work is lying.

I touched his leg to try to pass on her love. The leg was already dead, already gone. No longer part of him. The part of Henry that still lived was shrinking upwards. The fire dying. Dead ash left behind. . . .

You're not thinking straight, girl. You still stink of the sickroom and your own retch. Your thoughts are scrambled by close stools and shouting doctors. By seeing Death place its hand over the prince's face. By fear.

She will hear from others how it was. In time. The tongues, the tongues in this place! Rumour will not spare her.

How the doctors panicked. How they shaved his head and split open live doves to slap against the scalp to ease his headaches. How he screamed and fought them and clutched his head as if trying to pull it off. How they cut open his veins to let his blood flow. How they cupped him until he was covered in bloody welts. How leeches swelled like blisters on his skin and left marks like the small pox. How they dosed and then purged him until he vomited blood and black bile. Then dosed again until his poor body was almost turned inside out. How he struggled and writhed, loosed his bowels, emptied his stomach, and fell back, scarcely breathing. How they split a live cock and slapped it to the soles of his feet. How his pulse faltered. How he struggled for air so that his screams faded to the gurgle in a drowning man's throat.

'They are killing me!'

No doctor will report those words. But I heard them and don't know what to do with them. That was not wild raving. He knew what he said. I saw his eyes.

He knocked away hands holding the cup to his lips. 'You kill me!'

'He raves,' they said. 'That was always his favourite drink.'

I saw that cup then spilled on purpose onto the floor. It was no accident.

She will learn most, if not all, sooner or later. Then she will know that I did not give her truth. Please God, she doesn't wake and ask for a consoling tune. My hands shake too much to pull music from the strings.

I must tell her all these things, for both our sakes. But not yet.

59

'I knew already,' I said. 'By the ring you brought me.'

He would not have sent it if he had merely been afraid to die. He would not betray his own courage at the last moment. The ring had only one message.

Now Tallie had confirmed that message. Someone had murdered my brother.

'Learn who paid that doctor,' I said. 'The one who spilled the cup.'

We stood side by side like two figures carved in ice. I felt her desire to comfort me and was grateful that she did not try. Her simple presence was the best consolation she could give me. A touch, a gentle word would have shattered me into sharp cold fragments. I had failed to rescue my brother.

Until the message arrived from Sir Thomas Lake, acting as Chief Secretary, I had thought I grieved.

Then I learned that Frederick, too, was to be taken from me.

PART THREE

The Bride

We then are dead, for what doth now remain
To please us more, or what can we call pain
Now we have lost him?

— Lord Herbert of Cherbury

60

'Go back to Heidelberg!' my father shouted at Frederick. 'I can't stomach the sight of yer mooning calf-face! How d'you think I can imagine happiness? Permit music? Tolerate celebration?'

If Frederick obeyed my father and returned to the Palatinate, I knew the marriage would never take place. Frederick could no longer afford me.

I devoured news and rumour, although it made my stomach churn. With Henry dead, I was now second in line to the throne, with only the frail Baby Charles between. If he died, then I would be queen of England, the second Elizabeth. Many thought me likely to be queen. Some wise heads in the Privy Council feared a civil uprising to finish what the Gunpowder Plotters would have begun. The treasonable intention to make me queen grew suddenly more plausible, even likely.

Tallie put on her old re-cut gown from Southwark and went out into the streets of London. At night she whispered to me in little gusts of frosted breath what she heard.

Pssst, pssst! England still remembers its other Elizabeth on the throne. The English yearn to have a female monarch again. Pssst! They had wanted a man but are disillusioned.

371

They've lost the future king they had hoped for. They mock Prince Charles. Pssst, pssst, pssst! There are cries in the streets of London for the 'Elizabeth the Second'.

I wanted to tell her that it was too dangerous even to repeat such words, but I listened greedily, all the same, with the covers pulled up to my neck, unable to stop my shivering.

'Do they say how Henry died?'

'Poison,' she said flatly. 'That the doctors lied to save their necks.'

'Who is blamed?'

She clamped her hand over her mouth and looked at me over her fingers.

'Tallie!'

'The king,' she said.

Our father, still writing the Stuart history of blood and violent death.

Don't jump to conclusions, I told myself.

But the world about me boiled like a wave breaking over rocks and tumbled me on with it.

I had suddenly become a treasure too valuable to throw away on a minor German princeling. If the Palsgrave had been unworthy before Henry died, he sank even deeper now that my value rose. A rush of ambassadors brought renewed suits from abroad. The Scots again pressed for my marriage to the Marquis of Hamilton. My mother again argued for a Catholic match.

In the dark confusion of the days after Henry died, I missed Wee Bobby. I needed to ask him what we should do. I needed him to persuade the king to let the marriage go ahead. I needed Henry, to raise a popular clamour for the marriage by telling the world that it was his last wish.

I was saved by the need for mourning. The king refused to consider proposals till the mourning period was done.

In the meantime, no one dared even to speak of celebration, let alone be seen singing and dancing.

I tried to think who could advise the king in place of Cecil, and be heard.

At one moment, the king seemed to be without a care in this world and rode out hunting, noisy with his usual jests and shouting. Then he would sit without moving, staring at the earth, his fingers twitching as if he pressed the strings of a viol. Silent, refusing to answer anyone. He wouldn't lift his eyes. He neither ate nor drank.

Grief or guilt? I asked. If guilt, then no one was safe.

Then, suddenly, he would raise himself as if he had just remembered an urgent duty and stump off strewing orders and demands behind him.

Only his chamber groom heard him sobbing behind the hangings of his bed after he had ordered everyone to leave. As Tallie had proved, a groom is not truly 'someone' but goes in and out as freely as the dogs, collecting the close stool and renewing the candles that always burn in my father's bedchamber. A groom sees the truth.

I told myself that I didn't know why the king wept so violently, unless at the loss of such an expensive piece of gold which he had meant to trade. I asked again how much of his anguish sprang from guilt. I could not forget the look in Bacon's eyes the night Henry had banished him.

I put Henry's ring on a chain and wore it around my neck. I remembered what he had told me – that an armoured man is vulnerable at only two points. You can kill him if you know these points.

I would have died of my grief if it were not for Frederick. With one limb torn off, I found another beginning to grow. And yet, I almost wished I had never seen him. My father had ordered him to be sent away again. I might have lived without him if I had not known he existed. Now, I could not let him go.

Tallie brought me pieces of Bacon's writings, which I studied for signs of his true nature. A man of clear sight and no compassion, I decided. She had bribed one of Bacon's secretaries to make a copy of the *Eulogium* for Henry that Sir Francis had written but not yet published.

'It hinted at possible patronage,' she said.

I read it. 'The secretary is as much of a fool as his master then. It's a vile piece of work.'

Although nothing in it was false, these were clever, insinuating words that seemed to praise while nicking a vein here, slicing a tendon there. Bacon's praise for Henry was, in truth, his revenge for his public humiliation. A coward's revenge against a dead youth who could not fight back.

61

THE PRAISE OF HENRY, PRINCE OF WALES

Henry, prince of Wales, eldest son of the king of Great Britain, happy in the hopes conceived of him, and now happy in his memory, died on the 6th of November 1612 . . . being a youth who neither offended nor satiated the minds of men. He had by the excellence of his disposition excited high expectations among great numbers of all ranks; nor had through the shortness of his life disappointed them . . . In his countenance were some marks of severity and in his air some appearance of haughtiness . . . He was unquestionably ambitious of commendation and glory . . . he breathed himself something warlike . . . He showed his esteem of learning in general more by the countenance he gave to it, than by the time which he spent on it . . . His affections and passions were not strong, but rather equal than warm. With regard to that of love, there was a wonderful silence . . .

I saw the brutal truth in Bacon's words but also his blindness to my brother's true nature. This was truth without understanding. Truth tinged with malice. I wondered, too, at the man's strange inability to read the king's immoderate grief. I saw suddenly the terrible handicap of extreme Reason.

If a thing were true, he saw no reason not to say it. Anything else was unreasonable.

This failure to understand the power of other men's unreason had doomed him as a courtier. His trust in pure reason had undone him with my brother. If Henry had become king, Bacon's career at court and perhaps even his life would have been finished. Bacon had far more reason than my father to wish Henry dead.

When Tallie left me, I rolled onto my side, curled into a tight ball and pressed my kneecaps so hard against my teeth that my lips bled. I still could not wipe out the unbearable thoughts that filled my head. The guilt was not Bacon's alone. Nor the king's.

I clutched my granite fragment so hard that it cut my palm. I shoved the edge of my coverlet into my mouth so that I would not scream, and moaned like the wind between the rocks on the crags. My eyes swelled with tears I could not shed.

A kind of storm swept through me, as dry as dust. Exhausted, I threw myself onto the pillows and thought back and remembered all that I should have seen earlier. How Henry had tired too soon while playing tennis. His violent shivering in Cecil's boat, which I had blamed on the cold water. The effort it had cost him to rise from his bed to greet visitors.

Now that I let myself see it, my brother had been ill since Easter. I had blamed his pallor and the bruise-like circles under his eyes on grief for Cecil. I had accepted his reassurances to me.

If only I had let myself see what I had not wanted to see!

If only Henry had not been so determined to hide any weakness and to laugh off all concern. It was possible that he had been slowly poisoned ever since Easter.

A strong young man in good health strengthened by discipline and exercise might have survived a poison subtle enough to avoid detection. He had been weakened first.

A long, gradual weakening with one poison, followed by a ferocious, murderous finish with another.

If I had paid attention instead of being blinded by unspeakable fear . . . if Henry had been more willing to admit to frailty, poison might have been detected in time to save him. We might all have taken precautions. His gentlemen and serving people would have been alerted. The poisoner – whether Bacon or not – would almost certainly have been deterred from further attempts.

Henry would still be alive.

I kissed his gold ring, then held it in my mouth. The cold metal had a taste that eluded me, just as Henry's living face had already grown less clear. Blurred by the strangeness of his shaved, knobbed skull, and by the painted image on his coffin, that was like him but not him at all.

He had sent to me for help. I had failed him.

I got up, found Tallie's copy of Bacon's eulogy for my brother and tried to read it again by the light of the night-fire. I could prove nothing against him, yet I believed what Tallie had seen. I believed my brother's ring. I remembered Bacon's eyes when my brother had banished him from his presence – the eyes of a man who knew he had just made an enemy of the future king.

Bacon had not published this eulogy. Why not?

I was certain he had killed my brother. I did not know whether he acted alone or on the orders of the king. I read his writings again. Somewhere in the spaces between the words, he might tell me.

62

'Marry in secret,' advised Anne, who had been invited into the councils of war. 'Then it will be too late for the king to forbid you.'

'And finish in the Tower like my cousin Arbella?' Because I was a direct heir to the throne, my open defiance of the king's will would be clear treason. But I found myself thinking about what she had said, nevertheless. I had learned that I could be a secret traitor. I had studied my father, looking for the unarmoured gaps at armpit and groin.

'Walk with me,' I ordered Tallie after dinner.

We left my ladies grateful by the fire, even Anne, though her eyes followed us out of the room. We did not speak until we entered the long narrow tiltyard gallery.

Every third wooden shutter stood open, letting in enough gloomy light to show that the gallery was deserted. This year, it would not be decked with pine and holly for Christmas tilts. Instead of fresh pine, it smelt only of damp wood, sand, mice and horse droppings from the other side of the shuttered wall, in the long yard where horses were exercised during the worst of the weather. I stared down at the hem of my black skirt, barely visible in the shadows of the floor. I felt filled with shadowy dread, a darkness as dense and heavy and hard to move as a boulder.

'Tallie, help us. If I can't marry Prince Frederick, my wedding bed must be a grave.'

Our relationship had changed since Henry's death. She had taken my place at my dying brother's side. She was the hand that held both of ours and joined them across the distance my father had decreed. She and I were now one in a way I could not have imagined when she first came to me.

'Speaking plain, or courtier-like?' she asked. Whatever change I might feel in our relationship, and in spite of my letter of manumission, Tallie still pretended never quite to trust me and continued to tease me with tests of my willingness to hear the truth.

'I am distraught,' I said. 'I stare into the depths of hell.'

'You survived without the Palsgrave before.'

Our breaths made grey-white puffs in the dark, cold air of the gallery. Our shoes clacked on the creaking wooden floor.

'I survived by ignorance. Because I could not imagine a marriage that would give me joy!' I said. 'But now I know Frederick! I lost my Henry. I will not lose my Frederick too!'

I understood now the desperation that made my mother beat her fists against her own belly when the Countess of Mar refused to hand over Henry. Even though she murdered the babe inside. Nothing mattered to me now, either, but to be with Frederick. My only safety. My only husband. My only hope.

'La,' said Tallie. 'You surpass yourself in immoderation.'

'Don't talk so much like Cecil!' I wanted to pound my fists on my face, to tear out my hair. In my ignorance, I had once thought such acts to be poetic excess. Now I knew them to be urgent and inarguable. My fists clenched and wavered in the air. 'I can't bear it!'

'Someone must try to speak sense in the place of that poor

dead wee man.' Tallie was frowning at me with impatient concern. 'The country's been in the hands of fools and weasels since he died.' She rubbed her lower lip with the pink ball of her back-curved thumb.

'Spit it out!' I ordered. 'I know that look of yours. I pray you, save me from the "fools and weasels".'

She diverted her steps to one of the un-shuttered openings. She put her head out into the tiltyard, then pulled it back. 'You'll get nowhere by flapping about like a headless chicken . . . though I don't suppose Cecil would have said it in quite those words.' She glanced sideways at me. 'You and your sharp wits can do better than that.'

I wanted to tear out a handful of her hair. Or fling myself to the floor in hopes of sinking into it. Then, listening to the echo of her harsh words hanging in the dark air, quite suddenly, I saw that she was right.

I shook myself, a dog emerging from a sudden dive into the icy pond of reason. I wanted to clutch at her hands but protected my dignity with a little distance, and an edge in my voice. 'So what miracles of good sense does the ghost of the late Secretary whisper in your ear?'

We leaned close together so that our skirts met and the clouds of our breaths mingled. 'The Palsgrave must act the attacking general,' she said.

Attack and Frederick did not sit easily together.

'He's too much in awe of your father,' Tallie said. 'The king finds awe tedious. He sees too much of it and loves impudence. Awe turns the Palsgrave into just another favour-seeking courtier.'

Frederick had dignity and self-possession. But, impudence? With my father?

I suddenly saw my new love in a raw, exposing light, unclothed by my private knowledge of him. His youth made vulnerable, his fine limbs reduced to 'small stature'. I tried to imagine his wonderful gleam of laughter and collusion under attack from my harsh, raw-edged, canny father. Frederick's delightful gentle humour would be beaten senseless by my father's shouts of coarse, malicious wit.

'The king dismisses him as a half-grown boy,' said Tallie carefully. 'Calls him the "German Mouse" because of the fright he took at the gun salutes when he arrived. Or so the rumours run.'

'He's not a mouse!' I cried. 'You know it's not true!'

Tallie shrugged. 'What I know counts for nothing. Your father sees only the quivering boy of the gossip.' She hesitated. 'The king believes himself to be a man of reason . . .' Her words trailed away.

We both knew what she left unsaid. My father's reason was seeming less and less able to govern his actions. Since Cecil had died, no one had guided him honestly. Now that no one swept aside the smaller decisions for him, he foundered amidst too many decisions. His reason might urge one way, but if his impulse – or Robert Carr – urged another, that way he would lean. And wine was loosening his reason even further. To say nothing of the storm in his soul that stood for grief at Henry's death.

I tried to imagine Frederick outfacing Carr, the new *de facto* ruler of England.

'Your Frederick's as handsome as any of your father's chamber gentlemen . . .'

'What are you suggesting?' I demanded, my voice rising.

'Only that, just now, with Carr flirting openly with that Howard woman, the king may welcome a new, handsome young man who will tell him what to do next.'

At last, I nodded. 'My poor Frederick. This will be yet another test of his stomach.'

We turned together at the end of the gallery, like a pair of dancers in a figure, and started to walk back.

'Am I so immoderate?' I asked.

Silently, Tallie rolled her eyes to Heaven. But she didn't

deceive me. I could see that she was relieved I had taken her advice so well.

Frederick and I met on horseback in St James's Park. After his threat to arrest me, I did not dare to defy the king openly, but Frederick might.

'Ignore the king's orders to leave England,' I told him.

'But I have already acknowledged them,' he said miserably. 'I can't now pretend.'

'Tell your people to delay packing. Lose papers. Order a new suit of clothes that you must wait to have finished. Arrange for a leak in your flagship.'

Understanding bloomed in his eyes.

Arbella's stubborn refusal to hear or obey orders had delayed her removal to imprisonment in Durham long enough for her to attempt to escape to the Continent. I would have to succeed where she had then failed.

We leaned together and snatched a kiss under the trees with cold-roughened lips. Reluctantly, I straightened in my saddle. 'While your people dawdle, you must make a foray into the enemy camp.'

My chosen husband, my love, my sweetest Frederick, looked alarmed.

'I will have you and none other,' I said. 'Remember, you are also Henry's choice.'

Frederick nodded and swallowed. 'I am your true knight. Point me out the dragon's lair.'

In his voice, I heard both fear and resolve.

Uninvited, Frederick would accompany James to Hertfordshire, to console the king, he would say. With luck the king would not object. He seemed hardly to notice who rode with him.

Tallie and I rehearsed Frederick's part with him.

I told him how sorely the king missed the political advice of Cecil. Frederick must remind him that, with Henry dead,

Frederick was now the greatest hope of the anti-Hapsburg Protestant alliance in Europe, balancing the new threat of a conjoined France and Spain.

'And you must amuse him.'

'Amuse the king?'

'You must be a gallant.' I did not let myself look at Tallie. 'Show him how you can swagger! Take him hunting but never shoot the stag yourself. Then lean close and smile into his eyes. Tell him that he is the wisest, most handsome king in the world! And then ask him about . . .' I tried to think what investigation or philosophy was now the king's chief amusement. 'Tallie will try to learn the subject of the latest trial of wits at his dinner table. Ask anything and then listen. But above all, make him laugh.'

Frederick looked aghast. 'So soon after your brother's death?'

'Trust in me,' I said. 'Most of all, he wants to laugh. Don't fear. It won't all rest on your shoulders. While you're with the king, I will play my part.'

Frederick, Baby Charles and I then piled into a coach to visit my father in Kensington. Then Baby Charles and I returned to Whitehall, leaving Frederick behind to travel with my father to Theobald's.

'I want you to give me Belle,' said Baby Charles.

I had been staring out of the coach window, thinking of Frederick, who must now try to change the king's mind. I turned to stare at my younger brother. 'Want what you like,' I said. 'You can't have her.'

Baby Charles gave a sly look. 'You must. You have to be kinder to me now that Henry is dead.'

'Have I not been kind?'

'You treat me like a baby. And laughed when I couldn't lift Henry's sword.'

Please, God, I thought. Let Frederick hold his nerve.

'I want Belle,' Baby Charles repeated. 'She's prettier than any of my bitches.' He met my eye coolly. 'I will be the next king. I shall ask our father to make you give her to me.'

I shook my head in protest. 'She's my favourite dog.'

At twelve years old, my brother was still small and as spare as a miniature greyhound. His hair was still thin and baby-fine, but his voice had begun to break. Adult angles were beginning to sharpen his narrow, delicate child's face. A new, chilly consideration had replaced the hopeful puppy look in his eyes.

That is England's next king sitting there, I thought with a jolt. Instead of Henry.

'I will have her,' he said.

'Will you leave me nothing?'

'I want her.'

As we tried to stare each other down, I saw that I had lost two brothers, not one.

Back in Whitehall, I invited the Sir Francis Bacon to join me in my barge, telling no one what I intended.

63

'You're a crazed green girl.' Bacon looked away over the cold grey water as if he found my words tedious. We sat like two boulders of wool, wrapped against the cold wind off the Thames. The clouds overhead scudded in from the north, bringing icy mist from the Russian steppes. Moving slowly upriver against the descending tide, we watched the Surrey shore slide by. The dark towers of Lambeth Palace grew larger.

'Don't threaten me with the king,' said Bacon.

He did not see that he shared a boat with a wolf.

The dreary day had reduced the number of boats on the river. There were few pleasure seekers, many loads of cabbages and coal. My barge was not dressed in its royal livery. We were a well-wrapped man in a wide-brimmed hat, a shadowy young woman under the roof.

'What are you trying to say?'

Bacon shrugged, but the hazel eyes under his hat were alert and bright with malice. 'Do you think his majesty truly mourns the loss of the whelp that threatened him? Who has been replaced by a more pliable heir. I think the king would reward rather than punish me . . . if what you seem to be saying were true. Which, of course, it is not.'

We stared at each other.

Did he not hear how much he had just told me in the eloquent spaces between his words?

'Each of us is free to nurse his own suspicions,' he said. 'Those bats of the mind. I know that you were forbidden to visit your brother. In fact, I advised the king against it. I know that your pet blackamoor was spied in his chamber, against the king's orders, dressed as a boy. Soon after she first arrived, the prince died.'

Someone had recognised Tallie after all.

'If anyone poisoned your brother . . . for that is what you are accusing me of, is it not . . . who is the more likely poisoner? An Attorney General or a black witch employed by a daughter twice besmirched by treason and who advances by the prince's death?' His face performed an imitation of amusement. His heavy cloak made it impossible to read his body. 'I hear dangerous rumours against your woman already.'

Started by him, I had no doubt. I had seen for myself that he did not read the inner movements of a man's outward show. But I could not believe that he had seen me with Henry and still believed it possible even to hint that I might have killed him from ambition.

I understood suddenly that he could conceive it, because he himself could kill from ambition.

'If my woman were guilty, I would kill her myself,' I said. 'If you can't see the treacherous ground under your own feet, your reputation for intellect is mistaken.'

'I don't believe that you are the best judge of that.'

'Can the king be the judge?'

'His majesty outshines us all in intellect.'

'Has the king read what you write about Henry?'

'How is that relevant?' I felt a subtle shift as he re-arranged the pattern of his thoughts to meet my new direction. 'No. I have not yet published it for him to see.'

'But you have shown it privately.'

'Only to the closest acquaintance, a few discreet fellow scholars.'

His weakness, the gap in his armour. His cold detachment and imitation of emotion had failed to understand that most human souls are both unreasoning and curious. Even his fellow scholars. Most of all, the king.

I took a paper from my sleeve. 'A copy of your *Eulogium* for my brother,' I said. 'Which, like many of your other works, I have read with interest. I can't believe that the king has not yet seen this.'

'To the best of my knowledge, he has not. But what if he has? I say nothing that I do not mean. Reason will tell the king that all I say is true.'

'And you think that Reason rules the king, just now?'

He shook his head. 'You underestimate his intellect. He will recognise the force of what I say.'

'Then you underestimate his fears and passions. Do you think he will relish what he reads? You may see the intellect but you misjudge the man. As I think you misjudge most men.'

'The wisest counsellor is skilled in his master's business, not his nature.'

'Surely, his master's nature shapes his business.'

His eyes flicked away but quickly regained their steady authority. 'Nature is often hidden. I will not speculate. It asks a strong wit and a strong heart to know when to tell the truth and then to do it.'

'The king will see that you draw blood with your truth-telling pen. My father understands attack better than most men.' Had Bacon never read the deep import of that padded doublet?

I held the paper in a hand bright red with cold and damp. 'Listen to what you say here! Can't you even surmise the effects of these words on a father who imagines that he is about to go mad with grief? Or who wants the world to believe as much? He may change. He most likely will. Then you will be safe to tell the truth. But now? Just now, when he wants the world to observe how he mourns, how will he receive this opinion of his dear, lost child?'

I read: '... *ambitious of commendation and glory ... warlike ... haughtiness ... cold ...*'

'I see no harm in that,' he said stiffly. 'Does an untutored girl pretend to understand such matters better than scholars? Among his many other virtues, the king is a scholar.'

'He is my father,' I said. 'I know him. And I think that you suspect the truth of what I say, or else you would have sent this eulogy to him already, with an eager, oily dedication.'

The wool boulder of his cape shifted uneasily. At last.

A strand of hair began to whip into my eyes. I tucked it behind my ear. My skin felt tight and lips cracked from the cold. I changed direction again.

'Perhaps I can't presume to judge a scholar's work, but I do understand rumour. And I know that you understand its dangers. Why else warn me of the rumours about my serving woman?'

I licked the taste of blood from my cracked lower lip and was reminded of Frederick Ulrich, who must never be allowed to re-enter my life. The barge rocked in the wake of a passing lighter. I shivered and pulled my cloak tighter around my neck.

His arrogant silence angered me. As if he had only to stay silent and I would disappear, a temporary gnat buzzing in his ear.

'You misjudge me, as well,' I said.

He attempted a look of scorn, but the muscles of his face would not seat themselves properly. 'To the point, then. With what, exactly, do you threaten me?'

'I can loosen your grip on your late cousin's powers. Who will be believed by the Privy Council? A late-ascending, favour-seeking Attorney General – who has made enemies at court – or the king's daughter, second in line for the English throne? Think how much damage even the rumour of my accusation will do. Your enemies will relish the whispers.'

The wide brim of Bacon's hat flapped in the wind. Anyone watching us would have thought us both intent on the empty workmen's scaffolding that banged on its ropes against the chapel walls and towers of Lambeth Palace. The silence lengthened. Then he shook his head in amused disbelief.

I could not judge the effect of my threat. I chanced my last arrow. 'My brother told me all that you said to him the night he banished you from his presence.'

The colour drained from his face.

I felt a little dazed by this sudden easy victory. I had understood what Henry had not said. I had not been mistaken.

But Bacon rallied. 'The prince's illness may have begun long before it made itself known. It's widely known that he lost his reason. He raved and saw what was not there.'

'At the end. This was many months ago.' I chose my words carefully so that I did not entirely lie. 'That night, you made an enemy of the prince, and he made his feelings plain to all who were there. My death now would not save you. Your court career was over once he became king. There's reason for you.'

At last our gazes truly met.

'I believe that leaves us at an impasse,' he said. 'I denounce you and your woman on logical supposition and proven disobedience. In return, you denounce me without proof while unleashing the destructive power of rumour.' He made an impatient gesture with one hand. 'I suggest, your grace, that you set me down on the stairs and we agree to forget this monstrous conversation.'

I looked at him with steady wolf eyes. 'Impasse? I see a possible agreement that works to the advantage of us both.'

Bacon was watching me now without moving a muscle. The pupils of his eyes closed down to pinheads.

'The king hungers for wise advice now that your cousin is dead.' I said. 'I want you to step into your cousin's shoes and advise the king why England needs the Palatine marriage.'

He half-smiled. 'I believe that I may achieve my ambition without the advice of an ignorant girl.'

The young she-wolf refused to loosen her jaws.

'The world whispers that my brother was poisoned. Being already so close to the centre, you no doubt heard who is most often blamed. He must have had an agent. If you advise the king as I suggest, I will keep silent about who I believe that agent to have been.'

'Can it escape you that you weave your blackmail from a web of lies?'

'It won't escape you that my father will think twice before he risks advancing a man even faintly tainted by guilt in the prince's death, whether it's true or not.'

Even then, Bacon admitted nothing. He agreed nothing. But he was thinking. I signalled to my barge men. We turned and let the out-flowing current sweep us back downstream.

'Have you thought,' he asked suddenly, 'that your brother brought on his own death through his uncommon fondness for swimming at night?'

'I fear greatly that his night exercise might indeed have put him in danger.'

After a long assessing look, he said nothing more until we reached the Privy Stairs.

He offered his hand to help me from the barge. I could not bring myself to take it.

'Take care, your grace. The steps are slippery.' He acted the very picture of an attentive courtier. 'Did you imagine no one would learn of your spying?' he murmured. 'One of the clerks your woman bribed was in my pay. His majesty would not be pleased to learn of her theft of official letters. A capital crime, I believe.'

'She served the king's daughter.' I concentrated on placing my feet on the treacherous, damp green stairs.

When I had safely mounted the jetty, he added loudly enough for the men-at-arms to hear, 'Your grace speaks wisely. In these difficult times, we must all endeavour to help one another.'

Bacon might or might not do as I asked. The king might or might not listen. I felt I had lost almost as much as I might have won. I knew that Tallie, my betrayed intelligencer, was in mortal danger. She was my only witness, my only true weapon against Bacon.

Almost worse, even though he had called my accusations against him 'lies', he had not denied that my father had ordered my brother's death. He had implied that he had acted on the king's orders. He had even given my father a reason. 'A more pliable heir.'

If only Tallie were truly the witch that Sir Francis had called her. Together, she and I would trap him in a manikin, drive thorns through his head and cock, and wiggle them to and fro. Then I would push one, very slowly, into his heart.

Witch or no witch, Tallie was in danger from Bacon, because she had served me.

I did not stop shaking for several hours after he and I parted. After trying to be cheerful with my ladies, I took to my bed. I was past pretending.

Bacon was now my enemy, too. But if I had persuaded him, I would be happy. If I had lost my gamble, I would want to die in any case. Tallie's case was different. I had to send her away. Putting her beyond the reach of Bacon and his net of agents and intelligencers, meant also putting her beyond my own.

64

I told her at once what had happened with Bacon and what we must do.

She closed her eyes. Then she nodded.

'Nowhere in England is safe from Bacon,' I said. 'Nor France. Where would you like to go?' I glanced at her. 'Africa?'

'I would not be at home there,' she said after a time. 'Nor altogether a stranger neither. I have experience only of being strange.'

'America is strange,' I said.

Neither of us went to supper. While the other ladies dined in their rooms, Tallie and I sat together on a window seat in the Tennis Gallery, not speaking, clasping hands.

I felt hollow with coming loss.

Suddenly, she startled me by raising my hand and pressing it to her mouth. When she lowered my hand, I felt that the back was wet.

She released my hand and wiped her eyes with the heels of her palms. 'And I'm also afraid,' she said. 'And yet happy as well.' With an attempt at her usual dryness, she touched Diana. 'Can you understand?'

I nodded.

*   *   *

The *Speedwell* was soon to sail from London for Chesapeake Bay. I commissioned Simon Lynn to arrange passage for her, secretly. Though Tallie still refused his offer of marriage, I trusted him to protect her. Word of her intended departure would soon leak out, but I wanted Bacon left in ignorance for as long as possible.

I watched her packing. I gave her a coral necklace for protection. I gave her a case of *eau de vie*, and a box of apples wrapped in silk and dried herbs from an apothecary to treat every ill from the ague to the plague. I gave her a thick brown wool cloak that reeked of the sheep's grease used to make it proof against rain.

I put her up on Wainscot while I mounted Clapper and led her beside me along the Thames, to teach her to ride. I gave her a pair of riding boots and a woman's saddle and three embroidered saddle cloths.

I gave her a writing chest filled with paper and silver-mounted bottles of ink, so that she could send me letters.

'I will still expect reports,' I told her.

I tried to think what she might need in that unknown, distant land. I could not imagine what her life would be. I gave her a needle case, and coloured silks and a pair of silver scissors. I gave her a hunting knife and a clock. Nothing I gave seemed enough to keep her safe.

I watched her prepare to leave me, stocking by stocking, gown by gown. On the last day, when she set her lute case on top of the pile to wait for the porters, I had to run from the room.

My only cheer was that Lynn had decided to sail on the same voyage. Since my brother's death, he said, England held nothing for him.

He saw the unasked question in my eyes.

'I'm stubborn,' he said. 'As persistent as time.'

I kissed her. I found that I could not let go of her hands. The boatmen rattled their oars impatiently below the dock at

Gravesend. The weather was so far fine, but the winds were expected to shift. Tiny figures ran busily on the decks of the *Speedwell*, anchored out at its mooring. They lashed down the last barrels. A sail unfurled and shivered delicately downward. A flock of raucous gulls circled above us, ready to swoop on any hint of food.

I knew I must let her go. Reason told me that I wanted as much as Tallie herself to get her safely away from England.

I heard the distant sail snap in a rising wind. A gust whipped my hair into my eyes.

Time was pushing us onwards, out of our control. The moments before execution must feel very like this, I thought, though they would be unlikely to smell of salt water and fish.

The truth was that I wanted her to stay and she wanted to go.

'How will I manage without you?' I asked.

'Very ill, I'm sure.' She smiled. She had regained her familiar poise. 'You'll have to hire a new spy and learn to speak the truth to yourself.'

'Are you trying to make us quarrel so I won't mind so much?' I watched the last bale being winched up from the lighter that bobbed alongside the *Speedwell*.

'No,' she said. 'Merely playing my part to the end.'

'Was it no more than a part?' I asked. 'Tell me the truth! Did I force you always to pretend?'

She smiled down at the damp, heavy stone beneath her feet. 'You have no idea!'

'Then I don't know you at all!'

'On the contrary, you helped make me what I've become.'

I was afraid to ask her what she thought that was.

'I mean still to torment you from a distance,' I said. 'I shall have Lynn knighted. Then, if you do relent and agree to marry him, you'll be Lady Lynn and have to learn to be dainty and well-behaved. That will force you to act against the grain.'

'I'll never marry.'

'Marriage doesn't seem so terrible to me.'

'We've already spoken more than enough about this matter.' Her voice was more gentle than her words. 'You get yourself married to the Palsgrave. It's the closest you'll get to manumission.'

'I don't know if I can.'

'You did it for me. And trust your Frederick to work on the king.'

We stood in silence, listening to the waves slapping against the dockside. The gulls swung away with eager cries towards an approaching fishing boat.

If she wasn't going to weep again, neither would I. Weeping felt too dangerous, as if it might tear loose my inner parts. Anything we had left to say to each other could not be said now, in these last few moments, with sailors rattling their oars below us. It was too late to make good any omissions.

'Hey, ho. Onwards,' she said at last. 'I pierce the mirror and soar up with a great clap of my wings.'

I looked at her, puzzled.

She smiled and shook her head gently. 'An old dream I once had.'

'You have my brother's standard?' I asked.

'Of course. Already on board, wrapped up safe in my cabin. I'll write to tell you when it has been raised on Cape Henry.'

'I'm losing you too.'

'Now that you have the Palsgrave, you won't need me – or all those dogs.'

'*If* I have the Palsgrave.' My head rattled with unspoken words. 'I'm already teaching the dogs German.' The moments of our last chance were seeping away. Along with all the truths she had not had time to tell me.

'What if Frederick won't stiffen?' I burst out.

Tallie peered into my eyes. Then she threw back her head and guffawed. She waved a derisive hand. 'He will, never fear! He's young! And in good health. And you're . . .'

'. . . handsome enough,' I cut in. 'I know.'

'Are you in earnest?'

'What else should I be?'

'Your grace . . .'

'Please don't laugh at me when we're about to part!'

'Your grace . . . Elizabeth . . .' She took both my hands and shook them gently. 'Surely, you must look into a glass from time to time!'

'Please . . .'

'D' you not know?'

I turned my face away from her.

'You are a fool after all!' she said. With one hand, she hauled the medallion of Diana free from her cloak. 'Remember this?'

I nodded.

'Then open your stubborn ears and listen to me! You're more than "handsome enough". You're a real beauty – unless you've a taste for whey-faced prigs. Look at you! You're the envy of all your ladies.' She stepped back and swept her hands through the air from my head to my feet. 'All golden and ripe and full of life!'

'Don't taunt me, Tallie! We don't have time to quarrel and make up.'

'I promise you, you won't need to do a thing on your wedding night! Not one single Southwark trick. Not with that hair, and mouth and those big blue eyes! And those long legs hidden under all your skirts. And neat, round little titties that would earn you a pile of gold sovereigns in Southwark. Just show yourself to your Frederick in your naked beauty. He'll manage the rest. And that's the truth!'

With that unexpected farewell gift, she dropped me a curtsy and turned to give her hand to Lynn, who was waiting to help her down the stairs into the boat.

The sailors unshipped their oars. At the skipper's shout, the oars bit into the waves. The gap between us widened. Slowly, the boat grew smaller. Against the dark water, her skin disappeared, so that I had the curious impression that her clothing moved away by itself and that Tallie herself had not gone at all. I waved.

A pale silk sleeve waved back.

Tallie, Henry. Goodbye to you both. The Americas are so far away. Tallie, you show me how to leap. At least, you are accompanied by a man who loves you. I try not to fear for you in that wild unknown place . . . trying not to weep . . . I remind myself of your good sense, your stubbornness and your ferocity veiled by good behaviour. Your music. My unexpected sister. Queen of the Americas.

65

'Belle.' I called. She had not run to greet me when I returned from Gravesend to Whitehall after saying farewell to Tallie. 'Belle!'

I went into my bedchamber. Cherami, Bichette, and Mars, the dog pup from the king's kennels, all jumped off the bed and ran to paw at my skirts. I gave my maid my travelling cloak.

'Where's Belle?' I stooped down to stroke the other dogs. 'Do you know where she is?' Fragile with loss, I needed to hold her and kiss her head.

I looked under the bed, in cupboards, behind wall-hangings. I looked down into the orchard. She was not there, playing with a groom. I searched my apartments, calling her name. My ladies had not seen her that day. Nor had the maids, grooms or footmen.

Belle never strayed alone from my apartments. I could see her lying, flat and empty and dead under a bush, like the *paraquetto*. I saw her floating, swollen with putrefaction, in the Thames.

'Find her!'

The urgency in my voice sent my servants running, grooms, secretaries, maids, even my ladies.

With Anne's help, I searched the orchards. Then we crossed over the King Street Gate to the privy gardens, where we peered under every box and laurel, growing more and more certain that I was looking for lifeless fur.

I turned my head towards a scuffle at one of the garden gates. Two of my grooms were hauling a third youth between them.

'Your grace!' one of them shouted urgently.

They dragged their struggling captive towards me. 'Tell her!'

He swung his head into the face of one of his captors and almost escaped. Then the other groom elbowed him in the gut.

'Stop this!'

All three suddenly drew to attention. 'Tell her,' the first groom prompted again.

'He stole her,' said the other.

'Belle?' I asked.

'Yes!' chorused the two captors.

The captive stared sullenly at the ground, his mouth clamped shut. His right eye had already begun to swell. One of the grooms elbowed him again. 'Tell her what you told us.'

'Did you steal my dog?' I demanded.

'I had to, your grace. The prince ordered me.'

He wore my younger brother's livery.

I wrote to Baby Charles asking him to return my dog. He wrote back that he would not. I should have given her to him in the first place, when he had asked.

I wrote to the king. I had a reply from Carr. I had many other dogs, it said. I would not be able to take them all with me when I left England after marriage. The duke needed consolation after the death of his older brother. The king instructed me that, in the spirit of Christian generosity, I could not object, etcetera.

In short, Baby Charles would keep Belle, whether I liked it or not.

I tore the letter across.

My ladies all looked at me.

'He's to keep her!' I tore Carr's letter again and again. I crushed the pieces and threw them into the fire.

'Leave me!' I said. 'All of you!'

I saw my ladies exchange glances. Belle was merely a dog, their eyes said.

When I was alone, uncontrolled weeping overcame me at last.

66

Frederick returned from Theobald's before Christmas. 'I worked to charm him,' he reported. 'I am become his "sweetest little German mouse". He swears that he will have no son-in-law but me – but not yet. Not while England still drowns in tears for the Prince of Wales. He says that I must return to Heidelberg and return to press my suit again when the mourning is done. In the summer, perhaps.'

And before then, my father would have changed his mind yet again.

I pressed Frederick's palms to my cheeks. 'If he sends you away, I'll drown myself in the wake of your ship.'

'No!' He kissed my hands. 'No! No! I couldn't live, then. I would drown myself with you. Our souls would live together as dolphins!' He kissed my hands again, as if this were already our final farewell.

My father was toying with us. He dangled happiness, meaning to snatch it away. Thames and Rhine would never flow together. I dared not complain. He had made it clear what he would do if I ever dared to defy him again about my marriage.

'Drag your feet,' I said. 'Smile and say that you obey him

and prepare to go. Move as slowly as you dare. We must seem to obey while we find some way to keep you here.'

As if he had detected our strategy, my father devised yet another torment. He now kept Frederick in attendance on him almost day and night so that I never saw him.

I believed that Bacon would do as I asked but could not be certain. Even if he obeyed me, I did not know whether his advice would sway the king. I tried to think what more I could do. I thought I would go mad.

I tried to pass the time by playing my lute, but the sound felt thin and forlorn without Tallie's lute singing too. My fears sprang up between the notes and fogged the melody. The place in me from which music sprang felt hollow and dry. If I lost Frederick, I would never make music again.

I sat down to meals and rose again. I rode. I tried to play with my dogs but the absence of Belle destroyed my former pleasure. I accepted hands of cards and threw them down on the table again. Night after night, I picked melted wax from the candles and made it into tiny balls. I would arrange these balls in a straight line, then squeeze them together again into larger ones that I threw into the fire, where I watched them melt into the coals.

I drank wine with Lucy and probed her for court gossip. She told me enough to confirm my fears that the king still entertained the envoys of other suitors, whatever he might have told Frederick. The queen still wrote to Savoy. I myself had seen the hopeful arrival of another envoy from Brunswick. And I was inclined to believe the whispers that the king's waiting gentlemen were more and more often finding excuses to avoid his changeable, irritable presence. I was waiting for the ghostly abbot again, lying in the dark stiff with fear.

Send me the ghost! I thought. Anything but this waiting in ignorance!

In my imagination, I saw Frederick being seized and bundled aboard a ship before he could send me word. From seeming possible, it grew to seem likely. When I still heard nothing from Frederick, his secret forced departure swelled into certain fact.

I would dive deep into the dark water, I decided, as soon as his departure was confirmed. At night, when no one could see to fish me out. Gulls, or a curious dog, would find me washed up like seaweed on the estuary mud.

'I'm weary,' I announced one evening. 'You may all go now.'

'I shall make you a comforting posset,' said Anne. 'This is not an easy time.'

I nodded, called Cherami, Bichette and Mars and went into my sleeping chamber. Trey was already curled in his basket by the fire, stinking and wheezing in his sleep. Turning over a book from my table, I heard voices. I almost collided with Anne at the door.

'He's here!'

Frederick was warming himself distractedly at the fire. He looked at me with such open longing that I felt faint. 'His majesty was lost in drink. I escaped,' he said.

'Two possets,' said Anne firmly.

When she had left, I flung myself into his arms. 'I was afraid you were gone for ever,' I said.

'They would have to kill me first.' He kissed my mouth, my neck. I burrowed into his warmth, all shyness banished by my relief to find him still there. My place in the world was there, pressed against him, with his arms around me. My fingers touched his soft hair, the intricate shells of his ear, the dark down on his upper lip.

When Anne returned with the two warm, foaming mugs, we stepped apart, reluctantly. I held onto his hand, unable to break our contact completely.

Frederick looked down at the gold and enamelled collar, which I now saw hanging across his chest. 'The king gave this to me this afternoon, after dinner.'

'It's the collar and George of the Order of the Garter!' I exclaimed. 'My father has made you a Knight of the Garter, one of the highest honours he can give. This must be good news!'

Frederick looked doubtful. He fingered the pendant, a mounted knight spearing the dragon that lay under his horse's hoofs. 'I'm not certain. Perhaps because I'm unfamiliar with English customs . . . You must explain to me, Lizzie.'

With both hands, he lifted off the heavy collar and frowned down at the enamelled garters set with red enamelled roses, all linked by golden tassels. 'It did not feel like such a great honour to me. His majesty was still in bed, when I arrived.'

'My father takes pride in behaving badly,' I assured him and myself. 'Grown worse since Henry died.'

'But, undressed? In his night shirt, in the afternoon?'

'He suffers from gout and often stays close to his bed. Does he not, Anne?'

'Indeed he does.'

Frederick looked from one of our eager faces to the other, then down at the George again. 'At first, he stared at me with such a puzzled frown that I was certain he had forgot why he summoned me.'

'He often pretends that, in order to cause discomfort,' I said. 'What did you do then?'

'Ventured my good wishes for his recovery – to which he did not reply. Then I pretended to play with his dog, to try to make him laugh, as you told me.'

'But he didn't send you away again?'

'On the contrary, he seemed to remember himself all of a sudden and motioned me close to the bed. Then he mumbled a few words in English and dropped this over my head.'

My rising hope sank back down onto its haunches. 'Did he first dub you a knight?'

Frederick looked stricken. 'No.' He frowned at the wall.

'He did not,' he said firmly. 'I have created knights myself. I believe I would have known.'

Chilled by a sudden thought, I leaned close and looked more closely at the George.

Not a taunting counterfeit. Not a wheelwright or barber's livery badge. Not the arms of an executed enemy. I exhaled in relief.

'It was Henry's, the king told me. Then asked me if such a thing was known in Heidelberg.'

Henry's George. Henry, who might have been poisoned on the king's orders. A garter but no knighthood. The king had just given Frederick a gift of the most tender sort from a grieving father-in-law to-be, or else a taunting threat.

I had lost Henry, Tallie, Belle. I had lost my mother, if I had ever had her. My younger brother had become a chilly enemy. My father would continue to waver and change his mind. He had ordered my brother to be murdered – or he had not. I would marry Frederick – or I would not. I was to wed a Catholic. I was to wed a Protestant. I was never to marry at all and would wither in the Tower like Arbella when desperation at last drove me to folly. I could bear no more uncertainty.

I handed back the George. 'Enough,' I said.

'What do you mean to do?' Frederick had already learned to read my face. 'Bessie, you are frightening me. You know what he threatened, if you defied him.'

'I mean to be my father's daughter,' I said.

67

WHITEHALL, NOVEMBER 1612

Where did I get the stomach? The sheer effrontery? What gave me the courage?

I think it was the memory of courage, now almost forgotten, the memory of saying that I would rather die than submit, then turning my back and walking away.

Once she had been born, that fierce unthinking girl-child had survived secretly, hidden deep inside me, stubbornly, silently triumphant. She pulled a dark cloth over her face. She lay quiet and waited, a moth camouflaged against tree bark, detectable only by the faintest suggestion of an outline. Now, she sat up and revealed her face. She laid her hand over the face of reason. As if giving up were not a choice, she said, 'Do it.'

68

My father had dressed in a loose gown but wore his diamond-studded hat when I presented myself at his lodgings the next morning. He was still in his bedchamber, drinking beside the fire with his inflamed unshod foot propped on a stool.

Sir Thomas Lake stood near him, looking wary. Bacon leaned in the window alcove. Apart from Lake and Bacon, only two secretaries and Carr attended the king. The half-dozen grooms and running footmen waiting by the wall had a head-down-I'm-not-here air. The only creatures at ease in the room were the two hounds asleep by the king's chair.

I noted the absence of other attending gentlemen. The whispers of diplomatic reasons for absence appeared to be accurate.

'My honoured father . . .' I curtsied. 'I heard that you are troubled with the gout and have brought you a hopeful remedy.' I offered a tincture of crocus in a gilt-edged bottle.

He turned the little bottle in his hand, thoughtfully. 'So dutiful? So sudden?'

'I'll swallow some first, if you like,' I said.

'That's better,' he said. 'I know that impudence. What d'you

407

want of me, Bess? It's not like you to come crawling, all sweet as sugar, like an arse-licking petitioner.'

Sir Thomas Lake cleared his throat. Sir Francis's moustaches twitched in amusement.

'May I speak with you alone, sir?' I said. I watched the challenging swagger of Carr's back as he left the room with the rest. The door closed.

'England needs you to make a decision,' I said.

'"England needs"?' The king glanced at me with reddened, heavy-lidded eyes. 'Or "you need"?' He was too quick. Unlike Bacon, my father could read the true meaning hiding in the speech of others. 'Everyone seems to be advising me now on what England needs. Lake advises. Bacon advises. Now even my daughter advises.'

'Your majesty, England needs me to marry Frederick . . . the Palsgrave,' I said stubbornly. 'Now. The people need to feel solidity in the disorder since Cecil and Henry died. Only you can give them that solidity. They need to know that they are ruled again.'

He sucked on his imaginary sugar lump and studied me with eyes that suddenly reminded me of Sir Francis Bacon. 'The eyes of a hungry ferret,' Salisbury had said of his cousin. My father's eyes were less friendly.

'I need the advice of a lassie now, do I?'

Driven by desperate will, I ploughed on. 'Even in their grief, the English people need to feel the possibility of joy as well as sorrow. They need to know that happiness can return. That you will gift them with joy again.'

This, to a man who might have ordered his own son to be murdered. If so, he did it out of fear, I told myself. Out of weakness.

'The human soul hungers for joy,' I said.

'And when did you turn philosopher?'

I chose my path, which until that instant I had not known. I threw the dice. I chose truth, defiant or not.

I knelt and took his hand. 'Dearest father, my heart, not philosophy, tells me that you feel lost. As we all feel lost. But only you can lead us out of darkness . . .'

He gasped, flung off my hands so violently that I fell. He rose to his feet, forgetting his gouty foot, stepped on it, stumbled. '. . . Aiee! Shit!' He hobbled two painful steps to catch his balance.

I scrambled to my feet.

He turned on me, unleashing his rage. 'How dare ye?' he shouted. 'Who are you to dare counsel me? A smock! A vixen! Who are ye, t'think you know anything of what England needs?'

'I've learned a little while standing all those times like a prize heifer on show!' I shouted back, jutting my chin just as fiercely as he did. 'I've got eyes and ears! I've learned that I'm treaties and trade agreements and military alliances! I know enough to know that!'

I held out my hands and wiggled my fingers. 'I've learned that these are worth gold coins!' I pointed to my right elbow, bruised by my fall. 'Silver ingot . . . And here's another.' I pointed to my left elbow.

I kicked a foot out under the hem of my skirt. 'Worth Baltic oak.' My eyes? I pointed. 'Diamonds.' My teeth? 'Pearls.' I thumped my skull. 'D'you think I've nothing in here but dried peas?'

'And what about that little royal cunny? What's the value of that?'

This question, from a father, snatched the breath from me.

He nodded, pleased with his effect on me. 'Aren't ye glad you didn't challenge me before the whole court? There's none here now but the fish down there in the river to see ye go as red as a swollen cock.'

I recovered at last. 'Aren't you glad I've got a royal cunny? And that you'll be putting the price on it, not me?'

He didn't even blink. 'Why weren't ye the first born . . .'

For an instant, he disappeared into a private thought. 'And if you were a boy as well . . .' He tilted his head to one side in mock appraisal.

'But as I'm not a boy . . .' I began, giddy with that faint, extraordinary whiff of praise.

'Don't let kind words go to your head.' He took off his hat. The diamond flared in the sun, a deep pool of cold tiny fires, the size of a bantam's egg.

'Don't try to tell me your worth,' he said in impeccable London English, not a trace of Scots in his voice now. 'Do you imagine that I hold anything in this world to be priceless? Least of all, you?'

He straightened and seemed to grow taller. 'Bessie, your heart may well tell you all manner of nonsense. But my heart is as cold as this stone . . .' He paused as if listening to the echo of his words. 'Some plodding poetaster must have written that.'

He wiggled the hat to make the diamond flash until it seemed that a whole constellation of stars had been caught and compressed into its depths. 'I'll tell you what I truly feel. Nothing matters to me but to be entertained every minute until I die. In both flesh and in wit. When everyone else fails me, as they must, I amuse myself. You have just entertained me, but that moment is already passing.'

If I were a boy, I wanted to say, I wouldn't need a keen wit to entertain you.

'Those pious clack-tongues in Westminster call me greedy for wealth. Here's how I answer them . . .' He ripped the diamond from the hat, pushed open the window and threw the gem into the Thames.

Mouth open, I saw the flashing fall and the little splash where the price of a year's maintenance for an army sank into the water.

For a moment we both stared down at the opaque muddy water below the window. The king wore a slightly startled expression, as if he had taken himself by surprise as much as me. Then he slammed the window shut.

'That's how much I care for wealth. Or anything else, including you and your advice. The true value of wealth lies in other men's greed for it and how pliable their hunger makes them.'

All smiles now, the *rex victor* clamped his hands onto my shoulders and pulled me forward to plant a sloppy kiss on my forehead.

'There's a good lassie. Just don't think you can ever outwit your old dad. We think too much alike but my wits will always be sharper.' He lifted his hands and dropped them on my shoulders again, half blow, half caress. 'I'm glad I never had you educated. You might have been dangerous. Run along now and leave me to rule England. And you.'

Leaving the king's lodgings, I passed Frederick, again a helpless captive amongst the king's other waiting gentlemen in the great reception chamber. I caught his eye and raised my shoulders. I did not know what I had achieved, if anything.

As soon as I was clear of the king's lodgings, I wiped from my forehead the kiss of a father I suspected of murdering my brother.

Just then, I was grateful that I had escaped arrest. Later, sitting silent among my ladies while they gambled with dice, I felt the full damage of that meeting with my father. It was a clean wound, as I imagined a sword slice would feel. Almost unnoticeable at the time it lands. Only afterwards, when the sinews no longer connect, and the blood drains away, and the pain sets in, do you understand that the blow may have been mortal.

I kept seeing the diamond disappear into the water, as worthless as I was.

He was willing to throw me away, as valueless, except for what I could extract in return for other men's greed. No father has ever made himself more extravagantly clear about his paternal feelings. Why had I dared to hope for anything else?

I wanted to drop my head into my hands. Instead, I stiffened my neck and accepted the little leather cup of dice to throw in my turn. I had to decide whether my father had thrown away Henry in another fit of half-thinking rage. If he would have his own heir poisoned out of fear, I could think of no reason he would spare a mere daughter.

I set one of my grooms to watch all night on the Privy Stairs. 'Come at once to report any activity you see.'

Near midnight, the boy came to my elbow as I sat still dicing with a sleepy Anne.

'Your grace,' he said. 'The tide is out, and the king has his men dredging the river by torchlight.'

'Where?' I asked.

'Beneath his bedchamber window.'

'Please go to bed, Anne,' I said. 'This boy will accompany me. I want a walk in the open air.'

I had to see this for myself.

69

I never learned whether it was Bacon's advice that prevailed. Or my plea. Or Frederick's charm. It might have been any or all of them together, or perhaps no more than the king's own perverse, changeable nature.

The announcement was made and the news cried in the streets. Letters flew in all directions over England. Messengers of foreign envoys sprinted for their ships. The king had chosen his son-in-law.

Though lacking in true power, wealth or large territorial possessions, the Palsgrave Frederick, the Elector Palatine, was now, in the respect owed to him, the premier Protestant prince of Europe. In the interests of preserving the balance of his *via media,* the king of England wished to confirm his friendship with the anti-Hapsburg forces on the Continent by giving his only daughter to the Palatine. However, as counter-balance, Prince Charles, the new heir to the throne, would marry in Catholic Spain. On the 27th of December, three weeks after Prince Henry's funeral, the king's daughter, Elizabeth Stuart was to be betrothed. Thames would marry Rhine.

70

On the twenty-seventh of December, a dense crowd waited in the Banqueting House, packed into the long space, jammed between the columns, hanging from the secured boxes. Some of the younger men even balanced on the narrow plinths of the columns.

I had not expected so many people. The court was still in mourning for my brother. Many Catholics at court disapproved of this union that demonstrated the king's support for the Protestant League in Europe. My mother's displeasure infected those who followed her. Frederick's hugger-mugger Gartering had been lost in the general distraction of grief.

Perhaps, as I had told my father, everyone – like my father himself – yearned to forget the heaviness that sucked at their hearts. But in their mourning clothes, they made a field of purple and black, reminding us all of our grief when I should have rejoiced. Gloomy winter daylight fell from the tall windows, partly obscured by the columns marching down each side of the hall. Black silks, black taffetas, shiny black satins, with the darker pools of black velvets, blended into a single sombre shifting mass.

The hall had been designed for the performance of masques. My father sat on the royal dais near one end, under a canopy, with Carr's fair head close at his right side.

My mother had refused to attend. Gout, she had said by way of excuse. Her empty space sat beside my father, as vivid as a ghost.

I looked away from the other empty space where Henry should have sat.

Where was my beloved Hal? I still did not believe that he had gone. In my imagination, he had gone to the Americas with Tallie, to achieve his dream of being crowned in his other kingdom. He would have found a golden princess, a *dorada*, a golden girl. They would plight their troth as we did. The four of us, with Tallie in attendance, would . . .

I felt Frederick's grip tighten on my hand. He was gazing at me with concern. I smiled and winked. I straightened my back.

We walked forwards. Frederick in purple velvet and a cloak lined in cloth-of-gold. I in my black satin, joining the field of black. All that black must taunt my father with his loss, though his grief did not show today. His fingers darted and probed. He shifted his weight as if sitting on sharp stones, frowning at the colonnades, turning his head sharply towards a sudden movement at the side of his eye.

You'll soon be rid of us both, as you've always wished, I thought. You're already rid of Henry.

It was a thought from the devil, but I could not stop it. A deep trembling lurked in my bones, though I believed that I felt only determination and the will to joy.

I curtsied. The white feathers in my hair fluttered softly at the top of my vision as I straightened, before they sprang stiffly upright again. I heard the rustling of Frederick's clothing at my side as he, too, made a reverence. I saw Sir Francis Bacon and his mirthless courtier's smile at my father's other side.

I heard murmurs of admiration for my gown, my carriage, my jewels, my glowing youth. But I knew that many here would praise me even if I were a whey-faced ninny, just because I was the king's daughter.

I also heard unguarded surprise that Frederick presented such a brave appearance. The story of his fright at the gun salute from the Tower on his way upriver would not die. Nor would tales of my mother's snub and her 'Goody Palsgrave' shop-keeper jibes. Even my rescue of him when he arrived. None showed him in a brave light. I revelled now in the response to his splendour and dignity.

'Not tall, but a fine figure nonetheless . . .'

'Oh, yes! And able to amuse the king.'

I was still braced for a coarse jest from my father, or a shout announcing that he had been toying with us and would not permit the betrothal after all. That Spain had made him a better offer at the final moment.

He kissed us both and gave us his blessing.

Hand in hand, Frederick and I walked to the middle of the vast Turkey carpet in the centre of the hall where the Archbishop waited with Sir Thomas Lake. We stopped.

Sir Thomas raised the parchment he held and began to read in a sonorous voice.

'*Chairs bee-in aymays,*' he began.

I frowned, then exchanged glances with Frederick. What language was the man speaking? Frederick widened his eyes in bewilderment.

Then I realised. It was Lake's mangled rendering of 'Dearly beloved . . .'

'*Chères bien-aimés . . .*' the man had been trying to say.

The Archbishop had not warned me that Sir Thomas Lake had undertaken to translate the betrothal vows into French, as a compliment to Frederick, and meant also to read them himself.

I hid my smile. Frederick gave my hand a tiny squeeze. How had this man come to read our vows when so many at court spoke perfect French?

'*Desire charnel . . .*' Sir Thomas was saying, struggling with his French translation of 'carnal lust'.

In the edge of my glance, I saw smiles being suppressed among the crowd. The trembling in my bones grew more intense. I could not see my father without turning my head. Was it possible that he had arranged this travesty to humiliate me? Cecil would never have allowed it. He would have seen the risks, on all sides.

Sir Thomas now entered into mortal combat with the causes for which matrimony was ordained. He survived the Frenchifying of 'procreation of children' but was unhorsed by 'avoidance of fornication'.

I snatched a breath, not quite a snort, closed my eyes and tried to control myself. I could see my black satin sleeve trembling with suppressed mirth.

Sweet Lord, help me through this, I begged. Help us both. How much more? I raised my eyes to the gilded festoons and spread-winged angels high above my head. What are we to do when we must repeat his words?

Sir Thomas now addressed himself to Frederick's repetition of his vows.

'*Jew view prends,*' read Sir Thomas, landing heavily on the 'd'.

Frederick gave me a wild look. What is he saying?

Je vous prends, I mouthed. I take you . . .

'*Jew view prends,*' prompted Lake, a little more loudly and slowly.

Frederick inhaled.

If he corrected the man's execrable French, it would be insulting. And by nature, Frederick was civil. If he repeated exactly what Lake had said, I would explode into laughter. It might also discredit the ceremony.

Frederick's purple velvet sleeve was trembling like my black satin one. The Archbishop seemed to study the carpet.

Then Frederick spoke his part in faultless French.

417

I heard a faint rustle as looks were exchanged among the spectators.

'*Voter feem est oon raisin soor la vigny . . .*' Sir Thomas battled on. 'Your wife is a grape on the vine . . .'.

Poor fruit of the vine, I thought. Reduced by this mangling voice to a single wee grape. A wee grape in jewelled mourning. I had never before been called a grape. Nor a 'feem'. I could no longer control myself. I snorted.

Sir Thomas faltered. He frowned at my odd behaviour and resumed with resolution.

'. . . *oon raisin*,' he repeated.

Grape again. I gave a tiny squeak.

I gasped. I sucked in my lips and clamped down hard. It was no use. The demon laughter had possessed me just as weeping had possessed me after losing Belle. I fought it until tears came to my eyes. I tried not to breathe. I gasped again and heard the sound of a giggle escape. And another.

Then Frederick giggled. He tried to hold his breath, then giggled again. Then Anne snorted and ducked her head to hide her face. The silver lace on my dress now quivered visibly with the force of my held-in laughter. I could hear the mirth spreading, a contagion of giggles and suppressed snorts. At any moment, the entire crowd would explode into laughter.

My father sat rigid, fingers clamped onto the arms of his chair. He stared at us with frozen fury.

Lord help us! I thought. Lake is not his doing after all. He will stand up and stop the ceremony. He will cut off the contract to punish us!

But my terror only made the suppressed laughter worse.

'*Voolay voo posseday cet feem . . .?* The sonorous mangling continued. Will you possess this woman . . .?

Make the man stop! I begged.

The Archbishop was giving me a stern look.

But I felt a relief like the letting-go of a long held-in piss.

I remembered the last time I had wet myself as a child. Helpless. Shamed, but also relieved. I had held on too long, to too many things.

I'm a grape! I thought giddily. I'm a 'feem'.

If I stopped giggling, I would burst into uncontrolled sobs again.

Frederick's grip threatened to crack the bones of my hand. His arm shook. Mirth raced between us, still building.

The Archbishop gave us another stern look. I gazed back beseechingly.

Help us! I begged. I saw disaster.

The Archbishop stepped forwards. He cut across Sir Thomas, raised his hands and began the Benediction, far too soon.

'God be merciful unto us.' His stern voice beat down the last words from Sir Thomas, sounding so like my own thoughts that I was confused for a moment.

'And shew us the light of His countenance,' the Archbishop went on smoothly.

His oration still unfinished, Sir Thomas lowered his parchment and stepped back with dignity.

'Your feathers,' Anne later murmured in my ear. 'I could contain myself until I saw your feathers – how they quivered! By tomorrow, there won't be a white feather left in the markets. Every woman in Whitehall will be wearing them.'

I smiled. But I did not mean to marry and leave England as an amusing story whispered out of the hearing of the king. I had seen my father watching Frederick and me after the betrothal, with his lower lip stuck out, pulling on it absently. I remembered Bacon's over-obsequious bow as I left.

I must not let our first progress unravel.

Then Lucy told me that Robert Carr had approved the choice of Sir Thomas Lake. And Sir Francis Bacon had agreed.

The thought of a possible alliance between Bacon and Carr set a heavy stone in my belly. Even now, I feared that one or the other of them, or, indeed, my mother, had clerks hard at work sniffing out lost proof that Frederick and I were kin and forbidden to marry by the laws of affinity. Or else that someone would unearth a law against laughter, decreeing that any religious ceremonies thus interrupted were void.

We must not let it happen again. The wedding itself must defy any who might ever challenge it.

71

Frederick and I practised the English Wedding ceremony every moment we could snatch. After breakfast, seated before the fire in my chamber, while Anne prompted. And after dinner. And after supper.

Sometimes we worked wrapped up warmly in the privy garden, while our attendants and chaperones cursed us at a distance in clouds of frosty breath.

'Ordnunce . . .' Frederick twisted his tongue around the foreign English word, laying it on the air like a careful egg. He rolled his beautiful eyes, held up his hand to ward off my correction.

My eyes traced the lines of his ungloved fingers. Delicate but still male, not feminine like Cecil's.

'*Je sais!*' I know! He tried again without prompting. 'God's holy ord-i-nance . . .'

'You still speak in your nose like a Frenchman,' I said. 'Too much "awhh"'

We laughed for the pure pleasure of laughing, making little dragon puffs in the cold air.

'I think you're meant to hold right hands here,' said Anne. 'No! Wait.' She fumbled at the prayer book. 'Back here, it also says . . .' She moved her finger back to an earlier section and frowned as she read.

'I'm certain that I had never let go,' said Frederick. 'Nothing in Heaven or earth could have persuaded me to let go.' With a glance at my ladies and his two gentlemen, he reached out. I gave him my hand. The only parts of us that were free to touch. We both fell silent, taking note of the astonishing contact of our two skins. His cold fingers tightened on mine.

'I shall ask the Countess of Bedford how it was done when she was married,' Anne said.

Lucy presented herself at my lodgings before she could be asked. She brought disturbing news.

'I've had a letter from my father, your former guardian,' she said. 'I believe that he meant for you to see it as well.'

'I have lately received the disturbing news that customs officials of the Cinque Ports have confiscated a number of arms smuggled into England by rebel Catholics. It is thought that they meant to make an assassination attempt on the Elector, who is the chief Protestant prince of Europe. I have, of course, alerted the king and Privy Council to this possible danger, but feel certain that her grace, the princess, would wish to use every endeavour to keep her future husband safe. There have so far been no arrests . . .'

Nevertheless, the report was taken seriously enough by the Privy Council for my father to order extra men-at-arms to be put on guard in Whitehall and St James's. Everywhere we went, Frederick and I were now followed by armed men. In effect, Frederick became a prisoner, unable even to cross the park to visit me without an escort of soldiers.

The king meanwhile grew visibly stouter from the wearing of a second padded doublet. He no longer strolled on the roof-top walk of the river gallery, and a groom reported that he took care never to stand in line with a window, for fear that someone might shoot at him from a boat.

I gave Frederick my hand again when we practised, walking in the tiltyard gallery after supper with our attendants twenty paces behind and men-at-arms at the door behind us and on the sand below. The shadows of the gallery created the illusion of privacy.

'With my body, I thee worship . . .' murmured Frederick in English. 'I thee worship,' he repeated. 'If words were the action, we're already married twenty times over.'

My whole body went hot though my breath clouded the cold air. Yet my humour that night was dark. My thoughts still scattered when I tried to think of my wedding night. I kept seeing Frederick in the place of the mark in the brothel and wondered how much he knew of what we must do together. I imagined myself forced to carry out those cold, obscene manipulations I had seen through the spy hole. I could not imagine how our pleasure in each other would survive.

Grooms had run ahead of us to plant torches along the gallery walls when I said we wished to walk there. The juddering orange and yellow light unsettled me. Rather than illuminate, the spots of brightness blinded my eyes to the details of the shadows.

'The marriage of Thames and Rhine.' The phrase now rolled off tongues everywhere, a proud new possession. Poets and ballad-makers waxed geographical.

England and the Palatine. A kingdom and a princedom. The weighty words pulled at me. They named us, yet seemed to have nothing to do with the two of us here in the creaking, shadowed gallery, with our young bodies, red noses, cloaks brushing against each other and urgent need to touch.

'Thames and Rhine'. Thud, thud. 'England and The Palatine'.

The weighty words thudded at our sides, heavy-footed beasts that would never leave us. To the rest of the world, they were more real than the girl and boy who clutched each other's hands in the cold semi-darkness.

These heavy beasts would march ahead of us into the Royal Chapel on our wedding day, the trumpets and cheers truly for them, not us. Then, I feared, they would follow us into our wedding bed and hunker down between us on the sheets.

I glanced at Frederick. He stared straight ahead at the far end of the gallery. In the uncertain torchlight, his eyes were shadowed.

I felt moment of pure terror. Without him, I would be only a shard of my former self. A tree trying to grow with only half its roots.

Is this the underlying truth of love? I suddenly asked myself. This new possibility of loss? And seeing suddenly how many new forms loss can take?

'Let's go back!' I swung around and headed towards my lodgings. Our startled attendants scattered and pressed themselves back against the wooden walls to let us pass.

Frederick followed without question. I was grateful for his silence. I could not have explained that I had suddenly seen *trowies* waiting for us in the darkness at the end of the gallery.

72

England had not had a royal wedding since my great-grand-cousin Mary Tudor married Philip of Spain more than half a century ago. Boats were unloading at Whitehall Stairs after coming upstream from the Revels Office at St Johns. I watched them arrive with timber planks, scaffolds, rolls of painted cloths, vices, wires, metal, odd shapes of wood, glue. Crates labelled 'Rocks, Mounts, Battlements, Trees, Clouds and Houses.' Whole cities, heavens and underworlds waited to sprout in theatres and halls. Armies were carried ashore in crates. Monsters and demons arrived packed into wicker baskets.

In Scotland Yard, beyond the Chapel, I saw a forest of raw wood growing into the supports for all those bales of painted cloth, just to celebrate my marriage. Men hammered, sawed, cursed, and shouted instructions to each other as they stretched sails of cloud-painted canvas and nailed them taut to frames. I smelled the burnt hair stink of the hot glue pots. Wooden columns leaned against the walls of the orchards. A shimmer of gold leaf drifted in the air.

In one corner of the yard, a man wearing a tasselled Italian cap moved his head forwards and back like a pigeon, as he touched in the shadows of painted swags of golden fruit and drew back to squint at a bunch of golden grapes.

Songs and poems piled up in sliding heaps on desks and tables in offices, weighed down by fulsome dedications from hopeful poets.

> *. . . Eliza goes to breed and bring*
> *Forth to the light, sons of a noble kind,*
> *Whose worth one day shall make us Britons sing . . .*

A castle was growing across the river in preparation for Sir Francis Bacon's masque rumoured to enact a battle between a Christian Navy and the Turks. Another castle sprouted on the Court side.

I would be forced to attend, though I found a mock-battle offensive as a marriage celebration. I would have to pretend to smile at him and pretend to accept his humble respect and this supposed gift of his, which felt like an evil portent. I would have to watch him trying to oil his way into my father's favour and his cousin Cecil's shoes. Given the whispers of Cecil's corruption that Bacon has started, how did he have the gall? Unless he was acting on my father's orders when he killed Henry.

Being so close to escape, I was overwhelmed by fears of how I might be prevented. Though my father now acted as if he meant to marry me to Frederick, I could not be certain. If he had ordered his own son to be killed, I could be certain of nothing. I found myself tasting my food with extra care, trying to detect a foreign taint. Every time my stomach ached, I waited for the griping pains and for my heart to falter. A man who said that he could not feel love and who wanted only to be amused might well entertain himself with a fatal game of cat and mouse.

Sunday. The last asking of the banns in the Chapel. No one objected to the match, at least, not aloud, not even my mother. After the suspected Catholic plot to assassinate Frederick, the city of London had mustered five hundred musketeers to guard the ceremony and celebrations, and a supervising alderman. Shouts of their drilling carried each day from Scotland Yard.

Frederick seemed far out of reach. Our thoughts had to leap across the tops of playing cards and wine glasses. We were never left alone together. Avid eyes constantly judged how we looked at each other. Ears assessed our tone of voice. Even when they seemed to be busy with some other matter, people watched. Behind our backs, they discussed every nuance of our actions together. Careful as they were, no one could resist the game. I heard them.

'But he's much too young and small-timbered to carry out the duties of a husband . . .'

'In truth, she's wilful . . .'

'But they seem pleased enough with each other . . .'

Pssst. Pssst.

Though it was never said in my hearing, I knew what lay beneath this chatter – the planting of an heir for Protestant Europe.

Frederick and I both feared the new darkness that surrounded us after Henry died. Both of us felt how much had changed since that moment of our first meeting, when Henry had grinned at me afterwards and clapped Frederick on the shoulder and called him 'brother'. Then, Frederick had clutched my hand for safety. Now he was my safety line anchored at the far end to a piece of solid ground I could not yet see.

Kept apart and constantly observed, we learned to woo with our hands.

Sometimes, when we sat thirty feet apart at dinner or across from each other in a crowded room, our hands played a delicious secret game. Not seeming to look at him, I would curl my fingers and lay my hand on my sleeve with my forefinger pointing at the creases of my sleeve. As if by accident,

Frederick would do the same. Then, seeming to talk to the nobleman beside him, he would lift his hand and touch his chin. Talking just as animatedly to my neighbour, I touched my own chin. We found ourselves so much in harmony that we sometimes guessed the other's intent and dropped our napkins or scratched our noses at exactly the same time.

The king now seemed fixed on the match. My Frederick was a marvel, a wizard of seduction. My father hung on his words. He made him sit beside him on the dais and patted his cheek while Carr sulked. I suspected that Frederick's New Year's gift to the king might have played some part in his sudden rise in favour.

It was a bottle carved from a single agate. When giving it, Frederick also promised my father . . . his father-to-be . . . more gems from the mines of Bohemia, where, Frederick said, there was talk of making him the next king.

In the false, feverish gaiety that had replaced deep mourning, I didn't know whether or not to believe him. I didn't care. Cecil would have learned at once whether Frederick spoke the truth about becoming king in Bohemia or was merely employing new diplomatic skills to hold the king firm in his intent to let us marry. Truth or lie, it didn't matter, so long as my father chose to believe it.

When Frederick was engaged elsewhere and I was not needed to stand while my new gowns are fitted, I rode in the Park or wandered at a loss, driving Anne to distraction. I could take only so much silk grosgrain, tawny velvet, whalebone and fur lining. And so many beaver hats, fringes, tassels, spangles and brocaded flowers, and so many miles of gold and silver Spanish and Venetian lace.

One day, drawn by the nutty smell of browning butter and the bitter-sweet tang of burnt sugar, I visited the kitchens. Knives thumped down. Lids rattled shut. Hands were wiped on aprons as everyone stopped working to bow or curtsey. I admired a table of moulded jellies in the shapes of castles.

The men and women in the kitchen stood by their chopped blanched almonds, earthenware crocks of half-stoned olives, pickled cucumbers and salted spinach, as impatient as leashed dogs. Frozen in mid-act some held sprigs of sage and rosemary and handfuls of currants, lemons to be sliced. I felt them waiting for me to go so they could get on with their urgent work of preparing for my marriage. I had interrupted what truly mattered. I smiled and left again. I was a nuisance, in the way of the preparations for my own wedding.

As I walked in the privy garden one evening while Frederick was dining with my father, I heard a counter-tenor practising on the other side of the wall. He climbed towards his highest note. Fell off. Tried again. And again. Then he cursed, thinking himself alone.

> *Heaven the first hath thrown away*
> *Her weary weed of mourning hue*
> *And waits Eliza's wedding-day*
> *In starry-spangled gown of blue . . .*

An earlier self would have trilled 'Bluuuuue!' and flung it back over the wall in cheerful, mocking challenge. Now, Thames shook a warning finger at me. This poor singer might have to sing in front of me and the court. I must not be cruel, even in jest. More than that, I was afraid to jostle life in any way, lest I disturb its smooth running towards my marriage.

The cost of love – learning to behave myself.

I wandered. My life felt unreal. Who was that creature in the glass? That little face above all that sea of cloth-of-silver? Where was my wolf?

With no further help from me, the day arrived.

73

WHITEHALL PALACE, LONDON, 14 FEBRUARY 1613.

So many of the populace were curious to see me that I was to walk the long way round to the Royal Chapel. I stood in the great hall waiting to set out, with my hair loose, almost to my waist, interwoven with gold spangles, pearls, precious stones and diamonds. A gold coronet set with diamonds and pearls had been wired in place on the top of my head. I braced the muscles of my neck against the weight that tried to tip my head back.

'Worth nine hundred thousand crowns, the royal jewels!' my father announced at large, in case anyone had failed to notice the coronet's richness or his lavish spending on his daughter. His own clothes, however, made me uneasy, even now.

Oddly and ominously, he himself seemed dressed more for hunting than for this spectacle of splendour. A loose Spanish cloak, his stockings sagging around his knees. But the feather in his hat was anchored by the glittering diamond that his men had dredged out of the Thames mud.

My dress – more proof of his lavishness – was cloth of silver, its sleeves sewn with more diamonds. Neither white to proclaim my virtue nor black to mourn my brother, but a bright metallic silk embroidered with still more gold and silver. Diamonds flashed on my sleeves whenever I moved my hands. I stood at the heart of a chilly fire. In spite of the cold February air, a drop of sweat ran down between the tops of my shoulder blades before being dammed by buckram and whalebone.

'You will dazzle and amaze the eyes of the beholders,' said Anne. She and the other ladies who would carry my train wore white satin gowns embroidered with more silver and jewels.

It began to seem that this marriage was going to take place after all.

Our procession formed with the usual delays and false starts that plague such moments. The Lord Chamberlain and assorted secretaries sent grooms running in every direction with messages, throwing off bow waves of purpose. They debated precedence, waved people first here and then there. I stood in the still centre, both there and not there. I felt a faint tickle of nausea and the need to sit down. I needed to bury my face in Belle's soft fur.

My old guardian, Lord Harington stopped in front of me, wearing his familiar look of puzzled concern.

'Your grace,' he began. Then he looked at me more closely. He touched my hand. 'All will be well,' he said. 'The Duke, your brother, and I will serve as your hounds and lead the pack out. You have only to ride after us.' He leaned closer and lowered his voice. 'Your mother is arrived.'

She stood turned away from me. Her dress was no more reassuring than my father's. She wore plain white and almost no jewellery.

Then off we went. Lord Harington, with the two bridemen, Baby Charles and the Earl of Northampton, flanking him.

Then me, the tiny nugget of flesh encased in Protestant union and a fortune in gems, dragging a silver train.

My father and mother followed behind me, he in his

431

flapping Spanish cape, sagging stockings and jewelled hat, the great diamond rescued from the river, now perched above his right eye. My mother in undecked white like a ghost.

Through the palace, we went: through the Presence Chamber, the Guard Chamber, the Banqueting House, out by the Court Gate. People sprouted everywhere, in windows, doorways, leaning out of staircases, even on rooftops. Shouts and cheers rained down on us. Blessings were thrown like flowers. I tried to give them the smiles I knew they wanted from me. Radiant Thames on the way to meet her Rhine.

We progressed along Whitehall itself, where more people hung from every window, pushing for a better view until I feared that someone would fall. They jostled at the sides of the street, straining to see us.

An old woman pushed forward suddenly, ducking under elbows, and knelt to touch my silver hem. I raised my hand to stop the man-at-arms who would have beaten her back. We passed the Jewel House, under a window where a very old man hung perilously far out, shouting 'God bless you, your grace! God bless you!'

After walking almost from Charing Cross to the western-most part of Whitehall, we passed along a gallery to the great chamber stairs. The storm of cheers and shouts still pounded at us as we passed through the great chamber, into the lobby, and then, at last, through the quiet of a closet that led to the Chapel.

When we reached the Chapel door, I heard Lady Harington behind me, scolding my attendant ladies, pushing them aside and taking control of my train herself. Even at such a moment, her severity made me smile. My lady guardian sounded as determined as I was that nothing go wrong.

But as I entered the chapel door, I faltered. In the middle of the Chapel, a large scaffold had been built. My eyes counted. Six steps. I saw Sir Everard Digby climbing six steps to his death.

I remembered my own conviction that I too was about to be beheaded. Then the murmur stirred by my entrance roused me. I blinked away the image and watched Baby Charles mount the scaffold with the Earl. I followed.

It's only so that people may see better, I told myself, listening to the murmur that lifted me upwards. So that they may rejoice.

Then I saw Frederick, standing with his uncle, Count Henry of Nassau. My husband-to-be also wore silver. Henry's diamond cross hung on his breast. He looked more than ever like a young boy.

Another small, encased nugget of flesh. We reached for each other with our eyes.

I felt Lady Harington guiding me by my train as if I were a horse on a rein. I felt her tug. It seemed that I must sit. I sank onto a stool. My mother sat to one side of me, still not looking at me.

I'm sorry you were forced against your will to trouble yourself to come, I thought angrily.

The Gentlemen of the Chapel sang an anthem. Then came a sermon by the Bishop of Bath and Wells.

I pulled against the weight of the jewels in my hair, fighting to keep my chin down.

Still the Bishop talked. And talked. The marriage at Cana . . . and still the marriage at Cana.

My father yawned audibly.

Then another psalm. The king yawned again, more loudly. In the corner of my eye, I saw him fidgeting with his cuffs. Then he pulled at his buttons. He uncrossed his legs and thumped his feet on the platform floor. He slapped his hands down on his chair arms as if about to rise and leave, just as he had stormed out of the launching of the *Prince Royal*. Just as he left any event he found too tedious. I knew then, with absolute certainty. He had devised the ultimate punishment for me. At any moment, he would stand up and walk out, shouting for everyone to stop their gawping and go home. There would be no marriage after all.

Don't jump to conclusions, I told myself.

Suddenly, the Archbishop of Canterbury was nodding at me. I stood and gripped Frederick by the hand. I felt him trembling.

While the Archbishop intoned the many reasons for entering into holy matrimony, I heard my father sigh loudly. Then I heard the sound of vigorous scratching.

Trembling or not, Frederick spoke his 'I will' clearly, in English.

I did not look at my father as I made my own reply.

Then we came to it.

'Who giveth this woman to be married to this man?' asked the Bishop.

My father stood up in his wrinkled stockings and crumpled suit. 'Weel,' he said doubtfully, in his thickest Scots.

I closed my eyes. I heard the utter silence of several hundred held breaths.

'That I do . . .' He stopped. He gazed up at the ceiling. Still no one breathed.

I waited for the 'not'. The unspoken word flapped and crashed through the air of the chapel, careening off the walls and ceiling. NOT! NOT! NOT! NOT!

The king sat down again.

I remembered nothing after that, except that Frederick looked into my eyes and spoke his part in English almost without mistake. I must have spoken mine, because the Bishop led us up to the altar for the final Benediction.

We are married! I thought. It has happened! Helpless to stop it, I felt a wide smile pull up the corners of my mouth until I must have been grinning like a looby. I swallowed against a bubble of laughter.

Not this time! I swallowed again, holding in relief and triumph and joy.

The Garter King of Arms proclaimed us husband and wife. 'All health, happiness and honour be to the high and mighty Prince, Frederick,' he cried. 'By the grace of God, Count Palatine of the Rhine and Prince Elector of the Holy Empire; and to Elizabeth his wife, only daughter of the high, mighty and right-excellent James, by the grace of God, King of Great Britain.'

Wine and hippocras were brought from the vestry. Frederick gave my father a huge golden bowl for the toasting. I grew giddy with wine and good wishes. As we walked in procession back to the Banqueting House, the air was filled with shouts of 'God give them joy! God give them joy!'

Then, outside the Banqueting House, a press of well-wishers sent up such a cheer for Frederick and me that I saw my father frown and pull his lower lip. But I was carried onwards towards the feast, into the music of Frederick's trumpeters, blowing a shower of gold and brass notes from their silver instruments. From outside, the crowd roared back, 'God give them joy! God give them joy!'

Frederick and I left the Wedding Feast at last, together with the official bedding party of Lady Harington, Northumberland, the Count of Nassau, Sir Thomas Lake, and various court officials.

'I wish to visit the Privy Stairs on the way to my lodgings,' I said.

Lady Harington and Northumberland exchanged looks but agreed. Humouring the shy bride, no doubt. Not even Frederick knew what I intended.

During the preparations for my wedding, Abel White had returned to England, to introduce a visitor from Italy, a Count Francisco Cointo di La Spada.

'I was Salisbury's man, whilst he lived,' the newcomer told me. He was a tall fair man, clean-shaven and short-haired against the fashion. 'His fire master. Now on loan to a

435

demanding ruler in Italy.' He gave me a devastating smile. 'In truth, your grace, I'm also plain Francis Quoynt, of Powder Mote near Brighthelmstone.'

'I know of you,' I said. 'It seems that you were much missed on a number of festive occasions in the last three years.'

'My present employer is both demanding and jealous,' he said, with a private smile. 'The Principessa of La Spada in Friuli. But even she could not forbid me to carry out a final commission for my former patron, Cecil.

'At the end of your wedding feast,' he said. 'As you progress to your lodgings, I ask you, in memory of Lord Salisbury, to stand for a short time at the end of the Privy Stairs, as if for a last breathe the air. And look to the south.'

The bedding party hung back respectfully at the palace entrance to the Privy Stairs. Music from the continuing dancing reached us faintly. Holding Frederick's hand . . . my husband's hand . . . I stood at the very end of the stairs, under the light of the two permanent lanterns, looking out into the darkness of the river and the marshes beyond.

The lanterns of distant wherries bobbed and traced slow lines of light. Small waves lapped at our feet, marking the dark water with pale lacings of froth. For an instant, close to the stairs, I thought I saw Henry's shape surface and dive again.

Then a single rocket rose behind us. Before I could turn to see the source, a curtain of fire rose up from the flat darkness of the Lambeth marshes across the Thames. Then balls of fire began to climb, each one leaving a bright orange snake tail hanging in the night sky, before it exploded in showers of stars. Green, silver, gold, pink. More and more fireballs rushed up, chasing each other so closely that there was not a breath between them. They etched the entire sky with lines of sparks. The rumble of constant explosions beat at us like the irregular thumping of huge drums.

Frederick's hand tightened on mine. It was a rising storm, as if the earth had turned to heaven and threw lightning bolts upwards, instead of down. Each rocket carried my heart and breath up with it. Each explosion jolted my heart. Again, and again and again, before I could recover from the jolt before.

Then, when I thought that there could be no more rockets left on earth, a pair rose together with only the quietest of thumps, leaving no tails. Mere sparks that cut upwards with a quiet mysterious purpose, higher and higher, above the rest. In silence, they rose and rose, seemed to pause, then jump upwards again, arching high over our heads, while the air still seemed to shake with the memory of past explosions.

I tilted my head back, unable to breathe, sure that the two sparks must be tickling the toes of the angels by now. Just as it seemed that I had imagined them, there was a double explosion that made the water jump at our feet. Higher than the moon, I saw two bright letters floating down, made of stars, our initials, Frederick's and mine, F and E, wavering against the darkness like their own reflections in the river, drifting, holding their shape for a time, then blending into a new unreadable constellation.

Then the stars began to die, but so slowly that I held out my hand like a child trying to catch a snowflake, before the last one died far overhead.

Frederick gripped my arm and pointed at the far bank. The lantern-lit wherries had disappeared. The river was now dark and still. Then in the silence, from the far bank, I heard the faint sound of a Scottish pipe, so distant and strange that it might have played for a spirit dance at a loch-side, daring mortals to join the ring.

A torch-lit boat had pushed off from opposite shore and approached us silently, accompanied only by the single distant pipe and the splash of its oars. A mermaid with burning hair sat in the bow. The boat glided up to the steps. She held up her arms to me.

'Take care!' Frederick said sharply. But I had already descended the slippery steps to take from her hands the closed silver scallop shell she offered me.

The boat and mermaid pulled away at once, leaving behind a smell of burning saltpetre and sulphur. I climbed back up into the lantern light. I felt with my thumb, found the catch and opened the shell.

Inside was a fine single unset pearl, and a letter.

I knew that signature. I had seen it many times on letters and state documents, taller than it was wide, elegant, with neatly squared shoulders, and always larger than any other signature that might also be on the page. In every way unlike the man whose hand had written it.

'It's from Cecil.' I angled the letter into the lantern light to read.

'Your grace, my pilgrimage is done. Yours now begins, travelling roads I cannot see and cannot smooth for you. I would that I could serve you and your brother still . . .

My voice caught on those last words. If Cecil had lived, I might have learned whether or not my father had ordered my brother's death. If he still lived, his enemies and my brother's might never have dared to act.

Frederick added his hand to steady mine, so that the paper did not shake too much to read.

All I can give is yours to take, though I fear it be very little and far from sufficient for the likely need. I remain as discreet for your cause in my death as in my life. May any good advice I might by chance have given help to protect you in the darkness of shadows. Please accept from me, on this joyful day of new beginning, a final gift of hopeful light. Ever your most humble and obedient servant, Salisbury.'

In the bottom of the shell were some dark grey ashes. I touched them thoughtfully, then shook the remains of my dangerous letter to Henry into the river.

'This was a wedding gift from the late Secretary,' I managed to say to the party waiting at the palace door.

74

Then Frederick and I were alone except for my maid. Even my dogs had been banished to the antechamber for the night.

My ears throbbed with the sudden silence. For hours my head had been constantly filled with shouts, cheers, trumpets. Faintly in the distance, the dance music played on. Bursts of rowdy voices came from different places around the palace. I knew that the official bedding party had their ears pressed to my door, listening for whatever we might give them to hear, as if the maidenhead of Thames might ring like a bell when it was cracked by Rhine.

Earlier, the weight of jewels had been taken from my hair to be counted and locked away. But my elaborate night-dress pricked my neck with lace and gold embroidery and seemed to weigh almost as much as my wedding gown.

Just before she left me, Lady Harington had gripped my hands with unexpected warmth. 'You must let the prince do his duty,' she murmured. 'Even if it seems strange to you.' She sounded even more severe than usual. 'He must perform his part. Your duty is to allow it, no matter how your modesty might protest.'

She gave both my hands a little shake, as if jostling strength from her own body into mine, like shaking flour from a sack. She helped me into the bed, which had been decked with ivy, bracken and branches of rosemary. I slid my hand under my pillow to touch the iron knife I had place there earlier, for good luck, along with my piece of Scottish granite. When my fingers brushed one of the rose petals strew on my pillow, it felt like cold, dead skin. The dish of fortifying caraway seeds set on Frederick's pillow looked like mouse droppings.

Sir Thomas Lake, the Count of Nassau, Northumberland, Baby Charles and other groomsmen had led Frederick into the room. He had likewise been stripped of his wedding finery and clothed in a heavy night shirt and a fur-lined, brocade gown. Then Lady Harington left with Sir Thomas, Nassau, Northumberland and the others, to stand in the passage outside the door.

Frederick and I could not look at each other. How could it be right that the most private parts of our bodies should be so openly in everyone's thoughts? The heavy-footed beasts, our state selves, Thames and Rhine, had followed us, just as I had feared. For one instant, I was tempted to give a blood-curdling scream to see if all those listeners would run back in again.

Frederick, the bridegroom Elector Palatine, now studied the floor. I could not think how to free us from these other selves and the terrible burden of lifeless Duty they had dropped at our feet. I looked at the door. All those ears listening to hear if we performed our duty. I suddenly feared that I might need to use Southwark skills after all.

This was unbearable.

'Psst,' I said.

Frederick looked up.

I stuck my tongue out at the door. Frederick imitated me. Then he put his hands to his ears and waggled his fingers at the door. I imitated him. We smiled at each other uneasily.

It was a start.

'Let him see you,' Tallie had said.

I climbed out of bed and beckoned for my maid to unfasten the night dress, feeling a blank terror.

The maid peeled off my stiff silk carapace and folded it over her arm.

Wearing only a fine silk shift, I nodded for her to leave us. I did not trust my voice.

We watched the little door of the private stairs close behind her. She would guard the door to make certain that no one else left or entered my chamber that night. We were truly alone for the first time.

The silence grew until it seemed to fill my head.

'Let him see you,' Tallie's voice repeated. His eyes were now on my breasts, naked beneath the sheer silk.

I pushed my shift down to my waist.

'Oh, Lizzie!' Frederick stared at me, his face bright red. 'You are entirely the most beautiful thing I have ever seen!' He fumbled at the hook of his gown. 'Wait,' he said urgently, as if I could do anything else. He shed his heavy gown onto the floor like a pelt. His night shirt followed. Naked, he was the most beautiful thing I had ever seen.

I couldn't breathe.

Naked, he was no longer a boy. Men's clothing hid more than it revealed, and I'd never quite believed the paintings and statues of warriors and satyrs that littered my world. Now I saw that the clean lines of those rendered muscles were true representations of exquisite fleshly curves and planes.

We walked to meet each other. I felt the extraordinary sensations of a bare male chest touching my nipples. We stood for a moment with our arms around each other, forehead to forehead. Holding on carefully, as if the other might be fragile. I was no longer frightened.

Tallie had been right. There was no difficulty whatsoever. His cock seemed all of a piece with the rest of him, not red or pink but lightly browned like his hands, face and smooth flat belly. Already stiff. He desired me after all. I touched it in wonder, as if it were a new sort of pet I had never stroked before. I would have stroked it again but Frederick groaned and caught my hand.

It seemed that I was wonderful too. Perfect. Beyond belief, beautiful.

He ran wondering fingers down my belly and touched my navel and red-gold bush. 'I never thought a woman's tits could be so soft!' he whispered, cupping them with his warm palms.

His excellent manners and careful watchfulness in a strange world had disguised this woodland creature I now found exploring me with such an open joyful appetite. He was a faun, set free by my permission and by my own eager hunger. A young satyr, still downy with innocence, but a satyr nonetheless. I grew recklessly drunk on his delight, awash with exquisite sensations that even our exploring fingers and snatched kisses had not led me to expect.

There was just one moment of peril, when we looked at each other, like the instant before a leap. Then I opened to him and he found me, as if we had both known exactly what to do, all along.

It hurt far less than I had expected. And the small pain was nothing against the joy of his weight and warmth, there, with me, against my skin, pressing me down. It was nothing when set against our relish in each other. It was nothing compared to my sense that all was suddenly right with the world. Although I was a little sore, he soon entered me again.

Then, feeling pleased with ourselves, we curled damply together. Inhaling our mixed new odours, we suddenly fell asleep, felled by the weight of our day. Thames and Rhine had long ago slunk out the door to await our public daylight selves.

75

I stretched, deliciously, only half-awake. Every fold in the bed linens stroked me like a caress. During the night, the dogs had found their way back into the room and crept up onto the bed, where they lay in comfortable heaps around our feet.

My leg brushed against Frederick's warm calf. We pressed the sides of our feet together, my right against his left. His hand fell sleepily onto my bare thigh. His fingertips stroked. His nails scratched lightly.

'Do that again!' I begged.

'This?' His nails moved over my skin again. He turned his head on the pillow and looked at me.

Under the covers, I offered my arm. 'Oh, yes,' I murmured.

He swept his nails up my arm, then along the inside of my forearm to the elbow. I shifted position so that he could continue on to my upper arm. In the morning light that seeped between the bed hangings, I saw his beautiful lips curve into a smile.

'I swear this pleases you more than the other.' He scratched delicately with his forefinger between my fingers. My forearm again . . . palm . . .

'Perhaps,' I teased, watching his fingers move on me. 'Och, Lord! No wonder my dogs love it so!'

'Roll over.' He gave me a little push. I turned onto my side with my back to him. He pulled the coverlet close around us to close out the sudden leak of icy air and ran his nails lightly back and forth over my bare shoulders.

I quivered with delight. 'Again!' I begged. My skin was the surface of a lake, shivering under a breeze. The sensation spread in tiny rivulets of quicksilver into places I had not known were connected to each other – the muscles under my ears, across the back of my tongue, down my inner arms, into my toes. Time stopped running away with me and shoving me onwards roughly into the next moment. It sat back down on its haunches like a great dog, planting itself exactly where it meant to be.

'Again,' I murmured. Every inch of my skin grew urgent, and clamoured, me, too! Me, too! 'Oh, yes. And a little higher . . .' I begged. It was almost too much to bear. I felt him gathering intensity like a river nearing the top of a waterfall.

'I've married a hound,' he said.

'Please, don't stop!' The sensations were all the more delightful because I could feel his cock pressing against the backs of my thighs, impatient but biding its time.

'Don't fear,' he said.

We heard the latch rattle. The chamber door creaked open, without a warning knock.

'How are my little turtledoves?' My father threw the bed hangings open.

Behind him, Anne, in a loose gown and hair awry, held up her hands helplessly. His attending gentlemen had stopped outside the door and pretended to look elsewhere. The dogs scattered off the bed.

We turned and scrambled into a sitting position, clutching the covers up to our chins to hide our nakedness.

'Well, sir,' demanded my father. 'Is it done? Did ye enjoy my daughter?'

We gaped at him.

Anne went out and closed the door behind her.

The king sat heavily on the side of the bed. Frederick pulled back his legs to make room. The king still wore his night gown, with a loose gown over it, and slippers.

'Are you now my true son-in-law?'

It was the first time, in all his sad history of discomfort in England that I had seen Frederick truly lost for words. His hand reached for mine under the covers. It was as icy as my own.

This was unbearable.

The king leaned closer, speaking slowly and kindly, as if Frederick might otherwise be too simple to understand. 'Did ye ride her or did ye not?' He sniffed at the air.

We stared at him, appalled.

He peered closely at us both. 'Not dumb from disappointment, I hope! Let me see the sheet!'

He yanked the coverlet from our hands. With a yelp, I dived away into the cold sheets on the far side of the bed. Poor Frederick had nowhere to go, and lay exposed to the king's eyes. He drew up his knees.

My father pushed Frederick's feet aside and touched the rusty smudge on the linen under-sheet.

'We could have done with a wee bit more,' he said. 'Even your mother produced more blood than that. All that running after your brother like a boy must have shrivelled your maidenhead. But it's clear enough. The young man performed. Well done, sir.' He shook Frederick by the hand.

Rage began to rise in me. This is mine! I wanted to scream at him. What I have now is mine! Not yours any longer! I've done my part for England.

'Let's hope you planted an heir.' My father pushed down on Frederick's knee to straighten the leg and dropped his sharp gaze to my poor husband's cock, now shrivelled with cold. However, my father seemed satisfied.

'Now, don't forget that I must agree to the marriage of

446

the *bairn*. It will be a Stuart babe, with a grip on the English throne. No matter what backwater you take my daughter off to, remember that the babe is grandchild to the king of England and Scotland, and stands in this royal line after Baby Charles.'

Frederick's face had darkened to the colour of old leather. His bare chest rose and fell with quick, shallow breaths. His knuckles showed white as ivory through his skin.

I had gone so hot that I thought the coverlets would burst into flame. Danger, danger! I warned myself. You're so close to escape. Don't undo it now!

But if my father had troubled himself to look at me then, my eyes would have dropped him stone dead.

'I will send our royal midwife with you,' he was telling Frederick. 'And a nurse, to see that the child is properly reared.'

'I'm sure they have midwives in Heidelberg!' I croaked.

My father glanced at me and, surviving my eyes, turned back to Frederick. 'You'll need assistance in ruling her, Palsgrave. You're not built with the stature for the task. Don't fear. You'll have my support in the matter.'

Frederick darkened another degree.

I drew breath to speak. Frederick put out his hand to stop me. 'I thank you, your highness . . . father . . . for your kind offer, but we have very fine midwives in Heidelberg. But if Elizab . . .' His dark eyes turned to me as if to reassure himself that I was still there.

I gasped. Frederick's eyes were hot and opaque with anger. I had seen him uneasy, confused, aroused and alarmed, but never angry. This new anger felt as fierce as his desire.

But his voice remained steady. 'If . . . my wife . . . wishes a woman she knows, she shall have her. But only then.'

'Insolent Protestant pup!' My father stared back into those suddenly dangerous eyes, his jaw moving as if he were chewing on his tongue. He scratched his jaw, chewed two more times, then guffawed and clapped Frederick on the shoulder. 'You'll need every ounce of that spirit if you hope to ride my Bessie to a standstill.'

He raised himself from the side of the bed. 'Door!' he shouted.

When my father had gone, Frederick flung himself back against the pillows and stared straight ahead in silence. I lay watching him, uncertain what to do. Our joy lay shattered around us in knife-edged splinters. I did not know how to pick it up again. I tried to think what to say. I imagined words and rejected them. The moment felt too fragile to test in any way.

The silence grew. Only one thought became clear in my mind.

We spoke the same words at the same time. 'We must leave England as soon as possible!'

We looked at each other and laughed with renewed delight at this proof that our unity had survived. Then, watching each other as we had done across crowded rooms or dining tables, we raised our hands in our game of mirrors. In unison like a pair of wheeling swifts, we clenched our fists and knocked them against our temples in mock rage and despair, not knowing which of us followed and which of us led.

Weak with relief, I smiled back into Frederick's eyes, which were no longer opaque. Again they liked what they saw. I was also aware of a new feeling.

Though I already thought him perfect in every way, and had never minded that I was leading and protecting him through the complexities of the English court, Frederick had just surprised me. I felt respect.

Then he leaned over and kissed my nipple. 'Tonight,' he said. 'But we must barricade the door.'

76

APRIL, 1613 – MARGATE

We had to wait for favourable winds. Lord Admiral Northampton again insisted that I not be allowed to sail on an ill-fated vessel that never wished to be put to sea. But I had vowed to make my escape on the *Prince Royal*, even if not to the Americas. My determination was as great as Henry's had been to get his ship afloat. Charges of corruption in the Navy and delayed launchings never sank a ship that I knew of.

It was ten years since I left Scotland.

I could not eat for fear that something would still stop us. I had listened in the night for the hoof beats of those skeleton horses. I did not look down into the river as we rowed away from Westminster, imagining that bony hands reached up for me, to twine in my skirts and pull me down to stay with them forever, buried in muddy silt.

The weeks of celebration following our marriage were marred by the financial reckoning. My father had failed to raise enough money from his subjects, as custom allowed, to pay the costs of my marriage. To save money, he dismissed the household he had arranged for my husband so that most of Frederick's gentlemen had to leave for Heidelberg at once, without us. Lord Harington found himself out of pocket for the costs of my trousseau. I ran out of the gold rings and other trinkets I was giving as gifts to the followers I would leave behind. I had found one of Carr's men measuring up my apartments. The Golden Weasel could not wait until I had left England before claiming what had been mine.

'Please tell your master that I'm amazed he's willing to wait until I've gone!' I said. 'Why does he not wheedle and pout and work on the king to have me thrown out at once?'

On the other hand, Bacon's masque had ended in disaster. Fireworks failed to ignite. Boats were delayed, performers injured. The king left in impatience before the end, ordering Bacon to try again the next day. Then the king refused to attend. Gleeful rumour said that, beforehand, Bacon had refused all offers to help allay the costs, because he wanted full credit with the king and refused to share the glory. The champion of Reason had been undone by unreasoning chance, with no one else to share the blame.

Without the firm guiding hand of Cecil, the affairs of England still limped and changed direction. Bacon was the most able of the king's advisers but also widely disliked. Frederick and I wanted only to be gone but had to wait on the festivities and the vacillations of the king,

The royal family had travelled together by barge from Whitehall to Greenwich and from there to Rochester.

I said farewell first to my mother, who was setting out on a progress to Bath.

'Well,' she said. 'Here we are. As I said – you, going. To Heidelberg.'

I nodded. I laid my hand over the fragment of granite from the Edinburgh crags, tucked into my pocket under my skirts. This time, I had armoured myself.

She kissed me formally and stepped back at once as if my touch burned. She started to leave, then turned back to me again. She gave me a sly glance. 'Sometimes, it is possible to exact a small revenge,' she said with the air of bestowing a parting gift. 'His majesty does not yet know it, but I have shot Brutus, his favourite dog.'

She rode away in her carriage in tears.

Then I asked to say farewell to Baby Charles, the next king of England.

He agreed to receive me in his borrowed presence chamber.

I approached and curtsied to the small figure perched in an upholstered arm chair fringed with gold, with two spaniels curled at his feet. 'Sir, I come to take my leave,' I said. 'As soon as the wind permits, we sail for Flushing.'

'I wish you a safe voyage.'

We stared at each other a moment in silence. I wondered how much we both would have changed when I saw him next.

Suddenly, he leapt to his feet. 'You're leaving me, Bessie!' he cried. He sounded surprised. 'You can't go!' He wept and clung to me. 'There's no one left. What will I do now?'

It was on the tip of my tongue to reply, 'Very much what you have always done – exactly as you like.' Instead, I kissed his head and said that he must come soon to see me in Heidelberg.

Then, still at Rochester, I said formal farewells to my father.

77

We lingered together for a moment, a little apart from the others, looking down from the stone-paved castle terrace at the ships on the Medway.

'You're rid of me at last,' I said.

'Nae, Bessie,' he protested. 'Your old dad's heart is breaking.'

I waved away his protest. 'I must know before I leave you . . .' I did not know how to ask. 'Henry. How much did you hate him?'

His head jerked back as if I had struck him. The diamond in his hat flashed across my eyes. His mouth opened. His tongue heaved behind his teeth like a landed fish. I saw him attempt indignation.

'We may never see each other again,' I said. 'Tell me before I go. I must know.'

Then his eyes brimmed and overflowed. 'Bessie,' he whispered. 'Are you turned so cruel?'

'I am a little like you,' I said.

'I'm cruel?'

'You know that you are.'

'I should have died instead.'

'Answer me.'

He groaned and clutched his jacket as I had seen him do so often before.

'Stop that at once!' I said. 'It doesn't impress me in the least. An honest answer is the price I ask you to pay for being rid of both of your dangerous cubs.'

To my surprise, he dropped his hands from his doublet. His eyes sharpened and looked directly into mine for the first time since our conversation began. 'I hear your question, Bessie – the one you don't quite dare to ask.'

I held his eye, waiting.

'I never hated Henry,' he said quietly. 'That's what you want to know, is it not?'

I nodded.

'At times, I wished that you and he could change places. You'd have made a better king.'

'Never!' I stared suspiciously, wondering what new game he was playing with me.

'Oh, aye,' said my father. 'The people would have lost their taste for his Puritan fervour when he began to make them drop coins into all those official fine boxes.'

Of course, he had known about Henry's boxes. He would have placed spies among Henry's household. They might even have been Cecil's spies.

'You had reason to fear him,' I said.

'Very good reason. He would have undone my life work for peace on the continent.' He shook his head. 'But I did not want him dead.' He stared down at the river. Then, hearing my silence, he turned to me again. 'I'll wager that you've feared me, Bessie, but I doubt that you ever planned to kill me.'

'Are you certain of that?'

He studied me for a long time. 'Aye. That I am.'

I let out my breath.

'I think you understand the pitiful jumble of the human soul,' he said. 'You don't think only in straight lines as your brother did.'

'Do you swear that you did not order Henry's death?'

I expected another protest, Instead, my father seemed to dissolve before my eyes. 'Ah, Bessie . . .' His eyes overflowed. 'Never ordered . . .' His nose ran. He wiped it on his sleeve.

'Ah, Bessie, I fear . . .' He stopped again. 'Who knows what men may do when they imagine they serve their king? I fear . . . Dear Lord, I fear that I might . . .' He could not finish. 'That someone may have believed . . .'

'Whom do you suspect?'

'. . . who might have served me too well?' He looked out at the river. 'I reject my suspicions. What if I can't now do without the advice of a man I suspect of serving me too well? Can you tell me that? What is England to do? How do I reward too much service? Who is more dangerous – enemies or friends?'

'Can't any of your books tell you?' I asked.

I'm safe, I thought for the first time since I had arrived at Whitehall. I believe that I am safe.

He waved away my attempted flippancy. 'Can you prove anything against anyone, Bessie?'

I shook my head.

'Best to say nothing then.'

78

From Canterbury, I wrote a fulsome letter to my father.

> *... I shall perhaps never see again the flower of princes, the King of fathers, the best and most amiable father that the sun will ever see ...'*

He would recognise the irony. It might even amuse him for a few moments. Then he would wave my letter about, a trophy. My last gift to him.

Let rumour mutter what it likes ... His eyes would challenge. Look you! Here's proof that I never wronged any of my cubs. See here, how she writes, *I long to return again and kiss your hands once more.* What more do any of y'want? ... *most amiable* ... You know she's a lass who speaks her mind. Who dares to disagree now?

Though I had once feared that he would have me executed, I now believed that he valued me. I couldn't say 'loved' because he himself told me that he could not feel love.

As for Henry, my father would never have thrown away such a precious jewel if he could not have fished it out of the mud afterwards. I was quite certain. I would not risk the fragile balance that he and I had found by believing anything else.

Five days later, we moved from Canterbury to Margate, to set sail at last. Lord and Lady Harington (still carrying all her certainties) rowed out with us across the choppy water. A fleet of other boats followed us, carrying the rest of my attendants and luggage. Because of the cramped space on board, none of the women wore a farthingale. I would not wear one again until we reached Flushing and rigged ourselves to greet my one-time suitor, Prince Maurits of Nassau.

I won't miss it, I thought.

I missed Tallie, most likely now arrived. I didn't know if she loved me, but it was no matter. We were each of us a solid place for the other to place her feet. Even if she sometimes felt as out of reach to me as the sky, I wanted her there in the boat with me, to share this happiness with me. I wanted someone to hear my tumbling words about Frederick, whose shoulder pressed against mine in the brief intimacy of our journey out from shore. I wanted her to make my words real by hearing them. I wanted her to tell me when I was being a fool. I wanted a witness.

Old Nottingham, the ancient Lord Admiral, had received us on board. Frederick and I stood at the railing of the giant ship with the wind whipping at our hair, and looked down at our attendant fleet. There were shouts and whistles and a great deal of purposeful activity. We stayed out of the way. For the moment, a pair of royal highnesses counted for less than stirring the pulse of this great-bellied beast with a golden image of my brother on the bow, mounted on his horse, pointing the way forward with his sword.

The beast inhaled. Then let out its breath and settled back into itself. The wind had shifted easterly. Foul weather threatened. We returned to shore.

I felt sick.

Three nights in Margate. Three nights of listening for hoof beats. Of fearing another turn in my father's humour. Then back on board and at the rail again.

I thought of Henry and his not-quite confession about Frances Howard. His uneasiness . . . poor Henry! He never knew this joy!

I would have liked to tell him how happy I am, I thought.

At least, his ship supports me, holds me up, carries me across the water.

I looked back at England and saw white. If I had been a gull, I would have loved the place so much sooner.

I had escaped the demons. I had no doubt that others lurked, my very own, but I could not see any of them now. Just then, I pitied my father because he wasn't me. I pitied my mother, and Henry, because they never had what I had now, that moment. It was better than the moment of unlacing. Of feeling the air move freely against my bare skin.

My bare skin. A universe I never imagined.

I looked at my Frederick. My husband. My lover. My unexpected friend and ally. My gift from God.

I gave myself permission not to see the shadow in his eyes. It belonged to our future, which I would deal with when it arrived. As I would deal with all the other things I did not yet know. I knew now how much I could do. No matter what might happen, I would have known this time.

I am loved, I thought. I am his star. I make a universe for him as he does for me.

This was a perfect time. I would eat it, drink it, inhale it, roll in it like a hound in sun-lit spring grass. My wolf stretched on warm rocks. I was a child again, filled with the space below the Crags, cousin to the birds wheeling below me. I flew.

A sail shivered and thumped above our heads. A coil of hanging rope knocked gently against a mast.

We flew.

Frederick turned curiously when he felt me fumbling inside my cloak.

I kissed the granite fragment from the Scottish crags. Then I threw it high into the air. As it arched through the air, my stomach dropped in terror. Tears sprang to my eyes. I wanted to call it back. My eyes lost it against the waves, then saw the tiny splash where it entered the water. I could not look at Frederick for fear that I would see the same terror in his eyes that was washing through me.

Then I heard his clothing rustle. His warm hand found my clenched fist among the damp folds of my cloak. Still not looking at him, I clamped my fingers between his and held on. As we watched the strip of grey heaving water between us and England grow wider and wider, I leaned against his shoulder for balance and was slowly filled again with that odd, new contradictory sense of alert peacefulness that he had brought to my body and heart. I looked back at where I imagined my granite fragment had entered the water.

It was done. It was right. I was headed for my very own mountains. My husband's mountains. *Die berge*. The mountains. *Das volk*. The people. My people, who will love me as he does, Frederick said.

My husband. *Mein mann*.

In a few more days, I would be certain that I was not going to bleed this month. If my suspicions were right, I already carried in my belly a living testament to my new life. I would not tell Frederick yet, not until I was certain.

I imagined telling him. I imagined burying my face in my child's belly. I could relish again and again the perfect joy of imagining those future moments.

I glanced at Frederick's serious profile and the dark hair being whipped into his eyes by the wind. I smiled at the thought of his most recent wedding gift to me, now cowering in her wicker cage amid the strange creaks and smells of our cabin, beside my lute case. When my new husband last visited Charles at Whitehall, she had climbed eagerly onto his lap. Frederick had looked my brother in the eye, tucked Belle inside his coat and walked out, taking her with him. Belle, who had once been so jealous of him. She might again be jealous of the babe, at first, but again would soon learn to love.

CHARACTERS IN THE KING'S DAUGHTER

REAL

JAMES I OF ENGLAND AND VI OF SCOTLAND – King of England after the death of Elizabeth I. Previously King of Scotland from the age of two, after the forced abdication of his mother, Mary, Queen of Scots. He accepted the English throne from the woman who had signed his mother's execution warrant.

ELIZABETH STUART – second child and first daughter of James. Born in Scotland.

HENRY FREDERICK STUART, PRINCE OF WALES – oldest son of James and older brother of Elizabeth. Born in Scotland.

CHARLES, DUKE OF YORK – their younger brother, with the recorded nickname of 'Baby Charles' (later Charles I of England). Born in Scotland.

ANNE OF DENMARK – Queen to James, mother of Henry, Charles and Elizabeth.

ROBERT CECIL, LORD SALISBURY – English Secretary of State and chief adviser to James. The 'secret king'. Also known historically as 'the King's Little Beagle' and 'the King's Monkey'. In this book, also called 'Wee Bobby'.

SIR FRANCIS BACON – cousin to Cecil, and his frustrated political rival.

ROBERT CARR – favourite and likely lover of James. Subsequently replaced by the Duke of Buckingham.

LORD AND LADY HARINGTON – guardians of the young Elizabeth after James's accession to the English Crown. NB Not to be confused with his cousin, Sir John Harington, godson of Elizabeth I and inventor of the flush toilet (which Elizabeth I did not think had a future).

LADY ANNE DUDLEY SUTTON – childhood companion, then lady-in-waiting to Elizabeth. Niece of Lady Harington.

FREDERICK, ELECTOR PALATINE – German prince, suitor of Elizabeth.

FREDERICK ULRICH OF BRUNSWICK – German prince, suitor of Elizabeth.

MRS HAY – Elizabeth's former nurse.

OTHERS – real courtiers, ladies-in-waiting, doctors, ambassadors and political figures, including poet and dramatist Ben Jonson, royal architect Inigo Jones, and the suitors for the hand of Elizabeth. Even the put-upon playwright, Samuel Daniel, is real, and I ask his ghost to forgive the liberty I take with his reputation.

And BELLE, BICHETTE and CHERAMI.

FICTIONAL
THALIA BRISTO – 'Tallie'. With African parents, but raised in Southwark. Bought as a gift for Queen Anne and given by her to Elizabeth. Her presence at court is based on an often-overlooked demographic reality. The number of people of African descent in England at this time was large enough for Elizabeth I to have ordered them to be expelled in 1596. (See Historical Notes.)

PETER BLANK – serving man to Prince Henry. However, his alleged great-grandfather, of African descent, was historically real, one of the official trumpeters, first to Henry VIII, then of Catherine of Aragon and Henry VIII, who can be seen pictured in a procession on the Great Tournament Roll of Westminster at the Guild Hall in London.

MRS TAFT – and the whores at Fish Pool House in Southwark. They are, however, based on reported reality.

ABEL WHITE – Scottish stable groom to Elizabeth.

FRANCIS QUOYNT – fire master and fireworks expert, formerly employed by Cecil.

Author's Note

THE HISTORY BEHIND THE STORY

SOURCES
Elizabeth Stuart was much observed and described from a respectful, if not star-struck, distance, but almost nothing is known about her emotional life. Her many letters usually conform to the formulae of the period and don't give away much except her famous high spirits. A gossipy biography written later in the 17th century by one of the court ladies is now thought to be flummery. I have therefore tried to make the historical chronology of events correct as far as I could learn (and sources agreed) while having to imagine almost entirely what Elizabeth thought about almost everything. The challenge has been to imagine the privately plausible from the known public details, portraits, gossip, etc. The same challenge arose with most of my other main historical characters.

A little more helpfully, King James wrote extensively and spoke his mind with no thought of tact – and was much quoted, often in horror or indignation. Sir Francis Bacon left us his *Essays*, *Apophthegms*, and other treatises, which give glimpses into his formidable, if unhappy, mind. While writing, I sometimes found myself cursing as well as blessing that gossipy old letter writer John Chamberlain for locking in the exact dates of events at the Stuart court while leaving my real questions about the people unanswered.

Apart from the disastrous fictional masque, '*Niger in Albion*' I have not made up any major court events. (Mind you, all word of such a disaster would undoubtedly have been suppressed.) I have, however, compressed the time frame once or twice to avoid an endless sequence of masques, hunts, feasts, and other recreations. Frustratingly, Elizabeth is largely left out of historical reports while hindsight often includes Charles (at the time a minor figure not expected to survive into adulthood) because he later became king, led England into civil war, and had his head chopped off. I have occasionally inserted Elizabeth into occasions when, though not noted, she could well have been present.

If Henry had lived to become Henry IX, he would very likely have changed the course of English history by avoiding the Civil War. He might, however, have become embroiled in the religious wars on the Continent. He is oddly absent from most general history books, even though he was widely popular and his death in 1612 caused a nationwide outpouring of popular hysteria and grief similar to that following the death of Princess Diana. The reasons for this absence from official history should be apparent in the story.

Elizabeth's early life, treated in this book, held two peaks of interest – the time of the Gunpowder Plot and the time leading up to and including her marriage. Her greatest melodramatic adventures were still to come, very soon. To compare my imagined Elizabeth with what is known of the historical one, you will find a time line on my web site, www.christiedickason.com.

HISTORICAL REALITIES

The love of Henry's life was indeed his sister, Elizabeth. But, given his strict morals, stern temperament, and open distaste for his father's loose living, I did not rise to baited hints that their relationship was incestuous. In that dysfunctional family, it did not need to be sexual to explain their closeness. Henry may or may not have had an affair with Frances Howard (later famous for the Overbury murder case). But most sources, and his own character, suggest that he was still a virgin when he died at the age of eighteen.

Queen Anne was indeed furiously opposed to the Palatine marriage for Elizabeth, on religious, financial and status grounds. Her mocking of Elizabeth as 'Goody Palsgrave' is documented. Elizabeth did defy both parents to secure her marriage to Frederick. The scene of his first arrival in London is closely based on factual reports, as is the about-face that Frederick somehow produced in James after the (documented) near debacle of the betrothal ceremony.

Henry was deeply involved in and committed to settling the New World. However, one source reports that his interest was largely kept secret because of the political and commercial sensitivity of European interest in the Americas. In the book, I have suggested one particular reason for his secrecy. James did fear both of his older children and envy their wide popularity among the English. This was not paranoia. He himself had been used to depose his own mother while he was still a toddler. Later, he had tacitly acquiesced to the execution of his mother and accepted the English throne from her executioner. As a child, he had been kidnapped and manipulated by powerful Scottish lords who wanted to rule Scotland through him. He had every reason to fear a palace revolution that would put his son on the throne in his place – or his daughter.

Though Tallie is fictional, the presence in early 17th century England of people of African descent is well documented, although, until recently, scholarship has tended to focus on the development of the trans-Atlantic slave trade later in the century. A 1617 portrait of Anne of Denmark shows a barely visible, unremarked, groom of African descent holding her horse. Titania's 'Indian boy' in *A Midsummer's Night Dream*, Aaron the Moor in Shakespeare's *Titus Andronicus*, and other literary references (including the queen's 'noble blackamoor' who pulled a masque chariot in place of a lion) are further examples. Londoners would almost certainly have seen African envoys, merchants, scholars, and sailors. And, without doubt, their explorations, exploitations, piracy and commerce brought the 16th and early 17th c. English into contact with a wide range of peoples, from those (in the Americas) whom they considered 'savages' to the 'noble moor' like Shakespeare's *Othello*. Queen Elizabeth herself bought a white taffeta coat for a favourite 'lytle Blackamoor' – which did not stop her, in 1596, from ordering the removal of all blacks from England, 'of which kinde of people,' she wrote, 'there are already here too manie . . .'

There was undoubtedly fear and suspicion among the English of anyone who looked 'strange'. But one challenge in writing Tallie was to try to set aside our modern attitudes towards racism and the legacy of the slave trade, to guess what attitudes might have predated 'scientific racism'. The slave trade with the West Indies had only just begun and was still on a very small scale. In a period when you could also buy the guardianship of a wealthy orphan, apprentices and indentured labour, slaves, *per se*, were still most often thought of as captives of war, like Aaron the Moor. In the early 17th c. on the written evidence they left behind, the English seemed to be fairly xenophobic towards most foreigners, the French and Italians in particular. In that hierarchical society, wealth, status and education would have defined a person as much as colour of skin.

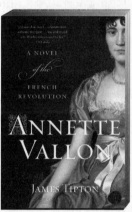

ANNETTE VALLON:
A Novel of the French Revolution
by James Tipton
978-0-06-082222-4 (paperback)
For fans of Tracy Chevalier and Sarah Dunant comes this vibrant, alluring debut novel of a compelling, independent woman who would inspire one of the world's greatest poets and survive a nation's bloody transformation.

BOUND: A Novel
by Sally Gunning
978-0-06-124026-3 (paperback)
An indentured servant finds herself bound by law, society, and her own heart in colonial Cape Cod.

CASSANDRA & JANE: A Jane Austen Novel
by Jill Pitkeathley
978-0-06-144639-9 (paperback)
The relationship between Jane Austen and her sister—explored through the letters that might have been.

CROSSED: A Tale of the Fourth Crusade
by Nicole Galland
978-0-06-084180-5 (paperback)
Under the banner of the Crusades, a pious knight and a British vagabond attempt a daring rescue.

A CROWNING MERCY: A Novel
by Bernard Cornwell and Susannah Kells
978-0-06-172438-1 (paperback)
A rebellious young Puritan woman embarks on a daring journey to win love and a secret fortune.

DANCING WITH MR. DARCY:
Stories Inspired by Jane Austen and Chawton House Library
Edited by Sarah Waters
978-0-06-199906-2 (paperback)
An anthology of the winning entries in the
Jane Austen Short Story Award 2009.

DARCY'S STORY
by Janet Aylmer
978-0-06-114870-5 (paperback)
Read Mr. Darcy's side of the story—*Pride
and Prejudice* from a new perspective.

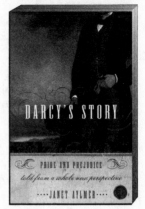

DEAREST COUSIN JANE:
A Jane Austen Novel
by Jill Pitkeathley
978-0-06-187598-4 (paperback)
An inventive reimagining of the intriguing
and scandalous life of Jane Austen's cousin.

THE FALLEN ANGELS: A Novel
by Bernard Cornwell and Susannah Kells
978-0-06-172545-6 (paperback)
In the sequel to *A Crowning Mercy*, Lady Campion Lazender's courage,
faith, and family loyalty are tested when she must complete a perilous
journey between two worlds.

A FATAL WALTZ: A Novel of Suspense
by Tasha Alexander
978-0-06-117423-0 (paperback)
Caught in a murder mystery, Emily must do the unthinkable to save her
fiancé: bargain with her ultimate nemesis, the Countess von Lange.

FIGURES IN SILK: A Novel
by Vanora Bennett
978-0-06-168985-7 (paperback)
The art of silk making, political intrigue, and a sweeping love story all
interwoven in the fate of two sisters.

THE FIREMASTER'S MISTRESS: A Novel
by Christie Dickason
978-0-06-156826-8 (paperback)
Estranged lovers Francis and Kate rekindle their
romance in the midst of Guy Fawkes's plot to blow up
Parliament.

THE GENTLEMAN POET:
A Novel of Love, Danger, and Shakespeare's The Temptest
by Kathryn Johnson
978-0-06-196531-9 (paperback)
A wonderful story that tells the tale of how William Shakespeare may have come to his inspiration for *The Tempest*.

JULIA AND THE MASTER OF MORANCOURT: A Novel
by Janet Aylmer
978-0-06-167295-8 (paperback)
Amidst family tragedy, Julia travels all over England, desperate to marry the man she loves instead of the arranged suitor preferred by her mother.

KEPT: A Novel
by D. J. Taylor
978-0-06-114609-1 (paperback)
A gorgeously intricate, dazzling reinvention of Victorian life and passions that is also a riveting investigation into some of the darkest, most secret chambers of the human heart.

THE KING'S DAUGHTER: A Novel
by Christie Dickason
978-0-06-197627-8 (paperback)
A superb historical novel of the Jacobean court, in which Princess Elizabeth, daughter of James I, strives to avoid becoming her father's pawn in the royal marriage market.

THE MIRACLES OF PRATO: A Novel
by Laurie Albanese and Laura Morowitz
978-0-06-155835-1 (paperback)
The unforgettable story of a nearly impossible romance between a painter-monk (the renowned artist Fra Filippo Lippi) and the young nun who becomes his muse, his lover, and the mother of his children.

PILATE'S WIFE:
A Novel of the Roman Empire
by Antoinette May
978-0-06-112866-0 (paperback)
Claudia foresaw the Romans' persecution of Christians, but even she could not stop the crucifixion.

PORTRAIT OF AN UNKNOWN WOMAN: A Novel
by Vanora Bennett
978-0-06-125256-3 (paperback)
Meg, adopted daughter of Sir Thomas More, narrates the tale of a famous Holbein painting and the secrets it holds.

THE PRINCESS OF NOWHERE: A Novel
by Prince Lorenzo Borghese
978-0-06-172161-8 (paperback)
From a descendant of Napoleon Bonaparte's brother-in-law comes a historical novel about his famous ancestor, Princess Pauline Bonaparte Borghese.

THE QUEEN'S SORROW: A Novel of Mary Tudor
by Suzannah Dunn
978-0-06-170427-7 (paperback)
Queen of England Mary Tudor's reign is brought low by abused power and a forbidden love.

REBECCA:
The Classic Tale of Romantic Suspense
by Daphne du ⎡ **3 1901 05305 3163**
978-0-380-730⌐⌐⌐⌐⌐ ⌐⌐⌐⌐⌐⌐⌐⌐
Follow the second Mrs. Maxim de Winter down the lonely drive to Manderley, where Rebecca once ruled.

REBECCA'S TALE: A Novel
by Sally Beauman
978-0-06-117467-4 (paperback)
Unlock the dark secrets and old worlds of Rebecca de Winter's life with investigator Colonel Julyan.

THE SIXTH WIFE: A Novel of Katherine Parr
by Suzannah Dunn
978-0-06-143156-2 (paperback)
Kate Parr survived four years of marriage to King Henry VIII, but a new love may undo a lifetime of caution.

WATERMARK: A Novel of the Middle Ages
by Vanitha Sankaran
978-0-06-184927-5 (paperback)
A compelling debut about the search for identiy, the power of self-expression, and value of the written word.

Available wherever books are sold, or call 1-800-331-3761 to order.